IN A FOREIGN COUNTRY

IN A FOREIGN COUNTRY

by

Hilary Shepherd

HONNO MODERN FICTION

First published by Honno

'Ailsa Craig', Heol y Cawl, Dinas Powys, Wales, CF64 4AH

1 2 3 4 5 6 7 8 9 10

Paperback ISBN 978-1-906784-62-1

Ebook ISBN 978-1-909983-06-9

Published with the financial support of the Welsh Books Council.

Cover image: Shutterstock

Cover design: Graham Preston

For Nick

ACKNOWLEDGEMENTS

A big thank you to all those who offered to read this novel during its long gestation but especially to Zarine Katrak, to Felicity and Christopher Martin, and to Siam, for their detailed feed-back: I hope I have done justice to the observations you all made. I would also like to thank Charlotte Spring, and my editor, Caroline Oakley, and Helena Earnshaw and Janet Thomas at Honno, for all their help and support. Most of all, of course, thank you to my husband, Nick Myhill, whose incisive comments and unflagging encouragement have kept me going through challenging times.

AUTHOR'S NOTE

Writing this book I have re-visited memories of Ghana more than thirty years old and used them as the backdrop of my fiction, so some details may well be inaccurate. All the characters, events and organisations in this book are fictional. As far as I know there is no Rice Corporation in Tamale and never has been, nor does the Mission of the Holy Redeemer actually exist. Indeed, the Mission of my imagination is a relic of earlier times: by 1976 Ghanaian priests would have been working alongside their European colleagues. One fact is true, however. Homosexuality was – and still is – illegal in Ghana.

'Thou hast committed
Fornication.'
'But that was in another country,
And besides, the wench is dead.'

The Jew of Malta

August 2007

It takes her thirty years to go back. She who had said she would go and come.

And when she does – tentatively, expecting everything to have changed beyond recognition – it is the un-changed which is most shocking. As she steps out of the aircraft, that colourless sun hanging mute and brooding just above the flat horizon. The loudness of the yodelling birds echoing all around. The soft intensity of the dawn heat, and the rich vegetative smell of growth and decay all mixed up together. And in a moment she is twenty-two again, and arriving for the first time.

1

Week 1: March 1976

Atta the tailor sat in an armchair discussing politics, elegant as a Roman emperor in the long green cloth draped like a toga, the thin electric light gleaming darkly on his bare shoulder. The light bulb was swinging backwards and forwards in the night wind that charged through the house. It made her feel slightly seasick. She closed her eyes.

She opened them again to a questioning silence. Atta was looking at her, waiting.

'Pardon?'

'I said, how come dis your first visit to Tamale-here when your daddy live in Ghana so long time?'

She had to concentrate on the singing cadences to hear the shape in them.

Because I was never invited, she might have said, if it hadn't sounded churlish. She couldn't say what her dad had always said, *Tamale is no place for children*, because at this very moment children were pounding past outside, squealing excitedly.

'Dey callin' up de rain,' Atta said, grinning.

From the table where he sat wreathed in tobacco smoke her dad said, 'Anne's been too busy with her studies up till now.'

So that was how he saw it! She glanced across at him, but

the conversation was veering off again, back to communism (Atta) versus democracy (her dad). She stopped listening and let her tired mind wander.

The day that spread out behind her had started in one life and was ending in another. My father's house, she thought, looking round her. Amused because the phrase sounded grand but the reality was strangely banal. She considered the drabness of the heavy furniture, the bare walls, the concrete floor painted a scratchy red, thinking *I could do something here.* She could make this little house homely in no time at all, if only he would let her. She watched him fiddling with the tobacco in his pipe: this man who used to seem so much more familiar, seen once a year on his brief visits home, than he seemed now, here in his own house.

He was laughing. 'Atta, how can you – a communist – say we should keep the Queen?'

Atta grinned. 'She a good lady.'

The house might be banal but nothing about today had been ordinary, from the moment she got off the plane in Accra and emerged into the tropical dawn. Waiting all morning in the airport for the internal flight to Tamale, everything so clamorous, so hot and so other. Feeling drab and white amongst the vibrant crowd of passengers pushing onto the plane. Glimpses of a distant land spread out remotely below her, but as they circled before landing in Tamale she had seen real thatched huts, and men hoeing bare red earth with shining mattocks, before the fierce glare of the tin roofs of the town came out to meet them and there was the little Lego airport and her father in it, so familiar and so out of place in the thronging, colourful, dark-skinned crowd. If she'd had to turn round and go straight back home the drive into town alone would have made the journey worthwhile, she thought, remembering the big shade trees that lined the busy road and the women in their bright wraps and bobbing turbans who sat at their treadle sewing machines at the roadside or walked erect under weighty head-loads. Was it only this afternoon she had witnessed all of this? Crowds of men and boys on gleaming bicycles; lorries with lively slogans painted on the back; goats, and humped cows. The featureless little town. The sprawl of the government estate. This house in the last road of all, looking out over the bush, the far blue horizon. And she didn't have to turn round and go home again because she had six whole months ahead of her. Six months with her father, to make up for all the years of his absence.

Atta said, 'But I say, in Ghana-here, when de power goes—'

At that moment the sky crashed down on their heads and the light went out.

'I'm really sorry,' her dad said, spreading over-bright jam across a slice of rubbery white bread. 'We've been waiting for these tractors for more than a year. It's really bad luck they should turn up just at the same time as you. Not to mention the missing hydraulics.'

'It's okay,' she said yet again. He had been waiting for her to come for nearly fifteen years, after all. Or maybe he hadn't.

'I'd meant to take at least one day off before abandoning you.'

'It's all right, Dad. You did warn me it would be difficult, with the rainy season coming.' She could tell how anxious he was – he didn't usually talk so much.

'I'll get back as soon as I can. By lunchtime, at any rate. Or soon after. I'll take you into town then. The later we go out the cooler it'll be, anyway. You know where the food is. Sorry there isn't any fruit – it's always difficult at the end of the dry season. It'll get better when the rains come properly.' She watched him over the rim of her glass of tea as he cut another slice of bread. He chuckled suddenly. 'The look on your face when it thundered just before the power went! You looked as if you thought the world was ending.'

'It felt like it was. Does it always make such a racket when it rains?'

'Can be worse…'

'I suppose it's the tin roof. It wouldn't be so noisy in a thatched hut.'

'Not so noisy but rather damper. Sure you don't want any bread and jam?'

She declined. He hurried his plate away to the kitchen, coming back to give her a few more instructions as he picked up a battered old briefcase from behind the door. Then he was gone. But she detected a note of relief in his leaving – the jaunty bang of the Land Rover door, the deep revving of its engine – which coloured the empty air left behind him.

It's tiredness making me feel funny, she reflected as she braved the dark reaches of the shower room with its cold water and broken tiles, the drain merely a hole in the wall through which snakes might come. *It will seem better when I get used to it.*

On the left of the shower room, a smaller, darker cubby hole housed a toilet, which would be a lot more presentable if it were treated to a good clean. She remembered her mother saying once, *Men and toilet brushes are never to be seen together*. And the toilet might have been merely a hole in the floor – she should be grateful.

To the right of the shower-room there was a small store room with a tiny window high in the wall, a metal bed with a mattress rolled up at one end, a sack of charcoal in the corner. And next to that was the kitchen. The strange, forlorn little kitchen. Just a room with a tap in it, really. Out of which her dad had magicked for supper last night… slices of tinned Spam with a mess of fried onion and tomato. If this is how he eats I really *can* be useful, she had thought, watching him tucking in to his own heaped plateful. All those meals out through the years of her childhood and it had never struck her that he might be a Spam person in private. Again that feeling of unfamiliarity swept over her. Her father.

She stood for a few minutes towelling her hair while she surveyed the kitchen with its solitary gas-ring on the floor, on which she must boil a pan of water if she wanted any more tea, and the low stool, and the big water jar, and the rickety shelves. And in one corner a brash new fridge. But her dad had warned her the power usually went off around eight and didn't come back on until the evening, so the fridge would not stay cold all day and should be opened as little as possible. So many instructions! Boil your water for drinking, don't drink from the water jar. Do this, don't do that, as if he thought she couldn't look after herself. She went back out into the corridor and looked through the open front door to the road, and beyond that the pale blue haze of empty countryside. People were passing on the road. They looked at her with curiosity and one or two shouted out 'Hey, sister!' She moved discreetly out of sight.

Blimey, she thought, this house really is small! You could

fit the whole thing into Mum's sitting room. She paced out the length of the hallway, holding the towel steady on her head, and through the door at the end into her dad's bedroom until she reached the far wall. Yep – just about!

How bare his room was, like a monk's cell. The bed neatly made, the sheet pulled tight and square and a garish cloth laid over it as a coverlet. There were hardly any objects in the room, beyond some books and a pipe-rack with three pipes in it. On the desk, a few photographs. One of her dad with a young African man, both of them smiling at the camera. Another of an African family dressed up in their best clothes, the young wife very pretty. The third, surprisingly, of her mother. No photograph of herself, she observed, not even the graduation picture she had sent him last summer. She shut her heart down firmly and went back through the living room to her tiny bedroom and hung the towel over a chair to dry. Everything felt warm and slightly damp. She could smell mud through the window. She shut the wooden louvres as instructed and blanked out the heat, but then it was too dark to read.

She put the light on in the living room and looked at the titles of the books on the small bookcase. Mostly well-thumbed sci-fi paperbacks, and a few hardbacks stamped *Tamale English Language Library* inside. The ceiling fan stirred the warm air but to little effect. She considered the heavy, utilitarian furniture. The only ornament in the room was a carved figure perched on top of the bookshelves. She picked it up and ran her fingers over the exaggerated shape – large head, small body – identical to the ones she had seen for sale in the airport in Accra when she was coming through yesterday. Probably turned out for the tourists. She stroked the figure thoughtfully before carefully putting it back as she'd found it. She picked up her book from the sofa.

The tin roof was creaking alarmingly as the house heated up in the sun. The light went off. She looked up in dismay at the precarious-looking fan winding slowly to a halt over her head. The light came on again and the fan stirred sluggishly back to life, but only for a moment. She looked at her watch. It was exactly eight a.m.

Had she known how late her dad would come back, she might have walked further than the bread-lady. But actually that had been far enough. The sun was dizzying, and a swarm of children came running to follow her as soon as she was spotted leaving the house. She climbed the path, marvelling at the multitude of ways the identical semi-detached houses had been adapted. One had been made into a bar with tables and chairs set out under a thatched awning. Another was being used as a carpentry workshop. Some backyards were swept bare and clean, some were miniature farmyards with ducks and goats. She saw a rabbit hop heavily into one house, pushing under the door-curtain. Roosters flapped onto fences and crowed victoriously, hens scratched busily in the mud. It was humid in the sun after last night's rain and the goats, which shimmied off the path in front of her, slipped and skidded in the red clay like naughty girls disturbed in their petticoats and high heels.

She stopped to look back down at her dad's house, memorising which one it was in the very last row at the bottom of the slope. A large mango tree loomed over it, and opposite, on the edge of the vast pale reaches of the empty Bush, more mango trees stood in a little copse, all bright and shiny in the sun, with an absurd row of white egrets pegged out along their tops. The troupe of children at her heels stood staring up at her, commenting freely to one another and laughing, but their laughter sounded innocent and she didn't mind. When she turned and went on up the path they turned too and followed.

At the top of the slope the path made a sharp detour round a big clay oven which had its own little shelter of thatch. A slender young woman was bending to take loaves out of the oven. A little boy stood beside her dressed only in a shirt. His eyes were big and round and he had one finger in his mouth. Anne stopped to watch the woman, smiling absently at the child. He burst into tears and hid his face in his mother's brightly coloured wrap. The woman laughed. She bent down and swung him casually by one arm, up onto her hip. Such a wonderful smile, she had, and big silver earrings bouncing merrily whenever she moved.

The crowd of children pushed closer until one of them knocked over the tray of newly made bread. The smiley woman stopped smiling and cuffed the perpetrator briskly round the ear. He howled. That really seemed to infuriate the bread lady. She dropped her own child and chased the others away, shouting and shaking her fist. Anne watched helplessly, horrified to be the cause of such an outburst. But the children didn't retreat very far, and when the woman turned back she was smiling again. Her smile was infectious, the kind of smile you just had to smile too. The woman reached out her arm and laid it alongside Anne's, pulling a rueful face. Anne laughed: next to the woman's rich brown skin her own arm looked unpleasantly anaemic. They bent together to pick up the bread. Should she buy some, since it was her fault they had fallen on the ground?

Perhaps better not. She gestured instead at the child: 'What is his name?' But the woman only laughed and jogged the boy up and down on her hip. He stared at Anne dolefully, his big eyes still flooded with tears.

'My name is Anne,' she said, pointing at herself.

'En,' said the woman, smiling broadly.

'I am Anne, and you are…?' she asked, pointing from herself to the woman.

'En,' the woman repeated cheerfully.

She tried again. Pointing to herself and saying 'Anne', pointing to the bread-lady and raising her eyebrows.

The woman's eyes gleamed suddenly in recognition. 'Abina,' she said, and pointed to the child: 'Kwame.'

They shook hands vigorously.

'Goodbye, Abina,' Anne said as she turned away. 'Goodbye, Kwame.'

'Bye bye, sister,' said Abina.

The children were waiting like an escort. She went back to the hot little house, shaking off her entourage at the door. Her father didn't come back until the heat was fading.

Outside the market, drummers in traditional smocks and conical straw hats were loudly drumming. Old men listened solemnly to the stories the talking drums were telling. All around them the market buzzed with the hustle and bustle of vivid women, arranging, carrying, tidying, or simply squatting motionless in long rows beside their wares, the energetic rise and fall of their shrill voices beating at the air. When they saw Anne they shouted, 'Sister! Sister!' She smiled at them over her shoulder as she followed her dad through the narrow alleyways. The light was the lovely neutral light of sunset fading. Soon it would be dark.

9

Hurricane lamps hissed and crackled, shedding warm light over small pyramids of withered onions, or bruised tomatoes, or battered green oranges. They went from stall to stall, her dad buying a little of this, a little of that, putting the goods into the string bag he carried on his shoulder.

'Peanut butter?' she exclaimed in surprise as brown paste was scooped from a big bowl and wrapped in a banana leaf with much careful licking of fingers.

'Groundnut paste,' he corrected. 'Staple crop of the Northern Region. We fry in the oil and cook with the paste.'

Not so you'd notice, she thought, remembering the Spam.

She followed him out of the market, jumping lightly over a deep storm-drain. She caught his look, and guessed that he no more knew what to expect of her, coming into this world, than she did of him living in it. She saw his teeth flash from the depths of his beard as he grinned. He seemed to be enjoying himself too.

They got back into the Land Rover and he drove her round the town. He pointed out the pottery market, the two small supermarkets and the shabby electrical shop – funny places with almost empty white shelves. He showed her the Bus Park, and the Lorry Park. He called it an 'Orientation Session'. She doubted if she'd ever find any of these places again.

'I don't know how you're going to fill your time,' he said the next evening as they sat in his living room. 'It's not a very exciting place, Tamale.'

It seemed exciting to her! She had ventured back into town this morning while he was at work. That extraordinary market, those streets over-spilling with people and traffic! All manner of life lived outdoors – women cooking, old men sitting gossiping in the shade of a tree. Everything exaggerated: the smells, the din, the narrow spaces choked with brightly clothed people. And some things had made her laugh out loud. The small bald pullet that goose-stepped its way into the kitchen this morning and looked her in the eye as she sat on the stool waiting for the water to boil on the gas-ring on the floor. When she leaped up to shoo it out it lifted the bare stubs of its wings and legged it outside like an ungainly white woman on the run. The insatiable children sitting on the doorstep had clapped their hands and laughed. She couldn't imagine getting bored. Besides, the air was electric with the expectation of rain. The ground had baked hard again after that first storm, though the clouds built up by day and the night air smelled of flowers. It felt as though big things were about to happen. But he was right, she did need to have some kind of structure to her time. She couldn't simply be a pair of observing eyes with a tail of excited children following her everywhere, waiting for the rains to come.

'I've been thinking of doing some research while I'm here,' she said tentatively. 'Something I could use towards a PhD.'

'Oh, you want to be a perpetual student, do you?'

She was stung into silence. Didn't a First count for anything with him? Even if it *was* a First in Social Anthropology.

'Mum thought it was a good idea.' (Which was a lie. Her mum had used every trick in the book trying to persuade her not to come to Ghana at all.)

He puffed his pipe and didn't say a word. She couldn't

11

read anything from his face. 'I'd be eligible for a grant. It wouldn't cost you anything.' Or maybe he was hurt that she didn't think father-daughter bonding was occupation enough. She stared at the page of her book but the words were swimming. Getting to know him properly at last, sharing his life for a little while – of course that was why she had come! But was it wrong to want more out of this trip than that?

'You could do worse than look at rice farming.'

She looked up in surprise. His own specialism! The sting subsided. 'I could,' she said, but not very eagerly because she would rather study something traditional. Carving or leather-working, perhaps… Or weaving. She'd been reading up on all of those before she came.

'And I meant it about wanting some voluntary work,' she reminded him, steering the conversation away onto safer ground. She went back to her book, he to his, but she wasn't concentrating. She was thinking about their outing this afternoon.

"That place today – TAT, was it? You haven't gone religious have you, Dad?'

'Religious? No, I just thought you ought to meet them.'

She couldn't think why. Nor, it seemed, had it been obvious to the pale-skinned, earnest American missionaries at TAT.

'And all the talk about that priest?' she added. Some story of a priest being cornered by an amorous pig in a pig-shed in one of the Catholic missions.

'Michael? Oh Michael's a good friend. Michael is *everybody's* good friend. Incidentally, if you're serious about looking for voluntary work his Mission would be a good place to start.'

12

'A Catholic Mission?'

'I'm told they're desperately short of teaching staff.'

'Wouldn't they mind that I'm not religious?'

'I don't think they'd hold it against you.'

She looked at him sharply. His eyes twinkled as he puffed on his pipe. She picked up her book again but it seemed dull and irrelevant, her head buzzing as it was with everything she'd seen in the last few days. TAT seemed a funny outfit. Officially the Tamale-America Trust but nobody seemed to refer to it as that, not even its own members. She had commented afterwards what a hairy lot they all were (the men bearded, the women with long hair down their backs, like a colony of hippies), and her dad commented that some expats thought TAT was a front for the CIA. She'd laughed out loud at that, thinking he couldn't possibly be serious.

She read another page, trying to concentrate.

'No, I haven't gone religious,' he said, but by then she had forgotten what they were talking about.

This evening she had cooked her first meal. It was clear from his cooking that her father needed looking after. No wonder he was looking rather gaunt. She sat curled up on the sofa, thinking about this and studying her bare feet (they were dreadfully dirty!) instead of her book. There was no reason why she shouldn't go to the meat market tomorrow on her own if he didn't have time to take her. The kitchen was tricky, split as it was between two worlds: the single gas ring on the floor and a charcoal brazier for barbecues, the fridge that didn't really keep the drinking water cool and the large clay water pot which did. *But we will boil your water*, her dad had said more than once, *and you can keep it in the fridge.*

Later, making a pot of tea after their supper, she sat on the stool waiting for the pan of water to boil on the old-fashioned gas ring and reflected that it wouldn't take much to make this kitchen an easier place to work in. Get a table, for a start, so the gas ring wasn't on the floor. She had even seen ready-made cupboards in the carpenters' section of the market this morning. 'Very expensive, all that stuff,' her dad said dismissively when she mentioned it. She could see she would need to go softly, softly on this one.

'Shall I do some cleaning tomorrow?' she suggested as she poured the tea. The house had got very dusty even in the short time she'd been here.

He shrugged. 'Don't worry about all that,' he said, as if the house would clean itself if they left it long enough.

She had to do something. The days were very long while he was at work and there was a limit to the amount of time she could spend in the market with her Pied Piper entourage in the glare of the sun. *So much for feminism!* she thought, laughing at herself. *All this cooking and cleaning!* She really was going downhill, but she didn't care. She had waited such a long time to be here.

2

Week 2: March/April

Her dad set out his pencils and pens on the table and eyed her quizzically over his reading glasses. 'I take it you weren't that impressed by Ursula's "At Home"?'

She didn't know what to say. He'd been so anxious that she should go, afraid that she must be getting lonely, and it seemed ungrateful to say she'd hated it. She shrugged. He grinned. 'Pity, because Ursula has an At Home every other Friday. As you probably know by now.'

She felt free then to say, 'It was so dull! They only seemed to have one topic of conversation, if you don't count face-cream.' He raised a questioning eyebrow and went on sharpening his pencil. 'Servants. How to get them, how to get rid of them. Actually I do them wrong: they did also spend a lot of time discussing that priest. Father Michael, is it? Whether or not he's gay.' She was surprised to see a shadow pass across her father's face. She hadn't meant to shock him. Had expected him to be more open-minded than her mother. 'Actually it sounded as if they were just covering up for the fact they all seem to fancy him. Is he some kind of a Lothario then?'

'Lothario? Michael?' He sounded amused.

She watched him draw careful lines on his notepad with a ruler. 'What's that?'

'A graph. To show numbers of rats trapped in the grain stores through the year.'

'Yuck.'

He was so neat, so precise. She watched him make his small crosses, not liking to disturb his concentration with idle gossip. She couldn't imagine *him* spending time as she had this afternoon. Such listless women! That luxurious bungalow with its throbbing generator so far removed from the scruffy, vibrant world surrounding it. She wouldn't go again.

'You never know when you might need them,' he said suddenly. 'Can get to be a strain sometimes, being a foreigner.' He drew a long, careful line joining up the twelve little crosses on his graph.

Did he feel that?

'At the beginning,' he added.

I wonder if he'll ever go back home, she thought. It was hard to imagine. Even as a teenager she had sensed how out-of-place he was when he came to visit, as if he were uncomfortable in his warm clothes, and ill at ease with English manners. There was an odd sing-song edge to his voice that made him seem more and more foreign as the years passed. Now she could see where that came from, his voice sounding so much more at home here than her own clipped accent did.

Fifteen years is a long time, she thought as she watched him discard first one biro, then another.

'These Chinese pens are bloody useless! I only bought these a week ago and they've dried up already.'

They had been complaining about that too, this afternoon: the way the dry season made the furniture crack and face-creams dry out. Those complaining women.

Ursula, short and unreliably blonde, watching Anne through narrowed eyes from the armchair where she sat with her head thrown back, a glass of lemonade in one languorous hand. The other women unmemorable, except for two: a thin English girl called Jo with an interesting face half-hidden under a mane of electrically charged black hair and a pale blob of a baby attached to her hip, and the woman who had given them both a lift home – the intimidating Deepa, an Indian woman with a cut-glass accent and a haughty profile. When they stopped to drop Jo off at the end of a drive not half a mile away from here, Jo had, out of the blue, invited Anne to tea the following Monday, looking at her directly for the first time and excluding Deepa, who didn't seem to mind.

'Deepa gave me a lift home, Dad. She says you know her husband.'

'Sunni? Yes, I know Sunni. He's in teak. But he's FAO, not Government, so he gets lots of money.'

Ah. She had wondered. Everything so sparse and shabby in this house. No vehicle of their own, just an old Rice Corporation Land Rover. And her mother's endless complaints, ever since she could remember, about alimony.

Sunday, and she had completed her first full week. She congratulated herself.

It was the first time she'd had her dad at home all day. They didn't talk much but pottered about in amiable silence, and in the afternoon they sat in the hot living room and read their books to a background of cheerful Sunday sounds outside. The flies were too irritating to sit out of doors. Some came in through the open front door as it was. She found it hard to ignore them the way her dad did. They

17

crawled around on your face, lacking any manners. You wouldn't think of flies being polite until you met these, she thought, batting at them ineffectually.

Suddenly there were men's voices at the front door, spilling into the house. Young men, giggling in the corridor, then muffled as they moved into the kitchen. She looked at her dad. He couldn't *not* have heard but he didn't look up from his book.

A young man appeared in the living room doorway. She recognised him at once as the boy in the photograph, but older. He grinned at her dad and nodded to her.

'Anne, this is Moses,' her dad said.

Moses ducked from the room and disappeared. Chattering and laughter in the kitchen. *How very familiar!*

'Who is Moses?'

'The houseboy.'

'I didn't know you had a houseboy!' she said at last, her voice sounding rather small.

But her dad merely said, 'He's been away this week. Went to his village. Now he's back he'll do the cooking. And the washing and the cleaning.'

The bottom had dropped out of her new world. How could he have failed to mention this before? She was quiet for a long time.

'Where does he live?'

'Here, of course.'

'But where does he sleep?'

'The room next to the kitchen.'

The room she had thought was a store room, though it was true it did have a bed in it. So she would not have the house to herself any more during the day, and no more private evenings, just her and her dad alone together. Her

18

stomach felt hollow with disappointment. It was a very small house to share with somebody she didn't know.

'What will there be left for me to do?' she asked, trying to make it sound like a practical question.

He shrugged. 'There's always shopping to be done. Talk to Moses. But really, you don't need to worry about it.'

So many questions she wanted to ask, but her dad had retreated into his book and didn't seem to want to talk. Would she be able to talk to Moses in English? She wanted to learn Dagbani, so having him around would be good for that. And when she could speak it he would be able to tell her all sorts of things.

It was just that it was a shock, her dad not saying.

The other young men left. Her father went to the kitchen and talked to Moses – in Dagbani, she could tell from the shapes their voices made. She heard them laughing. Then he came back and went on reading.

'Moses speaks very good English,' he said when she asked him.

Later she went to the kitchen to get a drink. Moses was sitting on a low stool preparing the meat she had been expecting to cook for tonight. He looked up when she came in and moved his long legs to one side so that she could pass to the fridge. She was startled by the edge of antagonism in the look he gave her. His body-language said very clearly, *This kitchen is my territory. You are not welcome.*

Moses banged the chipped enamel plates down on the table (three plates, she noticed) and three spoons. Sitting down, he started to dish out the stew.

Anne hadn't expected him to eat with them. Another

little corner of her expectations flipped the other way up. She looked at her dad. He was gazing anxiously at Moses.

'We usually have a *little* more formality, Moses. Knives and forks? And side plates perhaps, for the bread?'

Moses stalked off to the kitchen. She looked at the stew on her plate. The bit of goat she had bought this morning, thinking she would make a curry, swam in a thin gravy under a skim of orange-red palm oil. A few pieces of onion were visible, and a large number of coarse-looking brown beans.

'He does usually do considerably better than this,' her dad said, looking at his plate. Moses came back with the side plates and cutlery and a plastic water jar. He filled her dad's glass and was reaching over to fill hers but her dad put his hand over it. Moses tutted impatiently as the water spilled onto the table.

'Is that boiled water, Moses?' her dad asked, his voice apologetic. 'She oughtn't to drink water from the tap. She isn't used to it like we are.'

Makes me sound like a coddled baby, she thought, catching Moses' eye. His stare was not benevolent. She gave a small apologetic grin and he turned his attention back to his plate. Perhaps she had unwittingly trodden on her father's toes when she'd said that about all the discussion at Marion's being about problems with servants. He seemed to be having a few problems of his own. She studied Moses discreetly between mouthfuls. He had an easy, sullen grace that made him seem young but he might be much older than he looked. He certainly didn't seem at all in awe of his employer.

Later, when Moses was safely in the kitchen washing up and they were sitting, just the two of them again in their fragile solitude, her dad said 'I'm sorry about the meal. He's quite a good cook usually. He wasn't at his best tonight.' She looked at him questioningly. 'Well – you know,' he said, taking his pipe out of his mouth and fiddling with it. And said nothing more, though she sat waiting and looking at him. But ages afterwards, when she'd almost forgotten what they were talking about, he added 'Bit unsettling, you coming.' So that she didn't know whether it was only Moses who was unsettled by her coming, and the remnants of her embryonic happiness fell in a little broken heap at her feet. Again she looked at him waiting for him to explain, but he seemed to feel he'd said quite enough.

At the bottom of the concrete steps she paused uncertainly, but then she heard Jo's voice call out 'Come on up.'

The bungalow was a handsome building, built on pillars for coolness in the days before air conditioning. Modern air-conditioning boxes had been fitted at the windows and were humming laboriously. Jo stood at the top of the steps holding the screen door open, the baby balanced on her hip and holding onto her T-shirt with both hands like a monkey.

'He looks happier today,' Anne said, feeling she should say something.

'His teeth were troubling him on Friday. But he always gets upset if there's an atmosphere.'

'Was there one?' she asked, surprised, as she followed Jo across the large bare room to some easy chairs set awkwardly around a low table.

'Didn't you notice? I suppose it wouldn't have been obvious to you, it being your first time. And anyway, you were partly the cause.'

'Me?'

Jo laughed. 'Yes, you! Didn't you notice the way they were all sniffing about you, like dogs round a new bitch? Or should that be bitches round a bitch? News travels fast in Tamale. They've been waiting on tenterhooks to meet the beautiful blonde bluestocking fresh out of Cambridge. Your hair is a lovely colour by the way. Is it naturally like that? You're so lucky!' *On Friday Jo had been so silent!* 'You're about as threatening as you could be, without even trying. At least, I assume you weren't trying. You're old enough to be a rival but young enough to be free of all the ties which keep them down.' Jo took out a tobacco tin and started rolling a cigarette. 'Smoke? No, thought you wouldn't. You look much too healthy and sensible. Mind if I do?'

'A rival?'

'Yep.' Jo picked Joshua up and sat him on her lap. She held the cigarette away from him carefully and blew the smoke out behind his back while he sat like a small Buddha, swivelling his eyes from one to the other without moving his head. However dubious Anne might feel about babies, she couldn't help laughing.

Jo said, 'Anyone younger is a rival, even me – we've got youth on our side whereas they're all heading fast through their thirties and forties and they don't like that one little bit! Mind you, they've never found me unsettling for any other reason. Have they Chooky Chook?' She balanced the cigarette carefully on an ash-tray on the table so that she could jog the baby on her knee and clap his hands together. Joshua giggled.

The large room, shadowed by the deep eaves of the roof, was sparsely furnished. Like her dad's house, it looked as if they had half-heartedly moved in with no intention of staying. The furniture was the same PWD stuff – "Public Works Department" – dark and ugly. A printed cloth, this one a giant paisley in lime-green and yellow, had been thrown over the sofa in a half-hearted attempt to disguise it. The bookcase in the corner held some glasses, a bottle of whisky and one of gin, and a small collection of books. She read their titles while Jo went out to the kitchen to make some tea. *An Engineer's Handbook. The Reader's Digest Book of Practical DIY.* A baby book by someone called Doctor Spock. A collection of Ray Bradbury short stories.

Joshua, abandoned on his rug on the floor, sat and stared at her gravely.

'Hello, baby,' she said, cautiously.

Joshua blinked.

He was surprisingly beautiful. What in Jo was stretched and narrowed into pale, anxious lines was moulded in Joshua in perfect curves. His large eyes were, like Jo's, very dark brown, but his hair was a blonde haze framing the round head which balanced delicately on its slender neck. He sat like a small god, naked except for his nappy, the ubiquitous dust collecting in the folds of his rounded limbs in startling black lines.

Suddenly he spoke. 'Ga!' he said, and raised one eyebrow quizzically. 'Ga!'

She laughed.

'Is he talking to you?' Jo called from the kitchen over the rattling of tea things. 'He must like you. Usually he cries if I leave him with anyone he doesn't know. You can pick him up if you like.'

'I think he's quite happy as he is.'

3

Weeks 3 and 4, April

Moses did all the cooking, just as Anne's father had said. And he cleaned the house, sweeping officiously around her feet with his palm fibre broom while she sat reading, or writing letters. He washed Dick's clothes in the mornings and hung them to dry on a line outside, then ironed them with a heavy charcoal iron on a rickety table on the porch in the afternoons. Anne had been told to give her clothes to Moses to wash but she was too embarrassed, and she couldn't believe Moses would like being asked to do something so personal. Anyway, she hated the idea of having a servant.

After Moses had finished washing, she took the big purple plastic bowl and the box of Omo washing powder to wash her backlog of clothes.

He came and stood over her as she filled the bowl at the kitchen tap. 'I do dat,' he said accusingly. 'Washin' my job. You give me laundry, I do it.'

'Oh,' she faltered. 'I thought you wouldn't want to wash women's clothes.'

'I wash ladies' clothies. I not Muslim man.'

As if she had insulted him.

She could hardly make it worse by refusing to give way. He took the laundry off her and went to his customary place for washing under the big mango tree at the back of the house. He worked up a good lather in the bowl that would leave her clothes as stiff as if they'd been starched. He seemed to be beating the dirt out. She had upset his routine, she knew, and even from inside the house she could hear him muttering crossly.

That evening he presented her with a pile of immaculately clean clothes, folded small and ironed into crisp parcels, each sock and every pair of knickers included.

After that she compromised, secretly washing her underwear and hanging it to dry in her room. But she did take a stand about him cleaning her room. She must have some privacy.

However hard she tried, she seemed to be always upsetting him. And yes, she *could* see how idle and useless she must seem to him. She went out as much as she could, but the walk into town was very tiring in the sun and there was nowhere much to go. She hadn't come across any weavers yet, and Tamale was too far from the forests to be a centre for wood carving. One whiff of the leather-workers' section of the market persuaded her she would prefer not to spend too much time there. She began to have creeping doubts. Perhaps six months was going to be too long.

The signboard by the gate declared that the Mission of the Holy Redeemer Secondary School for boys took pupils from eleven years. Technical education was available, also Cambridge Exam Board.

The buildings were set back from the road among dusty neem trees, a large whitewashed church on the right and to the left two low rows of open-sided classrooms, empty now in the late afternoon sunshine. In the middle, another single-storey building where she had been told she would find the Head of the Mission's office.

It was a slow interview. Father Morrissey seemed prone to silences. He looked like a minor character dreamed up by Lewis Carroll and when he gestured with his hands his long thin fingers divided two and two like a saint dispensing blessings.

'Hmm, so your degree was in Social Anthropology. Pity. What A levels did you do?'

'History, Biology and English,' she said. 'I did Part One of my tripos at Cambridge in History.'

'European History has limited uses here,' he said. 'Father John covers what we need more than adequately. Whereas geography would have been useful to us because Father Simon is away on sick leave in Ireland at the moment. English, of course, we can always make use of, if only for language practice, but we have a biology teacher already – Father Klaus, who also looks after the pig enterprise. We produce very good fresh pork here, by the way. Your father may already buy meat from us. Most of the expatriates do. No *O level* in geography, I don't suppose?'

'Sadly no. My other O level subjects were maths, chemistry, music and French. And Latin. But no geography.'

'Never mind.' He sat up in his chair and eased out his shoulders, first one then the other, making her think of a dreary bird. 'I'm sure we can make *some* use of you. Father Michael is responsible for the timetable. Any problems you encounter in the classroom, you can take them to him. Unfortunately he's out of town until Saturday but if you would care to come again next week he will show you round the school and discuss the details of what you might be willing to contribute. On a voluntary basis, of course.' He raised his eyebrows sternly. 'I take it we're not speaking at cross purposes on that?'

'Oh no! I would very much like to contribute in any way I can.' She hesitated, thinking she ought tell him now that she wasn't religious. She didn't want to start off at cross-purposes either, and she had never been inside a Catholic church except as a foreign tourist.

He didn't flinch. 'Of course it would have been preferable, but I presume that you won't let your lack of belief come between you and the pupils?' He eyed her from under one austere eyebrow as she murmured, *No, of course not.* 'However, we do expect high standards of behaviour throughout the school, from teachers and pupils alike. And while we will not expect you to attend daily Mass we would expect you to attend church on certain school occasions such as end-of-term services.' He added, with a dry, thin smile, 'You could regard it as an anthropological exercise.'

Behind him on the wall, a sickly looking Christ gazed aslant from his torturous cross. A shabby thing of flaking paint, the lacklustre shine of the pale flesh looking like sweat, a stylized rictus of redemption on the averted face. She tried to keep her eyes on Morrissey's face, also pale and gaunt but in his case more prosaic. There wasn't much suggestion of redemption in *his* thin features, only the pinched nostrils of the congenitally adenoidal. He dismissed her with the slightest of bows and a limp handshake.

A few days later she was buying onions in the market when an Irish voice boomed just behind her, 'Could this possibly be Miss Foster?'

She turned in surprise and peered up against the glare of

27

the sun at a tall, solid man with a close-cropped head. 'How did you know?'

'There can hardly be two blonde girls newly arrived in town. I knew you were blonde before you'd properly got your feet under your father's table. My spies also informed me you were moderately tall, didn't have enough to eat in England, and you carry a blue bag big enough to hide a baby in but you don't have a family yet, although you are already twenty-two, and this is still more evidence of the inadequacy of white men. Martha!' he said, turning exaggeratedly to the woman on the onion stall, 'I didn't see you hiding there! And how are you today?'

'I fine, Father My-kel,' the woman said, grinning broadly. 'I jes fine.'

So this was the famous Father Michael. Anne picked up her onions and put them into her bag. She had expected a dashing, handsome priest, not a big clown.

'I'd better introduce myself,' he said, putting out a large hand and shaking hers so firmly it took her a moment to recover. 'Father Michael to some, Micky to me Mam and Dad, Mike to me more degenerate associates, but mostly just plain Michael. I hear from Father Morrissey that you've offered to give us a hand?'

'Yes,' she said uncertainly. 'But it wasn't clear that I'll be of much use.'

'What!' he exclaimed with such force that she jumped. 'Be of use? We can use you! Even if all you could do was talk in your mother tongue we would make use of you!'

'But I haven't got geography, even at O level.'

'Oh that! He's got a thing about geography. No, we can use you. How much time can you spare us?'

Before she could answer, a voice behind them called

out, 'If it isn't de good priest! Father My-kel, how are you today?'

A neat little man in shorts and a white shirt was standing just behind Michael, a large pile of carefully folded new shirts balanced on top of his head.

'Atta! How are you? Atta, allow me to introduce you to Anne Foster.'

Atta was grinning at her from under his bundle. 'We already met. I waiting to see if you knowed it was me. You not recognise me I tink in my weekday clothies?'

'Oh, I'm so sorry,' she said, and knew she was blushing, 'I didn't see it was you.'

The tailor laughed. 'We all look de same to you I tink.'

'It's okay, Atta is teasing you,' Father Michael said. 'He would have just the same problem if there were more white people in town. The only reason he recognised you just now is that there are so few blondes in Tamale.'

'That's right, Father My-kel,' Atta said with a grin. 'And if we trying to recognise you by *your* hair we have hard, hard time, since you not got hardly any.'

'Oh well, I'll let it grow back and then I'll dye it pink to save you any such problem. But for now I'm keeping my hairstyle just the way it is because it's cooler.' The priest ran his hand backwards and forwards over his close-cropped scalp. 'Anyway, it's much more useful for sweeping the floors like this. They just turn me upside down and there we go, who needs a piddling little broom?'

Each morning when she looked outside the house, there were children hanging about hoping to set eyes on her. Small girls carried babies nearly half their size, balancing them expertly on one under-sized hip. The girl babies wore

29

only earrings and a string of beads around their middles, the little boys wore nothing at all. They peered at her anxiously over the shoulders of older siblings as they were heaved about. The children brought things to show her – a baby goat, a lizard on a string, a newly hatched chick – and waited to see what she did and where she went so they could accompany her. The novelty, for her, had worn off quite quickly, but not it seemed for them. Wherever she went a group of children followed, grinning and calling out to her and shouting to other children to come and join them. If she went nowhere they hovered, hoping she would come out and sit on the porch so they could stroke her fair hair and ask how it was that her ears were not pierced. If she did not come out, the bolder ones would creep onto the porch and peep round the door. Moses shouted at them to bugger off, though he shouted it in Dagbani so she could only guess at his actual words from the way he scowled after the children as they retreated. Then he turned to her and said, 'It only cos you white dey come. Don' tink it cos dey like you.'

She recoiled, startled. He looked down at her through narrowed eyes. What had she done to upset him this time?

She got her bag from her room and went out of the house. She couldn't stay in it with him giving her the feeling all the time that she was encroaching on his territory. There seemed to be no air left for her to breathe. He was so touchy! The least little thing seemed to offend him. Yesterday it was that she had used his knife to cut up some oranges. The day before, that she had bought plantain by mistake instead of bananas.

Within ten yards of the house her little entourage materialised as usual. They went with her all the way into town to the funny Kingsway supermarket, but there they did not follow. She could see them outside the window as she walked round the nearly empty shelves, their noses pressed to the glass as they watched her every move.

When she came out again they vied with each other to carry her bag, but she was afraid she would be expected to tip them and she didn't know how much to give, so she declined the offers. Her bag didn't have much in it anyway: all she'd been able to find in the supermarket, apart from Omo washing powder, was French greengage jam. She went into the market. More children had swollen the ranks at her heels. It made it claustrophobic in the hot, narrow alleyways, and the crowd pushed behind her, knocking into the stalls, so that the stall-holders shouted and shook their fists. But the children only giggled and ducked and made even more mayhem as they hopped out of reach.

She was trapped between them; the kids outside, Moses inside. And the bold flies sticking to her, too, and going with her everywhere. As persistent as the children but not as polite. Some of the flies bit, and none of them called her Madam.

'Well,' Father Michael said. 'Why don't you just suck it and see? If you take to it you can do more. I can give you some help, if you need it.'

The empty classroom was shady and peaceful. Orderly, but dusty with Easter holiday quiet. Father Michael was sitting on the teacher's desk on the small dais in front of the blackboard, idly swinging his bare legs. A scruffy man, his shirt gaping a little to reveal a hairy belly peeping over the waistband of his shorts. She sat below him in one of the front desks thinking that she liked this quieter Father

Michael rather better. His love of the school was obvious, his enthusiasm alluring, his deep voice hypnotic. She wanted him to go on talking, so she asked if he'd always wanted to be a missionary.

He was silent for a moment, gazing out through the unglazed windows of the classroom to where the falling sun shafted the dusty air with its bright, late light. 'I don't think I *am* a missionary. I don't believe I'm here to convert anyone. But there I think Father Morrissey and I part company: he does believe that we are here for the saving of souls.'

'But you? Why be in the Mission then? Why not just be a teacher, if it's not about saving souls?'

'Oh that's the easy bit – I'm here because the Mission can raise money, it can get things done. Yes, sure there are loads of other ways of getting things done but they all have political agendas. The Church is different. It's not like Save the Children or Unicef where everybody's on an individual career ladder of their own.'

'Doesn't that apply to priests as well?'

'Of course it does. I'm simplifying madly. But less, I think. I believe there *is* a difference.'

'But surely you didn't become a priest just to come out to Africa?'

'Nope. Tell me about you. I know you're twenty-two and you've just finished your degree in Cambridge.'

'And that no hairy English man has thought to make me his wife,' she said, grinning. 'That's all there is.' If he wasn't going to be drawn then neither was she. She got up and picked up her blue shoulder bag. 'I really ought to be getting home. I told Dad I'd be back before dark.'

'I'll walk with you,' he said, getting up off the desk and

stretching. 'I haven't seen your dad in a while.' He had dark patches of sweat under his arms and as he stretched his shirt rose up over his pale, hairy belly. More hairy than his shaved head, she thought, amused.

He talked, as they walked through the early dusk, of the way the Mission had changed in the eight years he'd been there. She was thinking as she walked beside him that she was beginning to understand why the expatriate women should be fascinated by him. His energy was attractive, if a little over-powering. And of course, being a priest, he was safely unavailable.

'Tell me more about this research you're thinking of doing,' he said, taking her by surprise.

'I'd like to have a look at weaving. I've read up on it quite a bit and I went to the museums in London.'

'Ah. The posh stuff, then. There isn't anything like the Asante and Ewe weaving here. It's all very plain.'

'I know,' she said, 'but it doesn't matter. There was a study done in Tamale ten years or so ago. I want to see how much has changed since then. You know – supplies, markets, middle-men – that sort of thing.'

He laughed. 'Sounds rather like geography to me.'

'Geography with attitude. Not the same.' She could see the Land Rover outside the house. Her dad was home, then.

'Gonja district, just off the Airport Road – that's the best place to look for weavers,' Michael said as they climbed the steps of the porch.

He didn't stay long. As he was leaving he said, 'So that's agreed, then? You'll come and give teaching a whirl when term starts again? As much time as you can spare us, or as little – anything at all would be appreciated.'

Behind him, a brilliant star had appeared in the soft blue-black of the upper heavens, pinning the cradle of the swinging crescent moon to the sky. In the shadowed distance beyond the town the village drums were beginning to rumble.

'Yes' she said. Her own horizons had just grown a little wider.

It was, Michael thought, a fair swap: for one tired priest with halitosis (now sadly stricken with jaundice and returned to Ireland on sick leave), one pretty girl poised on the threshold of adulthood but not yet fallen over the edge. She reminded him of his cousin, also an Anne (though known to the family as Annie), when she was young. This Anne had the same mix of seriousness and sudden humour, of insecurity and bold confidence, all bound up in one uncomfortable bundle that his Annie had had, until she became responsible and mature, the possessor of a respectable husband and the mother of four children. He hadn't thought of Annie in an age. It must be eight years since he'd last seen her.

Going into the refectory for the evening meal he found the usual gaggle of priests standing hopefully by the serving hatch as they waited for Ishmael to open it and hand out the food.

'Nobody want you tonight then, Michael?' said Giovanni.

'No, nobody wants me tonight.'

Of all of them, apart from Father Morrissey, Michael was the one least often present for the evening meal. For which the other priests teased him ruthlessly. They liked to maintain the myth that he was wooed by all the expatriate women in town because it gave them the chance to get at him a little. And it was true that however much he preferred sitting round a communal pot of *fufu* by the light of a hurricane lamp to the indolent western meals in air-conditioned bungalows, he was much too well-trained to pass up any opportunity to wheedle funds out of wealthy expatriates. And besides, he made it a matter of principle never to say no to a free meal.

Ishmael threw open the hatch with an angry rattle and thrust forward a large pan of stew. The stew was watery, a few pieces of onion floating around gristly chunks of meat under a skim of palm oil.

Giovanni peered into the pan sadly. 'Is it goat again, Ishmael?'

'Dat all der is in de market.'

Ishmael slammed the serving hatch shut again, so sharply that the basket of bread fell off the ledge. Michael caught it deftly in mid-air and only a few pieces of bread fell to the floor. He picked them up, dusted them off on his tee-shirt and popped them back into the basket. 'Waste not, want not,' he said.

They sat at the long refectory table on benches, two rows of oddly assorted bottoms, some in shorts, some in grubby white habits, and talked idly as they waited for Morrissey to join them and say grace. John told a joke about a dog, a cat and a pigeon that was quite funny, and Giovanni remembered another about a nun that was funnier. And then Morrissey was taking his place at the head of the table and bending his head over his clasped hands and they all fell silent.

It is the tired time of year, Michael thought. The Biblical time between harvests. For a while yet there would be little enough to eat in the granaries and the food-stores, and if they were eating a surfeit of goat – old, tough and scrawny – and plain bread, at least they didn't go hungry. He glanced around at his fellow priests, tucking into their meal with varying degrees of enthusiasm. You could call it God's wisdom – if you never go without how can you appreciate plenty when it comes? But Michael read the secrets in his colleagues' eyes and constructed a private mythology: Vanni dreams at night of fresh young garden beans, of olive oil, of light crusty bread made with flour without weevils; Dominic hungers guiltily for a juicy steak; Christopher (barely out of the seminary as he is) writes home to his mother asking if she could possibly send him a packet of liquorice all-sorts and a tin of ham. And even Morrissey, Michael thought, would be nostalgic for the Irish stews of his youth.

Sitting on Morrissey's left hand, opposite Dominic, Michael grew conscious of the Mission cat under the table, furtively rubbing round Dom's white-robed legs in hope of the usual titbits. He saw Morrissey frown at Dominic just as Dom's hand went down under the table with a piece of bread. Morrissey said, 'Do you think you'll be able to make use of that girl after the holidays?' and Dominic blinked, then realised it was Michael, not him, who was being addressed.

Michael said evenly, 'Of course. Any English girl that you can send me – or boy either – will be made good use of. And who knows, she might prove herself able to contribute more than conversation and a bit of elementary grammar. If we're lucky she'll be able to take over some of the English literature classes and then we could give John geography until Simon gets back. I take it we *are* expecting him to come back?'

'That can by no means be presumed. A single attack of jaundice is one thing but this is getting to be repetitive. If nothing else, his constitution needs a good rest. It would perhaps be better if he were to stay in Ireland for six months or so recuperation.'

Michael caught John's eye. He knew John would love to take over the geography department, given half a chance.

'By the way, Michael,' Patrick said from the far end of the table, 'I was telling the others before you came in – I've had a letter from Benedict. He's enjoying his retirement in sunny old Hastings but he misses Tamale. He wants to know how the new science labs are coming on.'

There was a gust of laughter round the table. The new science block had long been the subject of energetic fund-raising but it was proving slow to rise out of its footings now that building work had actually begun. There had been a lot of political rivalry over this project before Michael took it over, and there was a certain amount of glee that all was not going as smoothly as it had at the money-raising stage. There were some who intimated that Michael (being full of hot air) was better at persuading people to cough up money than he was at organizing actual work. He couldn't help but know this since Patrick had carefully told him, veiling it as a joke. They were all looking at him now to see how he was taking this joke but he wasn't going to satisfy them by rising to the bait. This was why he preferred to eat elsewhere: they were a family, with all a family's worst vices hidden under a thin skin. The bickering, the manoeuvring, the petty jealousies and banal kindnesses. The loneliness beneath. They had all, except Christopher, been there a long time and they were heartily tired of one another's little ways.

No, that isn't fair. It's me, not Father Simon, who is suffering

37

from jaundice. Yes we bicker, but we have our little bits of fun too. Look at Dominic now, feeding that cat under the table. Morrissey scowling at him but Dom doesn't see because he's too busy looking at his plate and trying to appear innocent as his left hand goes down under the table edge with another bit of bread. Michael knows for a fact that Morrissey cannot abide animals in the refectory but he can hardly say so openly, this being God's world and all creatures in it God's creatures.

But just as he was thinking this Morrissey snapped, 'Dominic, are you feeding that cat?'

Dominic looked up guiltily and flushed. 'C-c-c-cat?' He couldn't say *No* without everyone knowing it for a lie. He couldn't say *Yes*, because the cat wasn't supposed to be in the refectory. All eyes were on him, waiting with interest. Except for Ishmael, who was coming round the table with a bowl of desiccated green oranges.

Ishmael tripped over the cat, which let out a fearsome screech and shot out of the room.

I do love them, Michael thought. We're all flawed but that's what families are: flawed, but all we've got.

4

Week 5, April

The dense, heat-heavy days were spreading out behind her, full of little things but nothing very much. Her dad at work all day, the days long and slow with just her and Moses in the house. Moses who seemed no more accepting of her now than he had been at the beginning.

She'd rather had her fill of Moses. She wondered how long it would be before he went off to visit his village again.

All the same, she couldn't help feeling a sneaking admiration for the nonchalant skill with which he operated. In the kitchen, she observed with interest how he squatted on a stool to prepare vegetables, cutting them without a board straight into the pan. After the meal, he washed up in a plastic bowl using cold water and lots of Omo washing-powder so that the bubbles rose up his arms and clung to the crockery, leaving faint rainbow circles where they dried. She could smell the Omo on the plates afterwards. She was sure she could taste it. Sometimes he cooked on the gas ring but he seemed to prefer the charcoal brazier (the one she had assumed was for barbecues), which raised the temperature in the airless room to dizzy heights. The window in the corner was too small. It allowed the sun in, but never seemed to catch any breeze. Sometimes Moses took the charcoal stove outside to the backyard to cook. If he did (unless he brought the stove straight back into the kitchen, still alight as it was) he was always agitated that it might be stolen while they were eating.

She observed these details like an anthropologist with an invisible notebook, safely remote. But he didn't treat her as one. He was brusquely familiar, clicking his tongue as if her every action annoyed him, and tossing his head impatiently. He showed no respect at all.

Did she expect him to? His relationship with her dad wasn't formal either. Sometimes Moses called him 'Sah!' but when he did it seemed to be some kind of a joke and mostly he addressed her dad by his Christian name. It wasn't respect that was the issue, she realised, it was his casually revealed dislike of her which hurt. He didn't even know her! She had to keep reminding herself of this when she caught him scowling.

She objected to the way his presence limited hers: he took up too much space in the house. Probably he would prefer it if she didn't come into the kitchen at all but she wasn't prepared to sink quite that low. She could make her own cups of tea, thank you very much, even if boiling water on the gas ring was the limit of her forays into his territory.

When the gas ran out, Moses carried the cylinder on his head all the way up the hill to the depot in town, and then he carried the even heavier replacement all the way back. She understood then why he preferred to use charcoal: it was bulky but it was much lighter to carry. She felt a belated twinge of guilt at her own free-and-easy use of the gas ring. No wonder he tutted.

Anne walked into town and found her way down the Airport Road looking for Gonja District, a crowd of excited kids at her heels. She couldn't find any weavers. Everybody seemed to know where to find them but it got lost in translation somehow when they tried to give her directions. She walked home again.

Home. So easy to say that word but nowhere else felt real and there was no other home but here. Her father's house was home now, strange as it was. Except for Moses in it. She came in through the front door and saw the light drain out of his eyes. She couldn't stay under the same roof. She went out again and walked back up the long weary hill to Jo's house.

At least Jo left no room for doubt that she was pleased to see her. And if Anne was subdued, Jo was too eager to tell her own life story to notice. How she'd met Kevin when they were both VSOs in Kumasi. Got married because she fell pregnant, to keep the parents happy back home. Stayed in Ghana because Kevin had landed this job with the Tamale Water Corporation. Anne asked – mildly interested but mostly to be polite – if Josh had been born in Tamale. Jo flashed back, 'No fear! Have you seen the hospital here? You really don't want to be hospitalised in Ghana, Anne – take my word for it! No, I went home when I was seven months pregnant. Kevin came back on leave. He tried to time it for the birth but he missed it.' She was silent for a moment, gazing at Josh. 'Story of Kevin's life.'

The idea of a baby was like something arriving off a different planet, but it must have been like that for Jo, too, until she found herself pregnant and had to see it through. Anne watched the little gestures and inflections between mother and child with a mixture of awe and revulsion. The nappy smells, the dribble. The two little dark wet patches on Jo's tee-shirt, over her pointed breasts, which Anne had been surreptitiously staring at, intrigued, until she realised with a shock that the wet was milk.

How could such a thin, tense person sustain a whole other life?

Joshua sat placidly on his mother's knee and pulled clumsily at her tee-shirt. Jo laughed and lifted her shirt to suckle him. Anne didn't know where to look. And then to her surprise she was moved. Discreet rhythmical sucking sounds came from under the rucked shirt, followed by an eloquent sigh.

'Do you like being a mother?' It was another question to plug a gap, but she did suddenly want to know.

Jo stared down at Joshua's head, half hidden under her tee-shirt. 'I wouldn't be without him for the world. But it's a funny thing – he's what stops me from being terribly lonely and he's what makes me lonely as well. Whenever we go out, the local kids follow us trying to touch him. If I carry him in the sling I'm hassled all the time.'

'Why?' Anne exclaimed, surprised, because all babies here were carried, there were no pushchairs or prams.

'Everybody shouts at us, all the time – men, women, even little kids. *On de back! On de back!* as if it's absolutely shocking – hysterically funny kind of shocking – to carry a child on the front. It's like I'm breaking some kind of law.'

'Why don't you just carry him on your back then?'

'If I did I wouldn't be able to stop them pulling at him. And I can't see what they're giving him if he's on my back. It's a conservative place but people feel so free to voice their opinions. Anything you do out of the ordinary, it's all right for them to comment.'

'Don't you think it would be the same at home?'

'I'm sure people would say it behind your back at home, even in provincial places like this.'

Anne nodded, but she had only ever lived in London and later in Cambridge, where nobody commented on anything much. She noticed Josh had fallen asleep, his head lolling back to reveal a wet nipple.

'When we lived in the other house over in Gonja District, before the Water Corporation gave us this one, the women would line up in the alleyway outside the window whenever Josh cried and chant *Feed dat chil'! Feed dat chil'!* Like a chorus in a Greek Tragedy or something. Only they thought it was funny.'

Joshua woke with a little start, surfacing like a drunken swimmer. Jo put him down on his belly on his blanket on the floor. She got out her tobacco tin, looking defensively at Anne from under her dark cloud of hair: 'I know I should give up but it's so hard! It is my only luxury!'

They sat in silence watching Josh doing press-ups.

'He'll be crawling soon, I guess,' Jo said proudly. 'Are you really not coming to Ursula's At Home on Friday?'

Anne laughed and shook her head.

'Wish I was as strong-minded,' Jo said. 'But it does make a change from being stuck at home. Deepa's all right, but most of the others are pretty dull. And Ursula always drinks too much – she used to be much more fun. Have you ever seen her with Michael? She flirts outrageously with him. It's as if it's some kind of a game but underneath you get the feeling that she's sort of serious. That's probably why she was so edgy with you last time. You're all the things she isn't – young, beautiful, single – and now you're going to be Michael's protégée as well.'

'I am?'

'Isn't he going to be your mentor?'

'I suppose so,' Anne agreed uncertainly.

'Well there you are then! Ursula would give *anything* to be you. Bar the actual teaching, of course. She's too sodding lazy to *work* for the pleasure of gaining anyone's attention. I wish you'd change your mind and come on Friday. It would be much more fun if you were there.'

Anne shook her head. 'Sorry. I really couldn't stand another afternoon like the last one.'

Jo laughed. 'Oh well, it was obvious that was how you felt. That's how I knew I was going to like you. But you should hide those feelings in front them. Hard as it may be to believe, in six months or so you might find you do need them after all.'

That's all right then, Anne thought, because by then I'll be on my way home.

The next day she came into the living room, silent on her bare feet, to find Moses standing in the middle of the small room with his back to her, staring down to his left. What was he looking at so intently? She glanced down to where her bag and book were lying on the sofa. There was nothing else. As if he sensed her presence, he moved and looked back at her over his shoulder. His bold, malevolent stare, so strangely lacking in curiosity. Shaken, she took her things to her room and sat miserably on the bed. She had to get out of the house!

Walking into town, her jangled feelings eased a little. She saw a child standing under a standpipe at the side of the road, wailing in protest as his mother vigorously soaped his gleaming little body. The woman bent to her task, the kerchief on her head nodding merrily as she rubbed and scrubbed her protesting son. Anne returned the woman's cheerful greeting as she passed, wishing she could understand what was being said to the child in that husky, sardonic voice. This life of the streets – so vigorous, so un-embarrassed and noisy – she would not like to live it but she loved to observe it. *I'm such an academic!* she thought. *Sitting on the outside looking in!*

She looked for the weavers but she didn't find them. Only a group of kids standing at a little distance, calling out cheekily. She called back, 'I can see you, you naughty boys!' It didn't matter what she said since they wouldn't understand. She turned to go back home, reluctantly. Home where Moses would be, anthropology come right inside the house. They were all miniature versions of Moses, she was thinking as she pushed her way through the crowds by the market, these small, nearly naked boys. But they hadn't yet learned to scowl. When had he? He smiled at other people – he had a beautiful smile, with his wide mouth and his perfect whiter-than-white teeth, his slanted eyes crinkling suddenly. She saw him smiling at others but whenever he looked at her his smile abruptly faded. It made her feel like a leper in his presence.

Meal times were the worst. Moses watching her closely.

'Delicious!' her dad said as he tucked into yet another greasy stew. 'But perhaps go easy on the chilli, old chap? While Anne is here?' The next night, when Moses passed her one of the plates he had served in the kitchen and brought to the table (his fingers as always carefully avoiding any chance contact with hers, as if she might contaminate him), she looked up and caught the expression on his face . She looked at her plate. There was surely more chilli in her serving than in either of theirs. She took a spoon as well as a knife and fork from the centre of the table and began to eat. If she laid the spoon and the knife casually on the side of her plate and ate with the fork she could push the bits of chilli quietly under them. Her dad cut the bread – Abina's bread, delicious-looking with its shiny crust but tasting of nothing. 'American wheat,' her dad observed, seeing her looking at it. 'Food Aid, destroying local markets. They should teach you that at university,' he added, as if whatever they had taught her had fallen short of the meaningful truths. She took up her fork and began to eat, feeling Moses watching her. The chilli made her eyes water and she knew he was waiting for her reaction but she would not give him the satisfaction of one. 'Plenty of traditional staples here,' her dad went on. '*Fufu* from yams. Cassava, sorghum. But Moses prefers bread. You think everything that comes out of the US is good, don't you Moses?'

Moses laughed and ducked his head in assent. 'But not de football. American football no good. All de same, one day I will live in America.'

She saw her dad wince as if he'd noticed her pushing another piece of chilli to the side of her plate. He said nothing. But later, when he passed her empty plate to Moses to clear away, he exclaimed 'Gosh, Anne! You do seem to have landed more than your fair share of chilli!' She waited in vain for him to say something to Moses. Why didn't he stand up to Moses on her behalf?

My father, my protector. Another childhood belief foundering.

One evening her dad got round to doing what he'd been talking about ever since she'd arrived and took her to the Tamale English Language Library. The Library was a small modern building set on a grassy knoll among some trees.

Inside, it was like any small local library in England, picked up and dropped down again in Tamale. Except for the librarian, a young and smiling Ghanaian with thick glasses and a big Afro, who welcomed her warmly.

While her dad browsed the sci-fi section she wandered round the shelves in amazement. There was a bit of everything here, from D.H. Lawrence to Mills and Boon.

When they went to the counter to stamp her dad's two books and two for her, Mr Issafu Nigeria had already made out tickets in her name. He handed them over the counter with a shy smile. He had got her name right without being told, even the 'e' on the end of Anne.

The library was somewhere else to go when she needed to escape from the house and changing her dad's library books was something she could do better than Moses. Moses was only interested in football magazines.

She wasn't going to let herself be limited to library books. She bought a pretty cloth and draped it over the unprepossessing sofa. In the evening it had been removed. She found it neatly folded on her bed. *Right, Moses!* She marched to the living room to put it back on the sofa.

Her dad was sitting in the armchair. 'Oh,' he said. 'I moved that.'

'*You* did? But why?'

'Moses wouldn't like it. Best to keep it in your room, I think.' He avoided her eye.

She put the cloth away in her cupboard, too hurt even to want it on her bed. All right then, if that was the way her father wanted it, she would submit.

Later that evening they sat out in the warm darkness at the front of the house, watching the lightning flash from behind a bulk of cumulus clouds in the night sky. Her dad smoked his pipe placidly in his chair and she sat silently beside him, listening to the din of insects, aware of Moses behind them on the porch steps. He spends very little time in his own room, she thought irritably. Then she thought it *was* a stiflingly hot little room, not much more than a storeroom really. She felt guilty, but not that guilty. 'Tell me about when I was small,' she said, choosing a subject which firmly excluded Moses.

'There's not much to tell. I've a memory like a sieve these days.'

She listened with half an ear to the shrill cricket lodged somewhere in the wall just behind her. 'But you must remember something!'

He took his pipe out of his mouth and knocked it on the sole of his shoe, spraying red sparks briefly in the monochrome night. 'Shockingly little.'

She was offended into silence.

'I'm not a very good dad, am I. No stories to tell you.'

But she suspected he was lying. She felt Moses sitting just behind her as if she could feel his eyes boring into her back. For a moment she thought her dad was talking to Moses and not to her at all. A crazy thought came into her head – could it be that her dad was *his* father as well? Wildly she thought of all the reasons why he couldn't be – Moses was so dark. And he was too old. Older than her by quite a bit. Her father hadn't come to Ghana until she was old enough to remember him leaving home. But it would explain why she felt the way she did. Twenty-two was much too old to discover sibling rivalry, let alone a real sibling.

'Moses has so many cousins!' she said to her dad the following night, after yet another gaggle of young men had called by the house. Moses had gone across the road with them to smoke in the grove of mango trees, their cigarettes glowing in the dark shadows as they squatted in a circle and chatted, leaving her and her dad in peace indoors.

'He has, but *we* wouldn't recognise most of them as relatives. What he calls a cousin might be his father's sister-in-law's second cousin once removed.'

She worked it out. 'You mean, not even a blood relative?'

'But still a cousin to a Ghanaian. Very important, all these family connections. They think we're very odd, you and me. A family of two is almost an impossibility here.'

'I know!' So many people had asked her in the street, *Where is your mother?* Shocked to find that her mother was in a different country. *And where are your sisters, your brothers? Your aunties?* Increasingly incredulous as she replied 'I haven't got any.' It wasn't quite true: she did have an uncle, and an aunt by marriage if you counted his wife as a relative, and two cousins, but she'd seen them too rarely for them to feel like family to her.

'Anyway,' her dad went on, 'they're only coming round to take a look at you. We don't normally get so many visitors, cousins or otherwise.'

'Hasn't the novelty worn off yet? I've been here more than a month!'

She didn't believe it was her they were coming for. It was true that they would hang around the porch and ask to greet her if she didn't come to the door, but they always scooted off pretty quickly to smoke and gossip under the mango trees with Moses. She could hear their voices now, from where she sat in the living room. A burst of laughter rang out.

'Getting a bit wild out there,' her dad observed. Their

high-pitched laughter made them sound like small boys. Not like men in their late twenties or older.

'Is Moses married?' She had no idea whether he was or not. He spent most of his time in her dad's house but he might have a wife and a whole lot of children tucked away somewhere, for all she knew.

'They get married late here,' her dad said. Rather tersely, she thought, looking up in surprise. He had returned to his book, shutting her out.

That's what he does, she thought. He shuts me out. Removes himself. Subtly, but as surely as if he's slammed down a hatch.

Suddenly she thought of her other home. The one so far away it no longer felt real, leaving her marooned in this one. Her mum's pretty little garden seemed suddenly very desirable, even with her mum in it. Busy weeding as she would be now in the long spring twilight of England, whereas here it had been dark for an hour or two already. Her mum who always had time for her (too much time!), and who loved to talk. Her infuriating, demanding, overly-dependent but in the end surprisingly endearing and terribly faraway mum.

She stood up abruptly, needing to be alone. Her dad looked up from his book and raised an enquiring eyebrow. 'Just going to write a letter,' she said, meaning to sound cheerful but her voice betraying her. If he noticed, he made no comment.

Her room was airless. She sat on the bed with her back against the warm wall and let the silent tears fall. It was a relief just to let go for a while. Then she got out her precious pad of airmail paper. The light in her room was terrible – a single ceiling light without a shade. No light bulb in Tamale seemed to be stronger than forty watts. She dried her eyes and started to write, in tiny writing to make the paper last.

Writing was cathartic. Remembering all the new things she had seen as she re-told them to her mother. Remembering, by the things she chose to leave out, why the distance was good. Her mum, not understanding how much it involved, would have preferred her to toil up to the public pay-phone in the post office but letters were better. Letters were more manageable. They could be edited by simple omission.

She wrote about all the things she had seen that week: the crowded buses, and the overloaded lorries emblazoned with artwork and idiosyncratic slogans. The pottery market, where thin women sold the fragile handmade pots they had carried on their heads from villages outside the town. In the main market, the stalls of smelly salt fish and dried bush-rats pegged out like small dark tiger-skin rugs but minus the stripes and with buck teeth. And stall after stall of vegetables where there was nothing to buy except poor quality red onions and bruised tomatoes arranged in sad little pyramids, and withered okra, and the women clamoured for her custom in shrill, angry voices as if their lives depended on it. Which, quite possibly, they did. She wrote about this, and then she described the lizards darting out into the sun and back again into the sharp shadows: small ones with bright blue tails, huge ones ugly as sin with yellow heads ponderously bobbing up and down on prehistoric bodies. She told about the mysterious *juju* stalls where dusty treasures were piled in untidy heaps. She described walking through the narrow alleyways with sweat running down her back and down the backs of her thighs, wrapping her shirt to her ribs, her long skirt to her knees, but she didn't mention how quickly she was exhausted. It wasn't just that she had yet to acclimatise to the savage savannah climate: tempers were rising all around her. Market mammies shrieked at small boys who jostled against their stalls. Men raised their hands threateningly to women in the street. Taxi drivers argued over fares. The heat was getting to everyone, the pent-up longing for the truant rain. She didn't mention these negative things, but she did describe the giant clouds building up by day, and the thunder rumbling, only to disperse at dusk and leave the night innocently clear, while in the villages surrounding the town the drumming reached new crescendos.

5

Week 6, April

She was in the market buying wizened oranges, on the day which marked the end of her fifth week in Ghana, when she looked along the row of stalls and noticed a white man standing at one of them. Her eyes picked him out involuntarily, just as her ear located the different, penetrating edge of his American voice. He was not eye-catching and yet he caught her eye. A tall man, slightly stooped, not old but not young either. Hair thinning, long over the collar. Wearing a loud African shirt, but like an insect wearing its disguise in the wrong place, the shirt only emphasized his foreignness.

He came up to her and presented a large hand. 'Don Seinfeld, Tamale-America Trust.'

She shook hands. 'Anne – Anne Foster. Have we met before?' She was trying to remember whether she'd been introduced to him that day at TAT, but it seemed like a lifetime ago.

'I think not. What are you doing here?'

'Um – buying bananas.' She remembered what her dad had said about TAT and the CIA, but surely not!

'I meant, what are you doing in Ghana?'

'Oh sorry. I've come to stay with my father.' He was still looking at her questioningly so she added (as if feeding scraps to a dog in the hope that it will be pacified and go away), 'Dick Foster.'

'Dick? Dick's got a *daughter*? Oh my! I did not know that!'

So much for the CIA theory.

'Well, be seeing you.' He shook hands again and ambled off, chortling as if she'd said something particularly funny.

She had meant to look for weavers again but it was much too hot. Besides, tomorrow was her first day in the classroom and it would be hard to concentrate on anything else just now. She turned round to trudge back home. It was a Sunday but her dad had sloped off to the office and Moses had gone to his village: the prospect of going back to an empty house wasn't enticing, even after so long wanting it. She had spent days preparing for school and now she didn't want to think about it any more or she would be too nervous to sleep tonight. She passed the end of the drive to Jo's house. *What the hell!* She turned back and went through the gate.

The sky beyond the bungalow was forbiddingly black. Gusts of hot wind sent dust devils upwards from the bare soil and turned the tired leaves of the neem trees pale-side out. The hot smell of burning charcoal drifted from the village huts just beyond the garden fence. Halfway down the drive it occurred to Anne that it was silly to come on a Sunday when Kevin would be home and they would be enjoying a family day together but it was too late to turn back without being seen from the windows.

Instead of happy familial sounds, when she came under the lea of the house she heard the dismal wailing of a baby, and then Jo's voice, admonishing. The baby's wail rose to a howl. Anne's heart sank but if she hadn't been seen coming

54

she would surely be spotted leaving. She climbed the steps and knocked on the screen door.

'I'm glad to see you!' Jo exclaimed, flinging open the door. 'We are *not* having a happy day here! Kevin's gone off to sort out an emergency. Typical, isn't it – he works for the Water Corporation and our own water has gone off completely! We haven't had a drop since Friday. So Josh and I are on our own, as per usual, and we're heartily sick of one another. Not to mention that he's having a spate of particularly revolting nappies. It's either his teeth or it's the bananas.'

She had to shout, to be heard over Joshua who was sitting on the floor, his howling having risen to an even higher pitch at the sight of Anne. Jo picked him up. 'Here, hold him for a bit while I get us some cold drinks. As cold as they can be, anyway, given the power's been off since seven this morning. Make the most of him while he doesn't smell.'

Joshua, as astonished as Anne was, stopped crying and looked at her, a tear trembling on each cheek. His lower lip pouted and his breath came in juddering half-sobs.

'Hello, Joshua,' she said softly, surprised by the feel of him. The density of his little body – and yet he felt light because of the way he held himself erect, leaning back a little to look at her, his fists still raised in mid-protest. 'Hello,' she said again, and smiled.

With a shuddering sigh he gave her a watery smile back. And at that precise moment she fell in love. She kissed the top of his head, breathing in his surprising baby smell. He gazed at her intently as she gingerly carried him to the sofa. An ancient man, half a year old. Then he said 'Da?' and pointed at the ceiling.

Jo came in with lemonade and they sat on the sofa with

Josh hemmed in safely between them happily banging two wooden bricks together. The sky outside was so dark that even though it wasn't yet five o'clock they could hardly see one another's faces. The wind was rising.

The storm broke suddenly with such a crash of rain on the roof that they all three jumped. Lightning ripped the shadows, thunder following on its heels. Joshua wailed and Jo hugged him to her, but she was laughing. They didn't hear Kevin coming back in the Land Rover. He banged through the screen door, soaked to the skin.

Later, Jo lit a single candle. The flame guttered gently, the storm safely pushed outside now that they had run round the house closing the heavy wooden shutters. They sat together in a circle of golden light. The drumming of the rain drowned all attempts at conversation. It got late. The lightning and thunder subsided but the rain showed little sign of easing. Jo fetched cold chicken and salad, bread and beer, and they ate supper at the table by the light of the candle.

Anne looked at their faces in the soft, enclosing light. Kevin's kind face glowed rosily, his brown beard Jesus-like. Joshua sat on his lap, very still, gazing at the candle. Jo was not still at all – jumping up to fetch things, worrying about Joshua, worrying about the roads which would be awash between here and Anne's house, and about whether the power would come back on that night. Her anxiety visible but inaudible, swallowed up by the storm.

Joshua was put to bed. Kevin got out the Scrabble.

It was nearly ten o'clock before the rain eased enough for Kevin to drive Anne back down the hill to the Low-Cost Estate. Everywhere was deep in water and mud, the storm drains full to overflowing. The headlamps of the Land

Rover flared oddly against the walls of the unlit houses as they followed the twisting road. Here and there the muted glow of a candle or a hurricane lamp lit up an open window but most people seemed to have gone to bed to keep warm. It was strange to be shivering with cold but already, now that the rain had nearly stopped, the heat was gently re-asserting itself. It wouldn't stay cool for long.

She saw the relief on her dad's face as she walked in at the door. She went to him and kissed him gratefully on the ear. He squeezed her in a brief hug. 'Go to bed,' he said. 'You'll need your sleep tonight of all nights. Big day for you tomorrow. Shall I wake you before I go out in the morning?'

A rush of happiness at this sudden gruff affection washed over her as she said goodnight. Such an unexpected and lovely evening it had been! Outside in the damp darkness, where the crickets were shrilling again, the triumphant drums had fallen silent and everyone slept.

'Do you not think our prayers for rain rather did the trick?' asked Father Michael when Anne reported to him in the staffroom next morning.

'Your prayers? I thought it was the drumming that did it.'

He put his finger to his lips and whispered 'Probably was, but don't let Him Above hear you say so!'

The morning was humid but fresh. Great puddles everywhere reflected the bright sky. The sound of vehicles splashing through the wet made a startlingly foreign sound, a misplaced sound of home, so profoundly had she been absorbed into Tamale life already. An intense array of smells had erupted after the rain, from fragrant earth and distant flowers to drains and sewage. As she had picked her way up the sticky road to the school this morning, trying to avoid the worst of the puddles, clouds of brilliant butterflies were feeding on old mango stones and dog turds in the warm red mud.

Here in the staffroom the air was pleasantly cool. Father Michael introduced her to his fellow priests and she shook hands, trying to memorise names. He showed her a gap on the crowded shelves where she could keep her books and cleared a bit of one of the tables for her to use whenever she wanted. 'We'll have to put your name on that bit of space,' he said, but she thought he might be joking. 'You'll find you have to fight for your corner in here.'

She put her bag down on the table, not sure what was expected of her.

'You're not nervous are you?' he asked suddenly, peering down into her face. 'Don't be. Though of course you are bound to be, to begin with. Remember – whatever your own time at school was like it won't have been anything like this. Every one of these boys is grateful to be here. It's an opportunity for them. A gift, not a requirement – one they grab with both hands.'

'That makes me feel worse! I might let them down.'

He gave her shoulder a reassuring squeeze. His hand was strong and comforting, like a doctor's. 'You won't. Whatever you know or you don't know, you can give them a lot without even trying – your youth and your enthusiasm, and your ability to speak good English in a clear voice. When you find you don't know something, take them with you. Teach them the process of finding out. If you can do that you'll have taught them the most important thing of all.'

He saw her worried look and grinned. 'Come on. The sooner you get started the sooner you'll feel better.'

They entered the classroom to a sudden silence. The boys crowding the undersized desks stared for a startled moment before rising eagerly to their feet and chorusing 'Good Morning Father My-kel.'

'Good morning, class. And what a lovely morning it is too! Boys, this lady is Miss Anne.'

'Good morning Missanne.' Fifty-two pairs of shining eyes looked her way.

'Miss Anne has come to help us in the school. She is from England and she has not been in Ghana very long so it won't be easy for her to understand you if you speak very fast, and especially not if you talk pidgin. But since this is an English lesson you will be speaking your best English anyway, and so will she. I've told her you are the very best pupils in the school but don't tell anyone else I said so, because I've told all the classes the same thing. Only with the others it was just to make them happy.'

The class tittered, a sea of smiling faces.

He turned to her. 'I'm afraid we've had to give you the overspill classroom – these desks are ancient, they used to be in the primary school and they're rather small. You'll need to give the boys a chance to get up and stretch a bit before the hour is up. They'll probably be too polite to say anything themselves.' He gave her a private, reassuring smile. 'Over to you, then,' he said, formally, and then he winked and whispered, 'Have *fun*.'

The door closed behind him. Fifty-two faces gazed at her expectantly. A hundred and four hands poised ready to shoot into the air with answers to questions. She cleared her throat and began: 'Okay...' but her voice seemed to lose itself in the space between her feet and the front row so she began again, notching her voice up a level – 'Okay, we're going to play a word game. And so that I can start learning your names, or trying to learn them, you can each tell me your name as we go along. The game goes like this: My name is Anne Foster. I went to the market and I bought a yam.' She pointed to a boy in the front row who was beaming at her. 'Now you say your name, and say *I went to the market and I bought a yam and a* – and then you add a word for something else you bought. And the next boy I point to has to tell me his name and say both those things and then add another thing that he bought, like a list. Okay? So, I am Anne Foster. I went to the market and I bought a yam.' She pointed to the boy.

'I am Joseph Appiah. I went to de market and I bought a yam and a cassava.'

'Good!' She pointed to the boy sitting next to him.

'I am John Aburiya. I went to de market and I buyed"

'Bought'

'I bought a yam, a cassava and… Missanne, how you say *agushi* seeds in English?'

'Oh – I don't know. We don't have them in England. I think they might be melon seeds, but *agushi* seeds is fine.'

'I went to de market and I buyed – I bought – a yam, a cassava, and *agushi* seeds.'

She pointed to a boy sitting in the third row.

'I am Thomas Nanfuri. I went to de market and I bot a got.'

'A got?'

'Yes, Madam. A got. I bot a got.'

She was puzzled. Somebody at the back of the room helpfully gave a faint bleat. 'Oh, you mean a *goat*. You *bought* a *goat*. But what about the yam and the cassava and the *agushi* seeds?'

'No, Madam,' he said.

A wave of smothered laughter washed through the class. The boy, still sombre, said, 'Madam, yesterdeh I went to de market and I bot a got only. I didn't buy cassava or all dat ting.'

This time the laughter rang out loud. The boy sitting across the narrow aisle from Thomas leaned over and said, 'It's a game, Thomas. It not de real market. And you should say Missanne, not Madam.'

'Let's start again,' she said quickly. 'This time we'll do it differently. Each thing you say you buy, make it start with the next letter of the alphabet. So, if we start with *agushi* seeds the next item could be bananas, and so on. They don't have to be real things you can really buy in the market,' she said, not daring to look at Thomas. 'It could be "giraffe", or "lorry", or anything at all so long as it starts with the next letter of the alphabet from the last item.'

They began again and she could feel the class relaxing as they got into the swing of it. They got to *F*. She pointed to the boy in the back row whom she suspected of the bleat.

'My name is Ezekiel Naah. I went to de market and I bought *agushi* seeds, bananas, cassava, a donkey, an elephant, and...and a fish!'

She pointed to Thomas, hoping to make him smile this time. He shrugged. 'Missanne, I only bot a got.'

6

Early May

He was so quiet that she didn't realise he was in the house until she went into the kitchen to make herself a cup of tea after school. He made her think of the Tailor of Gloucester when he sat like that on his low stool, his long legs folded under him. He had – surprisingly – a book in his hands. A scruffy blue hardback that was vaguely familiar. He looked up with his usual scowl and she braced herself for the usual barbed comment, but instead he asked, 'Mince – what is dis mince?'

'Mints?' she queried, startled. How would she begin to explain *mints*? As in sweets? As in Exchequers? She looked down at the book and saw it was a recipe book. But if Moses meant mincemeat, did he mean it as in beef or as in Christmas? Then she forgot the question all together as she realised with an odd, lurching jolt that she recognised this book. It used to belong to her mother. In recent history, it had been in her mother's kitchen.

She smelled that kitchen suddenly – its friendly, comfortable smell. She covered up her strangely jangled feelings by bending to look at the page. Beefburgers. Minced meat. She could not think that anybody they knew in Tamale would have a mincer, and the only butchers she was aware of were in the abattoir – they only went in for hacking. They certainly wouldn't mince.

Moses was watching her impatiently with hooded eyes, ready to take offence as usual. He would think she was being awkward but she couldn't think how to explain 'mince'.

'It's a machine,' she said at last, and his eyes widened as if she were crazy: this had been a type of meat a moment ago but now it was a machine? 'It grinds the meat up very small.'

His frown lifted marginally. 'You mean, make small-small meat?'

But she didn't think she did mean that. 'Not *small* meat, no. Smaller – like little worms.'

His delicate eyebrows shot upwards. 'Worms?'

'Smaller than small-small,' she said, hopelessly. 'Squashed. So that you can sort of press it into a little flat cake. I don't think it would stick together if you just cut it into small-small meat.' Moses was reading a recipe for something he had clearly never seen or eaten, and asking advice of somebody only a little more experienced than himself.

He stood up abruptly and turned away, ending the conversation.

At supper that night he came to the table bearing a plate covered with a clean cloth.

'There's a wonderful smell been coming out of that kitchen,' her dad said hopefully as he cut thick wedges of Abina's bread. 'I'm ravenous!'

Moses laid the plate in the middle of the table and whisked off the cloth with a flourish. Six perfect beefburgers.

Now how did he do that? Anne wondered.

Games were one thing but in Anne's second week, Father Michael was keen to move her on to teaching bits of the English Literature syllabus. In the open-sided classroom she was acutely conscious of the way voices carried: from where she stood she could hear Father Morrissey's prim tones teaching geography to her left and the sing-song ebullience of Father Giovanni teaching religious education to her right. Self-conscious, she dropped her own voice, until one of the boys informed her politely that they could not hear her in the back row.

Sometimes, as she walked through the school, she heard Father Michael's playful baritone and the excited laughter of his class. She listened enviously: she would never be able to share his skill, and had she herself been blessed with a teacher who possessed that power to make maths fun she would surely have learned a lot more maths.

Her various classes settled to a routine. She began to recognise faces and put names to them. She learned which boys to draw out of their shyness and which not to confront with failure by asking them for answers they could not give. In the staffroom, Michael helped her with advice and suggestions. He made her laugh at herself when she was inclined to take it all too seriously. When he talked about his classes he was often very funny, usually at his own expense.

The agreement had been that she would spend two days a week in school, but at the end of her second week, Father Morrissey stopped Anne in the corridor and asked her dolefully if she would be willing to do more. She said yes without hesitation. He added (as if he'd been testing her) that if she were willing to work full-time it would of course be on an employment basis. They would give her a local salary – not much by expatriate standards but better than nothing.

She hadn't thought of being paid. Nor that being paid would make her more independent. She told her father she would start paying her share of the housekeeping . He was startled, looking at her as if she were a stranger come in out of the afternoon and leaving by nightfall. For a moment it seemed as if he would say yes but then he changed his mind and rejected the idea, making her a child again.

The school day ran from seven-thirty in the morning until one-thirty, with a half-hour break mid-morning. The new routine was surprisingly comforting, making a dynamic shape in her previously shapeless existence, but she was relieved she wasn't required to attend Mass before school with the boys. She couldn't get used to the population of pale saints under whose scrutiny they all passed their days. This was an iconography of the white-skinned and the golden-haired but how did she fit into this world? Was she, in spite of her fair hair and pale skin, to be one of the Damned who trekked down to hell in the background of the painting that hung on the wall outside Father Morrissey's office? There were crucifixes everywhere, some with Christ upon them, some just the stark, solitary symbol. These white men and these black boys, moving so easily among their symbols! Were the symbols more potent to those on the inside, or to her, the outsider looking in?

But then she remembered, she was not the only one recently stepped into this Christian world. Not the only one at all. How did the world look to these boys who passed through her classroom?

My boys, she was beginning to think of them. Their faces

would swim into her head at odd moments as she walked the red roads or sat at her marking. The ranks of the youngest and newest so bright and childish still, nervously eager in their freshly ironed white shirts and green shorts. The Sixth Formers relaxed and confident, spilling out of the same undersized desks that comfortably contained the small boys. And then there were the middle-school boys, all sizes and shapes, their voices gruff and unmanageable, more turbulent and mixed in their reactions than the small boys or the young men, but wanting to learn. Wanting to please.

In her brother-less, as good as cousin-less, girls' school existence Anne had never had much to do with boys until she got to university, where they had outnumbered girls by eight to one. (And most of those sex-starved public school idiots didn't count as boys, she thought now, looking down at the faces watching her to see what she would do next.) She turned to the blackboard and wrote: *He clasps the crag with crooked hands*. It was much more difficult writing on a blackboard than she had realised. Keeping the letters even and large enough, fitting them in. *Close to the sky in lonely lands*, she wrote on the next line.

'What do you remember of what you learned in school?' Michael had asked. 'Mainly doggerel,' had been her reply but he said, 'Use it – if you can still remember it, they will find it memorable too.' A conversation they'd had right at the beginning, standing looking into the Mission 'library' – a cupboard, full of theological books with a couple of dog-eared Len Deightons stuffed in among them.

Above the azure seas he stands, she wrote. The First Formers licked the ends of their pencils and copied the lines into their exercise books with frowning concentration. Had she remembered it correctly, she wondered, standing back and assessing her slightly descending script? Was she promulgating a misquotation? The Tamale English Language Library hadn't been able to help. The only poetry books on its shelves had been Rudyard Kipling and Sylvia Plath, with a gap beside them where the Collected Verse had gone missing. ('We used to have it,' Mr Issafu Nigeria said sadly, standing in front of the shelves, scratching at his Afro, which had just tickled her face when he stopped suddenly as she followed him between the stacks.) She remembered Kipling writing about fuzzy-wuzzies: perhaps he was best avoided. Sylvia Plath might do for the Sixth Formers, given time, but she needed ideas right now. Michael's suggestion was a useful one.

Then like a thunder-bolt he falls. She put in the final full stop with a little flourish and turned to the class.

After the First Formers came the young men. They were reading the blackboard as they gathered in their places while they waited for her to tell them to sit. She could see the looks on their faces as they registered the unspoken meanings in the lines that had been so obscure to the First Formers. This was going to be a different journey that she would share with them. *I can do this!* she thought suddenly. A surge of excitement went through her, an exultant feeling of adventure and discovery. They took their seats and opened their exercise books and began to write.

On weekdays, after school, Anne worked on her lessons for the following day and caught up with marking, before sleeping the deep sleep of the exhausted. At weekends Jo and Kevin eagerly claimed her. She hadn't discovered any weavers yet and her allotted stay (which was due to run out in October) was beginning to seem painfully short.

The thought came to her suddenly, one morning as she walked up the road to school. So obvious, really. Her plane ticket was open: now that she was earning a little money she could choose to stay longer. If they would agree to take her on in the school for another academic year she could stay as long as she liked. Another year at least. Her mum would mind a lot but she was far enough away to be easy to deal with. Her father would be more tricky. She really couldn't guess what he would feel about it.

The conviction grew steadily as the rains came in earnest at last and the world transformed in front of her – bright green grass smothering the red earth, and fields and gardens everywhere sprouting great bursts of vegetation – she wanted to be here to see the shape of a whole year, and to witness this amazing eruption a second time round. Not merely to taste it and go away again in the middle.

7

Mid May

'Where's Kevin?'

Jo said, 'He's been called out to an emergency. All this rain, you'd think water was the one thing we'd got enough of now.'

It was Saturday afternoon. Anne had called round after marking fifty-two compositions on the subject of *The day that I was born*. A thorny subject, it turned out. She'd meant it to be an exercise in imagination but in the classroom they had taken it much more literally, especially the ones who didn't know when they'd been born. She'd missed a trick, she realised now as she watched Jo rolling a cigarette. She should have given them a simpler title, one that encouraged them to tell real family stories. That could prove fertile ground from an anthropological point of view.

Jo licked the cigarette paper and smoothed it down with her thumbs. She flourished the roll-up proudly. 'I'm only smoking when Josh is asleep now. Progress! Shall we go to the market when he wakes up?'

Anne laughed. 'That's the one thing I *don't* feel like doing, to be honest,' she said lazily. 'You can't exactly walk round the market discreetly if you've got a Joshua with you, can you.'

'Well aren't you just the lucky one. You can opt out. I

have to put up with it all the time. I can't just do babies when it suits me.'

'It is your life!' Anne retaliated, stung. 'And your baby. You made the choice.'

'But that's just it, isn't it! I *didn't* make the choice. I wouldn't have chosen all this, not in a million years!'

Jo turned away so that her hair hid her face. It looked as if she might be crying. Anne sat watching her for a moment, disconcerted, then she went and crouched next to the sofa. Jo ignored her. She looped a tentative arm round those bony shoulders. 'You wouldn't want *not* to have Josh, would you?' she said to Jo's mass of hair. 'Surely you're glad he's here? He's such a lovely baby!'

Jo broke away and marched off to the kitchen. She came back with a tea towel, wiping her face on it fiercely before blowing her nose on one corner. She sat back down but at the far end of the sofa. Anne went back to her seat on the armchair. 'I'm really sorry, Jo. I didn't mean to offend you. I didn't think. I suppose I just don't have much idea what it's like being you.'

'No, you don't.'

Anne bridled. If Jo wanted her for a friend she would have to accept her as she was, however inadequate. But she held her tongue and suggested, 'It must be very annoying, shut in the house all day and followed everywhere if you do go out.'

'It is.'

They sat in silence.

'You *wouldn't* choose to be without him, would you?'

'That's just the problem, though,' Jo said, bleakly. 'I *didn't choose*. If I'd chosen maybe I wouldn't feel like a victim. But I don't even know if I'd be with Kevin if I'd *chosen*. I'll never know now.'

'Oh, Jo!'

'Well, it's the truth, isn't it? He's a good man but he's…
He's dull. I'm sorry, but that's what he is. Good-hearted and
doggedly, doggedly dull.'

'Is he?' Anne thought of Kevin as amiable, a kind friend,
and sometimes surprisingly humorous.

'Dull, dull, dull.'

But if she hadn't thought of him as dull, neither could
she imagine choosing to live with him, so there wasn't much
she could say in response.

'Perhaps it's not just Kevin,' Jo admitted grudgingly, after
a silence. 'Perhaps it's the life we lead. I don't suppose I'm a
bag of laughs either. Trouble is, nothing ever happens in my
life.'

'You can't have it both ways, Jo! You gave birth to Josh
within the last twelve months – of course things happen!'

From the far end of the house Joshua began to wail in
his cot.

'See! That's how it is! One long round of obligations. I
can't even have a crisis in peace.'

'Let's go to the market,' Anne said. 'I was just being
stupid before. Come on! It will do us both good to get out.'

As they walked into town the sun came out from behind
turbulent clouds and lit up the shabby streets with golden
light. Jo was fragile but cheerful, like someone recovering
from illness. Josh was at his best after his sleep, crowing and
gurgling in his regal seat on Jo's back, in the brand new
backpack Kevin's mother had sent out from England. The
crowd of fascinated children that clustered around him was
bigger than anything Anne had to put up with when she
went out on her own. From time to time the kids laughed

excitedly as Josh reached out for a sweet or an orange on a tray balanced on a child's head, making Jo frantic because she couldn't see what was happening. Anne prised the goods out of his hand and gave them back. Through the market they went with the crowd close on their heels. They rambled past the busy stalls admiring the glowing purple and white aubergines, the shining tomatoes, the pert okra. Nothing was withered now. There were tall baskets containing enormous edible snails, which seemed to be in a constant round of escape and recapture. Josh stared, big-eyed, gripping the edge of the backpack with both hands. They walked through the shea-butter section where a line of big calabash bowls stood on the ground, each with its owner squatting behind it with her back against the mud wall. The women shouted good-naturedly, inviting them to buy. The mounds of shea-butter in the calabashes glooped in strange, fixed droops of pallid yellow under a film of dust. 'What do you do with it?' Anne asked Jo, but Jo didn't know. Above them, in the trees, the yellow and black weaver birds were building their nests furiously, apparently oblivious of the crush in the alleyways below.

They bought vegetables for supper. The crowd of children got bored at last and faded away. It was cooler, as well as more peaceful, without them. 'Let's go and look at the *juju* stalls,' Anne said.

'What for? They're just a load of dusty old rubbish, aren't they?'

'It's always worth looking – you never know what treasures you might find. There was a tortoise shell last time I came.'

Jo looked unconvinced. 'Can't say I'm exactly short of tortoise shells just at the moment. And I bet it was full of germs.' But she turned down the *juju* alley.

When they came abreast of the second *juju* stall they found Michael seated inside it.

'What are you doing here?' Anne exclaimed.

He laughed. 'Moonlighting.'

'*Moonlighting?*'

Jo dug her in the ribs with her elbow. 'He's teasing you.'

Michael said, 'I'm waiting for Iddrissu. He's gone to fetch some tea and I'm guarding the goods in his absence. What brings you girls here? Are you wanting *juju?*'

Anne looked down at the dusty pile of dried skins, fly whisks and porcupine quills. 'I always feel there might be something exciting lurking among all this junk.' The empty tortoise shell was still there, lying upside down to one side of the pile. 'Why are you here really?'

'Iddrissu sometimes helps swell the congregation at Mass.' He saw the astonishment on her face. 'Oh I know what you're thinking – *juju* and Christianity don't go together? Well, Iddrissu is one of those who likes to keep himself covered both ways, just in case.'

'What's all this stuff for anyway?' Jo asked, prodding the tortoise shell with her foot. Joshua leaned over the side of the backpack to look, too.

'Now this,' said Michael, picking up a leather pouch on a plaited thong, 'This is one of Iddrissu's best-quality general charms to ward off the evil eye. See here – tucked inside there's a written charm. No, no,' he said, whisking it out of reach as they moved closer to look, 'It's all hieroglyphics – we mere mortals can't read it. But if you wear this against your chest no harm will come to you. Or if it does, you come back to the *juju* man and make a complaint and he tells you that it must have worked a bit or you'd be not just cross but dead. Or if you *are* dead and it's your relatives who come round demanding retribution, then it will be that you hadn't been wearing the charm the right way round, or your wife gave you the wrong things for dinner and weakened its potency, or the bad magic was so bad that if you hadn't been wearing the charm it wouldn't have been just you that died but all your family too, so by implication the relatives should go away grateful.' He put the charm back on the pile. 'Don't laugh,' he said, laying one finger along the side of his nose and looking at them sternly. 'You can never tell which *juju* is going to work best, this kind or the kind we dispense at Mass. Ah – Iddrissu! Any chance of giving those teas to these young ladies and I'll go and fetch some more for you and me?'

'Oh no, we can't,' Jo said quickly. 'We have to get back. It's Joshua's teatime.'

Anne didn't say anything as they walked away. If she had been on her own she would have stayed without hesitation. It would probably have turned into one of those times you remember long afterwards, quite different from your everyday life. As they walked out of the market she was tempted to observe to Jo that her life would be more eventful if she didn't fence herself off from the small, unlooked-for pleasures, but perhaps she was being unfair. If she had a child, would she be as anxious over germs and teatime as Jo was?

Jo said suddenly, 'Do you fancy him?'

'Who? Iddrissu?'

'No, stupid! Michael.'

'No, I don't!' she snapped, surprising herself. 'How could I? He's a priest.'

'Since when has that fact stopped everyone else fancying him? Except me, of course. I don't go for big brawny men.

Anyway, how significant is it, really, him being a priest? Okay, he made all sorts of vows twenty years ago or whatever, but maybe he's moved on since then, only he's stuck with being a priest. And you know what they say, there's nothing like the priesthood for providing access to young choirboys and the confessions of young girls.'

'I wondered too, when I first met him. But I think he *is* a priest, through and through. Just an unusual one.'

'It's funny, though,' Jo retorted. 'Have you ever heard him talk about God?'

No, she hadn't, Anne realised, except in banal half-mocking euphemisms – *Him Above, The Boss.* Even *Him Upstairs,* occasionally. But rarely *God.* Yet she thought of Michael as someone who was totally comfortable in his priest's skin.

'Wouldn't Ursula and co just love it if he turned out to be a full-blooded sexually active individual after all!' Jo said wickedly. 'But they'd all be so jealous of the lucky one that got him.' She laughed suddenly. 'It would be one in the eye for them if it turned out it *was* the choir-boys he fancied! He'd never be forgiven for that!'

Not sure I'd forgive him either, Anne thought, but she didn't say anything.

'I suppose there *isn't* anything going on there?' Jo mused.

'Where?'

'Between Ursula and Michael. He seems so open but I bet he's good at being discreet when he wants to be. If there *was* something going on he wouldn't let on, would he? But then, if there was she wouldn't talk about him the way she does.'

'Does she particularly talk about him?'

'Just a bit! Thinking of which, hasn't she been in touch

with you? She said she was going to ask you over one weekend, if you couldn't make it during the week.'

Anne groaned.

'I told you before,' Jo said, 'you should keep them sweet. You never know when you might need them!'

There must have been a football match, because the roads were filling up with excited young men and as they walked out of town past the Take De Wife Chop Bar they had to push against crowds coming the other way.

'*Leave De Wife At Home* Chop Bar, more like', Jo said, looking across at the handwritten sign. The shaded enclosure at the front of the Take De Wife was full to overflowing. 'Isn't that your houseboy?'

Anne looked, and there, sitting at a table under the tin awning, was Moses. She saw him just at the moment that the youth next to him saw her and pointed her out. Moses stared at her, unsmiling, and the boys around him stared too and grinned. Their grinning had an insolent edge, it did not feel friendly. Then Moses bent to his neighbour, his eyes still holding hers, and said something. The youth looked shocked for a moment and then he burst out laughing. Moses did not smile.

'Well!' Jo exclaimed as they walked out of earshot. 'Looks like your houseboy isn't overly weighed down with respect!'

Jo was a Marxist: it was supposed to be a joke. But it didn't feel like one. Anne looked up at the sky, carefully not thinking about Moses. The sky was a glorious blue between the great piles of white and gold cloud. A light breeze rustled the leaves of the acacia trees. They trudged along in silence for a while, Joshua singing quietly in his seat. They turned into the road that led past Jo and Kevin's bungalow and down towards the Low Cost Estate. As the sun dipped lower the colours became more intense. You could feel the curve of the sun's descent in the falling off of its heat. The sweat which had run freely all day – down the spine, down the backs of the thighs – began to dry off, creating a micro-climate of near-coolness all its own.

They passed a child with an intricate lorry made of wire which he was trundling carefully along. When he saw Joshua the boy whooped with delight and scooped the truck up in his arms to come running across the road. 'Beby! Beby!' he called, holding the truck up to Joshua, who leaned over the side of the backpack and made a grab at it.

'Oh no, Joshua!' exclaimed Jo, laughing. 'You can't have it!'

'He can, he can!' the boy said. 'Take it, Beby.'

'But he'll break it!'

'Then I make another,' said the boy, beaming. 'Take it, madam. It for him.'

Jo stood nonplussed in the road. Anne could see her thinking, *Germs!*

'Take it, madam,' the boy repeated.

'It's a wonderful present,' Anne said, 'but Jo is thinking Joshua will break it.' The boy looked up at her uncertainly so she dropped into the lilting Tamale-speak her father used. 'It such a beautiful lorry and he very clumsy boy. Why don't you make small-small car, give him that instead? Then it not such a sad thing if he break it.'

The boy's smooth, round face lit up. 'I make small-small car and I bring beby's house. Yes?'

'Yes' she said, and couldn't resist patting his earnest head. His hair was surprisingly tough and springy under her hand. 'Do you know where Jo lives?'

'Certain sure!' said the boy. 'Bye-bye, Beby. I make you small-small car and bring it you. Bye-bye Beby bye-bye!'

He stood with his lorry at his feet, grinning and waving until they had turned the corner.

'Doesn't it make you feel dreadfully small,' Jo said. 'These children with so little, and then to give it away so freely to us who've got so much more than them.'

Perhaps it was the power of suggestion that made her connect it the way she did, but when Anne found the small triangular hole in her favourite shirt she didn't think *nail*, she thought *Moses,* and she thought *amulet*. It was such a neat little hole. A nail *could* make a v-shaped incision as sharp as any cut made with a knife, but a nail didn't take the third side of the triangle out to leave an empty little hole. Just the right size piece missing to be inserted into one of those leather charms Michael had been talking about, like the one which Moses wore (along with most of the population in Tamale). She hadn't noticed the hole at first, her clothes ironed and folded so crazily small – flat little packages with razor sharp creases. But when she shook the shirt out to hang it up she saw it at once in the middle of the back.

Through the wooden louvres at her bedroom window she could see Moses outside in the yard languidly sweeping. His tall slender shape stooped casually over the short broom, one arm crooked behind his back as if he were dancing. A voice called from the other side of the matting fence and he spoke back in Dagbani. His voice seemed to come spookily from right by the house though she could see him clearly on the far side of the yard.

She shivered. Moses being quietly and consistently rude to her: she could hope to get used to that. But *juju – juju* was scary.

Later, when she went to the kitchen to make some tea, he was sitting on his stool peeling potatoes and cutting them directly into the pot which was boiling on the gas ring on the floor at his feet. It was stifling in the little kitchen so why wasn't he cooking on the charcoal stove outside? Perhaps he had run out of charcoal, or perhaps he was doing it just to annoy her. It was early to start cooking supper and there was only the one gas ring. He knew she liked to make herself a pot of tea around this time in the afternoons while she was sitting over school books. Now she would have to go without.

She went to the lifeless fridge to get some half-warm water instead. Moses studiously ignored her as she stepped round him. The air between them was empty and dead. As he leaned forward to his work the leather charm around his neck swung backwards and forwards.

Little things, little things. But they added up. Passive hostility, persistently displayed, felt like active aggression.

And affection withheld, like dereliction: that night, going to kiss her father goodnight as usual, Anne actually observed him flinch. What was wrong with her to make him flinch away?

Her face must have betrayed her because he covered himself rapidly and patted her on the small of the back. She could feel, even before she turned, that Moses was staring at her. And he was, his black eyes boring into her. She felt he was staring right through her soul.

8

Late May

There is a book, remembered from somewhere in Michael's childhood: a book of fine colour reproductions of medieval illuminations. A Book of Hours, it might have been. He cannot remember now. But he thinks of this book sometimes. His fellow priests are like illustrations from it. There is an element of caricature in each of them.

Father Stefan is *The Gardener*. He who must dig and delve. Michael sees him as a crooked figure in medieval clothing, bent over his spade. In reality, ageing Polish priest that he is, Stefan has retreated further and further from the vegetables (grown now by his Ghanaian assistants) and spends his declining years among his beloved flowers, which he assiduously brings to the church every Saturday to decorate it for Sunday Mass. And it is true, Michael thinks, that in his own way Stefan may do more than any of them to bring local people to the church: Sunday Masses in the rainy season, when Stefan's garden is at its best, attract surprisingly large congregations. In his mind's eye Michael spices up the illumination of *The Gardener* with banks of lilies behind the figure of the toiling Stefan.

Then there is Father Klaus *The Swineherd* with his long-nosed pigs. A Brueghel-like figure in Michael's imaginary Book of Hours, large-snouted like his pigs, a little anxious.

For the purposes of imagery Michael leaves the goats and rabbits, which are also Klaus's labour, out of the picture.

Father François in his carpentry shop strikes a pose with an old-fashioned wood plane. Behind him the tools of his trade are arrayed on shelves and at his feet the long curls of shaved timber drift into the corners of the picture.

Father Christopher is *The Musician*, black notes on a stave above his head to signify his occupation. Michael takes away his dusty harmonium, which – because it must be pumped by hand – makes Christopher painfully dependent on the (sometimes woefully lacking) charity of his brother priests, if he is to practice, and gives him a viol instead. Although, Michael reflects, a viol would probably fare no better than the recorder that Christopher brought with him to Ghana: the first rainy season after his arrival, termites attacked the wood and it crumbled to dust. In the image Christopher (a gawky figure in heavy glasses) is bent awkwardly over his instrument.

Father Jeremiah is *The Apothecary*, busy in his pharmacy with brightly coloured bottles arrayed behind him, a tiny set of scales in his left hand. Jeremiah stands for health, and bodily healing. Or in the urbane language of the modern age, for primary healthcare clinics and mobile vaccination units.

Father Marcos sits bent over his ledgers: *The Scribe*, keeping the accounts. And although all of them except for Stefan teach, he is the one whose Book of Hours image has a blackboard in it, hovering at his left shoulder. There are figures and calculations on the blackboard. For what could be more international, more essential and inter-changeable, than mathematics?

Father Simon's image shows him as a dark figure in a

monk's hood, *The Teacher*, turning a huge globe with one thin hand. Simon the geography teacher, now sadly dislocated geographically. Sent back home to recuperate, not knowing when he will be allowed to return.

Father Giovanni, elderly now and nearing retirement, is known for his fine singing voice, leading the Mass. Michael thinks of him as *The Cantor*, one finger raised to heaven as he sings. But sees him not in church, but instead reclining in a rose-covered arbour while maidens bring him delicacies to eat and drink. Because Giovanni, for all his holy singing, is a suppressed epicurean with a mischievous glint in his eye and a rounded belly.

Dominic the animal lover has to be *Saint Francis* in a field of flowers, with clouds of birds coming to him and a cat at his feet. Caught between the perpetual tensions of his earthly love.

Father John, who teaches physical education as well as English (or these days geography) appears in his image kicking an inflated bladder, with his monk's habit tucked up around his knees. Though in reality John is fat and jolly and prefers shorts, and his physical exercise is limited to shouting from the side-lines.

Father Patrick has his nose deep in a book. Wickedly, Michael places him in his imagination behind a tree as if in hiding. Because Patrick is never there when there is any work to be done and must always be sought out.

Father Morrissey is the austere *Abbot*, humourless, hooded, his hands tucked into the sleeves of his cassock.

These are the images of Michael's private Book of Hours. He tinkers with them in his mind's eye when meal times are tedious: Christopher drops his viol and the notes on the stave above his head slide into one another in a glissando;

John's football disappears down a storm-drain; Father Morrissey puts his hand up the sleeve of his cassock and draws out an embroidered hankie. Each of them caricatured into a neat little emblem in Michael's mind. Not without love, and there is respect too, for the clarity of their personalities which permits him to caricature them in the first place.

But what of me? he wonders. Which one am I? *The Joker, The Clown, The Entertainer*? Or the one with no image, remembered when I am present but forgotten when I've left the room?

He has many such moments of secret self-doubt. Technically Father Morrissey is Head of the school. The school is Morrissey's duty. It is Michael's lifeblood, but he has no autonomy. Everything must be done through Morrissey. And Morrissey does not like Michael. They have been together before, in an earlier life and they did not expect to wash up together again. Michael tries to be patient and to bide his time. He hopes it will not be long before Morrissey moves on to another Mission. He has only to hang on. But he misses the quiet, gentle wisdom of Father Benedict, latterly Head of The Mission of the Holy Redeemer in Tamale, now Retired of Hastings.

'I'm taking Moses with me,' her father said. 'I'm going on a field trip, he can do the driving.'

She stood on the porch to wave him off, her throat aching with disappointment. He had never once suggested she might come with him to see what he did, not even when he thought she might like to study the development of rice farming. He knew how much she wanted to see everything, and she hadn't been out of Tamale once. But it wasn't just that. It was the triumphant look Moses shot her as he jumped into the driving seat. Moses had somehow won and she had lost. She went back indoors, and tried not to mind as she busied herself with collecting her stuff together for school. After all, she couldn't have gone; she had classes all day.

The next week it happened again, on two consecutive days, and again on the Saturday, which was supposed to be only a half-day for her father. Off he went with Moses at the wheel, saying they wouldn't be back before sunset.

When they'd gone, she looked at the rising tide of dust in the living room. I'm buggered if I'm going to clean up after them, she thought, and went out to look for the weavers.

Jo assumed she must have been happy once, but she couldn't remember what being happy felt like. Tamale was a difficult place to be happy in, especially with a baby in tow. There were too many things to worry about for a start: the biting insects, the germs, whether snakes could climb stairs. Whether soaking the salad in the stuff she used for sterilising Joshua's water bottles was enough to kill the nasties from the night-soil in which all vegetables were reputedly grown. She worried whether Joshua was late starting to crawl, and then when he suddenly started crawling at the precocious age of seven months, whether he was picking up germs off the floor. She worried whether his teeth were coming through straight. Whether she had ironed the nappies well enough to kill the eggs of the fly which lays its eggs on washing and the bugs burrow into your skin. Sometimes she would get up in the night and iron the nappies a second time just in case.

The Water Corporation employed a gardener to come and cut the long grass in the grounds of the bungalow: she saw the tell-tale bandage round his shin and knew the man had been drinking well-water, like many others did now the piped water was so erratic, and he'd got a guinea worm. Guinea worms can grow the length of your arm or your leg, inside a vein. She started boiling the drinking water twice, to be safe. And when Kevin came home exhausted after long days at the Water Corporation she berated him as if it was his personal fault. He heard her out patiently and patted her on the back.

So damned patient, was Kevin. He never told her to shut up, never said she was being unreasonable. Really she wished he would. She sounded just like her mother.

They'd always been like this, Kevin and her. Jogging along together, getting by. But now there was Anne, and suddenly Jo was conscious just how how fed up she was. Anne was everything she was not, that was the trouble. Anne was tall (taller than her, at any rate). Slender but not skinny, she had what Jo was sadly lacking: she had flesh. She went out and in at all the right places where Jo was just straight up and down. And where Jo's hair stuck out all over her head in an unwilling Afro, Anne had beautiful hair, glossy, straight and heavy. It was a lovely ash-blonde colour, too, and mostly she wore it tied up in a casual knot on the back of her head and it made her seem even more graceful. Anne was perfect without even trying. Sometimes Jo found it difficult to take her eyes off her as they sat casually chatting.

But a bit of her hated Anne for all these things.

So when Anne came to see her, all upset because apparently her father was taking the houseboy with him as a driver-cum-cook whenever he went out on field trips, Jo felt sort of hard inside. She couldn't see what the fuss was about anyway. If Anne minded so much, why didn't she just say something to her dad?

Some evenings Michael came to the Low Cost house, an easy-going arrangement that seemed to go back years. Sometimes they would sit there, nobody speaking at all: her dad smoking his pipe and reading; Moses sorting beans or rice for supper, or cutting up fruit to put in front of them on a plate, or simply sitting doing nothing, a dreamy look on his face, clicking his knuckles one by one; Michael reading. Anne could see it must have been disruptive when she suddenly turned up in their midst, but now she too was just another reader sitting quietly in the lamplight while the hectic sounds of another Tamale night went on all around the house: fowl being slaughtered, fires stoked, yams pounded, pots and pans banged, mice scampering in the roof. And the local cockerel, confused as ever, crowing proudly from his roost in the nearby tree.

Usually they sat indoors. The mosquitoes made it too frenetic to sit outside unless a particularly warm night, or a splendid moon, tempted them, or a power cut drove them out. The evenings that Michael came – as far as she knew without any prior arrangement or signal – he would knock with vague formality on the open front door, kick off his sandals in the porch and walk in to join them in the small living room. Sometimes, like Moses, he would just sit, if he didn't have a book with him. Occasionally he and her dad played chess. And the conversation lifted and sank, lifted and sank, with a placid ebb and flow like a tide.

One Saturday night he was there reading. Moses was safely out of the way in the kitchen cooking supper (a meal

Michael had agreed to stay and share) and her father was talking to a colleague outside. She sat in the hot armchair with her book, Michael on the equally uncomfortable sofa with his.

He looked up from his book (*North South East West – The Twentieth Century Pathway to God*, by a Father Heinrich Stott) and saw her gazing into space. 'Not a gripping read, then?'

She laughed ruefully. She liked these times when Michael came. At such moments she didn't feel like the odd one out in the house, the perhaps not-quite-wanted invader. On nights like this they were like a family, all of them together, made so by his presence. She reached over and turned up his book to look at the title. 'More gripping than yours!'

'Touché!'

She closed her hefty paperback and smoothed down the cover: Henry Fielding's *Tom Jones*, set text for the Cambridge Board A-level English students in the autumn. She was nearing the end of her first read-through.

He said, 'Isn't that next year's curriculum? You've decided then – you'll be staying?'

She put a warning finger to her lips. 'I haven't told Dad yet – don't say anything.'

He looked surprised but made no comment. She sidestepped: 'I don't know what the class will make of this. It's bad enough expecting the average eighteen-year old back home to read such a mammoth book but it's even more irrelevant here.'

'Why so?'

'It's too remote!' she exclaimed, surprised he should question something quite so obvious. 'Eighteenth century rural England? A comedy of London manners?'

'From what I remember of the story I'd have thought there are lots of parallels. Arranged marriage, for example – that's a reality for lots of people here too. And going to Accra is still one hell of a journey if you're not rich enough to go by plane. Think of the possibilities! A young man trying to get to Accra, beset by all sorts of adventures on the way. Vagabonds too – it's not unknown for the occasional *trotro* to be held up and robbed, so for stage-coach you could read *trotro*. And how about swapping the Take De Wife Chop Bar for the Inn at Upton? Yep, I think you could put *Tom Jones* in a modern Ghanaian setting pretty neatly!'

'You're in the wrong job,' she said, wishing she'd thought of all that for herself instead of having it pointed out by a maths and physics teacher. 'You should be taking my English class!'

'Nonsense, you'll be great. You've got to find your way into it, that's all. You should be grateful it *is* such a hefty book – it'll keep them quiet for a long time just reading it, especially with so many of them having to share books. Four copies is all we could fork out for, and one of those has to go to you or whoever is teacher, so that leaves only three for the students. There are sixteen in the A-level class, which means at least five sharing each copy.'

She turned the book over and read the price on the back. Two pounds ninety-nine pence. If they bought ten or twelve more copies that would come to nearly thirty-six pounds. Call it forty-five pounds including the postage. She had that much and a little more tucked up in an envelope in her underwear drawer. She could give Michael the money now and tell him to order the books at once. Even if they had to wait a month or two after the beginning of the new school year for the books to arrive, it would still be worthwhile. Such a nice thing to do! she thought. And more meaningful than buying mementoes to take home. She said it at once, before she could have second thoughts.

Michael whistled. 'Well that would be noble of you! Are you sure? It would certainly impress Father Morrissey.'

'Really? I assumed he couldn't be impressed.'

He pursed his lips as if measuring his reply. 'He can, but not by the likes of me, and still less by you. Don't take that amiss – he just doesn't like women. That's why he was pretty iffy about taking you on in the first place. Anything you can do to gain his approval would be money well spent! But seriously, the kids would love you for it. It would make the difference between passing and failing for some of them, and while you're about it you might as well make a good impression on old Morrissey too.'

She looked across at him, slumped untidily in his chair. 'You don't like him much, do you?'

He was idly spinning one of her dad's pencils between his fingers. (Her dad was always complaining that his pencils kept disappearing. Maybe they went home in Michael's shirt pocket?) 'It isn't that I like or dislike him. What I'm unhappy with is the way he runs the Mission. I wish you'd seen it when Father Benedict was here, Anne. *He* wouldn't have had any qualms about signing you up! There's something a touch mean about Morrissey.' He sat up abruptly. 'Nope, you're quite right. I do not like him. It was vanity made me say otherwise.' And he changed the subject by asking her whether she'd found those weavers yet, and she had to admit she hadn't, but then she hadn't spent as much time looking as she'd meant to.

'You're working me too hard,' she said.

9

May/June

Without her quite noticing it, Michael was becoming more than a friend: he was her guide and mentor. The one who explained the local greetings. The social niceties. That it is rude to gesture with your left hand. Also, to stare or to point.

'But they point and stare at me all the time!' she objected, surprised.

'They do, but they think each other terrible rude doing it. It's just far too much fun to desist.'

Almost invariably, if he passed on his bicycle when she was walking in to town on a Saturday or after school, he stopped to walk beside her for a while, even when he had been passing in the opposite direction. They talked about school, and about Ghana. He was a fund of jokes, and of things she needed to know.

'Mind the goat!' she warned as he rode across the road to join her.

'That's not a goat, it's a sheep.'

She looked back, surprised. She thought those goats with the drooping ears and glossy brown and white coats were called *Nubian*. 'A sheep? How can you tell?'

'Easy. If its tail goes up it's a goat. If it goes down, it's a sheep.'

Another time, running into him in the middle of the market, she bemoaned the gaudy Chinese plastic bowls and buckets that were rapidly replacing the local pottery. 'Yes,' he said, 'but have you ever picked up one of those pots when it's full of water? The plastic ones are so much lighter and easier to carry! *And* they don't break if you put them down too sharply, wasting all the precious water you've just carried miles.'

She was slightly ashamed for not having thought this for herself. I am an anthropologist and you are a sociologist, she thought.

'This fly which lays its eggs on washing and the grubs burrow into your skin – is it true?' she asked another day as they sat in the staffroom at mid-morning break. His clothes looked decidedly as if he did his own washing, and no ironing at all.

'It's true.' He scratched his hairy belly absent-mindedly where his shirt gaped and turned the page of the *Ghana Times*.

'I thought you had to iron everything to kill the eggs.'

'They say so. I've never had any trouble but maybe that's my thick Irish hide.'

'Moses uses a charcoal iron. It looks like something out of a museum and weighs a tonne. I shouldn't think any flies eggs would survive his ironing. I'm not sure my clothes will survive it.'

'Yep,' Michael said. 'The sun wears clothes out quick enough here without laundering them to death besides. But about the fly grubs – I think in the end it's mostly a question of luck. I've known people iron everything religiously and still get them, but most people get away with it whether they iron or not.' He went back to his newspaper.

He was always crumpled but it was more than just a question of ironing since he usually had frayed collars, and buttons missing as well. All the Fathers looked like that. It made them seem unworldly, and for all that the Mission appeared to be segregated – as Jo often observed – along archaic lines of foreign white priests and Ghanaian servants, in practice the lines were so blurred there was no feeling of inequality. Perhaps it wasn't such a bad thing, employing servants, she thought as she gathered her books together for the next lesson. It wasn't really logical to do as Jo and Kevin did and deprive local people of jobs for the sake of theoretical principle. She stood up and picked up her bag. All the same, even if her dad was doing the right thing employing somebody, did it *have* to be Moses?

Friday was pork day. Which seemed a little strange to Anne, having always thought that Friday was fish if you were Catholic. But this was something to do with the climate, the killing of pigs, and the need for fresh meat for the weekend, and so at the Mission of the Holy Redeemer in Tamale, Northern Region, Ghana, Friday was pork day.

She was in school all day teaching so it was logical that she should be the one to go and buy pork, instead of Moses, when Father Klaus at last began killing pigs again after the long dry season.

It was the first time she'd been down to the small farm at the back of the school since Michael had shown her round the Mission before she started teaching, and that had still been the dry season. The sandy lane running down from the school was unrecognisable now. Every dry stick and withered vine had fizzed awake. All was leafy exuberance: great trumpets of flowers hung out of the hedge and twining jasmine tumbled. Beyond the hedge there was a whole garden where before had been bare red soil. Green shoots were striking upwards out of the long neat ridges, and tomato plants had been neatly staked. Beyond the orderly rows of vegetables an elderly priest in a white habit was just visible as he moved gently among beds of bright flowers, accompanied by a young boy with a basket on his head. The priest waved when he saw her. She waved back. She was getting used to everybody here knowing who she was.

At the bottom of the lane, a white-washed building with a tin roof seemed to be the butcher's shop. She knocked on the open door and stepped inside. Everything was very clean and neat but the room was empty. She called 'Hello!' several times. Nobody came.

She was turning to go when Father Klaus put his head round the far door. 'Did you call me?'

'I wanted to buy some pork.'

'But we sold all by ten this morning!'

'Oh!' she said, disappointed. Pork would have made such a nice change. 'What time should I have come?'

'Well, it is first come first served – there's always more want it than we got to sell. We open at nine but people queue from long before that.'

'But I'm teaching first thing on a Friday morning, and I wouldn't be able to keep it cool during the day, anyway.'

'I tell you what,' he said, 'as you are working in the school – how about I reserve you some and keep it here in the cold room until you can pick it up? Only please not to tell anyone. I don't do favours for nobody, normally. Only for you, because you are working here. And I could do it for only small amount of pork. We'll be killing another two pigs in two weeks' time. How much you want then?'

93

'Only six chops. It must be nice to be able to eat your own meat,' she added, to be sociable.

'Oh we can't afford to eat it. We sell everything we produce. The income goes to Mission funds. It costs a lot of money to run a place like this mission – you can imagine. And pockets at home run dry. It is better we earn our own keep, as far as we can. The farm,' he said proudly, 'is good little earner. Better than the school. And a good training ground. All that academic learning – what good will it do most of your pupils? Better they come down here and learn real-life things.'

She walked back up the sandy track past the garden. The elderly priest was standing just the other side of the jasmine hedge and peering over the top. His face lit up when he saw her.

'You are Anne? Who is teaching English classes? Wait there!'

Again, that strange Ghanaian lilt, masking his European origins. She waited while he hurried off along the far side of the hedge. A moment later he came out onto the track through a little wicket gate.

'For you!' he said, handing her a single red rose. 'For de pretty miss who comes to brighten our lives.'

'Thank you!' The rose was a spindly, fragile little thing but she guessed from his face that it was very special.

'I am Father Stefan. I look after de garden. Come!' he said eagerly. 'Come see my garden!' He tucked her hand under his arm and led her back through the wicket gate, past tall, orderly ridges of earth where yams had been planted, past blocks of young maize and millet and cassava, past bushes where peppers were swelling, or pale aubergines, or small, pointed okra. Past the staked pyramids of tomato plants, whose heavy fragrance hit her as she passed, to a

94

fenced-off area beyond, and another wicket gate. Through this they went, and into what seemed like Tamale's very own Garden of Eden. At the far side stood full-grown mango trees, their leaves dark and glossy in the sultry air. High above them soared four slender paw-paw palms. As they walked round the garden she smelled the pungent aroma of guava but what was startling was the flowers. So many of them! Huge gushing lilies, hot little daisies. Other flowers she didn't recognise. Flowering shrubs, sprawling plants and spiky ones, oleander bushes, and jacaranda trees with their blossoms like blue lavender. At her side, the skinny old priest kept patting her hand in the crook of his elbow, trapped between his bony arm and his hot bird-cage ribs as he hurried her from one glory to another. 'Dis de best time!' he kept saying, as if she had successfully kept an appointment. 'All dat long waiting for de rains to come and den – woooof! He flung his free hand up in the air to signify all that growth and laughed excitedly.

The poor little rose in her free hand was withering fast. She noticed that the thorns had been carefully trimmed.

'You take tea with me?' He giggled like a school-boy suggesting a midnight feast. 'We have our own tea-place, you know. We don' go to de refectory in de daytime, we got our own special place here. Come, I show you and you can meet Emmanuel.'

At the bottom of the slope at the far end of the garden there was a shelter of poles supporting a thatched roof. Electric-blue Morning Glory climbed the poles and sprawled in a mass over the thatch. Inside the shelter an elderly Ghanaian was sitting on a low stool, boiling a kettle on a charcoal stove.

'Emmanuel, my boss,' said Father Stefan.

Emmanuel grinned. He had grizzled hair, kindly eyes, and very few teeth. 'Yeh, yeh, I de boss and you de assistant I suppose? Assistant who don' do no work hardly at all and boss who do it all?'

'Emmanuel, dis is Anne, de new teacher.'

She sat on the stool Emmanuel offered her and the priest sat on another, gathering his white habit about his thin legs. His skirts were stained with red dust as if he'd been kneeling on the ground. Emmanuel, who was wearing shorts, had dusty knees. He handed her a glass of hot, strong tea sweetened with Carnation Milk. They sat quietly, the two old men slurping loudly and contentedly.

'It is a wonderful ting, God's world' said Father Stefan dreamily. 'All tings in their order.'

'What – no weeds?' she teased.

'He send us weeds but He give us de knowledge to pull de weeds and leave de good plants to grow.'

'Not dat boy He don' give de knowledge to,' Emmanuel said tersely. 'Dat boy still don' know de difference between de millet and de chic-chac, though I tell him every day.'

'Poor Kofi,' Father Stefan confided to Anne. 'I tink his days working for dis boss is numbered.'

Emmanuel affected not to hear.

Suddenly he jumped up from his stool and seized a heavy stick that was leaning against one of the roof supports. 'Dat snake agen! I seed him dis morning!'

Father Stefan twisted on his stool to look behind him. A slender snake was sliding along the sand at the bottom of the hedge with his head held delicately up and his forked tongue flicking in and out. 'Leave him be, Emmanuel. He only one more of God's creatures. You leave him in peace and he'll leave you.'

Emmanuel grunted and began to whack lustily at God's creature but the snake slipped away under the thorny hedge.

She took her own leave soon after. She was not afraid of snakes but it is never comfortable to sit with your back to a hedge containing a cross one, and besides it was getting late and Moses was expecting her to come home with pork chops for supper. The old priest walked her back to the gate. 'Any time you want to rest your brain from all dat book-learning you come see old Father Stefan. A garden always better dan a classroom. You come, any time.'

When she got home she went to the kitchen to confess to the lack of pork. Moses gave her a caustic look. For supper that night he served fried spam, with a tomato and hot chilli sauce.

'Delicious,' said her father.

Next morning, as it was a Saturday, she went to the abattoir on the Airport Road to buy penitential meat for supper. But there was no meat, there were only gangs of flies, and idle men who grinned when they saw her and said 'Come tomorrow. Tomorrow we get mountain beef from Switzerland!'

Failed again! She could hardly bear to imagine how Moses would react when she returned home empty-handed. She decided to put off the evil hour: she kept on walking.

The Airport Road was its usual chaos of trucks, cars and bicycles, and pedestrians spilling into the road along with goats, sheep, and the occasional herd of cows. In the leafy trees overhead the yellow and black weaver birds were busily feeding their young in the hanging nests. Soft silky down floated everywhere. She stopped to gaze up at the *kapok* trees, soaring tall and graceful on their winged trunks, and a small crowd stopped to stare upwards too. She walked on. Never alone, here. Always a child or two following. Cheeky faces smiling up at her whenever she looked down. The usual string of questions and statements – *What you name? Where you live? Madam, you hev beautiful eyes.*

And then, suddenly, there they were! Between the mud houses to her left, a strip of bright colour, taut as a rope, trembling rhythmically just above the ground. Weavers! Michael had said this was where they would be. She turned down the alleyway.

In an open space between the mud-brick houses three men sat weaving at narrow looms set up under thatched shelters. The bright lines of colour were the long warps, stretched out twenty or thirty feet in front of each man and attached to drag-stones on the ground. She knew they would look like this, when she eventually found them, but the real thing was so much more exciting than reading about it in books and looking at photographs. The men called out to her when they saw her standing there. She returned their greetings and moved closer. They worked so rapidly – she hadn't imagined *that* when she read about it. Nor how soothing it would be on the ear, the clack-clacking rhythm of moving wooden parts. One of the men paused and called out to her to sit out of the sun, pointing with his shuttle to a vacant stool nearby. She sat down gratefully. Answered their cheerful questions with tentative questions of her own. She had always known she would find them in the end.

Her precious weekends acquired a new pattern. In addition to evenings preparing lessons for school and afternoons with Kevin and Jo, she spent the mornings talking to the weavers. The ones near the Airport Road, and then others too, in the jumble of huts beyond. At last she could start filling her notebook. So many questions to ask: what tribes were they from? How long they had been in Tamale? How did they organise their work? Who sold them the yarn and who bought the finished cloth? They told her what she wanted to know and volunteered more: the different patterns all had names (*topari* was the bold cloth in red and blue stripes, *tambuona* the blue, black and white one). She feasted on the words, storing them up in her notebook, running them over her tongue at night as she lay in the hot and sleepless dark. *Bankobro*, the word for 'guinea fowl', was the name of the indigo weave with a faint check. *Paludare* was the loom, *kokolaga* the bamboo spools, bobbins were *gambo*. A whole tradition unfolding through the poetry of its vocabulary.

The Dagomba first learned to weave through inspiration from God, said the old man who was head of the family. Each time they could not get any part of it right they would go and rest until it came to them from God how they must do it. Then they told everyone else in Ghana how to weave. 'Write this in your book,' he said. And she wrote it, knowing from her background reading that the elaborate weaving in fine cottons and silks of the Asante a long way to the south of Tamale, and of the Ewe to the east, is famous throughout West Africa, and in the museums of the rest of the world too, and that neither the Asante nor the Ewe thought the Dagomba had taught them how to weave. No one mentions the simple cotton weaving of the Dagomba in the big expensive books. She didn't tell them this. They felt they were at the centre of the weaving world.

It was soothing to sit quietly and watch the rhythmical

progress of each long strip until it was taken off the loom and rolled into a tight reel like a brightly coloured millstone. She was pupil here, not teacher, stumbling along in her few words of Dagbani but mostly in English. The weavers were Muslim but they weren't affronted by her femaleness, nor that she came visiting them alone. Weaving was man's work. If she wanted to know about it, she could not quite be a woman. It was the same old question of the Outsider, she realised, sitting unobserved in the shadow of their thatched shelter and watching a small boy shin up the terrifying height of a paw-paw palm to pick the heavy fruit from the crown. She was not the first white woman to have come asking questions: she was one of a kind with which they were already familiar. And it was not their kind. Therefore, they could treat her as an honorary man.

Each time she came they told her more.

The best blue dye was made from natural indigo but it was a long process and only the old men bothered with it now. The others used factory-made thread in brilliant synthetic colours that smelled of chemicals. The best cotton was hand-spun but it was more difficult to work with. The old traditions were dying out. Weaving itself was. She could tell by the way they talked that they knew this too, but they hung on, and many of the weavers were young: it wasn't only the old men who worked the looms.

She made notes. She sat in the shade and watched the young goats jumping the stretched-out warps until chased off with a well-aimed stone.

The old man who was head of the family agreed to weave her a *fugu,* the traditional smock that many men still wore, for her dad's birthday present. He said he would make it out of hand-spun cotton dyed with natural indigo, just for her. She went to see how the work was progressing. The old man peered into the oil drum where the indigo was fermenting. 'It not ready yet'. Four or five small boys of different ages hung round him, watching her.

'Are these your *pikkin*?' she asked.

He looked down at them and rubbed his chin meditatively. 'Dese all my *pikkin*.'

She went home to finish her marking. Moses was outside the house, pounding yams into *fufu* in the big wooden mortar which he kept on the front porch. He worked bare-chested in the sun, lifting the heavy pestle high above his head between each blow. The pestle was as big as a fence post and polished with use. The mortar was big enough to serve as a tall stool when it was inverted between pounding sessions. Sweat stood out in a band across his forehead and ran in streams down his lean back. His muscles rippled. Whose imaginary head was he pulping? She could see it in her mind's eye, a white face upturned at the bottom of the mortar, eyes shut, features bloodied. Whose face? She shivered and went indoors to her marking.

In the living room she sat at the table and opened the exercise book on the top of the pile still to be marked, trying to block out the rhythmic pounding as she stared at the awkward script. The mice were busy this afternoon too. They seemed to be running races from one side of the ceiling to the other. She frowned. Put her hands over her ears and tried to concentrate. If a First Former writes *De man had many ships but only wun wife and wen de wyfe dyed he ate all de ships for his sadness so den he had nuffing*, should she put a tick for inventiveness or a cross for the spelling? She thought about it for a moment, concentrating hard against the thumping outside and the scurrying overhead, then she wrote in the margin, *Very good, but we need to work on your spelling*. She put a line through both 'ships' and wrote *sheep* in the margin.

Later, the *fufu* came to the table in the big aluminium cooking-pot, looking innocent enough – a bland mound of glutinous starch. The catch was, as always, in the thin sauce, which was liberally laced with chillies. Since it was a local dish this was a hands-in-the-pot day, not plates-and-cutlery. Moses liked to alternate haphazardly between European and local but sometimes only the presence of the plates and cutlery revealed that it was indeed a European meal. Snails in particular (he seemed to be very fond of snails) were for some reason always served with cutlery, though the snails were too rubbery for a knife and fork. He's just trying to expose me, she thought grimly whenever yet another bit of snail bounced off her plate and Moses eyed her sneeringly across the table. Her father grinned. *I'm outnumbered*, she thought. If he were challenged, would her father align himself with Moses, or with her?

As shitty days went it was, Jo thought, a bottom-of-the-pile sort of shitty day.

'What am I going to do with you, Josh?'

He had slap-slapped his laborious way, crawling along the corridor after her, only to have her pass him again before he got halfway. He sat on his very sore bottom and wept a small tear from each eye.

'Oh Joshua!' she scolded, coming back and picking him up. 'Pooh-er Joshua! Again?'

She couldn't believe how often a teething baby could dirty his nappy. And the more he did, the more sore his poor little bot got, and the more he wept, and the harder it was for her to get to the mounting pile of nappies in the stinking bucket and wash them out. And there was no water in the tap, either – only in the tanker-trailer which Kevin had wheedled out of them at work. All of Tamale was having water problems, but she felt she was perhaps the only one who was living quite such a complicated life. Who ever invented nappies anyway?

'It's all right for that lucky old Anne,' she said to Josh as she took him off to the bedroom to change his nappy yet again. '*They* get water most days, being at the bottom of the hill.'

Lucky old Anne. Always so lucky, that Anne.

Too busy with this weavers thing now to have much time for us, Jo thought, spreading a towel out on the bed and lying Josh down on it. 'No you don't!' She gripped Joshua by the chubby thigh as he twisted round and tried to crawl away. 'You stay there, you little bugger!' Anne's friendship was like having a juicy morsel dangled in front of her only to have it whisked away again just as she was beginning to allow herself to enjoy it. She sniffed, and pulled out the cotton wool with one hand while she held Joshua down with the other. Where did the time drain away to? It was late morning already and she had achieved absolutely nothing. Every day she got up thinking 'Today I will do *something*…' But she never did. The days sank without trace. Some days she didn't even get the nappies washed. What had she got to show for her life but a long trail of un-washed nappies?

And there was Anne, she thought sourly as she took the soiled nappy to the water-less bathroom. So busy, so fulfilled. Throwing herself into this teaching. Behaving as if it was a serious job, though they were paying her peanuts… Personally, Jo thought the Mission had a cheek, accepting Anne's labour full-time but acting as though they were doing her a favour. Jo had only met Father Morrissey once and she hadn't liked him, thinking him cold and disdainful. But she was surprised at Michael.

Perhaps it's all too easy to take advantage of someone like Anne, she reflected, carrying a clean bucket of water up the stairs from the water-trailer parked at the back of the bungalow. Too easy – when it was twelve shabby old priests and one beautiful Anne – to see themselves as somehow doing her a favour. It must make such a change in that musty, dusty old Mission to have *her* wafting about. 'You all right, Josh?' she called. He didn't reply but she could hear him making little crowing noises not too far away. She wondered if perhaps Michael fancied Anne. Very matey they seemed, the two of them.

She tutted into the nappy bucket as she thought this. Really, it seemed pretty dishonest to her, even if it was unconscious self-deception: Michael pretending he was above all that, Anne declaring she wasn't the slightest bit interested. Not that Jo believed her for one minute. She poured the revolting nappy water down the toilet and began to rinse the nappies in the bucket of clean water. Behind her Josh had arrived at the bathroom doorway on his hands and knees. Bugger. That meant he'd be trying to join in nappy washing any minute now.

'Go and play, Josh,' she said, to no effect of course. He crawled into the bathroom and grabbing hold of the back of her tee-shirt as she knelt on the floor he pulled himself up onto his feet.

Sighing, she began to peel off the stinking rubber gloves. God, how she hated this life.

A few days later the source of all Josh's trouble broke through his upper gum. When Anne called by in the late afternoon on her way home from school he was sitting on the floor gnashing his three teeth.

'I'm afraid he's still enjoying the horrible noises you can make when you've got a top tooth as well as two bottom ones,' Jo said as she went to the kitchen to fetch drinks.

'I've told Dad I'm thinking about staying another year,' Anne said from the kitchen doorway.

'Really? What did he say?'

'Actually he seemed quite pleased. For Dad. I told him I wasn't expecting to stay with him unless he actually wanted me to and he looked quite put out that I had even considered living anywhere else. I must say I was relieved – it would be quite difficult making what they pay me stretch to paying rent as well as everything else.'

Jo wanted to say that they had room here – she should come and live with them and there would be no question of rent! But although the bungalow was spacious it only had two bedrooms. It would be a major upheaval now to move Josh back in to sleep with her and Kevin. She said nothing. If Anne decided she didn't want to go on living with her father after all, that would be the time to suggest it.

After Anne had gone, though, the same old miserable mood descended. Apart from Anne there was nobody she could really share a good laugh with, nobody she would *really* call a friend, but she knew Anne had only called today because she was passing on her way back from work. She'd come in saying she couldn't stay long because she had so much marking to do.

Jo sat on the floor with Josh in the middle of the living room, spooning mashed banana into his mouth and thinking she'd feel so much better if only she could have Anne to herself for a bit instead of having to share her with everybody else.

Anne could come with them in August when they went to Kumasi! The thought hit her like a bolt of lightning. The house they were borrowing while friends from their Kumasi days went back to the UK on leave had three bedrooms. It would be the school holidays, she would have no excuse not to say yes – perhaps not for the whole two months but at least for a bit. It cheered Jo up, just thinking about it. Got her all through the bedtime routine and out the other side. But by the time she was sitting in an exhausted lump on the sofa, sipping Kingsway Supermarket gin and waiting for Kevin to roll in from work, she realised her plan had a flaw: Anne might say no.

There were her small boys, bright-faced and eager, and her big boys, nonchalant and self-confident. And in-between there was the Fourth Form with their up-and-down emotions and their unreliable voices, and this class was secretly her favourite. Which made it all the more shocking that it was with them that she had her first really difficult lesson.

She never did identify where the trouble came from. One moment they were laboriously going over the plot-line of *Portrait of the Artist As a Young Man* for the benefit of the weaker in the class. A moment later the boys were suddenly debating religion. Not an area she would have let them loose in – on the contrary, she had to tread around this subject so delicately that she was extremely careful about the structure of these particular lessons.

She stepped back (quite literally) against the blackboard

and let the argument rage for a few minutes, simply because she wasn't sure what was happening. The boys had discarded their classroom English and lapsed completely into pidgin. They seemed to have split suddenly into two factions, possibly more than two. She could see Ezekiel Naah in the back row glaring at Thomas Nanfuri, who was turned in his seat with his back to her gesticulating, but she couldn't work out what it was that he was shouting at Ezekial. Ezekial swiftly retaliated, and then the boy beside him leapt to his feet and started shouting furiously at Thomas.

'Boys!' she said sharply, but nobody heard her.

Joseph Appiah in the front row gave her his usual radiant smile. 'Thomas want to be a priest,' he said helpfully, as if this explained everything.

She managed to call them back to order at last, wondering what the classes on either side could be making of the din. Her own voice sounded silly and weak as she struggled to make herself heard. The boys who had got up from their desks sat down again. Thomas turned unwillingly back to face her. She got them back to the structure of the plot but for the rest of the lesson there were strange undercurrents rumbling and tugging. A dark energy, which she couldn't quite pull back or contain, threatened to erupt again.

She could have dissipated it – she could have ordered them to get out their exercise books and write an essay – but she didn't want merely to repress them, she wanted to harness the passion that seemed to have been let loose. She felt weak and ineffectual, as if she was running behind the class hastily picking up pieces instead of being in control. When the bell went it felt like a reprieve.

Michael laughed sympathetically when she told him and observed that she had gone a remarkably long time without any major hiccup. 'There had to be a first time, and it won't be the last,' he said. 'Fourth Forms are nearly always difficult – you've got them all together still, whereas in the Fifth they're split into the O Level group and the non-exam boys and that makes it easier.' He told her to go home and not to worry about it.

When she came out of school, Joseph Appiah was lingering by the gate. He lived on the Low Cost Estate somewhere. She often saw him passing the house, looking towards their front door, ready to wave if he saw her. As she came towards him now his face lit up as it always did. It was impossible to go on feeling glum once she had been showered with that smile. He offered to carry her pile of books and turned to walk beside her, down towards the Low Cost.

'Dis Thomas Nanfuri, he very difficult boy,' he volunteered when they had gone a little way down the road.

'Is he?' She was unwilling to focus blame on Thomas. It seemed to her he had merely got in the way of something else.

'He always telling, *You must do dis, God say do dat.* As I tell you, he want to be a priest.'

Thomas had always been such a stolid, silent boy in class: she had difficulty fitting Joseph's version to the boy she knew, with his impassive face and his apparent diffidence, his unwillingness to expose himself intellectually and the obstinacy which was revealed if he was pushed into exposure. She glimpsed, suddenly, a hint of the complex inter-relationship of the playground and the school corridor that lay beneath the class she was familiar with, sitting so demurely at their desks. A hint of a different dynamic to the one she had understood – Thomas as ambitious, not as scapegoat. She looked at Joseph, wondering who *he* was, beneath that disarming grin.

A clever boy, Joseph. He would most definitely be in the O level group next term. Thomas might or might not be. She wondered how the decision would be made and who would make it.

10

Early June

The scampering in the roof had got so bad it was beginning to make the thin ceilings shake. Not mice, she was guessing now.

'Couldn't we put a trap down for those rats?' she asked her father one Sunday morning.

'Rats?'

'Well I suppose they might be mice,' she said doubtfully, 'only they sound a bit big. I've seen traps in the market but they don't look strong enough for rats and I wonder where we'd put a trap anyway. We couldn't put one in the roof, I don't suppose?'

He laughed. 'Even if you could you wouldn't catch rats in them. That's not rats, it's lizards.'

'*Lizards?*'

'Monitor lizards. We always get them during the rainy season. It's the young ones running about. If you think they're noisy now, just wait until they're fully grown.'

She thought he was joking. She bought a mouse-trap anyway and set it in the kitchen, in case the rats made their way down from the roof and got amongst the food.

Moses went groping for an onion that had rolled behind the sack of rice by the wall. She heard the snap of the trap and her heart sank guiltily as he surfaced with a yell of pain, the trap clamped firmly on his finger. 'What dis crazy ting!'

Surely she had told him she had put a trap there? Or had she only told her father, expecting him to tell Moses? She couldn't actually remember.

His finger was bleeding badly. She did penance (she always seemed to be doing penance): he sat on his low stool, cradling his bad hand in his good one while his bright blood splashed in little puddles on the concrete floor at his feet and congealed like garish red counters in the dust, and she went looking for the first-aid kit which he said was in the cupboard of her father's room. Then she bandaged his hand.

As she stood over him, winding the bright white tape around his dark finger, she saw how clean-cut the lines of his face were, like the statue of the Indian dancing god with the slanting eyes and curling lips. She had never noticed the similarity before.

She had never touched him before either. He let her do it, but only because he couldn't do it himself. She tied the little tapes of the bandage in a reef knot. As soon as she had finished he stood up roughly, shrugging her off. She offered to cut up the rest of the mountain of onions, peppers and garlic that he'd been in the middle of chopping for chutney (another of his forays into Elizabeth Bramwell's *Young Housewife's Book of Cooking*). He sat down again on his stool, watching over her, his injured hand conspicuously cradled in his good hand, and took a bleak glee in criticising her chopping.

He was cutting them up just the same way! Anne thought crossly. But out of the corner of her eye she could see the blood seeping through his bandage. She chopped smaller, as instructed.

The scurrying in the roof got louder.

She was walking back from the market one afternoon, a string bag laden with tins of Ideal Milk cutting into her shoulder when a loud rustling in the coarse grass at the side of their road stopped her in her tracks. She peered cautiously into the storm drain. Between the clumps of grass, a short section of snake fully a hand-span in circumference quivered as if it knew she was looking. She jumped back. Strange that *a snake* should have been crashing about so loudly, she was thinking, just as the snake leapt straight out of the drain. It trundled away from her on four stumpy legs, across the sprouting new grass and up the side of their house and into the roof. *A monitor lizard! Just like Dad said.*

No wonder the ceiling was beginning to bounce.

She went indoors, buzzing, but her dad was out and Moses just shrugged, as if being excited to see a monitor lizard only proved she was stupid. He took the tins of evaporated milk and turned away sourly into the kitchen, clicking his tongue in that impatient way he had.

Suddenly it was too much – his bad temper, the way he was always there, and was never pleased with anything she did. She banged out of the house, no longer caring if he noticed that he had riled her, but that was as close as she dared go to letting him know she was angry. All this time she hadn't dared react when he was rude, afraid to upset some mysterious balance in the household, but now she wanted to be rude back, and that scared her.

Why? She walked quickly up the road, barely able to return the greetings as she passed their neighbours. It wasn't her way, getting angry. Emotions in their family had always been her mother's territory, but this was more complicated than that. She had long ago given up any hope of being

112

liked by Moses. Why was she so fearful of offending him when he had no qualms about being offensive to her? Was it because she was white and he was black? ('Hello sister!' shouted the man who owned the little bar. She waved, and hurried past before he could start chatting.) It would be a strange, inverted form of colour prejudice if she failed to react simply because Moses was black and she was not.

She shook her head sharply at the thought and the woman passing with a sack of rice balanced carefully on her head gave her a surprised, sideways look. Such a pretty boy, Moses was too – tall and slender, very neat. She might have been attracted to him in another life. In this one she was beginning to hate him, moving about like a gazelle that had wandered delicately out of the wide bush and into the narrow confines of the house. The whites of his eyes glinted brightly in the shadowy rooms but towards her they were veiled and sullen as if a transparent inner eyelid came down and shuttered them off. He didn't merely dislike her, he recoiled from her. That was what made it so bad. She walked out of his shadow feeling unclean. She needed to keep out of his way simply to feel normal, and each time she left the house she felt as if she were climbing back inside her own skin. Jo was right, she should say something to her dad She stopped in the road. Did she really want to go to Jo's house and hear her say it again? How could she say out loud, *What if he were to choose Moses instead of me?*

But there was nowhere else to go.

'Sounds as if Moses is a woman-hater,' Jo said. 'You should talk to your dad.'

That night when Moses was safely washing up in the kitchen she made herself ask (squinting at her biro as if just checking the ink level), 'Doesn't Moses like women?'

Her father seemed surprised. 'Moses? Oh I don't think he *dislikes* women. No.'

It was only her he didn't like, then. Can I really manage another whole year of this? she wondered in a panic. A year was such a very long time.

She could always move out. But if she did, Moses would have won.

Moses was winning anyway. That sinister talisman he wore, and the way he mumbled as he washed her clothes as if he was casting bad spells. The place on her foot where she had trodden on a thorn had gone septic and would not heal. Do they stick pins in effigies here? she wondered. They surely did.

Michael called after her as she walked down the corridor ahead of him, 'What's wrong with that foot of yours, Anne? You're limping!'

She stopped and waited for him. It was break-time. They walked together to the staffroom. 'I trod on a thorn. It won't heal.'

'How long ago was this thorn?'

'A week. Maybe more. I wanted to ask you about Dublin.'

'Wrong country.'

'I know that! Even without geography O level, I do know that. But have you ever been there? I want to know what it's like.' She hadn't had another bad lesson but *Portrait of the Artist* was still causing difficulties: if she could convey something of Dublin to boys who didn't know what mist was and had never seen the sea or even a river, it might be easier to win their interest. 'If you can't do Dublin, do Ireland generally for me. What five words would you use to sum up Ireland?'

Michael whistled. 'You don't ask for much, do you! But luckily I *can* do Dublin.' He ignored the allotted five words and told her about the city, and the smell of the river, and the way people look at you in the street, and the music and the singing in the pubs. By the time they got to the staffroom she had forgotten her foot was hurting. She was taken aback when he sat down in the chair next to hers and leaned down and grabbed hold of her left ankle. 'Let's have a look at this then.' He had her plimsoll off in a jiffy. She gazed down at her patchwork foot, striped by the sun, hoping it didn't smell too cheesy but bare feet in plimsolls inevitably do.

'I'm not surprised you're limping!' he exclaimed when he saw the angry swelling distorting her little toe.

'I got the thorn out straight away – it's not that there's anything left in there. It just doesn't want to get better.' She longed to say more, she had to bite her tongue to stop herself. It had been a small thorn, it had come out easily enough. Really it should have cleared up all by itself. But it hadn't. She could just imagine the pins in the effigy. It would be such a relief to say it, to put the word outside her head and cut it down to size: *juju*. But it would sound stupid and Michael would laugh at her, so she didn't say anything.

'Wait there a minute.' He got up and went out of the room. When he came back he had a small glass jar in his hand.

'What on earth is that!' she said suspiciously. The paste in the jar was a dull, sickly green.

'This? Well it's not out of Jeremiah's pharmacy, that's for sure. This is one of Stefan's little potions. Don't ask what's in it! It won't kill you, and it usually clears things up a treat.'

He pulled his chair closer and put her foot back in his lap. She could feel the warmth of his hard, muscular thigh through the fabric of his trousers. She watched idly while he carefully hooked out a little of the paste with his forefinger. The paste smelled nicer than it looked. He rubbed it gently around the swelling.

Jo hooted with laughter when Anne told her this story later. 'Whoohoo! If only Ursula could have been a fly on the wall! Wouldn't she have been pissed off! Or any of the others, for that matter. They're all of them besotted with bloody Michael, it seems.'

And Anne had to laugh too, though actually she was irritated with Jo for constantly harping on about Michael as if *she* was the one who was besotted.

A few days later, after a night of solid, homely rain, she went to see her favourite weavers, the ones off the Airport Road who had been her first find. She was sitting with them in companionable silence when she saw Michael on his bicycle. He had turned into the muddy lane in front of her, between the low-roofed huts, appearing quietly out of the green gloom of the shadowy bushes beyond the houses, and shortly afterwards he turned into another lane and disappeared. He didn't see her. Appearing like a ghost against the glower of the leaves and passing from right to left across her vision, he might have been a figment of her imagination. But the sudden unexpected beating of her heart when she saw him felt like an internal betrayal. He was a friend. A friend and a priest. It was Jo's fault, constantly harping on about his reputation with the ladies of Tamale.

She didn't want her heart to go into such complicated places.

Michael, on his bicycle, took his usual short-cut from the Airport Road to the Gonja Road. He cut off several miles by doing this but it was pleasant, too, on the outer edges of the town, to be amongst what a little while since had been separate villages. There were thatched huts in among the tin-roofed, mud-brick houses, and many gardens. The twisting lanes were fenced with woven sorghum, the bushes and small trees grew thick in places. There were accompanying hazards, of course. He had once nearly taken his eye out on a stick protruding from the low eaves of a hut as he cycled down a narrow lane. You could drop your front wheel square into a storm drain and fly over the handle-bars in an undignified heap. And there was a tale amongst the expatriate community – and therefore probably apocryphal – of a man cycling clean across the middle of a big snake which had promptly reared up and bitten him. Fatally, but then that is in the tradition of apocryphal tales. It was a short cut he took, therefore, for the sake of his leg muscles and for its own aesthetic pleasures rather than for speed.

He turned to the left into the lane leading to the weavers, and then after a few yards he turned right onto another track, ducking to avoid hitting his head on the overhanging eaves of corrugated iron at the back of a house. A little further on, he got off his bike to lift it over a deep ditch.

He patted the bike fondly as he climbed back on. *Old Paint*, he called her, remembering the cowboy dirge one of his sisters used to sing (to his adolescent irritation).

Actually his bicycle had no need of a name, *Old Paint* or

anything else. It had its own name, proudly emblazoned along the cross-bar. His good, solid, sit-up-and-beg Chinese bicycle, built like a tank. His one luxury, virtually his only possession after his clothes and his razor, costing him nearly £100 new. All black, except for the silver exclamation between his pumping thighs. *!FLASHER!* However low he might be feeling, this never failed to make him laugh.

The door was opened by a young girl. Her face cleared when he spoke to her in Dagbani. No, she replied, Master wasn't at home but Madam would be able to say when he was expected back.

The little housegirl led him into the reception room. He could see at once there was trouble. In the middle of the big bare room Issa's pretty young wife was sitting on the enormous black plastic sofa, flanked by her four young sons, and all five of them were weeping. Whoops, he thought, composing his face suitably for a bereavement, for a second wife, but Issa's wife gestured towards the large television that faced the sofa. She looked at him hopefully. 'It is not working,' she said, in Dagbani.

The ceiling fan was whirling briskly overhead, so it was something more technical than the power being off. Michael hadn't been around tellies much since he was a teenager but he examined the set gravely and twiddled the flex a bit the way a good physics teacher does, and pushed in the cable at the back. The five expectant faces watched him from the sofa, and a sixth from the corner where the housegirl was sitting on the floor. He twiddled again and nearly jumped out of his skin when the set suddenly crackled into life. A cheer went up. Michael stood back to admire his handiwork. There was the Lone Ranger, no less, staring impassively out of the black and white screen while Tonto stood behind him with the wind stirring his hair. The six faces were beaming now. It felt like switching on the sun.

He asked when Issa might be expected back. 'Try later, try five o'clock,' Issa's missus said absently without shifting her gaze from the screen.

It was a long, grinding cycle ride back up the hill into town. A dark day, threatening rain, hot and heavy. And so far, nothing at all achieved.

Later that afternoon Michael sat adrift in the centre of the same black sofa that Mrs Issa and her sons had occupied earlier. He sat where Issa had put him, in front of a bottle of Fanta. On the far side of the low table Issa sat in the big armchair with a second bottle of Fanta.

Issa was a big man in every sense – a business man, the owner of a construction company (though he was only about thirty-five, therefore younger than Michael by some). And he was built like a wrestler. A sleek bull of a man with his shaved head and his massive shoulders. He was sitting hunched forwards in his chair, huge hands cupped loosely around the frosted bottle on the table. Michael sat adrift in the depths of the sofa, unable to relax into either corner, pinned in place as he was by Issa's glowering presence on the far side of the coffee-table. He had the uncomfortable feeling that he was being stage-managed, even though it was he who had initiated this meeting.

'I bin tinking, tinking, tinking,' Issa growled.

Bad sign, Michael thought. Usually they communicated in Dagbani.

'I bin tinking, dat price no good.'

Ah, not religion then. Merely building contracts. Michael relaxed a little. 'You're meaning the contract we signed for the science block?'

Issa looked at him pityingly. They had no other agreement involving money.

The contract was already eighteen months old and inflation had been precipitous during all that time. However, the funds had been available since the beginning. It was Issa, not the Mission, who had caused the delays.

'Well,' Michael said carefully, 'tell me what you are thinking.'

'I am tinking, I don' want you cheat me.' Issa glared at him from under heavy, hairless brows.

He hadn't noticed before that Issa had no eyebrows. Did he shave them or was he entirely and naturally hairless? Whichever, the glare was even more effective without them. 'The Mission doesn't go in for cheating,' Michael said, unconsciously stroking his own over-active left eyebrow and hoping Issa was not as close to hitting him in the chops as his boxer's face made it seem. 'If you're no longer satisfied with the price we agreed you'd better tell me what sort of money you're thinking about.'

Issa clicked the knuckle of his forefinger. Then of his second finger. 'Dat price we said too too low. Building prices gone crazy dis last two years. I say now… ' Issa paused and clicked a third knuckle, then named a price nearly double the original sum they'd agreed.

Michael took a sustaining sip of his Fanta. He'd been told the original price they'd agreed was far too high. Other contractors would apparently have taken on the job for much less, as he'd been told only a week ago. That builder might, of course, have been lying, but it did look as if he'd been naïve accepting Issa's confident persuasions at the outset. The new science block had become a thorn in Michael's side. He knew he was too lazy, too willing to trust to the good nature of others to drive a hard bargain and then to see things through. But now the delays were getting downright embarrassing and he'd been wishing he could be free of Issa for some time.

He said, taking care with his words, 'It was a fair price when we both signed the contract. We *have* been waiting eighteen months for you to do the work…'

Issa said quickly, as if he'd been waiting to parry this charge, 'We put de foundations long long time ago.'

'Yes, but nothing else. I've been coming to see you once or twice a month for getting on for a year to remind you we need more than footings.'

'We made de footings long time ago. But you no pay me nothing.'

'The agreement was,' Michael said, keeping his voice neutral 'you would build to the roof, then we would pay you half. The rest when you had finished.'

'You no pay me nothing,' Issa repeated testily. 'You expect all but you pay nothing! All my costs go sky high and you pay nothing!'

'We had an agreement, as I just said.'

'It not enough! I want new price, and I want you pay me half-half now. Half-half when we made to roof, the rest when we finish.'

'We can't do that.'

'Then I no want contract,' Issa said, slapping his big hand down on the table and looking at Michael triumphantly.

'In that case the Mission will be happy to release you from the contract.'

Issa's face fell. Michael saw it and had to steel himself not to feel sorry for the man. 'Actually, the contract was broken when you failed to complete the work within twelve months, but I didn't like to bring this up before. Perhaps we should start again? You say your price and a date when you can promise to finish the work, and I will talk to other builders who might like to take on the job. We'll make a new contract with whoever offers the best deal.'

For the second time that day Michael toiled up the long hill into town. It was getting late but the heat still hung grey and heavy. A passive, inert kind of heat, the lowering sky darkening early, the night coming in ponderous.

When he reached the main road he turned left, away from the centre of town, and cycled a few hundred yards to a row of low-roofed houses which stood beside a small lorry park. It was not a good time to call on Mohammed, who would be at his prayers, but Michael was in need of quiet conversation with a good friend and he could wait until prayers were over. He seated himself on the step of the little house. Children passing called out his name in their sing-song voices, 'My-kel! My-kel!' He smiled and waved. The little boy, Mahmoud, whom he had carried in his arms to the hospital last year when the child had a ruptured appendix, came and stood as he always did, in a touching mix of shy silence and affectionate familiarity, leaning against Michael's knee and answering his questions in whispered monosyllables. The child's mother called a cheerful greeting from their house across the road. The pungent fragrance of groundnuts roasting on a brazier drifted. The women who sat by the road selling soaps and combs, spread on cloths on the ground, were lighting hurricane lamps and the smell of hot kerosene mingled with the smell of the roasting groundnuts and of charcoal and woodsmoke. As it grew darker even white-skinned Michael ceased to be noticed.

Except by Mohammed, when he came from his prayers inside the house. He sat down next to Michael. 'Ah, My-kel.'

'Ah, Mohammed.'

They shook hands warmly but awkwardly, seated side by side as they were.

'Mohammed, my friend,' Michael said in Dagbani, 'I have a problem.'

'Uh-huh?'

'The building of the science laboratories.'

'Ah,' said Mohammed. 'The building which is not done.'

'Yes indeed.'

'I told you, that man is not a good man. He made you a bad price, for a job he did not want enough. I told you all of this a long time ago.'

'You did. You did, Mohammed. And I should have listened, my friend. But I had already made the contract when you and I spoke of it. Now he has broken the contract and says himself he wishes to be free of it.'

'Uhuh?'

'He wants more money.'

'More money? He already asked too much! How much is he asking now?'

Michael told him, and Mohammed snorted derisively. 'So what is your problem, My-kel? Now you start again.'

'I know, I know – I was a fool not to come to you for advice in the first place. But Issa was so very convincing. And I am worried now that he will make life difficult for anyone who takes on the contract in his place. He can be very threatening, this man. When I went to see him just now he was praying, as if he wanted me to feel that his God was on his side and that I had no God at all.'

Mohammed said calmly, 'I told you before, this is a man who uses God but he is not a man *of* God. Yes, he will be angry that someone else gets the money, but he will not be angry that they do the work. What you should do is this. Find your builders, ask each of them what they will charge, and when they promise to do the job. This man, too, can name his price and his time, if he still wishes, along with the others. If he has already broken the terms of his contract he will not have a case against you if you do not choose him.'

'You are a wise friend, Mohammed. When you put it like that it sounds very easy. But what if he will not let it go at that?'

'This man is the cockerel who jumps up on the fence and puffs out his chest so far in his crowing that he cannot see the little birds on the ground are taking the grain while he makes noises and does not eat. But he does not want your work. That is why he has not properly begun it. He has heard there is government work coming. Big, big work. He is crowing to the bigger roosters even now.'

In the dark, the passers-by had become mere silhouettes of bare legs passing in front of the hurricane lamps, the occasional flashing spokes of a bicycle wheel, the cheerful murmur of many voices. The best hour of the day, this, between the pressure of the light and the oppression of the dark, and such a pleasure to be had, sitting side by side with a friend, watching the world go by.

'I am still afraid there may be trouble.'

'My-kel! You are a good man, but not enough of the world. Bad men can see you coming! Go to the Builders' Quarter on the Zigbili Road and look for three or four who could do this work. My friend Kwame will help you find them. We will write in a list what they each will charge and when they say they will start the work and when they will finish, and then you will choose and we will make a contract. And this time, if the contract is broken it will be clearly laid down what the penalty will be for the one who fails his side of the agreement, and that the next person on the list will take over the work.'

'You make it sound so simple!'

'In Ghana it is never simple. A man says *God willing I will do it today* when he means *I cannot start it before next week*, but some men are known to say this when they mean *I cannot start it ever*. My friend Kwame will take you to men who keep their word. You will have your science buildings, and the workmen will have their money. And your friends in England will be glad for the fine work you are doing and then they will send more money to Tamale-here and all will be well. God willing.'

'God willing, it will!' Michael said, getting to his feet. 'And now I cannot resist the smell of those roasting groundnuts a moment longer. Wait there, my friend, and I will go and get us some.'

He had already missed supper in the Mission. He could think of no nicer way of spending his evening than to share a newspaper cone of piping hot roasted groundnuts with his good friend and adviser Mohammed while they attempted to resolve their long-term debate on the question of whether a man's responsibility is first and foremost to his God or to his fellow man.

11

June

'Dad! There's a snake!'

It was side-winding along the corridor. She glimpsed the strong markings along its back, the flicker of its tongue and its clear, glittering eye as it slithered past the living room door.

He was at her side in a moment, his voice urgent: 'Where?'

'Heading towards your room.'

He moved cautiously into the doorway and she stepped up beside him. The snake, halfway into the shadow of her father's room whisked back on itself in an evil figure of eight, its head raised towards them as if it would strike.

He pulled her back inside the living room. 'Where's Moses?' he hissed. His hand gripped her upper arm so tightly it hurt.

Where was Moses? He wasn't in the house. She had last seen him out on the road, talking to a man carrying a cardboard box.

She stared, startled, as she too made the connection. Surely not! But it would fit. Oh yes, it would fit. All the little things that had been building up!

Her dad bent forward to peer round the door-post and so did she, just in time to see the snake's tail slip round the doorpost into his bedroom.

He went out into the corridor but when she tried to follow he said sharply, 'Close the door and don't open it till I say so!'

What he was going to do? She hovered in the doorway and watched him creep away from the bedroom towards the open front door. He picked up the heavy wooden pestle which Moses used for pounding *fufu*, which lived just inside the front door. *In case of burglars*, Moses always said, laughing. Her dad very quietly closed the front door and came back towards her, silent on his bare feet. He's trapping it in the house! she thought wildly. She looked down at his pale white toes with their tufts of dark hairs. Such vulnerable, bony feet he had.

'Dad! You have to put your shoes on!'

He didn't hear. 'Get inside and close the door,' he said tersely, and this time he stood over her impatiently until she obeyed. 'Stay in there till I tell you it's safe to come out.'

She put her ear to the door, listening: the sound of his bedroom door closing, then silence. Such a silence!

The pestle thudded heavily on the floor. Once, twice. Three times.

Silence again. So long a silence that she couldn't wait – she opened the door. From inside the bedroom she could hear the faint sounds of him moving about but they were ordinary noises.

He jumped as she came in, nearly letting go of the bloodied snake he was holding up by the tail. 'Close that door!' he snapped, though the snake wasn't going anywhere – its head was beaten to a pulp. She did as she was told and watched him drop the snake into a pillow-case and roll it into a bundle.

'Was it a bad one?' she asked, her voice sounding strangely loud and calm.

'Carpet snake. One of the worst. I've made a bit of a mess. Clean it up, would you, while I dispose of this.'

Another command. He must be very shocked, to be so brusque. It was a shocking situation. At least it was obvious now that something must be done. She went to the kitchen for a bowl of water and a cloth.

Kneeling to her task on the concrete floor, the snake's blood bright against the dull red paint, her heart whisked back on itself as she thought of snakes under sofas, under beds. Her father's bare feet. Her own.

Her father came into the room. She stood up, trying to read his ashen face. He took her by the arm and his grip was painful. 'You are not to say a word about this to Moses! You understand? Not one word.'

His sternness frightened her. She looked up into his face, wanting it to be explicit between them, the danger that they were in and Moses at the root of it, but it was too terrible a thing to put into words. 'I promise.' Her voice coming out hoarse, not much more than a whisper. The skitter of Moses' flip-flops on the front step interrupted them. Her dad let go of her arm abruptly and went out of the room.

She rubbed her arm, hearing his voice, painfully cheerful: 'I was wondering where you'd got to, old chap. D'you want me to take you into town now?' Moses laughing and saying something she couldn't hear. A few minutes later she heard the sound of the Land Rover doors slamming and the engine starting. And they were gone.

She sat on the floor and leaned against the bed. How calm her dad had managed to sound! Would he tell Moses to leave at once? If he did, wouldn't that make Moses even more angry? Snakes weren't superstition. There was nothing quaint about a venomous snake.

She got up and took the bucket of bloody water to throw it under the mango tree. She washed out the cloth under the kitchen tap and hung it on the line to dry in the sun, her pink flag waving bravely to tell Moses she didn't care.

Only, she did. And she was scared, too.

They didn't come back. It was hard to concentrate on marking when her mind was skidding all over the place. What else might be sneaking its terrible way into the house? Another snake, a scorpion, a biting spider? Or a bad spirit.

That was what she found most disturbing: the bad spirit of malevolence, the desire to do harm. She had laughed at the whole idea of *juju* (hadn't she?) but now she was staring the reality of it in the face.

Had Moses done it himself, or had he got somebody else to do it? The questions raged through her head. Nobody to talk to. Certainly not Jo – the very idea of a snake coming into the house would make Jo too hysterical to listen. Jo was expecting her this afternoon but she couldn't go and say nothing. She couldn't go and say something. Jo would just have to assume she was sick. There was nobody else she could talk to. No space for her to put the words out into the air and bring them down to size. Inside her head they multiplied and magnified. Perhaps they wouldn't have done, if her dad's mind hadn't instantly worked the same way that hers had.

In the afternoon he came back, and Moses with him. It was obvious nothing had yet been said because Moses was too cheerful. Her father was being strangely solicitous towards Moses. Almost protective. (Not towards me, she thought, with new bitterness. Not towards me!) Had Moses somehow got round him? On his shoulder, clutched close to his ear, he was carrying a brand new transistor radio. She was astonished, knowing how much those things cost here.

If it was some kind of strategy, her father gave her no signal. She could understand nothing from his expression and she couldn't ask. He had been so unnervingly stern before he went out that she couldn't help feeling the prohibition about saying anything to Moses was a prohibition about saying anything to anybody, including to himself.

'Could I talk to you about something?' she asked Michael as she packed up her books in the staffroom. She had lingered after everyone else had drifted off at the end of school in order to speak to him alone.

'Of course,' he said cheerfully. 'You know you can ask me anything at any time. You seem to be wonderfully in the swing of it now. I heard you racketing along this morning with great gusto.'

She thought he was fibbing. She hadn't been racketing along at all today. She sat down suddenly because her legs were trembling too much to stand up. 'I didn't mean school work. Could I talk to you about something personal?'

He looked at her quickly and pulled a chair round to face her. 'Fire away. What is it that's troubling you?'

She hesitated. She had gone over and over this conversation in her mind all day yesterday and most of last night, but now that she needed them the words had evaporated. 'On Saturday we had...a snake. In the house.' She watched his face, trying to read his expression. He went very still, his eyes not on her but on the floor. So there *was* something! It wasn't just her imagination. 'Dad said it was a carpet snake.'

Michael looked up at her, waiting.

'It was just Dad and me in the house,' she said slowly,

wanting him to understand ahead of her so that she wouldn't need to spell it out.

'Ah,' he said as if he did. But still he seemed to be waiting for her to say it out loud.

'Moses was outside. Talking to a man carrying a box.'

Michael frowned, but he said nothing.

'Ever since I arrived in Tamale Moses has been waging a kind of war on me,' she said desperately. It did sound terribly lame. 'He seems to really hate me.'

Michael sat up. 'What are you saying, Anne?' His voice was sharp.

'The snake!' she said miserably, fighting tears. 'I've thought for ages Moses was trying *juju* on me, but now…'

'Stop, stop! Go back a step. Are you saying you think *Moses* put the snake in the house?'

She nodded. 'Or he got somebody else to.'

Michael breathed out so forcibly that she felt the hair on her forehead lift and settle back, but when he spoke his voice was gentle. 'I don't think so, Anne. I don't think so. Did you not know? Moses has a phobia about snakes. His sister was bitten by one when they were playing together as children. She died in front of him. Dick has to be careful never even to say the word *snake* in his presence because Moses gets serious panic attacks at the mere word. Did he not tell you?'

She looked up at him in horror as all the pieces in her head shifted about wildly and settled back any old how. She must be wrong, but she so believed she was not! The ignominious tears spilled over and coursed hotly down her cheeks.

'Well, well, well, what's happened to my big bold new teacher?' He took hold of her hands and pumped them gently up and down. 'Annie! Annie sweetheart! What's all this about? Hadn't you better tell me from the beginning?'

She was offended by the laughter she was sure she could hear in his voice. She took her hands away and wiped her eyes. He pulled a large hankie from the pocket of his shorts, none too clean she noticed as she dried her eyes with it.

'Come on, tell me!'

She couldn't trust her voice, but Michael waited. She cleared her throat. Said it small. 'Right from the start Moses has acted as if he hates me.'

He was silent. She tried to read the silence without looking at his face. 'He certainly despises me.'

'Even if that were true, which somehow I doubt, there's a mighty big difference between not thinking much of you and wishing ill on you. Don't you think?'

'He looks at me so...venomously. I can't explain. You'd have to see it to know what I mean.' She really needed him to understand! 'That amulet he wears round his neck. And he has a sort of ritual in the way he leaves the kitchen knives on the shelf – he gets angry with me if I so much as pick them up. And last week I found an aubergine with sewing needles stuck in it, hidden behind a big pot in the kitchen. And you remember how that place on my foot wouldn't heal, and now the snake, and of c— '

He took hold of her hands again and she stopped. His hands were warm and slightly rough, the big, capable hands of generations of farmers only recently come to town. 'Annie, you're upset, you're losing sight of other possibilities here. Let's go backwards. Snakes in the house – well, that's not good but it does happen. They like the cool, and your house is on the edge of the bush – it's not that big a surprise if you get a snake indoors now and then. That's a reason to be careful but not to be scared. More snakes get killed by people than people get killed by snakes. Moses's sister was very unlucky, but she was only little.'

He squeezed her hands, waiting for her to look up. 'So now you know it couldn't have been anything to do with Moses. He wouldn't even have been able to arrange it, had he a mind to do such a thing – he'd have passed out first. Do you believe me?'

She looked away, biting her lip. Gave an unwilling nod.

'And the aubergine? Well that was probably nothing. Just boredom, or maybe he was doing some mending and used the aubergine as a pincushion. Did it look like you by the way?' She glared at him, but he grinned shamelessly back. 'It probably only seemed like *juju* to you because you were already sensitised to the thought. It probably didn't look that way to Moses. And your foot – it did heal after, didn't it? I don't think Stefan's ointment works against *juju*.'

Really offended now, she tried to pull away, but he held on to her hands.

'I think there's something here you're not seeing.' He sat silent for a moment, looking the floor, as if he was pondering how to explain, his rough thumbs rubbing backwards and forwards across the backs of her hands. 'How old is your father?'

'Fifty-nine,' she answered, startled into participation.

'And how old is Moses?'

'Late twenties?'

'Do you not think that before you came along Moses might have been the child to your father and that your coming has rather pushed him out?'

'Moses couldn't – ' she began, before she realised she was taking him too literally.

'It would be hard, wouldn't it? You with all the credentials on your side and him with none, not even the right colour skin. Did you know your father put him through technical college?'

'Technical college?'

'Yes. He did a course in agricultural mechanics. But afterwards he went to work for your dad and I don't know that he's ever used his training. So you see, before you came, there was Moses running the household and looking after your dad, being like a son to him perhaps. And then you arrive and it seems he's only the houseboy after all.'

'But that's how he was introduced to me – I didn't just assume he was the houseboy!'

'I didn't say you did. Probably your father thought it would be easier if you thought he was only that. In any case I don't *know* any of this – I'm only surmising. All I know for certain is, in the old days before you came, Moses always used to sit with us as an equal and join in the talk but now he lurks behind us a lot of the time or out the back all together and he serves the tea as if he's only the houseboy.'

'Why would Dad tell me he's a houseboy if he isn't? That's weird!' But the implications were beginning to sink in. 'What an idiot I've been!'

'No, Anne, you haven't. You weren't to know it was more complicated.'

'It's dreadful!' she said, not listening. All her sins were lining up in a new formation. 'I really did think he was a servant!'

'Don't punish yourself over it. Maybe he is a houseboy, maybe he isn't. But that isn't all he is. It's more complicated than you might have been seeing.'

A new thought struck her. 'Dad does pay him, doesn't he?'

Michael looked uncomfortable. 'I don't know the detail of their arrangements. Look, Anne, I don't really know what's been going on – I'm merely hypothesising. All I know is that Moses led a somewhat different life before you came than he does now and I guess that might have been hard for him. All the more so now that you've said you're going to stay on. Moses thought he only had to last out six months but now you're going to be a permanent fixture.'

'I'd better talk to Dad about it.'

'Actually I wouldn't,' he said, cutting her off. 'Not unless Dick says something to you first. The best thing you can do is be as tactful as you can with Moses. A little bit of kindness might work wonders. Think of him as a usurped child and feel sorry for him and he'll probably come round in time. But don't be scared of him. Forget the *juju* rubbish. We're talking bruised egos here, not magic.'

'The trouble is' she said, her eyes filling again so that everything blurred, 'I came to Ghana to get to know Dad, not to share him! I'm his only child! I don't know that this isn't even worse.'

He leaned forward to look intently into her face. 'Listen to me, Anne. Whatever Moses is to your father, he can never take your place. Your father loves you, I'm sure of that. But perhaps he does find it difficult suddenly having a full-time daughter on his hands. It's very different from annual visits and meals out in restaurants, isn't it? You said yourself this is the first time you've actually lived together since you were small. You're a lovely girl, Annie – it must have hurt him badly when he left you behind. If it's not straightforward now, don't you think it might be a little bit that he's afraid? If he lets you get close, how the hell will he feel when you do go back to England?'

She sat quietly, thinking this through. He shook her hands: 'Look at me, young woman! You are not—'

The staffroom door opened and Father Morrissey walked in. He surveyed the empty room. 'I was looking for John.'

'He was here about fifteen minutes ago, I don't suppose he's gone far,' Michael said, still holding her hands. Father Morrissey went out leaving the staffroom door ajar behind him. 'Where were we? Yes. Look me in the eyes, Anne!'

She looked, dutifully, but a part of her was absurdly disappointed that he hadn't in the least minded Father Morrissey walking in on them.

'You are not to go away and brood on this all by yourself. Okay? No broo-ding' he said, shaking her hands on each syllable. 'Come and talk to your Uncle Michael about it instead. You know I've always got time for my most promising assistant teacher. Any time at all, if you need to talk, just come.'

He let go of her hands. They felt quite pummelled. 'I don't know where to find you outside school.'

'You know where our Rest House is?'

'The building round the back?'

'Yep. If you come to the front door there's always a watchman around, you only have to ask. Come on now, get along home with you or that Moses will be thinking you've run off and he's won.'

They left the room together and walked along the corridor past the Head's office. Father Morrissey's voice called through the open door, 'Michael – a word, please.'

He winked at her. 'See you in the morning,' he said.

She walked home, her mind reeling. How spoiled Moses must think her, walking in on their household and assuming the superior role. She couldn't quite let go of all those signs which seemed to add up so differently: the talisman, the snake. The man with the cardboard box. The way Moses left his knives on the shelf, not lined up but always mysteriously aligned at the same angle. And that aubergine. Above all, the way he looked at her as if he hated her. But a little voice said, *As he would. As he would.* She could see it all differently if she leaned down and looked up at all the same things from a slightly different perspective.

It didn't excuse her dad. Her father who had let her make these errors. Who hadn't protected her from her own mistakes by explaining. Why hadn't he? Did he think she would be more jealous if she knew? Did he not understand the way jealousy works, feeding on ignorance and false understandings?

As she turned into their road, the empty bush stretching away to her right and the busy houses to her left, she suddenly saw another truth that had been lurking half-hidden, waiting to jump out at her. Her dad had been protecting Moses all the time. Not her. *Not her.*

12

Second week of June

She had been poised, but now she slid.

All this time Anne had been assuming she was safe. A priest – a large scruffy priest. And she an atheist with a taste for dark, slender men, preferably good-looking ones – she would never have predicted that an overhang of belly, a close-cropped head, builder's hands, could come to this, making her heart hot and her voice hollow with emotion. I'm as bad as Ursula, she thought, exasperated.

'It must be awful being a priest if you change your mind about religion,' she said to Jo one Sunday afternoon as they sat limply in the uncomfortable easy chairs in Jo's house (what Jo called the Uneasy Chairs); she had just been telling Jo about the supper at Ursula's the night before.

Joshua crawled round their feet, his hands and knees slap-slapping on the floor tiles. 'Doesn't say much for the cleanliness of my floors, does it,' Jo said idly, prodding his rump with one foot. Josh sat back on his grubby nappy and grinned. 'What were you saying? About a priest changing his mind?' She scrutinised Anne's face. 'Are we talking Father Michael here?'

'No, I—'

'Liar!'

'No!' Anne was laughing. 'No, I was just thinking in

general. It's a hell of a thing to change your mind about, isn't it? Like being married but without the option of divorce.'

'Do you *know* he's lost his faith?'

'I'm not talking about Michael! And I wasn't thinking of faith so much as all the convictions it takes to be a priest. All the limitations you have to take on. It's a big thing, isn't it, to decide you can do without love when you're eighteen or nineteen and still feel the same thing when you're thirty or forty?'

'I thought the whole point was that priests *don't* do without love,' Jo said drily. 'They sublimate it into love of God, don't they? And love of the Church, and spiritual love of the congregation. And love of the pupils, if you're Father Michael.' She stared at Anne for a moment and burst out laughing. 'Come off it, Anne! It's written all over your face! We *are* talking Father Mick here, aren't we! And you as the beautiful damsel who will bring him human love and rescue him from a lifetime of austerity?'

'I'm not!'

'You are! You fancy him, don't you? I *knew* you did!'

'I don't!'

'You do!'

'Don't!'

'Do!' Jo picked up one of Joshua's toys, a cloth brick with a bell inside, and threw it at her. Anne promptly threw it back. Joshua appeared between them, pulling himself up onto his feet by holding onto his mother's skirt and grinning with his tongue sticking out. 'Joshua Matthews, how very stooooopid you look!' Jo cried, bending down to rub noses with him. Joshua gurgled gleefully. 'But seriously, Anne – it is a bit of a dead duck, isn't it, fancying a priest? It's not got a lot going for it as the Big Romance.'

'No, but since I don't fancy him that's all right.'

After a bit she added, 'But wouldn't it be difficult to know what to do if you did?'

'Can't see why,' Jo said. 'It's obvious! You should run a mile and find somebody else to fall in love with instead. Not that there's much choice in Tamale.'

Anne might have pointed out that actually Tamale was full of men, but she didn't want to go sideways. Not just at the moment. 'It would be a terrible moral conundrum, wouldn't it. If you did happen to like a priest that way, and if he *did* like you as more than a friend, what would be the right thing to do? Keep away and save him from temptation, or tell him so he could make his own choice? Which would be like being the devil's agent, wouldn't it, putting temptation in his way?'

'Really? I thought this particular priest was already charging down that path all by himself. The way he and Ursula behave when they're together!'

'Last night was the first time I've ever seen them together,' Anne said. (And it *was* true that Ursula had been embarrassingly flirtatious, popping pastries into Michael's mouth in the kitchen and calling him Mikey.) 'He managed to sidestep her very neatly without seeming rude.'

'Or he wanted it to look that way because *you* were there!'

She decided to ignore that remark. Actually she had been thoroughly taken aback to find Michael at Peter and Ursula's last night. She had been overcome with awkwardness, not knowing whether you kiss priests socially the same way you do everyone else at a supper party, but more than that, she had barely seen Michael to talk to since their embarrassing conversation about Moses. So she had stood tongue-tied in the corner of Ursula's kitchen while

140

Ursula flirted, and Michael parried as neatly as any knight on horseback, deflecting all Ursula's approaches without moving from his seat on the kitchen table.

Jo was watching her so she said, 'Michael's very friendly and open and all that but he's also very good at steering round people when they act inappropriately. Haven't you noticed?'

Jo shrugged. 'I like Michael but I've never understood what all the fuss is about. Do they *really* fancy him, all those bored women, or is it some kind of an in-joke? Or is he leading them on for a bit of titillation himself? Quite honestly I've even wondered if the flirting with the wives is a kind of cover-up for really being interested in the husbands. I'm probably not a very good judge. I'm not sure I *like* men all that much. Except for Kevin, of course. But he's hardly a man.'

'Jo!'

'Well he's *Kevin*, isn't he? Which is different. And I don't think I ever really fancied him either, if the truth be told.'

Anne looked at her anxiously, but it *was* hard to think of Kevin in those terms, it wasn't just Jo. He was so dependable and good. Neither good-looking nor attractively ugly, he was... just Kevin. And Jo was as unlikely as Kevin was. It was hard to imagine how they had ever ended up in a relationship.

As for herself, Anne had to share the few men in her life, it seemed. Her father with Moses, and Michael with Ursula (along with all the other women in Tamale and every passer-by in the street). But bizarrely, last night it had not been Ursula and Michael, or Moses and her dad, who had caused the stabs of jealousy (Michael had spent all evening talking engineering with Peter, and Moses hadn't been invited). It

141

was Ursula flirting with her father. She knew that it probably meant nothing. But how she wished her dad could be as free and easy with her, his own daughter, as he was with this woman. She had never seen him so animated. While she herself had sat rather forlornly between the two camps – Michael and Peter on her left, Ursula and her father on her right – forgotten by both, wondering if perhaps she was just not very interesting.

But at least it had left her free to observe Michael secretly as he talked. Dressed in white trousers and a colourful shirt – it was the first time she'd seen him looking so smart.

As they were leaving, they had all lingered for a moment outside the house to breathe in the night air, warmly fragrant after the rain. Ursula had turned towards her then, apologising for neglecting her all evening. 'Come again on Friday afternoons if ever you're not teaching,' Ursula said. *How short she is!* Anne noticed with surprise. Standing in that characteristic way Ursula had with her head tucked back on her shoulders like an egret, looking out from under her eyelids.

She was aware of Michael standing behind her. It was too dark to see whether Ursula's eyes were on her or were looking over her shoulder at him. Was he looking back at Ursula? Then she felt his hand on her shoulder – his comfortable teacher's gesture. 'Your dad's just offered me a lift home,' he said. 'He's gone to get the Land Rover.'

Sitting in the back as they bounced homewards along the rough roads, her shoulder still hot with the echo of Michael's casual touch, she could study the line of his head in the safety of darkness: the cropped fuzz of his hair against the glare of the head-lights, his big-boned profile and angular nose as he turned towards her father to say something. She wondered how old he was and whether the difference in ages between him and her was impossible anyway.

And for thinking this ridiculous thought she punished herself by doing a whole batch of marking when she got home, before going sleeplessly to bed.

Anne didn't recognise him for a moment – the elegant young man walking down the road in front of her with a transistor radio clamped to his right ear – but she had been able to hear the music from fifty yards back and she'd been amused by the way his long-legged gait adapted itself to the crackling rhythms. 'High Life': the pulse which drifted from nearly every alleyway of the market and from most of the Chop Bars, always distorted, always crackly. Of course it was Moses! He had been welded to that radio ever since her dad had given it to him a week ago.

She came into the house just behind him. He turned, the radio still clamped close to his ear, and shot her a rare grin. '"High Life",' he said. 'You like?'

'Oh yes!' she said hastily. It was just as well that she did: for the past week the radio had been spitting out its insistent beat in the kitchen while he was working, and going walk-about on his shoulder in his spare time, dominating the house with its hissing crackle. But it also ate up batteries. This morning she had heard him asking her dad for money to buy more. Batteries were expensive here. She had watched with covert disapproval as her father handed over the money. Why was he so indulgent? Whatever Michael said, it *was* indulgence!

But she could see that she did have some bridges to build.

'Who is the singer?' she asked, cautiously. And in his

143

enthusiasm for Big Daddy and the Takoradi Boys, Moses talked to her for the first time as if she were a fellow member of the human race.

It was a shaky beginning: he scowled at her as usual when she came back to the kitchen half an hour later for a drink of water, and it was snails again for supper, for the second night in a row. Still, he was not to know that she was trying to be generous.

It didn't come easily: she had so small a share of her father's time and attention. He already spent a lot more of his time with Moses than he did with her, taking him out as his driver as he so often did. But really she had no choice. So she tried to draw Moses into their precious space in the evenings, to signal that she no longer saw him as an outsider. (A part of her laughing at the consternation this visibly caused him. She wondered if he would prefer her to remain his enemy?) Occasionally she even made Moses tea, the way he liked it, with sugar and evaporated milk. He frowned at her suspiciously when she did, but he stopped being quite so aggressive.

The next Sunday Moses had gone out to buy bread when her father suddenly said out of the blue, 'What are you up to with Moses?'

She looked up, startled at the hostile edge in his voice. 'I'm not up to anything.'

'Come off it, Anne,' he said (and she remembered suddenly being a little girl and being caught in the wrong), 'First you seemed to dislike him, now you're all over him.'

'Me? Dislike him? That wasn't how it was! *He* was the one who disliked *me*!'

'Don't be ridiculous!' he said irritably, clicking his tongue that same way Moses did. 'And even if that were true, what's changed? Because something has. *Moses this* and *Moses that* – you don't seem to be able to get enough of him now.'

She stared at him but he wouldn't meet her eye.

'Has somebody said something to you about Moses?' he asked, brusquely, opening his tool box and fishing out a screwdriver.

She considered whether to be truthful, or whether to tell a white lie. 'I did talk to Michael.' He looked up. 'Well,' she retaliated, stung, 'Moses was being very aggressive. You probably didn't notice but he was giving me a really hard time.' She decided she wouldn't mention *frightening*. She certainly wouldn't mention *snakes*. She said, 'It was so bad I was wondering if I mightn't be able to stick it.'

'Stick what? You mean you'd have gone back in October after all?'

She nodded, watching him to see if the thought of her only staying another few months upset him. The answer was reassuring.

'You should have said.'

'I tried to, but you didn't… Well, I guess I didn't explain it very well. You didn't seem to hear what I was saying.'

'No, I couldn't have done.' He stared down for a moment at the broken plug he was mending. 'I'm sorry, Anne. I thought we were mucking along pretty well. It's hard, you know,' he said, squinting inside the plug. 'It's very hard being a full-time father, after all this time. I don't suppose I'm all that good at it.'

'It's all right, Dad,' she said, going over to him and giving him a hug. He responded, albeit stiffly, and she let him go. It was early and the barred daylight slanted at an angle through the wooden shutters and patterned his greying hair in stripes. His hair was still thick. She was rather proud of her dad's looks. His thick crinkly dark hair, his neat beard.

An elegant wall-wasp with long trailing back legs like filigree banners had been flying in and out through the open front door all weekend. Anne went over and stood on tiptoe to admire the neat little mud nest on the living room wall, nearly ready to receive the wasp's single egg. What would it do tomorrow when they were all out of the house and the front door was locked?

Her dad asked nonchalantly, 'So what did he say?'

'Who?'

'Michael.'

'He said… ' (What did she want to reveal of what Michael had said?) 'He said, that I needed to be aware that Moses had been your protégé up until now, and perhaps I had pushed him out a bit without meaning to.'

'Oh, he said that, did he!'

'Wasn't it true then?'

'Oh yes, it's true. So you thought you'd push him back in a bit, did you? And has it worked?'

She grinned. 'Like a dream, Dad. I can't exactly say we're friends, Moses and me, but at least I've stopped feeling he might be trying to do a bit of *juju* on me on the quiet.'

He burst out laughing. 'You thought *that*, did you? Silly girl!'

He put the plug back together and plugged it back in the socket, but the power had gone off. 'Michael's put it pretty well. Of course Moses has been feeling jealous but he seems happier now, so maybe it's all for the best.'

All for the best? What about my feelings? Anne thought indignantly. What about my feeling jealous! But she couldn't think of anything to say so she stayed silent.

A couple of days later Anne witnessed something she was not supposed to see, that disturbed her all over again but in a very different way. She came back to the house at break-time for some school books and found the Land Rover pulled up haphazardly outside, the driver's door hanging open like a drooping wing. She kicked off her plimsolls on the porch step as usual and slipped into the house on her bare feet. In the living room Dick and Moses were standing facing one another – she could only see her father's face, but she could see from the way Moses was holding himself that he, too, was very angry. She hastily said something meaningless as she moved past them to her room, pretending she had seen nothing. When she came back Moses had gone. Her dad was sitting at the table as though nothing had happened, but when he looked up his face was strained. She was late, she had to rush off. She kissed him hastily on the top of his head.

It must have been a very serious argument! It had almost looked like a fight, the way they were standing.

The thought worried her, but more powerful was the strange elation that buoyed her up all the way to school. Moses might have softened a little and there was certainly less chilli in his stews, but she would be oh so happy if he were to quietly disappear out of their lives!

All through the day, at odd moments, this thought slipped into her head, so that by the time she came home in the early afternoon she was in a state of suppressed excitement. And the Land Rover *was* still there, though it had been parked up neatly now. Her dad had obviously not gone to work today. She hurried indoors.

He came out of the kitchen as she came in but he seemed surprised to see her. He tried to avert his face but she had already seen his red-rimmed eyes. 'Not feeling too well,' he said in a dull voice. 'Think I'll just go and lie down for a bit.'

It wasn't really surprising – everybody at school had been going down with the same thing recently. She went into the kitchen. No Moses. She put water on the gas to boil and stood listening to the silence of the house. It was a subdued silence, with a sad taste to it. Was her dad really sick? Was it possible that Moses had gone? A sound at the door behind her made her look round. Moses was standing there, looking at her with an expression she could no longer interpret. It might be animosity, it might not. 'Would you like some tea?' she asked. His eyes were bloodshot. Was he sick too? He nodded yes, distractedly, and went away.

When she brought the tray to the living room Moses wasn't there. She went back out into the corridor. From behind the door of her father's bedroom came the sound of low voices. The door was firmly shut.

Going into the refectory at lunch-time, Michael stopped to talk to Ishmael the cook about his brother. Ishmael stood by the kitchen door flicking idly at flies with a tea towel. 'Yes, yes, all dat trouble gone now. De fish and de donkey drink in de same pool.'

Out of the corner of his eye Michael noticed Christopher at the refectory table, pulling out his notebook and writing hurriedly.

Ishmael went on talking but his voice took on a hard edge. 'De donkey sings to de moon in his morning voice,' he said loudly, and glared pointedly in Christopher's direction as he stomped off to the kitchen.

Stomps off, Michael thought. Ishmael always *stomps*. He took his glass of tea to sit at the table.

'Do you suppose that was *mourning* with a *u*?' Christopher asked.

'I think that was *Ishmael* with an *e* telling *Christopher* with two *h*s that he was getting a little fed up with his pearls of wisdom being written down before they've even dried on his lips. *Morning* without a *u*. He means the donkey always speaks in the same voice. He doesn't put on any airs or posh accents.'

'I know what he meant,' Christopher said crossly. 'I was just checking.'

It was particularly hot and humid and lunch had been an irritable and sparsely-attended meal. Patrick had left halfway through in a huff. Sickening for the same thing that had laid most of the others low, probably. Anne had had to go home early yesterday and hadn't appeared today. It's terrible hard to feel entirely well when everyone round you is going down like flies, he thought. Now only he and Christopher were left in the refectory. He looked at the undersized, unprepossessing younger man and thought that you could never tell who the tough ones would turn out to be.

'Seriously, Christopher. I think Ishmael *is* getting rattled. He says things in his inimitable Ishmael way and you pounce on his words and write them down. You're making him self-conscious. What are you doing with all this stuff anyway?'

'Well, they're proverbs, aren't they? I'm making a collection of proverbs.'

'Who else do you collect them from? Students?'

'I haven't as yet,' Christopher said, somewhat sheepishly. 'But I will. Ishmael's just the beginning.'

He sounded like someone else suffering from a dose of anthropology. Lord help us, Michael thought.

'The trouble is,' Christopher was saying, 'he's got so he's conscious of me. I feel he's waiting till I'm out of the room before he says anything interesting. And when I do hear him say one he'll never repeat it, however nicely I ask him.'

'Look,' Michael said. *How it was that he kept getting himself into this avuncular role?* 'I think you're putting the wind up him. He speaks and you rush to write it down. I don't suppose he has any idea why you're doing that. To him it's a perfectly normal way of speaking but you treat it as if it's not. Have you asked him if he minds you recording his *bon mots*?'

'No.' Christopher sounded surprised.

'Well, wouldn't that be a first step? You don't need to have any reason – simple interest would be enough. That would be flattering. But what you're doing is just…' (he sought about for the right word but it was too hot for tact) '…weird.'

He finished his glass of tea. From the kitchen, Ishmael banged open the hatch and peered through at them before banging it shut again, making the crucifix on the wall above the hatch rattle.

Had he just said what he thought he had? He hoped not. *Weird* wasn't even one of his words. He'd caught it off Anne. And it was unkind to say so to Christopher, even if it was true. He should have said, it's like when people feel that being photographed is somebody stealing their soul.

The door from the kitchen opened and Ishmael stomped back into the refectory and along the table towards them. He took Michael's empty glass.

'You finished?' Ishmael said, gesturing at Christopher's half-full glass. Without waiting for a reply, he added crossly 'De flea can live with the tortoise in his house but the lion cannot go dere,' and stomped back to his kitchen.

'I think he was telling you in a roundabout way to leave him alone,' Michael said, but Christopher was already scribbling.

'Three in one day!' he said. 'Things are looking up!'

A day later and Michael was still holding his own, but only just. He lay on his narrow bed watching the afternoon tossing itself into dusk on the backs of the heaving neem trees. His room was only a little wider than the bed. The high window revealed little except for a section of the tree tops, shaken about now by a sultry wind.

It had been a dark afternoon, and soon it would be night. Storms had been hanging all day without breaking. And inside Michael the bug which had waylaid nearly everyone else was still hanging without breaking, just the other side of pain. He could feel his guts churning, desperately fighting off the enemy. He might succumb, or he might not. It was never possible to tell until the risk had clearly passed. In the meantime he felt tired and miserable: even if you fight off the bug you tend to pay for it with a dose of the blues, though it didn't help that one of his father's rare, spare letters had arrived in the post this afternoon.

He lay watching the wind in the trees, the phrases of the letter knocking about inside his head.

Pauline and the kids came Sunday.

We went to the Grave and changed the flowers, may she rest in peace, God bless her. She was always so proud of you, to have one of her children called to do God's work.

Gary grown so you wouldn't recognise him — nearly two inches this year already. We marked it on the doorpost.

That was almost all there was. Hardly worth the cost of the envelope, let alone the stamp, Michael thought. Not a hint there as to how Pauline was coping with Ian's awful death, let alone how the poor wee lads were doing. How strange human beings are. He thought about Issa, whom he'd been to see yesterday. He'd found Issa – big bruiser that he was – hovering just inside his house trying to drop a cloth over a small frog. He was astounded when Michael picked the frog up with his bare hands and carried it outside. So astounded that he made no comment when he heard he hadn't got the new contract for the science block.

Big bruisers tend to bounce back, Michael thought pessimistically. His stomach gurgled ominously. He wondered if Christopher had succumbed yet. Funny boy, that Christopher. This morning Michael had done the simple, obvious thing: at the end of one of the lessons he'd asked the class what proverbs they knew. In the space of ten minutes they'd come up with more than a dozen, which he'd written down and at break-time he'd presented them helpfully (and yes, in all honesty, just a shade triumphantly) to Christopher. But Christopher had been surprisingly uninterested.

The proverbs might be just an excuse, he reflected. Could be a fixation on the teller of the proverbs rather than on the proverbs themselves, though it was difficult to imagine anyone having a crush on Ishmael. No less difficult to imagine Christopher being capable of a crush, limp individual that he was. He remembered the twinge of protective jealousy he'd felt at the thought of Christopher and Anne sharing an enthusiasm for anthropology. Ridiculous! Christopher definitely was *not* interested in women. You could see it in his body language and hear it in the way he talked.

If only it would rain. The clouds were holding in the

heat. The closing in of the day was bringing little relief. The alarm went off and he hit it shut without looking at it. He'd had that clock since he was at school but he'd never felt any affection for it.

The trouble with dozing in the afternoon, he thought as he got up wearily from the bed, is feeling so shut in and claustrophobic afterwards.

Time to go and get the church ready for Mass. It would be dark early tonight.

13

The end of June. Such a short time she had been in Tamale but so much living fitted into those few months that it was hard to believe in any existence outside this one. The life of the school, unexpected and intimate, like a new family in which she was a strange, female fish swimming with or against the tide, she was never sure which. The extraordinary world beyond the school gates that was growing familiar now, but never ordinary: there was always some startling new detail she hadn't seen before. In that world, too, she was still a strange fish, a pale one swimming among the bright fishes.

Bright fishes. Bright colours. So much colour everywhere, strident, demanding, eye-bending. Sometimes comic, making her laugh out loud: an old man grinning toothlessly, dressed in a gaudy young-man's shirt; a woman bending over her pots, her ample rump picked out in riotous patterns of gold and crimson and fluorescent greens. Out of bare earth the sorghum and millet plants (shooting waist-high, then shoulder-high, then higher than her head) made a shifting pattern of luminous greens, waving against the sun. Trumpets of crimson and orange flowers thrust among the ferny leaves of the trees along the sides of the streets, and the weaver birds flitted, the broken shadows blending with the patterning on their wings and backs so that in spite of their audacious butter-yellow and jet-black colouring they were perfectly camouflaged. In the streets below, the women were not camouflaged at all. They were conspicuous, bold. Clothed in every colour that ever came out of a chemical dye vat.

When she thought about colour Anne always remembered a scene which began in black and white: she was sitting with the weavers and she'd been watching a woman carry out two guinea fowl and leave them on the ground at the back of her hut with their legs trussed together. Anne sat idly looking at them, admiring the intricacy of their black and white plumage. The woman came back and bent over the birds. The blade of her knife glinted silver in the sun. She went away again, leaving the guinea fowl squawking, flinging their half-severed heads from side to side. It took Anne a moment to understand the brilliant red drops spraying in the sunlight. A study in black and white mutated into a study in black and white and crimson.

She wished she could draw. She didn't want the invasiveness of a camera. She wanted to be a pair of eyes only, without a body. To observe without the disruption her own presence made, spoiling the picture. When she stopped to gaze, an audience always gathered to gaze at her. Except when she sat with the weavers. Everywhere else she made a stir. Women called out 'Heh-heh-heh!' on a rising note. There was a particular way they moved, turning back to their work from the distraction of her passing. A hoisting and tucking-in of printed cloth under armpits, and then the flexing of glossy flesh as their shoulders leaned back into the task of stirring a pot over a fire, of lifting a child onto one hip, picking up a hoe, pounding yams. There was a particular shape in a woman's stillness as she sat brooding by her cooking fire at the side of the road, chin on one elegant hand as she stared into the middle distance, the other hand absently patting her wailing child. What was the woman thinking about? But if she knew, Anne wondered, would she recognise the thoughts?

She too would sometimes sit outside, when it was late enough for the falling sun to cast a shadow from the house towards the road. She would sit on one of the uncomfortable metal chairs marking essays written on cheap paper in flimsy exercise books. In the darkening sunlight the clothes of the passers-by were brighter than ever. The whites of their eyes and their teeth flashed as they turned, laughing, to look into the sun towards her. With her white skin and her yellow hair she felt like a blank in the picture, a pale hole in the middle of the canvas.

She worked quietly, correcting the stiff prose and tortured spelling, while the sun set and all the crazy colour darkened and finally neutralised. Dusk was the brief grey pause between day and night when the pi-dogs ventured out from the shade to lie panting in the hot dust. The feral cats sat washing and yawning, watching unblinking as a phalanx of guinea fowl passed like a gang of screaming fishwives in the opaque light. This was the hour when the skin recollected itself and stopped trying to hide, and the eyes relaxed. The hour of gentling and reprieve because, having made it to nightfall, there would be twelve hours' respite now, before the glorious renewal of the life-giving sun. Dusk turned to night, rendering the egrets invisible, the mango trees mere silhouettes against the stars, the people on the road unseen but still calling. Night hawks flitted in and out of the light of the street lamps. Or were they bats? She didn't know. Night was the time of shadows, of half-known things. The colourless time, broken only by the orange streaks and dashes of cooking fires here and there, and – flickering in the distance of the bush – of village bonfires, from where the sounds of drumming came: all the raw Technicolor of the daytime world condensed and simplified into these few colours, and the mute, navy velvet of the sky around the moon.

Sitting on the sofa, papers spread all around her, she was still preparing lessons though it was nearly ten o'clock. At the table her dad was writing by the light of the table lamp. How nice he looks, she thought as she glanced up at him. The lamplight made a pool around him and etched his face in ruddy highlights and sharp shadows. Glinting on his reading glasses it made him look wise. *And kind,* she thought, as he steadily wrote his report, unconscious of her gaze.

Moses was outside, smoking with his cronies in their usual place across the road, under the mango trees.

Suddenly Michael was standing in the doorway.

He looked tired and grey and only half his usual self, as if he was an empty husk and the Michael within had got left behind somewhere. And he looked older, she noticed as she hurriedly cleared her papers off the sofa to make room for him to sit.

He sat down in the armchair. 'Sorry to drop in so late.'

'Nonsense – you know we don't go to bed early,' her dad said.

'Would you like some tea?' she asked.

'Or a whisky?' her father suggested. 'You look like a man in need of a Johnnie Walker to me.'

Michael inclined his head slightly. 'You know, I wouldn't say no to a whisky.'

157

He and Anne watched in silence as her father poured out two small glasses from the precious bottle.

'Well,' her father said at last, when Michael still said nothing. 'What have you been up to?'

'I've been at the hospital.' He sipped, then held the glass up and squinted through it at the bare bulb overhead. 'Damned fine whisky, this.'

The silence was swollen with the thrumming of insects. Through the window she could hear the next-door neighbours clattering noisily in their backyard. A gust of laughter sounded from the grove of mango trees. A monitor lizard tramped across the ceiling. She sat very still, curled up at one end of the sofa, her eyes on Michael's face. At the table, her father sat fiddling with his pen.

At last Michael said 'I'm sorry. I shouldn't have come. But they're all in bed by nine o'clock at the Mission and I was in serious need of some company.'

Her father murmured encouragingly. Silence again, the two men sipping from their glasses. Anne studied the place on the side of her foot by her little toe where the thorn had gone septic but you would never know now, only the slightest of pin-holes showing where it had been. Michael cleared his throat but did not speak. Her dad put the pen down and picked it up again.

'I went to the hospital to see the boy who broke his leg playing football last Friday. You heard about Jonathon, Anne? He's not doing so badly. Should be home tomorrow – they've had to plate the bone but he'll be as good as new in a few months' time. In the hospital I saw someone else I know – a woman whose kid I carried to the hospital last year when he went sick. Burst appendix, but he got through it. Such a lovely little chap, Mahmoud. About four years

old. Never said much but – very trusting. Affectionate.'
Michael paused for so long she looked up, thinking that
was all. 'She'd brought him in this morning with malaria.
By this evening he was dead. Nothing they could do.' He
wiped his face with the back of his arm.

Anne's father kept his eyes fixed on the table. She glanced
at him, then let her eyes slide back to Michael. She longed
to comfort him – to say something, or to put her hand on
his shoulder in that still, small gesture of calm, just as he
did to her. But she couldn't: as soon as she wanted to, the
innocence drained out of it. She folded her arms and tucked
her hands away.

Her dad began to talk about malaria and how many
people died of it here. Replying, Michael's voice steadied
itself. She half-listened, thinking about the child – *this*
child, of whom Michael had spoken more than once, as if
he was especially fond of him.

Her dad was speaking to her. 'Why don't you go and make
that tea, Anne? I expect Michael could manage one now.'

Michael looked straight at her then, with a weary smile
of thanks. She walked past him keeping her hands carefully
to herself.

When she came back with the tea he had moved to sit
with her dad at the table and seemed himself again. She put
the tray down beside them and poured out three glasses of
tea. Fished the ants out of the sugar bowl as usual before
stirring two spoonfuls into her dad's glass. Michael, she
knew, didn't take sugar. The powdered milk dispersed feebly
in a gritty scum on the surface of the pale tea.

Michael peered into his glass and said in an exaggerated
Irish accent 'Dis tay's so weak, Anne, it's leaning against de
saide of de cop!'

'Sorry! I forgot you like it strong.'

But she hadn't really forgotten. She'd been eking out the little that was left in the packet so that they should have some left for breakfast, but she didn't want to say so. She didn't want him to feel in any way at all that he shouldn't have come.

Anne picked up her two warm loaves and stood up, smiling at Kwame who was playing peek-a-boo from behind Abina's skirts. She ruffled his little head and made him laugh. 'I must go,' she said. They had been talking a long time in their funny mixture of pidgin and her woeful Dagbani, and Abina had a bread-oven to stoke up and she had marking to do.

Her bag of books weighed heavily on her shoulder as she walked down the path. She could see their house at the bottom of the slope, the mango tree cutting the corner of the zinc roof with its sharp shadow. Snow seemed to be spilling out into the sunshine from under the tree. When she came down by the house Moses was sitting in the shade plucking a chicken.

Ripping feathers out of a chicken, more like, she thought, pausing to greet him. He looked up, his eyes as veiled as the dead eyes in the floppy head which bounced loosely on his knee. 'Supper?' she asked, trying to be friendly. He gave a curt little jerk of assent. *Stupid question.*

She kicked off her plimsolls on the threshold and went indoors, pausing as you must always pause, stepping inside, for your eyes to adjust to the abrupt dark. At the far end of the passage the open front door framed the view of empty bush, bright now with the intensity of green grass, the different glossy greens of the scrub trees, the sharp blue of the sky. She glanced out at the view as she passed. The hot air coming in hit her forehead like the blast from a furnace.

When she went to the kitchen a little later Moses was still outside, his knife glinting in the tree's shadow as he quickly disembowelled supper. Will he read the entrails looking for signs? she wondered briefly, but Michael's voice chided gently inside her head and she took the thought back. In the kitchen, Mrs Elizabeth Bramwell was lying face down on the table. She lifted it, curious too to see what he was planning to cook. *Coq au Vin*. Now how would he manage that without any *Vin*?

Later, Moses – with his usual ceremony – slapped the big fire-blackened aluminium pot down on the table and lifted the lid. The familiar aroma of groundnut-stew. So, he'd ducked the *Coq au Vin* and cooked one of his stand-by meals but with chicken instead of mutton or goat. At least tonight the chilli wasn't overpowering. Her father, as usual, gazed earnestly at Moses and said 'This is delicious!'

What would I have done with that chicken? she wondered as she ate. Chicken curry? Or chicken in beer, or chicken risotto. Fried chicken, if it was young enough. When she had plucked it. And gutted it. Nothing was simple here. And what do you do with all the bits? she wondered. Throw them out and feed the vultures on the local rubbish dump, probably.

And would her father have said *Delicious!* if she had cooked any of these things? Maybe, but maybe not. And certainly he wouldn't have said it in quite that tone. He looked at her as if she was a part of the fixtures and fittings. Which was strange, considering that most of her life she hadn't been there.

Joseph came from the road to greet her, as he always did if she was sitting outside the house when he passed. She was marking grammar exercises. Never exciting. She looked up as he came towards her but this afternoon there was no disarming smile. He was unusually quiet, standing there scuffing at the dirt with the toe of one flip-flop.

At last he said that his father wanted her to eat with them. Midday on Saturday, if that would suit her. He looked relieved when she said she would be glad to come.

It was her first invitation to a pupil's home. What protocols might be involved? Was she representing the school or was she just going as herself? She would have asked Michael, if he hadn't been away at a conference in Kumasi.

When Saturday came, she got there promptly and found Michael placidly ensconced in the one easy chair in the cramped living room. Mr Appiah greeted her formally and went back to talking to Michael about tax reforms, leaving her to sit side by side with Joseph on the narrow bed that took up most of one wall. Joseph grinned at her shyly and swung his bare legs. She had never seen him so reserved. She would almost have said he was jittery. It made conversation difficult. She asked after the boy who had broken his leg and Joseph livened up a little in the telling. She looked covertly round the room as she listened. It was fascinating how two houses of identical layout could be so different. Their own house was small and bare. This one was small and crowded. She knew Joseph had four brothers and two sisters: probably more than one of them used this room as a bedroom. A column of folded clothes was stacked neatly in one corner. A tiny table against the wall was piled with books, some of which she recognised from school. A white-skinned Christ closed his eyes on the wall above the cramped dining table where Mr Appiah sat, half-turned to Michael, who looked thoroughly at ease in the single armchair. Through the window from the backyard came female sounds, and the hot smell of burning charcoal and the savoury smell of cooking. Anne's stomach rumbled, reminding her she hadn't had any breakfast. She gave Joseph an apologetic smile and he grinned back nervously. A girl came in with bottles of Fanta and shyly handed her one. 'Can I come and help?' she asked, but the girl shook her head and fled.

'My sister,' Joseph said.

She asked him about his brothers and sisters. He was the youngest. Two brothers were married, two more were still living at home but they were working today in the family shop – The Electrical Goods Emporium (Joseph said this importantly as if he was quoting), in the centre of town. Ah – the bare shop with hardly anything in it, she thought. The two girls helping his mother in the backyard were his twin sisters. No, she really must not worry about offering to help, she was their guest.

'Our honoured guest,' Mr Appiah interrupted himself to bow in her direction. 'We are most pleased you could come.'

She smiled back politely and glanced at Michael. Who winked.

The conversation limped stiltedly on. The cooking smells grew stronger. A large fly buzzed inside the insect netting at the window. If Joseph, so articulate in the privacy of the classroom or the street, was dumb and awkward in his own home it wasn't really surprising, given how severely his fond parent kept eyeing him. It made her nervous too, and nearly as tongue-tied as Joseph. It was easier to sit quietly, listening to the two men, who were talking politics now. Her grasp of Ghanaian politics remained vague, but she didn't get the feeling that her failure to join in the discussion made a negative impression on Mr Appiah. Was that because she was a woman, or because she was overshadowed by Michael? He overshadowed her in every respect, she reflected as she listened to them talk. It wasn't only that he was a large male, and a priest (both of which surely impressed Mr Appiah). It was his energy and his enthusiasm, his fun and his sudden seriousnesses as well. In his company she too felt coloured by these things but in his absence she felt less, and lesser. She thought, *This* is why women talk about him the way they do! He gives and he takes away, both at once. He can't help it, he doesn't even know he's doing it.

Or does he? She watched his face. Anyone looking at Michael now would think Mr Appiah was the most interesting man he had ever met. And yet, she reflected, he probably didn't much like Mr Appiah. Something in his voice suggested it. Joseph fidgeted on the bed beside her. He shot her an apologetic look as if he could hear it too.

Who was he, this Michael? When he smiled at her (her heart turning over hotly every time) did he really see *her*, or was she just one of the crowd in his busy, priestly life? A Virgin Mary, or a Mary Magdalen? Either way, she thought sadly, she was only a part of the Michael mythology, safely out of reach as he passed on his very private trajectory through the world.

At last the girl came back with plates and spoons and laid the table, which was barely big enough to seat four. Mrs Appiah came in with the other sister carrying steaming pots.

Anne and Michael were ushered to the table, the two girls and Joseph took their plates and cutlery and sat on the bed. Mrs Appiah, a stern woman with straightened hair and very large spectacles, took her place at the table and picked up the big serving spoon. She looked down at the table top and enquired 'Grace, Father?

'Dear Lord – ' said Michael just as Mr Appiah intoned 'Lord God our Father – '

'Of course! We have two Fathers in de house,' said Mr Appiah. 'As de official Father – ' (he gestured gracefully) 'please, after you.'

Which he meant literally: he followed Michael's short prayer with a long and rambling one of his own which seemed to include, amongst other things, hopes that Joseph might do well in his exams.

So *that* was why they had been invited. She sneaked a look at Michael's impassive, closed-off face, his eyes calmly shut. Across the table Mrs Appiah, head bowed and ladle in hand, coughed meaningfully. Mr Appiah, not to be hurried, ambled to his amen. Anne did not dare look at Joseph, sitting on the bed with his sisters.

Rice was served, and chicken stew. Mr Appiah was talking to her now, as if he had only just fully registered her presence. His wife filled the plates and handed them round the table, first to Michael, then to Mr Appiah, then to Anne, before serving herself and the three children on the bed. Anne looked down. The pile of rice on her plate was draped with two well-cooked chicken's feet. She looked up and caught Michael's eye, steadily signalling something to her. She looked at his plate. Eyes closed, serene, the head of a cockerel lay inert on top of his rice.

She smiled bravely and picked up her knife and fork.

The feet bounced about disconcertingly under her cutlery the same way snails did, but at least the feet had flavour. She finished one and bravely set about the other, wondering what dirt they had happily scratched in, on what roosts they had perched. The rice tasted of weevils – that at least was familiar. All rice in Tamale tasted of weevils, even in their Rice Corporation household, and would do until the new crop was harvested.

After the meal was cleared away and the table had been pushed back against the wall the girls and their mother disappeared outside again, refusing her offers of help.

As soon as the women were out of the room Mr Appiah started talking about Joseph's prospective exam results and said he would like to make a transfer of money to Mission funds. Thank goodness Michael was here! Michael looked at his fingernails as if he was discussing the price of fish and said Joseph needed no help, he would do very well on his own.

Though if Mr Appiah wanted to, Michael added as an afterthought, he would be welcome to make a donation at the beginning of the next school year.

It was a shame, she thought, sneaking a sideways look at Joseph who was squirming uncomfortably beside her. Joseph was a clever boy but now his successes would be discoloured by the suggestion that the marking of his papers might have been influenced by his father's offer of money.

A short time afterwards Michael signalled to her discreetly and they made a dignified exit.

As they walked away from the house, Michael pushing his bicycle, he said through gritted teeth, 'I wish to goodness they wouldn't do that! The Northerners do it too but they're not usually Christians so they're rather more tactful. But some of these Southerners seem to think the church is their direct line to God! It's stupid to muddy the waters like that – Joseph will do well enough in his own right. And besides the critical time isn't now, it's next year when he does his GCEs, and his success in those lies between him and the Cambridge Exam Board.'

'Poor Joseph, he looked so mortified! But surely Mr Appiah wasn't intending it as a bribe?'

'He damned well did. They all do it, these pushy businessmen. At least he was subtle enough to make it a payment to the Mission and not the straight hand-in-the-pocket I was afraid of – I wangled my way into your invitation, by the way. I guessed what might be on our Mr Appiah's mind when I ran into him last night and he said he'd invited you. I was afraid you might feel somewhat compromised so I looked hopeful and underfed until he got round to inviting me along too. I hope you don't mind?' He glanced at her questioningly.

He hadn't been seeking out her company then, he'd merely been protecting her. Or more precisely, the school. Of course she didn't mind, she said, minding quite a lot but not in a way he would ever dream of. If he hadn't been away all week, she added, she would have mentioned it to him anyway.

'That poor kid!' Michael said. 'He looked as if he wished the earth would swallow him up. Still, he'll do okay, with or without his father's interference. We don't really need to worry about Joseph Appiah. But it would be nice to be invited there just once without any ulterior motive.'

'Has it happened before then?'

'Oh, every exam time it happens. First with the older brothers, now with Joseph. I suppose our Mr Appiah thinks my lame suggestion that he pays his donations at the beginning of the following term is merely a deferment for appearances' sake. Bloody hell, I never thought of that!'

They walked up the road in silence. She wondered if he were exaggerating.

A heavy dust haze hung in the air, making the light red. There was a smell of rain, perhaps from somewhere a long way off.

Michael chuckled suddenly. 'Your face sure was a picture when you landed those chicken feet! I'd been trying to catch your eye to warn you. I didn't know whether you knew that's what they do here – they regard the head and the feet as the best bits of the bird so the guest of honour usually gets them. You're a good girl, Anne – most people would have baulked at that, but you didn't just *eat* them, you went over the top and said they were delicious! Annie, you're a star!'

He put his arm around her shoulders and gave her a brotherly hug. For a moment, holding her breath in surprise, she walked stiffly in his easy embrace. Then his bicycle fell over and he let go of her to pick it up.

'I'm grateful you were there to share the honour then,' she said, 'because I'm not sure I could have managed the head!'

'Those sleeping eyes! I have to admit, in spite of a certain amount of practice, I still find that bit hard-going.'

'And all the rubbery bits!'

'It's a good thing I was there, girl, or you might have had to manage feet *and* head, rubbery bits and all.'

'But I noticed you did leave the beak.'

'Even a delicacy has its limits,' he said. 'I think you'll find that most Ghanaians leave the beak.'

That night she couldn't sleep. She lay in the half-dark, lulled by the sound of next-door's washing-up in the corner of the backyard just next to her window, thinking about her love life. Or rather, about the lack of it. Her one great passion, which had turned to dust. He had been her Supervisor in her third year. Dave. A clever, disillusioned man. Tired of Cambridge, caustic with the young women who passed through his door. But to her, for some reason, he had been kind. He'd given her extra supervision in the subject she was weakest in, when she panicked just before her Finals. And then, in the giddy weeks which followed Finals, when the early summer rain swelled the flowers of the Fellows' Gardens along the Backs and dropped circles in the green, impassive surface of the River Cam, he made love to her, first in words (such heady murmurings in a secluded arbour under the dripping clematis and the yellow roses…), then in his bed in the cultured little house he shared with his wife, Eliza. But Eliza had recently left him and he was living alone, a little drunk on his solitude and his sorrow. A little wild.

She hadn't understood his wildness. In her dizzy intoxication she'd taken him at face value – a solitary man with the freedom to love her. Every morning she woke in his bed, and every evening, after the last concerts and parties and farewells of her university life, she went back to Dave's house and he welcomed her in with wine-fragrant kisses and a firm hand squeezing her bottom and she began to take it for granted that she would stay with him after term ended.

Then one night, when she went to the house as usual, he staggered drunkenly as he opened the door. She knew at once something had shifted fundamentally in their relationship but she wasn't ready for the shock of him saying, almost before she was over the threshold, 'Sorry. The idyll's over. Eliza's agreed to come home.'

Even now, a year later, she could hardly bear to think about it. The stark way he told her, and even worse the way she'd pleaded until she made him angry. 'Get out,' he'd said then. Something she had never thought a man would need to say to her. And then he'd added, 'Quite honestly, Anne, all you're looking for is your daddy. If you had any sense you'd go and find him.' The insult cut her to the quick.

She remembered this now, lying on her hot, narrow bed. How he would laugh if he knew what she was doing here! Not just that she had trotted out to Ghana to find her father as bidden, but that she'd found herself another kind of Father all together, the religious kind, and was in danger of falling seriously in love with him. Because she *was* falling. She acknowledged it now, exasperated. What was the point? Perhaps Dave was right. She was hopeless, she could only love men who could not be hers.

She looked down at her pale, hot, naked shape, lying on top of the thin sheet in the gloom and longing to be touched. Such a waste. All this body, all this energy, but no one to love. No hands on her flesh, no voice breathing in her ear. No small tendernesses and shared privacies.

There had been others in the twelve months since Dave but only cold fumbles in the park near her mother's house and in the backs of cars with young men she wasn't much interested in, the memory of them all tied up with the disaster of going back to live at home while she worked in the local library to save the money to come out here. Her mother half-clinging, half-resentful. The old life cold and clammy, dragging her back down into childhood. It all seemed trivial now and worth putting up with for the sake of getting her to Ghana, but at the time it had seemed a dreadful mistake, going *home*. Whatever that is.

Would her life always seem to be a mistake? Would it always feel as if something was lacking, even when – as here in Ghana – life was at its biggest and gaudiest and most engrossing? Her unused body would sag and fade. Time was passing, the precious years of her prime ticking away, but she could see no knight riding in from the dusty horizon, only the big Irish knight on the battered bicycle who had hugged her on the road, however much he didn't mean it personally. She would give anything to have that moment back again. But she couldn't have him, and surely, surely she wouldn't really want him if she could. A priest, with all a priest's baggage!

Weary of herself she got up to go to the bathroom. A thin line of light showed under the door of the tiny room where Moses slept. He must be having difficulty sleeping too. She was surprised to hear a sudden, suppressed snort of laughter, and then his giggling whisper. Someone was in there with him! Did her father know? How he would react if he did?

It was disturbing to think of a stranger in the house, of hanky-panky going on under their noses. She went back to bed feeling thoroughly jangled. She would tell her dad about it in the morning. But the thought of Moses happily entertaining some woman in his room rubbed so much salt into her wounds that she was confused about her own motives. Besides, it would hardly endear her to Moses, if she told tales on him. Perhaps she should say nothing.

The world had fallen silent, except for the occasional mistaken crowing of cockerels, by the time she fell into a fitful sleep. Michael pursued her through her restless dreams. Her shoulder glowed with the memory of his brief embrace and she raised her face to his, longing to be kissed, all her cells aching to align themselves with his, only to find that he was no longer beside her but leading her on, up and down corridors, across crowded rooms, through a strange wood full of people she half-knew whose names she couldn't remember. But when at last they were alone and she reached up to kiss him, it wasn't Michael at all. It was Moses.

14

July

From her retreat on the sofa, Jo croaked 'I know it's malaria, I've had it before. I'll be okay now I've taken chloroquine.'

Anne gazed down at her, unconvinced. 'Are you sure? You look awful!'

'Gee thanks!' Jo muttered.

The coffee table and the easy chairs had been pushed up close as if to hem her in. 'What is this? Fort Knox?'

'It's to keep Josh out.'

Right on cue, Joshua came crawling noisily across the floor with a large wooden brick in each hand. He pulled himself up onto his feet, dribbling cheerfully, and banged his bricks on the table top.

Jo shrank back, screwing up her eyes. 'Don't, Josh! I've got the most terrible headache.' She opened one eye and looked at Anne. 'You haven't had malaria yet, have you? Well count yourself lucky!'

Josh banged his bricks again and squealed excitedly.

'Oh God!'

'Can I get you anything? What do you want me to do?'

'Just take him away! Please…'

'Do you want me to take him back to my house?' Anne asked, startled. Jo nodded, not opening her eyes. 'Should I go and fetch a doctor?' A vehement shake of the head. 'Kevin, then?'

'No. Just get me a bowl from the kitchen. I think I'm going to throw up.'

She ran to the kitchen and brought back the largest bowl she could find. 'Jo, you're frightening me! You really do look bad.'

Jo hugged the bowl to her bony chest. 'I'll be okay now I've taken the chloroquine. If you could just take Joshua away for a bit. For a couple of hours, even?' She leaned over the bowl.

Hurriedly, Anne picked Joshua up and went in search of a clean nappy, and a shirt for him, in case it got cool later. It was strange going through the drawers in the bedrooms. Jo was such a haphazard housewife but everything was put away so neatly.

She changed Josh's nappy the way she'd seen Jo do it, though it didn't look very tidy when she'd finished and she didn't know what to do with the wet one so she just left it on the tiled floor by his cot. In the sitting room, to her relief, Jo was lying down again, looking as if she was asleep. She must be feeling pretty terrible to let Josh out of her sight.

Out on the porch, Anne put Josh into the backpack and swung him awkwardly up onto her back. Joshua went very quiet. She was afraid he might be going to cry but as she walked down the drive she felt his little hands come stealing round her neck, and when two large blue and white crows flew up into the trees he greeted them happily. She was surprised by how heavy he was. In the few minutes it took to get to the road the sweat started running down her back in rivulets. She stood uncertainly for a moment, not knowing whether to turn right towards the Mission to go to look for Michael and ask him whether she should call a doctor, whatever Jo said, or left towards home where her dad might possibly be in, if he had got back from taking the Land Rover to be repaired. She was tempted to turn right and go to Michael but the very fact that it was her preference made it seem inappropriate. She turned left.

On the road a gang of men were scything the long grass on the verges, singing a musical shanty as they worked in unison. Their arms and backs were burned very black by the sun. They looked up as she passed and broke off singing to call out in excitement at the sight of a white baby. The gang-master frowned at her. 'Dat chil' sho' have a hat.'

She could have told him she had tried to put one on, only Josh had kept pulling it off again until she'd given up, but it was too much effort to argue so she just smiled innocently as if she hadn't understood. As she walked on down the road Josh twisted round to look back at the men. 'Heh, heh!' the men called after them. 'Hah!' said Josh. Judging by her discomfort, he was waving.

She had nearly reached the Low Cost Estate when she saw Michael pedalling laboriously up the slope towards her. 'I've just been down to call on you,' he said, and her heart soared. 'Or rather, your dad,' he added, and her heart dropped back into its proper place. 'But you were all out. What are you doing stealing Jo's baby?'

He offered to go back with her to see if Jo was all right but, on reflection, Anne thought perhaps they should take Jo at her word, now she'd taken the chloroquine, and let her get a bit of sleep. 'Or do you think I should get a doctor out? She didn't want me to.'

Michael looked uncertain. 'Well... If it *is* malaria the

175

chloroquine will soon knock it on the head. But she should be careful. There can be complications. How about we give her a couple of hours to catch up on some sleep and then I'll come back with you and see how she is.' And to her delight he turned and walked with her towards home, pushing his bicycle. 'How are you planning on entertaining this young rascal?'

'I have absolutely no idea!'

'I tell you what – you make us some tea and I'll do the baby bit. I need some practice, ready for going home.'

'Home?'

'Two weeks today. I get a month's home-leave every third year.'

Her heart plummeted so suddenly that she nearly stumbled. She'd had no idea! She'd been blithely assuming the summer holidays would be just like now but somehow with lots of Michael filling up the gap made by there being no school. 'Why do you need baby practice?' she asked, as brightly as she could.

'My sister Claire's had twins since I was last at home. I've got lots of nephews and nieces but I haven't been round any babies for a while. I could do with getting my hand in again. By the way, I meant to ask you – how's that Joseph Appiah been this week?'

'Subdued,' she said. 'But that's probably just the exams looming. Can't say I'm looking forward to next week either. All that invigilating!'

The house was shut up, her dad not yet back and Moses away for the day. They went into the living room and Michael helped take the carrier off her back. She put it down and awkwardly lifted Joshua out. She sat him down on the floor and she and Michael stood there looking down at him as they might at some small animal.

'Is he crawling yet?'

'Like clockwork. He's into everything. I don't think this peace will last long.'

'Put that kettle on and I'll watch the wee man.'

She filled a pan with water and put it on the gas ring. She had never entertained anyone to tea here, not a proper tea. Jo hardly ever came to the Low Cost and when she did she would never stay to eat or drink anything. Probably she thought their house wasn't clean enough. And if Michael stopped by for a meal it was always Moses who cooked. She looked in the store cupboard to see what she could offer. No limp biscuits left, but that wasn't much of a loss. She wondered if she could make some drop scones. They would be quick and easy. She lifted down Mrs Elizabeth Bramwell from the shelf and looked up drop scones in the index.

Michael appeared in the doorway with Joshua in his arms. 'Now what is that Auntie Annie up to?' he said to Josh. They stood there, watching her gravely, making her self-conscious. 'Could that be drop scones I see materialising, by any chance? My favourite – how did you guess?' Anne blushed with pleasure, though she knew he was probably lying through his teeth. 'Joshua and I are both particularly partial to a dropped scone. Aren't we, Josh?' Joshua looked up into Michael's face very seriously and grunted.

'The trouble is,' she said, cracking the second egg into a glass, 'I might be in real trouble when Moses gets back and finds I've used up the last two eggs.' She peered into the glass. 'Well, only one egg really – this one's off.'

He laughed. 'Anne! You sound as though you're still scared of him!'

'It's not funny,' she said tartly. He stopped laughing and

177

peered at her carefully. She cleared a space on the small table for the gas ring. Moses always used it on the floor but Moses was not here. She was flustered and clumsy, painfully conscious of Michael's presence as he carried Josh round the tiny kitchen showing him things and keeping up a running commentary that made her laugh in spite of herself: 'This here, Mr Joshua, is a fly whisk. This is what you do with it. And if there aren't any flies that need whisking we do find the ladies might be not averse to the occasional slight whisk, just to keep them on their toes. See – like this. That's the way, Josh – whsssk, whsssk. That is why we call it a whissssk. Ah, hello, Moses!'

'Moses!' She paused in the act of spooning scone mixture into the hot frying pan. 'I thought you'd gone to your village!'

Moses made a bee-line for Joshua, crowing and laughing and holding out his pink-palmed hands. She watched in amazement as he took the baby in his arms and bounced him on his hip. Josh looked very anaemic against Moses' dark skin. He didn't cry as she expected him to but looked up at Moses in wide-eyed wonder. And then he smiled.

'That is one very amiable baby,' Michael said. She wasn't listening. She was watching Moses, seeing him differently – as an older brother, a young uncle. A man not much older than herself, who had been forced to leave his family behind to come to town to work, missing his family. As Michael missed his.

Moses disappeared into the living room with Josh. Michael followed. She was left in peaceful possession of the kitchen.

A few minutes later Moses reappeared holding a naked Josh in his left arm and a vacant nappy, Joshua-shaped, in his right. 'Dis come off. How you put it on?'

'Oh dear!' she said. 'I was so scared of sticking the pin in him I must have put it on too loose.' Behind her, the frying pan was beginning to smoke. 'Oh God, now I'm burning the scones!'

Michael came in. 'Give him to me,' he said, taking Josh off Moses. 'I used to be a dab hand with a nappy. Let's see what we can do.'

They disappeared again and from the living room (as she rescued the burned scones and spooned the last of the mixture into the hot pan) came the sounds of their laughing voices, and Joshua's gusty giggle.

Then her dad came in. From the kitchen it was beginning to sound like a party.

She took the teapot and glasses to the living room. Moses and Michael were on their hands and knees having a crawling race with Josh. She went back to the kitchen for the plate of scones, listening to the laughter – Michael's deep boom, Moses' light tenor laugh, Joshua's an excited squeal. Her dad silent. He'd been standing there with a bemused expression on his face when she took the teapot in.

When she went back with the scones he was still standing there, awkward as an intruder. She caught his eye and he grinned. She grinned just as sheepishly back. The complicity of outsiders, she thought, pouring out the tea. Father and daughter. No good at families, never were. The thought sent a hot rush through her: he hadn't been that bad a dad! She handed him a glass of tea and a drop scone to tell him so, avoiding his eye.

'Never knew quite what to do with small babies myself,' he said.

That could explain a lot, she thought, her eyes on the antics on the floor.

The sun was sloping down towards evening when she and Michael walked back to Jo's house. Michael carried Josh in his arms. She had the empty baby carrier on her back and pushed Michael's bike up the hill. Joshua was tired and grizzling a little, his head leaned drowsily into Michael's neck.

'I think I might have found another reason why our friend Moses could have been feeling displaced,' Michael said.

'You didn't say anything to him did you?'

'No, no, of course not. He said something in passing which made me think of it. Where does he sleep?'

'In the little room next to the kitchen,' she answered, surprised at the question because she'd always assumed the room was intended as the houseboy's quarters.

'I thought so. Before you came that was a storeroom. That's where they used to keep the sacks of rice and charcoal and stuff.'

'But where did Moses sleep then?'

'That's rather my point. I thought he was still living in his cousin's house near the hospital but he says he's been living with your father for more than two years now. I think your coming might possibly have put him out of his room.'

She was silent, thinking about it. You had to walk through the living room to get to her bedroom, which was small and hot and caught the afternoon sun but it was a palace compared with where Moses was sleeping now.

'Don't brood over it,' Michael said. 'It's not a big issue. I don't even know that he minded being put out of his room, if indeed he was. Some houseboys sleep on the floor in the kitchen. But I thought it was something to bear in mind, that's all.'

'*Is* he a houseboy or isn't he?'

'Does it matter? It's only a label. Moses is Moses. This little chap is falling asleep! Let's go up and see how his mum is.'

Kevin flung the screen door open when he heard them coming up the steps. Jo, on the sofa, looked a little less grey and shrunken after a long sleep. Kevin pressed them both to stay for supper but Michael made his excuses and pedalled off into the night and Anne stayed on a few minutes for form's sake only before walking home alone.

One fine, luminous night she and her dad were sitting outside the house after supper when Michael called by.

'Another hard day pacing the aisles, then?' he asked as he sat down in the chair Moses had just vacated .

She had been invigilating all day. 'Worse than working in a supermarket,' she said.

They sat quietly for a while, the three of them in a row in the sultry dark. Her dad in the middle, placidly smoking his pipe.

Michael observed casually, 'Morrissey's just announced he's staying on at the Mission after all. I'm sure now he'll want to be rid of me.' He said it in such a matter of fact way, as if he was saying *Morrissey's eyes are blue*, she didn't realise what he'd said for a moment. She knew he'd been expecting Father Morrissey to move on to another posting soon but she hadn't realised he felt his own position depended on it. She looked across at him, sitting on the far side of her dad in the warm enclosing night. Her dad was filling his pipe again.

'There's a moon coming up somewhere,' Michael said.

'*The* moon is behind us, just coming up over the hill. I

think you'll find we have only the one,' her dad observed, before putting his pipe back in his mouth and sucking steadily as he put a match to it.

Plaything, she thought. That pipe was just a glorified dummy really. Had he not heard what Michael had just said about Morrissey? Or was he thinking what to say before he passed comment?

'How could he want to get rid of you?' she asked. 'The school would be nothing without you!'

'I knew him before, don't forget. He didn't like me then and he doesn't like me now. He's ambitious – for the Mission, for the school – and he feels I'm holding things back.'

'Why?' she asked indignantly. 'Of course he can't think that! I mean, look at the new science block!'

'Exactly. Look at it. Walls three feet above the ground now – which admittedly is three feet higher than they were last month, but the money was raised for the new labs nearly two years ago. If I were a more ambitious man I'd have that block in use by now. We need it badly enough.'

'If you were a more ambitious man,' her dad said, still sucking on his pipe, 'you wouldn't be here at all.'

'True. I don't think Tamale is quite the career move Morrissey had in mind for himself either. That's why I'd assumed he wouldn't stick around very long. But his plans didn't work out, apparently, and now that he's been landed with another five years here I'm sure he's going to want to do a bit of pruning. I'm not the only one he doesn't like. He sees people like Stefan as so much dead wood.'

'But that's awful!' she exclaimed. 'You told me once that you became a priest so you could step outside the career ladder. Are you telling me now you're still on it?'

'I'm not but Morrissey certainly is. He wants to make the

school bigger, the Mission more important. He wants to retire to a seaside bungalow in Ireland with longer school photos on his mantelpiece – five hundred pupils, not two hundred and eighty odd.'

'That's a long way from being the same thing as wanting to get rid of you,' her father said.

'I can feel his beady little eyes on me all the time just waiting for some excuse.'

Nobody said anything.

'Not that I'm paranoid or anything,' Michael added. She could hear he was smiling.

The end of the week, the end of exams. And very nearly of the term, and the school year. The suppressed excitement all around her wasn't reflected in her own feelings. She had only just got going! And even worse, when term ended Michael would be disappearing.

He called across the staffroom: 'Hang on a minute Anne, I'll walk with you. I need to see your dad – he's got hold of a socket set for me.'

She put her books into her bag and waited. The complex bush telegraph by which such arrangements were made, without a telephone, still amazed her. Not to mention Michael's ability to wangle favours, loans and gifts of cast-offs out of anyone and everyone.

'Let's go the scenic way,' he said as they emerged from the protective shadow of the building into the fierce sun. They headed towards the yam field at the side of the school. Somebody called his name. A stubby little man was running clumsily across the school yard. 'Oh no,' Michael groaned softly. 'It's Mr Solomon Dabuo. I know what this will be about!'

'Father My-kel! I saw you leaving as I came from the road but I couldn't catch up.' The man clutched at his chest, panting. 'Oh dear, I am not fit! Can I have a word, Father?' Mr Dabuo drew Michael to one side and murmured. 'No, Mr Dabuo,' Michael said firmly in his normal voice, 'as I told you before, that just won't do. We don't work like that.'

'I hear you, Father. But a man must do what he can for his son, you know?'

'Another Chicken Head Moment?' she asked when Mr Dabuo walked away, shoulders drooping. She followed Michael onto the path between the neat, steep banks of red earth in which turbulent yams were sprouting.

He laughed. 'Another Chicken Head Moment indeed! Another bloody Southerner.'

'Isn't that a bit…um…racist?'

He looked at her, startled. 'What? Oh you mean stereotyping along lines of race?' He pondered a moment. 'You're right! It was.'

'What are you doing!'

He had dropped to his knees in the middle of the path, hands clasped as if in prayer, eyes shut and face turned up to heaven. 'Sorry God.' He bent his head and boomed at the ground, 'Ninety-nine Hail Marys, O sinner, and two chicken heads on toast once a week for a year.'

'Get up, you fool,' she said, looking about her and laughing. 'Get up before somebody sees you!'

He stood up and dusted off his knees.

'Don't you have *any* scruples?' she asked.

'Had one somewhere. He was right here just a minute ago.' He peered round his feet. 'Scruple, scruple, scruple! Ah, here he is,' he said, scooping up the imaginary scruple from the ground. 'Naughty boy.' He wagged a finger sternly at his cupped hand and put it into his back pocket.'

'Well reverence, then?'

'Yes, plenty, as the actress said when the Bishop asked her the very same question over tea. *Only none as good as you, Reverend.* Whoops – sorry Anne, I'm getting over-excited. I'm going home next week! Whoopee!'

As they came out of the yam field onto the road he said, 'Actually it's not that easy going home. My sister's husband was killed by a car bomb this time last year. She's been having a hard time of it.'

The words silenced her, they were so unexpected.

'She's got two boys. Nine and eleven. The younger one's taking it terrible hard. I'll be needing all the jokes I can dredge up to make *him* crack a smile, from what Pauline says.'

'Perhaps not the-actress-said-to-the-bishop jokes, then.'

'You're right. Yet again. I'd better steer clear of those.'

'Ooh!' said Jo later. 'He must have forgotten who he was with. He must have thought you were Ursula, telling jokes like that!'

Moses watched as she cut up the pineapple. It made her self-conscious but she wouldn't let him intimidate her. She arranged the pineapple on the plate and carefully rinsed the knife under the tap, the way he did, letting the water fall on the floor, there being no sink. She dried the knife and put it back on the shelf.

He slid across the room and turned the knife so that it lay at right-angles to the other knife instead of parallel with it. She always forgot he liked to arrange them in this way because it seemed so arbitrary.

Curiosity got the better of her: 'Why do you put them like that?'

He raised his eyebrows tartly. 'So de sharp don' come out,' he said, as if stating the obvious.

She looked at the knives, and looked back at him. Was he having her on? He'd been to Technical College, hadn't he? Or was Michael mistaken about that? Moses stared back. 'Sorry,' she said, 'I didn't know.'

His shoulders relaxed and for a moment she thought he was going to smile. 'Well, now you do,' he said, and he almost sounded friendly.

'Ever thought of becoming a Bride of Christ?'

She looked up from her marking. Michael sat at another table in the staffroom, piled high with exam papers. John's chair was empty – he'd gone to see if he could wheedle some tea out of Ishmael. They were working their way through the last of the exam-papers. 'What?'

'If you were to become a Bride of Christ we could have you as a Sister. You'd look very fetching in a wimple.'

She didn't imagine he was expecting a reply but he'd disturbed her concentration. She frowned at the exam paper in front of her.

'Sorry, sorry! Don't mind me,' he said. 'I wish John would get back with that tea – I've had it up to here with these Religious Education papers! This one's bogged down in a rather literal interpretation of Brides of Christ. E for Effort, I'm afraid.' He wrote a mark at the bottom of the page and turned the paper back to look at the name on the top page. 'Aha! It's our young Joseph. If I'd known it was him before I read it would I have marked it any differently, I wonder? With or without the prospect of boosting school funds?'

186

'Don't you look to see whose paper you're marking before you start?' She was startled into paying attention. It had never occurred to her not to look. He must actually cover the name up, not to see it there on the top of the page.

Before Michael could reply, John came in and put a tray down at his end of the crowded table. There were three glasses of strong tea on the tray, well-laced with powdered milk which made its usual scum on the surface. And a plate with five small biscuits on it.

'I've just found where that Patrick is skiving,' John said in his perennially happy voice. 'He's in the refectory having tea right now, the lazy worm. I got him to promise to come along at five – he swears he can't get here any sooner. And it was like milking blood out of a stone getting this tray out of Ishmael. I don't know what's got into *him* today! I could only wangle five biscuits. How shall we divide them?'

'Break each of them into three and five pieces each,' Michael said promptly. 'I was just saying to Anne – she could keep her foot in the door here indefinitely if she signed up as a nun.'

'She surely wouldn't want to go that far!' John said. He shot Michael a startled look and saw he was teasing. 'I suppose if Morrissey is serious about us going co-ed, he's going to have to sign up some more female teachers. It's funny, isn't it – he doesn't like women much but he wants to bring girls into the school.'

Michael said, 'He doesn't like anybody much. But he does like their money.'

They went back to their marking. It was terribly hot – an airless, brooding sort of day. The sweat welled up and rolled wherever limbs touched anything solid: under the backs of the thighs, and between them wherever they touched, under the arms, under the wrists where they lay on the table. And down the centre of Anne's back, which wasn't touching anything at all. She had to keep a clean sheet of paper under her right hand to stop her sweaty wrist smudging the ink on the papers she was marking.

John laughed suddenly, his puffy body quivering. 'Listen to this: "*In those days all England was a poor place. The houses had crude pictures on the walls and rough matting on the floor.*" Only he's left a *t* out of matting.'

Morrissey came in and they stopped laughing. 'I take it those exam papers will be dispatched by the end of today?'

They went back to their work like three naughty children. But every now and then there was a snigger from John's end of the table as he muttered 'rough matting' into his beard.

Later, in the evening, she told Jo about the Bride of Christ.

'He was joking, wasn't he?' asked Jo, who always took things too seriously. 'He *must* be queer, Anne. Otherwise he'd never tread so close to the mark.'

But Michael wasn't leading her on. He always stayed just the right side of the loony-uncle line. And although he made her laugh, sometimes it could be tiresome.

'He's going home soon,' she said. 'He's just getting a bit over-excited.'

Ursula's house seemed to be full of boxes. And only Deepa was there, sitting in a tall, upright chair flanked by her two adolescent children, home for the holidays from their Indian boarding schools. Deepa looked more than ever like an Egyptian queen. 'My offsprung,' she drawled, waving a hand towards them. Her voice was Delhi overlaid with

South Kensington. She picked a stray thread off her crisp dark slacks and the two girls smiled from under their thick fringes but did not say a word. 'Ursula won't be long.'

'I thought she was only going on leave,' Anne said, watching Jo haul Joshua back as he crawled from one tempting open box to another. 'Isn't she coming back in September?'

'She doesn't know when she'll be back. She might stay on until the kids are settled in their new schools.'

Across the room Jo looked disapproving. Josh was unlikely ever to find himself being settled into a boarding school, Anne thought.

Ursula came in with a jug, the houseboy following in her wake with a tray of glasses. 'Anne! Good – you got my message? There's someone here I want you to meet.' She put the tray down on the table and looked towards the door. '*Now* where's the woman got to?'

'De other madam still in de kitchen, Madam. I tink she doin' de washing up,' the houseboy said.

'Oh for goodness sake! What does she think I pay you for? Go and tell her to come in here.'

The boy grinned good-naturedly and went to the kitchen.

'Do sit down, you two,' Ursula said irritably to Deepa's daughters. 'You're making me feel nervous. Do you like magazines?' She picked up a *Woman's Own* and chucked it across to them on the sofa. They smiled politely and bent their glossy heads over the pages. 'I'm glad you've been able to find the time to come, Anne. We have a little favour to ask of you.' Ursula poured out the lemonade. A small, colourless woman came in. 'Ah, Mandy. Come and meet Anne. And Jo.'

The woman was in her early thirties, perhaps, but already running to seed. The red gash of lipstick only emphasised the pallor of her English skin, and somehow Anne wasn't surprised when Mandy shook hands limply and didn't quite make eye contact.

Ursula said, 'This is the girl I was telling you about, Mandy. The one I thought might be able to help you.'

'Me?' Anne exclaimed in surprise.

'You're a clever girl, Anne. And diplomatic. Mandy has a tricky problem and she needs your help. I can't get involved because I'm much too busy packing up to leave, and there's no one else I can ask.'

Jo scowled. Anne looked from Jo to Deepa. If the children had come back from India surely that meant Deepa was going to be in Tamale all summer?

'I mean,' Ursula said, 'no one who's free of family ties. You'll be here most of the summer, won't you Deeps, but you've got the girls with you.'

'Anne's coming to stay with us in Kumasi so she won't be here all summer either,' Jo said.

'This won't take much of your time, Anne. Half a day at the most. And it needs to be done as soon as possible. You finish school next week don't you?'

Anne nodded but said nothing.

'Oh you explain, Mandy,' Ursula said impatiently and turned away to open the gin bottle.

Anne didn't dare look at Jo, who had bet her five *cedis* that the gin would appear long before the sun got anywhere near the yardarm.

Mandy said, 'It's like this. I was married to a Ghanaian doctor. In London.' Her voice was as small and pale as she was and it was difficult to hear what she was saying. 'We had – we

190

have – a little boy. James. He's just two-and-a-half. Last year we got divorced and my husband came back to Ghana and me and James stayed in London. Then a few months ago my ex came over to visit. And when he left he snatched James.'

'Snatched?' Jo exclaimed, horrified.

'Yes. It's a long story – but the long and the short of it is, he said he was just taking James to the park, only he never came back. By the time I realised what he'd done it was too late. I think he might have brought James back to his village here.' The woman seemed uneasy, as if the heat itself disturbed her. She wiped her face with a handkerchief and took quick, urgent drags at the cigarette she had just lit from the stub of the previous one. 'I know the name of the village. Ursula says it isn't far from here—'

Ursula interrupted. 'He comes from Zigbili. Forty minutes away by car.'

Mandy swallowed painfully as if she was on the verge of tears. She gave Anne an imploring look. 'Ursula said you might go to see Yiri. My ex, that is. Be a kind of ambassador for me?'

'Wouldn't it be better if you went yourself?' Deepa would be so much more appropriate than me, she was thinking, but Deepa was studiously examining her nails.

'Well, that's one of the reasons for asking you,' Ursula said. 'You're thinking of doing some research, aren't you? Yiri comes from an important family in Zigbili. You could say you wanted to interview him.'

'Interview him? What would I be interviewing him about?'

'Well, I don't know! You'll have to think up that bit. Something that sounds plausible. You could pretend it was about health care services – he *is* a doctor.'

Anthropology, not sociology! Anne thought.

Mandy said, 'You see, if I go to his village they'll just hide him and James. That's what happened in London. They closed ranks, all his friends and relations. Told me they hadn't seen Yiri, and afterwards the police found the two of them had been in that house all the time, even while I was stood at the door!' She lifted the cigarette to her lips, her hand shaking so much she almost missed. 'We thought,' she said as she ground the remains of the butt onto the ash-tray, 'if you could get to talk to him about something that wasn't threatening, like something for your research, you'd have a better chance of getting his confidence, and then you could just say *Oh by the way I met your wife*, or something like that, so that he'd know I'm here in Ghana and wanting to see him but you could reassure him I'm not going to try and do the dirty on *him*. Though God knows he deserves it.'

Anne looked at Jo, wondering what to say. Jo stared hard back, but whether willing her to say yes or no, she couldn't tell.

'All right,' she said at last. 'I can't promise, but I'll see what I can do.'

'That's my girl,' said Ursula. 'You do that.'

Mandy was wistful. 'If you did manage to see James you'd be able to tell me how he is...'

'But what do you want Anne to actually say?' Jo asked.

'See if you can get Yiri to agree to see me, and let me see my little boy.'

They were still in earshot of the bungalow when Jo blurted out: 'You do know Ursula's just using you? She thinks this Yiri will respond to the bait! It's disgusting – she wants to dangle you under his nose like a piece of fish!'

'I thought Mandy was rather sad.'

Jo snorted in reply, thrusting her hands under the straps of the backpack to ease Josh's weight on her shoulders.

There were puddles on the drive, reflecting the turbulent sky. It might rain again before they got home. Too wet, probably, for the weavers to be working today, and anyway Anne knew Jo would be put out if she was left to walk back on her own.

'She was a bit of an odd-ball, wasn't she! So pale and plain. So *London*.' As soon as Mandy had opened her mouth Anne had heard her mother's voice saying *common* in that tone which always made her want to do the opposite of whatever it was her mum was advising.

'Another class, do you mean?' Jo asked, having grown up in the northern reaches of London herself, on the very edge of middle-class respectability. 'Anyway, what's wrong with coming from London? You do!'

Anne heard the bitter edge again and steered carefully away. 'You do have to feel sorry for her, don't you. It must be dreadful to lose your child.'

Jo looked back at Joshua in the carrier on her shoulders as if to check that he was still there. (He had fallen asleep.) 'It's the worst thing about thinking about splitting up – which of you gets to keep the baby.'

Startled, Anne gave her a sideways look. Was she thinking of herself and Kevin?

Jo said, 'Will you go to Zigbili then?'

'I don't know. I'll have to think about it.' They trudged on in silence. After a while she asked Jo what she would do, if she'd been asked.

'Yeah, I did notice I wasn't. Probably they thought I'd care about it too much and make a hash of it.'

'Do you mean I don't care?' Anne said, bridling.

'No, I just meant I'd take it too much to heart to be objective. You're much more rational than me. I don't mean you're cold or anything,' Jo added, seeing her expression, 'but it's different when you've had a baby. One day you'll know.'

'Hmm,' said Michael when she told him the next day.

'What?' Expecting his approval, she was taken aback.

He looked at her quizzically over the books he was packing into a box. 'Why are they off-loading this on you?'

'I suppose because I'll be here and Ursula won't.'

'She's not going on leave for a week or two yet. And you're not the only English woman who'll be in Tamale over the summer, merely the youngest. I think she's taking advantage of you.'

'I don't think so!' she said, stung. She hadn't wanted to be burdened with a stranger's messy domestic problems but the woman's plight *had* stirred her sympathy. And Ursula's comments on her diplomacy had been flattering, whereas Michael's reaction was not.

He said nothing, merely looked at her over his boxes as he went on packing up books. 'What does Jo think?'

She was saved from replying by the staffroom door opening. Ishmael came in.

Michael looked up. 'Ishmael! What brings you so far from your kitchen?'

'Even de cockroach leave de kitchen when de stove is hot,' Ishmael said cheerfully. 'For somebody leaving us you don' look happy, Father.'

'Oh but I am, I am! As a man is, going home. Did you want me?'

'I jes tellin', no chop-bar tonight! No street food! Anybody wan' feed you, you say no. I cook you big-big dinner – you very best. You no spoil it, heh? Don' forget!'

'Ishmael, I'm touched. After Mass – seven o'clock on the dot. The Last Supper.'

Ishmael nodded vigorously and clomped out of the room. He was wearing a large pair of old sneakers with no laces.

'What did you say the husband's name was?' Michael asked.

She had hoped Ishmael's interruption would save her from the interrogation, but apparently not. 'Jebuni something? Yiri Jebuni? Mandy is afraid that if she goes herself they'll do what the relatives did in London. She said they kind of closed ranks against her.'

'As of course they would. And he's a doctor, did you say?'

'Yes.'

'Doctor Jebuni,' he said musingly. 'Well there are a few of *them* about – I wonder if he's one of the ones I know. Does your dad know him? If his is an important Zigbili family they probably own rice farms.'

She gave a non-committal shake of the head, such as might suggest that her dad didn't know this doctor, rather than that she hadn't actually asked him. They'd come in so late last night, her dad and Moses, tired from the field trip, and then they'd gone out again early this morning. She hadn't wanted to bother him.

Michael looked at her. 'What is it exactly that they want you to do?'

'Ursula asked me to go to Zigbili and find out where he lives, see if I can get to talk to him. She suggested I could pretend it was part of my research.'

'Go in on a lie then?'

She shifted in her chair – she was uneasy about that too. Indeed, if she could, she'd happily drop the whole thing. She should have stood her ground yesterday and said no outright, but at the time she'd been able to think of no good reason for refusing.

The funny thing was, the more Michael looked sceptical the more she felt the urge to resist him. Why did he not have as much faith in her as Ursula did? He was treating her like a child.

'Did you particularly like this Mandy woman?' he asked suddenly.

'I didn't see enough to like her or dislike her.'

He shot her a piercing look.

'Well I'm not at all convinced,' he said at last. 'I don't know what the hell they're off-loading this on you for. Quite frankly I think it's outrageous.'

'They only want me to find out if the little boy is okay, and if I can to get the father to agree to see Mandy. I've said that's all I'm willing to do. I don't want to get embroiled in their quarrels. I'm not that naïve!' she added defensively.

'I wasn't meaning to imply otherwise,' Michael said. 'But you're not experienced enough to know when to refuse to get involved.'

Her hackles rose. What experience could he (a priest!) have that would make him so much better placed to judge? She was probably more emotionally experienced at twenty-two than he could possibly be at forty-one! She bit her lip resentfully but said nothing. She thought of Jo saying she couldn't understand because she hadn't had a baby, as if motherhood was a club she hadn't joined yet. And here was Michael implying that adulthood, too, was a club she had not yet joined.

'Come on, Anne – admit it! You'd be out of your depth. You haven't the first idea what it is to be a parent and lose your child, so how can you hope to liaise sensitively in a situation like this?'

'I think I can empathise with her enough to have *some* idea what she's going through.'

'I didn't mean the mother. I meant Yiri Jebuni. There are two parents in this, remember. Either way, one of them gains and one of them loses. I think you've just proved my point.'

She looked at her hands and said nothing, angry with herself for appearing to confirm his prejudices. Even more angry with *him,* for his apparent wisdom and his actual distance from the world. How could he choose to stand on the outside looking in from the pinnacle of priesthood, wise but essentially unknowing? It struck her suddenly that this was the root of her strange turmoil of feelings about him: he was part of the world but he was removed from it, a character in the play but standing in the wings. More the prompt than the protagonist. She had thought that the muddle she felt was because she was falling ridiculously in love with him. Now she realised it was just as much that she was angry with him – angry that he was separate from the world, somehow ducking out at the most important bits. How could he presume to judge her? He knew nothing of her emotional past, of her inner life, her loves and her hurts, her precious, painfully gained experience. For all he knew, she thought, hotly, she might have a secret love child herself! How dare he suppose he knew her when they never talked about their innermost selves! Would she assume she knew the secrets of his past? If a priest could *have* any secrets…

She sat half turned away from him, her emotions heaving about like kittens inside a heavily pregnant cat. Michael started to speak but seemed to think better of it. He packed the last of the books and began to move the boxes out to the storeroom along the corridor.

She hadn't been decided until then. She had floated the idea in front of him out of curiosity to see what he thought. But now she thought she *would* go to Zigbili to help Mandy. Just to prove she could.

As she sat there inwardly debating, and he took his boxes out of the room and she was too cross to offer to help, she suddenly wanted to say out loud, *Don't go! Why do you have to go? Stay here with me!* But of course she couldn't say any such thing, and of course she did not. He must go home to Ireland and live his own life, secrets and all, if he had them, and she must go back to the Low Cost House and live hers.

15

Zigbili

The Zigbili bus pulled out of the Bus Park with people hanging on its sides and perched on the roof. Anne watched it go, relieved to be one of the crowd left behind.

'*Trotro* is better,' Moses said when she got home. So next day she tried again.

The little bus-trucks were lined up in a section of the Lorry Park. She asked the big market mammy standing by the door of the *trotro* on the end of the row if it was going to Zigbili. 'Yes, yes, you sit down right here,' the woman said, pointing to the seat behind the driver. 'You no remember you buyed cloth from me den? I am Alice! Today I go to Zigbili market to sell cloth.' She wagged an emphatic finger, her elaborate headgear bobbing: 'You don' let nobody else sit here, only me!' and stepped down off the *trotro* to supervise the men who were hauling her awkward bundle up onto the roof along with some battered cardboard boxes tied up with string, a large number of bulky sacks, and a trussed goat.

Satisfied at last, Alice clambered back on board and took her seat beside Anne. The driver started the engine.

Squashed up against the window, Anne watched the countryside speed past, wondering why she hadn't done this before. There'd been nothing to stop her catching buses or *trotros* and going out to explore. Nothing at all, except that she'd been so caught up in school. She was conscious of the irony that it should be insular Ursula who had pushed her into it now. She shielded her eyes against the fierce downward glare of the sun and stared out at the fleeting figures bent over their shining hoes in the fields and the clusters of round huts topped with grey, gleaming thatch. Over her head, muffled among the luggage, the trussed goat bleated balefully all the way to Zigbili.

'Doctor Yiri Jebuni? Well, why you not say before it Yiri you wantin' to see!' Alice sat down heavily on the metal chair in the shade of the *kapok* tree and fanned herself vigorously with a piece of cardboard. The table in front of her was piled with bolts of brash new cloth. 'I'd have taken you dere straight-straight if you only said. He live by de old school.'

'I went to the street by the school but no one there seemed to know of him.'

'Not de new school! De *old* school.' Alice waved a deprecating hand. 'De new school district, dey all southerners. Nobody dere don' know Doctor Jebuni an' dey don' know de old school either 'cos it don' be a school now for long-long time.' Alice leaned forward in her seat and yelled suddenly into the middle distance. A small boy appeared.

'Take dis lady to Doctor Jebuni compound.' The boy looked puzzled and Alice spoke to him quickly in Dagbani. His face cleared. 'Don' give dis boy no money,' she commanded Anne in a stage whisper, wagging her finger. 'He owe me favour – I help him out of bad-bad trouble last year.'

Anne looked at the boy. He was very small to have been

in *bad-bad trouble*. He smiled shyly and signalled to her to follow him. As they walked up the road together she tried to make conversation in her limited Dagbani but the boy grinned amiably and shrugged. He led the way into a narrow lane. On either side of them the high mud walls of old compounds flowed between the backs of thatched huts, which the walls absorbed in passing as undulating bulges. Everything here was in shades of brown, except for the sweep of the over-arching *kapok* trees. And the bright white stones set into the mud around the open doorway of the small hut in the wall where the boy stopped. He gestured to her to enter. She hesitated. The hut was like a gatehouse in a castle wall: through the narrow doorway in its further wall she could see two women sweeping an open space inside the compound. Should she call out, or just walk in?

The boy stood watching her. She stepped inside the hut and gave a cough. One woman had moved out of sight, the other went on sweeping, so she stood and coughed again, a little louder.

The boy laughed. He went to the inner doorway, cupped his hands round his mouth, and yelled. The woman looked up. She saw the boy, and Anne standing just behind him, and rushed off in obvious panic. There was distant shouting – female voices. They seemed to have assumed she was Mandy. The boy looked up at her, bemused, as she stepped back awkwardly into the shadows of the hut. Michael had been quite right. She was hopelessly out of her depth.

A man was coming swiftly across the open space towards them, a tall, graceful figure dressed in a traditional white *fugu* and loose white cotton trousers. She saw the look of fury on his face and her heart jumped into her mouth as he ducked through the doorway.

He straightened up under the low thatch and his manner softened abruptly. 'I am sorry. I thought you were someone else. Whom are you seeking?' A deep voice. Oxford English with a rich Ghanaian lilt. The boy seemed to have fled.

'Doctor Yiri – I mean, Doctor Jebuni?' she stammered, flustered by his penetrating gaze. He nodded. 'I'm sorry to come to you out of the blue but I didn't know how else to get in touch with you…' She trailed to a limp halt. His eyes became hostile again. 'Doctor Jebuni, I – '

'Did Mandy send you?'

'She asked me to c—'

'Why does she not come herself? Why does she send strangers to me like spies?'

'I am not a spy, Doctor Jebuni! And she didn't *send* me…' She faltered, remembering Michael saying *You will make him angry. He will feel attacked.* 'Please…' she said, hearing the ignominious note of pleading in the word. The faint quaver of tears threatening (because she had been told, but she had presumed to know better). It made her angry with herself. 'Please!' she said, more sharply than she intended.

'She asked you to come?' Anne nodded unwillingly. 'Well then she *has* sent you. I think we will not quarrel over semantics. But we may well quarrel over what is right and what is wrong. She should have come herself.'

Mandy's ravaged face loomed up like a pale beacon in Anne's consciousness. 'Wrong? It was wrong of you to seize a child like that. Very wrong!'

Too late, she realised she should have just said *Of course she will come herself, I am here only to arrange it.* He was staring down at her through narrowed eyes.

A movement in the alleyway distracted him. The small boy was lingering outside, openly curious. Dr Jebuni sent him packing with a sharp sentence. He turned back to face her. 'We had better go somewhere more private.'

The brightness of the light in the inner compound made her screw up her eyes as she followed Dr Jebuni blindly across bare, sun-scrubbed earth to a thatched shelter, open on three sides to the hot midday breeze. He drew up an incongruous metal chair with the back missing and gestured imperiously for her to sit. He sat at a little distance, half turned away from her, on a similar chair. She was painfully aware of his graceful elegance, of her own grimy sweatiness. She waited for him to say something.

The silence grew awkward.

'I should explain—'

He raised a hand to silence her. A tiny, elderly woman with a wrap tucked tightly over wrinkled breasts was bringing bottles of Fanta. She glared at Anne. Doctor Jebuni said something softly to the old woman and her face cleared suddenly to a toothless grin.

'My grandmother,' he said.

Anne smiled and held out her hand to the old lady who hesitated, then took it in both of hers with a sudden stream of lisping sentences.

'She says she is glad my son's mother has not come because she does not want trouble but that when trouble comes she hopes it will be as beautiful as you.' He stared at Anne stonily. 'My grandmother is a great flatterer.'

She was silent, wondering if they were making fun of her.

The old lady went away.

Doctor Jebuni said 'So, you are acquainted with my former wife. I heard she is in Tamale. What has she told you?'

She said carefully, watching his face, 'I've only met her

203

on one occasion. She told me that when you divorced she was given custody of your son and you returned to Ghana.' He nodded once, staring at the ground by his feet. 'But she said that when you went back to London to see James a few months ago you failed to return him after taking him out for the day, and that is the last contact she has had with either of you.'

'And she told you this, no doubt, in some indignation? Because it is quite true, I have broken the order of the English courts and "stolen" my own child. I have been forced to act in this way by the English law.'

'Your child was born in England?' The slightest of nods. 'And he is a British citizen?' Another nod. 'And you were living in England, so you were subject to English law.' But she couldn't keep it up. Such a mean little word, *indignation*... 'A child shouldn't be taken away from his mother! Not under any country's law. Especially not a very young child.'

'In my country we believe a child should be with the father, *especially* a son. In any case we believe a child should have a whole family – grandmothers, grandfathers, aunts and uncles, cousins. No child should live with one person only.'

I did! she thought. How dare he judge! 'But you weren't in Ghana, you were in England. By your own choosing.'

'Yes,' he said. 'By my own choosing.' He frowned. 'I am well aware, Miss – Miss – ?'

'Foster, Anne Foster.'

'I am well aware of my responsibilities, Miss Foster. They are not as simple as you seem to think. I did not see *sharing* in the decision made by the court when they wrote me out of my son's history. I did not see the real interests of the child addressed by the court. I could offer James a home here full of loving people, a rich and interesting life lived not just with me, his father, but also with his grandfather, his uncles – the men who will help him become a man. Instead the English court decreed – without much consideration, I might add – that he should be condemned to a narrow life in a small flat, seeing only his mother, who was out at work all day, and a child-minder with whom he had no blood-ties.'

'But she had to work! Since you had left her, I don't suppose she had any choice.'

'Clearly you do not know my ex-wife very well. She did not tell you, then, that her refusal to give up her career and put our son in the care of a child-minder was one of the reasons for our separation?' He saw this hit home and firmly closed his lips as if he could say more but to do so was beneath him.

She was too ignorant of the facts to be arguing Mandy's case for her. All the same, his chauvinism was outrageous. 'If male example was so important why didn't you stay in the UK and spend as much time with him as you could? You didn't need to seize him in such an underhand way!'

'I did not seize him,' he said. 'I simply did not return him.'

'Oh come on!' *Semantics indeed!* 'If it was so right, you bringing him out here, why didn't you do it properly? Arguing your case, explaining to James what you were going to do, working it out with Mandy?'

'You think a two-year-old can be explained to in that way? Or a woman – God forgive me – like Mandy? Women like her will fight like a tigress for what they want, but that does not make them right.'

'But what about James! Are you telling me *he* hasn't been

205

hurt by all this? It must have been terrible for him, being taken from his mother like that!'

'Sometimes we must suffer before we can reach a better place. James is young enough to forget his other life quite quickly. Better to go through that now than when he is older. The culture shock would be far greater then.'

She stared at him, too outraged to argue.

'I do not feel I need to explain to *you*,' he went on. 'But before you go away, your English indignation set in stone, your convictions unchallenged, just consider this: in your country James would be looked on as a second-class citizen. Always understood to be less than he was capable of, never more. Always seen to be less significant. Remember, I lived in England for a long time before my son was born, I know what I am saying. But here in Ghana he is part of a significant family. When he grows up he will have opportunities to do significant things himself, if he so wishes. Ghana is a young country; a man can make his mark here, if he chooses. Enough! I do not need to explain my reasons to you. I have done what I have done after much careful thought, and that is all you need to know. You can tell her, she should come herself.'

'I will tell her.'

Silence. The wind stirring the leaves of the kapok tree. Somewhere, an unseen child giggled.

'Can I see James?'

Dr Jebuni hesitated.

'If everything's as wonderful as you claim, you surely can't be afraid of me seeing him? Don't you *want* me to be able to tell Mandy that I've seen him and everything's fine?'

'It would not be healthy for James. He is just beginning to settle.'

'Do you mean you wouldn't let *her* see him if she came?'

'If she comes she can see him, of course! But I honestly believe it would be better if he were left in peace, and probably easier for her too, in the long run.'

Peace! she thought. Poor kid. Poor woman. 'It's hardly likely that she'll accept that, is it? Not after all the trouble she's gone to, coming here to find him. Especially if I'm not able to reassure her that I've seen for myself that he's doing all right.'

He sat with his elbows on his knees and his hands clasped at his chin, clicking his thumbnails against his teeth.

'Is he unhappy? Is that what you don't want me to see?'

Shooting her a swift, angry look the doctor got roughly to his feet and strode towards one of the huts, from which children's voices had been audible for some time, talking in bubbling whispers.

What now? She watched him stooping at the door of the hut, talking to someone, his grandmother perhaps, inside.

She looked round at the compound. Intrigued – in spite of her jangled state – by the broad space enclosed within a circle of thatched huts linked by the meandering curtain wall. In front of several of the huts (the ones at the lower end of the compound, she noted with her anthropologist's mind) women stood over their smoking fires, stirring large pots and watching her with open curiosity. A *kapok* tree cast its abundant shade over one corner, its winged trunk like the jawbones of a whale

Doctor Jebuni came back with a pale-skinned child in his arms. He sat down, staring at her challengingly over the child's haze of light-brown hair. From the safety of his father's lap the child gazed at her steadily. No one spoke.

James, she noticed, had green eyes and clear, honey-coloured skin. His hand on his father's neck relaxed. For all that had been said, he seemed strangely unperturbed by her presence.

Poor Mandy, she thought, returning the child's calm gaze. How she must be hurting at the loss of such a lovely little boy. But by the same token, how must Yiri Jebuni have been hurt by her. Such a bloody mess... Could they not have stayed together for the sake of the child?

She looked at Doctor Jebuni. He raised one eyebrow but said nothing.

Afterwards it was the strange quality of the silence between them that lingered. And that sense of communal space around them, reverberating with activity all presently suspended by her intrusion. The breeze rustling the leaves of the *kapok* tree, the blue smoke rising, the goats noisy, the children giggling in the hut. In the background, the hot smell of burning charcoal and the cool smell of moist earth, the smell of cooking, and from a distance, of latrines. And how this enclosed world had seemed, suddenly, so very beautiful. And how she no longer knew for certain what was good and what was bad.

'He said *that*?' Jo was shocked. 'I hope you told him where to get off!' She shivered, and hugged the sleeping Josh tighter to her bony bosom. Josh murmured in his sleep and flung out one hot arm in protest. 'I could never leave Kevin,' she added. 'Because of Josh.'

Anne looked up quickly but Jo was calmly stroking Josh's sleeping hand. His fine hair was dark with sweat and dust had collected in grimy lines in the folds of his small limbs. How like maggots we white people are, she thought. Little maggots and big ones, surrounded by beautiful, dark-skinned, vibrant people who can walk out in the sun while we must hide away indoors.

'I don't think I made a very good impression,' she said.

'Nonsense! All men are impressed by you!'

'I think not. Not this one, certainly. This one was mad at me. And I got pretty mad back.'

'What was he like?'

'Tall. *Very* handsome.'

Jo gave a whoop of laughter. 'On your toes, Father Michael!'

'Oh don't! Michael told me I wouldn't do any good and he was right. I've probably completely messed up what little chance Mandy had. All I've done is find out where this man lives and seen that James is okay.'

'But how can he be, without his mother?'

'That's the funny thing. Before I got there I was sure it was all wrong. But now… I don't know.'

'You can't know, you haven't had a child,' Jo said, casting her out of the club again with one easy sentence.

16

1st week in August

The following day, when she came out of the house to walk into town, Joseph Appiah, and his friend, John Aburiya, were sitting on the side of the road near the copse of mango trees. They scrambled to their feet when they saw her. John was grinning his usual mischievous grin but Joseph kept his eyes fixed on the ground. His expression was unusually sullen.

'Hello you two,' she said. 'How are you both? Missing school?'

John said cheerfully 'We fine, Missanne. And no, we not missing school. Not yet.'

Joseph mumbled a token agreement.

'I'm going to the market,' she said. 'Are you going that way?' They could walk with her if they wanted to, and Joseph could get whatever was bothering him off his chest – if he wanted to. She had already guessed what it might be.

'I carry your bag,' John announced.

The blue cloth bag hung limp on her shoulder, having only her purse in it. She laughed and shook her head. 'Where do you live, John?' He gestured vaguely up the hill towards town. He looked older than Joseph, and perhaps he was: boys were sometimes taken out of school by their families if they were needed elsewhere for a while.

They walked beside her, up the road into town, talking gently about this and that (but Joseph still largely silent) until John said suddenly, 'My friend Joseph got something he wan' to ask, Missanne.'

Joseph turned on him fiercely. 'I have not!'

The boys stood in the road facing each other, Joseph angry, John grinning. John said affably, 'You have, Joseph. You like a chicken sitting on a bad egg.'

'Why don't you tell me what's bothering you, Joseph? I might be able to help.' Anne kept her voice carefully neutral, knowing his pride was at stake.

He made a little face and kicked at the ground, but when he looked back at her he had stopped scowling and looked wistful instead. 'It my daddy. He *very* angry.'

She waited, knowing what was coming. A passing goat did a detour round them.

'I not do so well in my exams.'

'You did very well in most of them!'

'Yes, but not in all. Religious Studies I not do well at all, at all. And English is my next lowest mark.'

'I told you in school, Joseph – you didn't answer the right questions in the English paper. You answered three in Section One and only one in Section Two. I could not give you any marks for one of your answers, otherwise you would have done very well. I explained this already – I had to mark the way the Exam Board will mark next year.'

'I know, I know. But Father My-kel did give me a bad mark in Religious Studies also!'

'How do you know it was him who marked your paper?' she asked. The Religious Studies papers had been marked by several of the priests.

'He told me.'

211

'So he will also have told you that you had got confused in some of your answers?'

He shrugged and said nothing, looking away over the treetops below them to the blue distances beyond the town. She turned and began to walk up the hill again. The sun was too fierce to want to stand still in it for long.

'My daddy say, why Father My-kel tell him not to pay de money till next term and den he go and mark me down? Why he no say what he mean so my daddy pay de money straight-straight?'

'Joseph, you know that money has nothing to do with it! Father Michael marked your paper fairly. He didn't even know it *was* your paper. Not until after he'd finished marking it. He never looks at the name on any paper before he marks it. Besides, your daddy has misunderstood. Father Michael didn't want him to think that *any* money your daddy gave the school would affect how well you do in class. But you understand that, don't you?'

He nodded, keeping his face averted.

Father John had an explanation for this sort of muddle. It's only like placating the gods, he said. They believe in the Christian God but they can't quite leave the other gods behind. She sneaked another look at Joseph as he walked beside her. His daddy was probably angry with her, too, for marking Joseph down in his English exam. No more chicken head moments for her and Michael, then. But she would be sad if Joseph stopped being the brightest spark in her class.

Just as she was thinking this, he looked up from under his brows and caught her eye. He gave a small, apologetic grin. 'I know my daddy wrong. But he very angry man and he did beat me, so den I angry too. But I tinking, maybe

Father My-kel punish me for what my daddy say about de money?'

'No, Joseph – he wouldn't dream of punishing you. And I didn't either. I wish I could have given you a better mark but I'm sure you won't make that same mistake again about answering the questions. I am very sorry your father beat you.'

His face lit up in his familiar big grin. 'He always beat me. But soon I be bigger dan him. He no beat me den!'

They parted company on the edge of the market. They had cheered her up, pulling her out of the emptiness she'd been suffering in the wake of school. She knew it was really the Zigbili trip that was weighing her spirits down. Her mind turned on it continuously in futile circles. Smarting for the way the handsome doctor had glared at her, but knowing that the sharp edge of his criticism had been at least partly deserved. She had been angry, too, but she was no longer sure why, and she regretted the impression she must have made. It didn't matter: she was unlikely to see him again. But it left a bitter taste, and an unexpected feeling of shame. She was an outsider. She'd had no right to judge.

The days passed and the feelings shifted. The big compound with its patterns of sun and shade lingered seductively in her thoughts. She would have liked to have gone to Doctor Jebuni's compound as a friend. To have played with the children, sat and talked with the women, got to know that big sprawl of family. Her own life was strangely empty of the familial and the doctor's words had struck home. Her experience of family had been made up of pairs: herself and her mother, and now herself and her

213

father. She had grown up sadly. A house of two people can be a lonely place, and all the struggles in it so exposed.

She couldn't put these things into words, and anyway who was there to tell? Her father wouldn't want to know, and Jo always understood the things Anne said differently than she'd intended. She missed Michael: his clowning self who would have made her take herself less seriously and told her where she needn't chastise herself, and the quieter Michael who would have told her (painfully) where she should.

She brooded quietly as she found herself small occupations around the house. Mending the skirt she had torn on a thorn bush. Sewing an errant button back on her dad's shirt. Reading the texts for next term. Jo and Joshua and Kevin went away to Kumasi. It was strange to pass their empty house as she walked the long hot road. Dagbani lessons with Rose, the daughter of a friend of Michael's, plugged some of the gap, though Anne wasn't making much progress. She wasn't a linguist and neither was Rose. Rose was an engineer: she didn't find it easy to explain what to her seemed blindingly obvious – just like Anne's dad, which was why he'd given up trying to teach her himself. I'll ask Michael to help me, she thought, when he gets back. But if Michael was there she would have to tell him about the Zigbili fiasco.

She could take another *trotro*, go and explore other villages within reach of the town, but the pleasure had gone out of the idea. She skulked about the house instead, writing notes on *Tom Jones*.

Rose came, and cheered her up. A lively girl, plump and plain but full of laughter, she was hoping to go to London very soon to start a university course, if the British Council funding she'd been promised came through, so she was anxious to improve her spoken English. The Dagbani lessons mutated without regret into discussions of all things English instead.

Sitting in the little living room in the Low Cost House, it was a struggle to answer questions about faraway London. Would Rose be able to walk to Oxford Circus from her aunt's house in Peckham or would she have to take a *trotro*? Peckham – where is Peckham? Anne thought wildly, staring at the knife blades of sun poking in at the louvres of the window. London no longer existed.

Moses came in with a tray and placed it with exaggerated care on the coffee table.

'Tea, Madam?' he said, and she had to bite her tongue at the sarcasm. As usual, Rose was self-conscious in Moses' presence and Moses played up to it by flirting outrageously. But he was playing games, like a sleek cat with a plump and earnest mouse. Anne shooed him out of the room, steeling herself against the look of pained regret on Rose's face.

'Next time I'll meet you in town,' she suggested, as Rose stood up to leave an hour later. That would bypass Moses. 'We go to a chop bar and I buy you a Fanta,' she added, lapsing as usual into semi-pidgin, because in this lilting, lyrical world a proper English accent sounded out of place and ugly and longed to camouflage itself.

Rose beamed. 'Yes – we do dat.' Adding cheerfully, 'I come fetch you when I ready.'

Anne couldn't really argue.

Moses was leaning pointedly on the front door-post. He looked up from picking his nails with a kitchen knife and grinned. 'Bye-bye, Rose,' he said, making the poor girl blush.

Anne stood on the porch waving as Rose walked self-consciously away, conscious herself of Moses lounging just behind her, graceful on one leg, the other braced against the door-frame. She remembered her own question: *does Moses not like women?* He plays with them, she thought. Even their own fighting, his and hers, had been a kind of game. She turned, knowing he would not be watching her now. Had he ever? Experience is very strange, she thought as she went back into the house. It changes us and then we can't remember quite what it really was.

17

August

A car tooted gaily just behind her as she walked up the hill. She turned to see the battered old Renault belonging to the Mission stopped on the other side of the road and Stefan waving at her excitedly from the driver's seat with Emmanuel grinning beside him.

'You goin' into town? You wan' lift?' Stefan shouted in his reedy, old man's voice.

She crossed the road gratefully. Emmanuel got out and lifted the seat so she could clamber into the back beside a large cactus in a pot.

'Careful!' Stefan giggled. 'Careful dat cactus don' bite!' His accent was such a funny mix of Poland and West Africa, it always made her laugh. The car leaped forward abruptly. 'Sorry, sorry. I don' drive dis car so often. What you say?'

'I said, where are you going with so many plants?'

But Stefan's driving didn't allow for idle chat. He peered over the wheel. Whenever they came near a bicycle he leaned hard on the horn, so that the startled cyclist nearly fell off in front of the car. 'We goin' to market! Emmanuel's cousin goin' to sell our plants. He hev special plant day today jes for us in his shop in de Old Market.'

Emmanuel grinned at her over his shoulder. 'Dis our last trip. We make lots of trips dis morning already.'

'What will you do with all the money you make?'

'Pay dis man,' said Stefan, nodding towards Emmanuel. He lifted his shoulders and tittered. 'How else he expect to be paid?'

'Dat not true,' Emmanuel reassured her.

'No,' Stefan agreed. 'It is a joke. No, we use de money to buy new seeds. I go to Ougadougou next time with John and Dom and buy French seeds. Very smart French seeds, and some special vines. Baby ones, jes young cuttings. You goin' to market or where you goin'?'

She said she was going to see the weavers but when he wanted to take her there, the prospect of kangaroo-hopping all the way down the busy Airport Road was more than she could face, so she said that actually she had changed her mind and the market would suit her better as she did have some shopping to do first. Oh good, he replied, because in that case she could come and see their shop. 'You know,' Stefan said, turning right so suddenly the cactus threatened to fall on her, 'Emmanuel eldest *pikkin* in your class?'

'Is he?' she exclaimed in surprise. 'What's his name?'

'He called Ezekiel.'

'I didn't know Ezekiel was your son!' In her mind's eye they instantly both looked different: Emmanuel as the father of that son, Ezekiel as the son of this father.

They parked precariously on the edge of the market and she helped carry the pots and baskets through the narrow alleyways to Emmanuel's cousin's shop. The small tin shack was full to overflowing with plants, and vegetables and fruit from the garden. There were even cut flowers (scarlet gladioli, yellow dahlias, white lilies) and Emmanuel's cousin was guarding them carefully against the crowd that had already gathered. Stefan – perspiring and harassed – was

218

getting querulous. She wondered if he would survive the morning without having a heart attack. But as she said goodbye he grinned suddenly and seized both her hands in his.

'You come to de garden tomorrow!' he commanded. 'We no see you in de garden since too long time. You come see your old Father Stefan and your old Uncle Emmanuel, now you no teachin'! Tomorrow or next tomorrow!'

Laughing, she promised she would.

The Airport Road seemed almost quiet, after the crowded market. She pushed her way against the steady stream of people walking into town. All along the sides of the road the treadle sewing machines clattered and the women operating them called out to her, 'Sister! Sister! How are you?' That perpetual cry that travelled with her everywhere. Occasionally somebody called out to her by name. Just as she had been teaching Emmanuel's son English for a whole term without realising it, she couldn't begin to guess at the connections by which people might know who she was.

She turned off the road and down between the small mud houses. Even from a distance she could see the bright warps trembling with the to-ing and fro-ing of the shuttles. All seven of the weaving places were set up today: the boys were back from school in Yendi and working for the summer. She was introduced to them, grave young men who seemed no younger than she was. One of them, Mustafa, spoke good English. They would do an exchange, he said. He would tell her all the weaving terms, she would correct his English.

She went, as she had promised, to see Stefan and Emmanuel

219

in their garden the very next day. In the few weeks since her last visit the garden had changed yet again. Heads nodded on the millet stalks high above her head. The tomato vines were full of ripening fruit. She found Stefan on the path beside the maize plot. He looked calmer than yesterday in the market. His white hair was amiably fluffy rather than wild, his white habit less grubby. He was supervising Emmanuel's weeding of the maize: Emmanuel was on his hands and knees among the tall plants, almost hidden.

Stefan's eyes lit up when he saw her. 'Dis man not so happy,' he whispered. 'He done hurt his knee. *Wah, wah, wah,* he all complaining!' He laughed, and yelled towards Emmanuel's rump, 'Our girl is come, let's go now make tea.'

Emmanuel backed out of the greenery towards them, grumbling. Stefan tucked Anne's hand in the crook of his elbow and they followed Emmanuel towards the thatched shelter, Emmanuel limping noticeably.

'I thought you had a boy to do the weeding,' she said.

'Sick,' said Stefan. 'He always sick – he not strong like you. Very bad childhood, dis boy, and always sick.'

'Plenty more where dat one come from not so lazy,' Emmanuel observed.

Stefan patted her hand and changed the subject.

Emmanuel began the familiar ritual of lighting the charcoal stove and setting the pan of water on it. A half hour of stillness as they waited for the water to boil, sitting on their stools under the riot of growth and decay that tumbled in front of them, and up and over, so that the roof of the shelter was bright blue under its smother of Morning Glory.

'How did you hurt your knee, Emmanuel?'

'Caught my foot in a rat hole an' twisted my leg.'

She sat listening to Stefan's chatter and watched Emmanuel's capable hands making the tea. Emmanuel the father of Ezekiel. Perhaps he wasn't as old as she'd thought. It was hard to tell, looking at Emmanuel's greying hair and weather-worn face. Nobody knew how old Stefan was, himself included. Or so he said, but Michael thought it a strategic amnesia – Stefan was afraid of being forcibly retired and sent away. He had no home to return to. He had lost that long ago during the Second World War and had never made another, except here. He could, like Father Benedict, retire to some home in England provided by the Church but that didn't sound like *home* to Stefan – a country he didn't know, living among strangers.

She looked at him, a small old man perched on a low stool, totally at one with his surroundings, totally absorbed in the tiny details of his life, and she envied him.

In the Low Cost house the tiny details of life were becoming increasingly solitary. Anne's father was out more and more of the time, often taking Moses with him. 'The growing season is always like this,' he said, as his working week spread into the evenings and the weekends.

Most days she went to see the weavers, filling her precious notebook with tiny writing, and sketches of loom parts. Back in the house she spent hours glueing in scraps of different cloths with the name of the pattern and technical details written alongside. Three different groups she was visiting now, but one group was her favourite and they were Muslim so Sundays were working days for them. Which was good, because Sundays could feel especially lonely.

Mustafa called her over to sit beside him in the shade so

he could talk while he worked. He had thought of more words for her to write down in her notebook. His father worked on the next loom, throwing in comments from time to time. 'Dat is our word,' he said of one of the words Mustafa offered. 'Dat is not their word here.' *Our word*, because they were Mossi people, Mustafa and his father and the other weavers in this group. They came from another town; they spoke a different language and they had different customs. *We are strangers here,* they said. *Like you.*

'Will you stay in Tamale?' she asked.

Mustafa shrugged. His father said, 'Home is Yendi.'

Home is Yendi, she thought. Home was Yendi, though Yendi was not where they originally came from: if they were Mossi, they must once have come south into Ghana from Upper Volta.

What would I say? she wondered, watching the hypnotic process of shuttle and beat, shuttle and beat, the steady growth of the cloth. Home was... Not with either of her parents, not now. She had grown out of that kind of home.

'These are my people,' Mustafa said, pausing for a moment and gesturing with his shuttle.

She too was with her people. Her father, obviously. Less obviously, with Jo and Kevin and Josh, with Michael and Father John. And with Stefan. And of course with Emmanuel also, so that then it got muddled. And home was *not* Ursula or Mandy or any of the other limp European women that she knew. So it was not simply *with my people*.

Home is where the heart is. The old saying came into her head, making her smile. Home had indeed become Tamale – scruffy, exciting/mundane place that it was – because her heart had rooted itself here. But sitting in the shelter with the weavers, lulled by the rhythm of the battens beating in

222

the wefts and the murmur of their quiet voices as they talked amongst themselves, the smile died away. She knew where she most felt *at home*, but it was an awkward, difficult, dead-ended kind of thing to know. The place where she felt most at ease and most challenged, most herself and most inspired to be more than herself, was when she stood within the circle of Michael's attention. That was where she felt *at home*, more than any other place she had ever been in. That was the one place in the world where she wanted to be. It was like a cloud passing over the sun, this realisation. As if the body heat went out of her. She stood up and took her leave, walking quietly away.

She was walking back to the main road when the sound of drumming caught her attention. It drew her sideways like a magnet, across a piece of waste ground to where a crowd of women were swaying in a shuffling dance. 'It is a wedding!' a woman shouted over the insistent beat of the drums. 'De bride ceremony.'

A large bossy woman spotted her standing at the back of the crowd of onlookers and came over to seize her by the hand and pull her out in front of the dancers. She jogged self-consciously, trying to move as the other women did, her eyes drawn by the hands of the drummer moving fast on the drum skins – his fingers beating tack-tack on the edge, the deep thrum of his palms on the centre. She watched his intent absorption as he leaned over the drums as if he was listening to the spirit of the drum speaking. She could hear the rhythm with her diaphragm. Suddenly she understood. These were people suspended between gods, the old gods which were here before and the newer gods that had come. The drummers were like Moses and Moses was like them, sharing another world, remote from hers although they were living side by side. And she would never have a proper grasp of it, however hard she tried.

She walked away, the sadness come back. Turned onto the main road towards the centre of town. *Sister! Sister!* She hadn't got the energy to return the greetings, or even to smile, but then a voice called her by name and there was Rose on the other side of the street, waving excitedly, and then the sun glinted off her glasses as she dashed dangerously across the road in a gap between cars and bicycles.

'What luck I see you! I was coming to de Low Cost later for tell you – I got de British Council grant! I goin' to London! It was mistake in de London office, dat why I not hearin' before now.'

'Oh Rose, I'm so glad for you! When are you leaving?'

'October – October 1st I have to be there. You must teach me plenty-plenty English! I do truly need it now!'

They walked into town arm in arm, talking busily about London and what Rose would do when she got there, and how the weather would be, until they parted near the Old Market. 'I go buy okra for my mother,' Rose said. 'See you Wednesday?'

Homesickness welled suddenly in Rose's wake. How dull and distant London seemed, how alluringly gentle its dullness. Anne shook the thought away sharply and made herself focus on the moment. A boy was bowling a bicycle wheel along the side of the road, driving it with a stick like something out of an eighteenth-century painting of rural England. An old man passed, leading a young goat by a piece of string tied to the stick round which its ear was folded. No wonder the goat was docile! She couldn't help laughing. Life was so vivid here. Ghana was alluring but never dull.

She picked up a taxi on the main road.

'I know!' the driver interrupted her as she started to tell him where to go. At the house they went through the usual good-humoured routine: he asked double what the fare should have been and then when she halved it he suggested she dash him the rest anyway. She, equally good-naturedly, refused.

'You take my taxi next time!' he ordered as he drove away in his backfiring yellow vehicle, as if she had just given him the full amount he'd asked for.

Joseph and John were sitting on the side of road. They jumped up when they saw her get out of the taxi. John had a small book in his hand. When they came closer she could see it was the ancient hardback copy of *A Midsummer Night's Dream* which she'd handed out at the end of term so they could take turns reading it during the holidays.

'Dis very-very hard book, Missanne. All funny words.'

'Why dis Shakespeare-man not write in good English?' John said, indignantly.

'He did, but good English was very different when he wrote this, three hundred years ago, just as good Dagbani was different then. Language changes. You would have difficulty understanding your own great-great-great-great grandfather.'

John looked sceptical.

Joseph said, 'But what is dis *fairy*, Missanne? My daddy say it all pagan stuff. He say it bad we learning pagan tings.'

'You know that in England there are big universities, some of them very old, where people go to learn? Well, tell your daddy that in the universities this Shakespeare is their special man. Many, many teachers study this special man in big libraries, and then they teach other people about him.

Anyway, the point is, you can write about something that doesn't really exist. When you write about a pretend life, which nobody believes is real, you can say something about your own life and times that might be dangerous to say out loud. It is what is called an allegory.'

Joseph said, 'But we can't see what he say in dis story at all at all, Missanne. It so hard to read! And what is dis donkey man?'

'Are you really struggling?'

They nodded. She looked back at the house, thinking. She was tired, but she could take the two of them home with her and go through a bit of the text with them. Just get them started, perhaps. But Moses was in the house today and he would listen in with his cynical, aloof expression and make her self-conscious. Perhaps she could take the boys to see Stefan? He surely wouldn't mind if they sat in the shelter in his garden and had an impromptu English lesson.

'Do you want me to read it through with you?'

Their eyes lit up. They set off up the road together, John carrying the book on his head because he needed his hands free to talk.

In the garden shelter Emmanuel made them tea, and then he and Stefan drifted quietly away and left them in peace. They went through the text, taking it in turns between the three of them to read a page each. An hour passed happily. Then she shooed them off home, anxious they shouldn't outstay their welcome in Stefan and Emmanuel's outdoor tearoom – and anyway she was exhausted. As they parted at the Mission gate, she to go home, John and Joseph to go off on an errand, they asked shyly if they might read some more with her tomorrow. She could think of no good reason to say no, apart from the risk of imposing of Stefan and Emmanuel. But they would probably enjoy the company.

Next afternoon, when she came out of the house at four as agreed, there was quite a little crowd waiting on the road. Joseph and John, and five other boys from the same class.

Joseph grinned and shrugged: 'Dey heard you is givin' classes. Dey wan' to come too.'

They wouldn't all be able to squeeze into the garden shelter. As they walked up to the Mission, the boys gambolling round her noisily, she pondered alternatives. Perhaps Father Morrissey would let them use a classroom? He surely would approve, given that it was educational. Especially since it was at no cost to the Mission.

Two days later and the little crowd had swelled to fifteen. They had been given the use of one of the classrooms. Even Thomas Nanfuri was there, the would-be priest who had *only bot a got* in her first-ever class. As gruff and unbending as ever.

Now that they were so many she allocated them each a part and they read aloud scene by scene, switching around now and then so that they all got a turn, even the taciturn Thomas. Their reading was sing-song, they stumbled over the words and had to stop frequently for explanations, but she was enjoying it as much as they were and was quite sad when the weekend came and they had to leave off until Monday.

The day they got to Act Five almost the entire class turned up. There was the usual noisy discussion of where they had got to, and what had happened so far, for the benefit of the newcomers. She had already decided that, as there were more than fifteen characters in Act Five, they might try acting it. She shared out the parts carefully, trying to make sure that everyone had something to do. Those who were there for the first time were attendant lords. She gave the part of Nick Bottom the weaver, playing Pyramus, to Joseph, and the part of Francis Flute the bellows-mender, playing Thisbe, to John, because really this had all been their initiative. She noticed the wistful shadow that passed across Thomas Nanfuri's face and gave him Snout, playing the Wall. He ducked his head stiffly in acknowledgement and peered over his friend's shoulder to look at his part.

'We'll skim through first and you can ask me questions so that you understand the text,' she said. 'Then we'll make a little play out of it. It will be a play within a play, because this is the scene where Bottom and the others put on their play for Theseus the Duke. This is the one they were rehearsing in Act Three Scene One, for those of you who were here that day.' Several of the boys laughed: they had enjoyed that scene so much they had asked to read it twice. 'When we stand up to act it you will have to share out the books so that the main characters have one each. The rest of you will have to make do. Yes, Thomas?'

'Madam, is I a speakin' part or is I a warl?'

'You are a man called Snout who is pretending to be a wall, and yes, you do speak.' Thomas looked alarmed and she wondered if she'd done the wrong thing giving him a speaking part but she could hardly take it away from him now and give it to somebody else. 'You do have some lines to say but not very many. You and Moonshine could share a book.'

She took them through the text. Thomas had more questions about his ten lines than everybody else put together but he was unusually animated. She got them to push the teacher's desk to one side so that they could use the dais as a small stage. It would be cramped, but Theseus and the courtiers could sit on the teacher's desk out of the way. They worked out roughly who would stand where and how they would move about in the small space. One of the boys hastily drew the outline of a palace on the blackboard to serve as a backdrop, and another added some cartoon flowers along the bottom.

She went to sit in one of the pupil's desks, their solitary audience of one.

They stumbled through the scene, reading their parts, some of them shyly but most of them really entering into the spirit. One or two, intentionally or otherwise, adlibbing shamelessly. She was transfixed by their faces. Even the self-conscious boys were totally absorbed. In their rich, musical voices the text began to come alive, like a new animal a god had breathed life into, even if at times the sense disappeared.

Pyramus and Thisbe, Moonshine, the Lion, and Thomas as the Wall stepped forward into the cramped space in the middle of the dais.

When his turn came, Thomas declaimed woodenly (but not inappropriately for a wall, she thought): '*In dis same interlude it doth befall Dat I, one Snout by name, present a warl*'. He got through the rest of his lines rapidly, partly because he left half of them out, standing stiffly to attention in the centre of the stage and reading awkwardly from the book which Moonshine held up for him.

'You got to make de crack, Thomas,' Joseph said,

229

straightening up suddenly and speaking in his normal voice. Thomas frowned. 'Like dis,' Joseph said, grabbing Thomas's hand and manhandling it into position to represent the hole in the wall.

Joseph bent down and peered exaggeratedly through Thomas's fingers, rolling his eyes from side to side: '*No Thisbe do I see,*' he said, in his most melodramatic voice.

A few lines later, when Thisbe said '*My cheery lips have often kiss'd thy stones,*', a look of such alarm spread over Thomas's face that it was obvious that, for all his questions earlier, he had not until now understood what was coming. His stretched-out hand quivered and he turned his head away, his eyes screwed up tight. Anne bit her lip, trying not to laugh. Joseph and John were crooning at one another through Thomas's fingers. The more everyone laughed, the more they hammed it up. Thomas's hand started to tremble. She saw it and thought he too was laughing.

'*Oh kiss me through de hole of dis vile wall,*' Joseph declaimed and John replied in his mincing falsetto, '*I kiss de wall's hole, not your lips at all.*' John bent down belatedly to match the action to the words and Thomas jumped as if he'd been burned, his flailing hand flicking up into John's face.

'Ow!' John stood up and clutched his nose, glaring at Thomas. 'Thomas, you s'posed to be a warl! Stand still den!'

The onlookers had collapsed, one boy laughing so hard he lay on his back on the floor and howled. Only Thomas and John were not laughing.

'I no want you kissing in my hand!' Thomas glared at John.

'It in de play, Thomas. You is de warl, de warl have a crack, I is de woman kissing in de crack.'

'Dis play is stupid!' Thomas said crossly, looking as if he might leave the stage at any moment.

'We'd better do that bit again. Do you want somebody else to take over your part, Thomas?' she asked, trying to keep her voice serious. Several hands shot up but Thomas declined the offer. There was something heroically tenacious about this boy, doomed always to be in slightly the wrong place at the wrong time. Though possibly – she thought as she watched him take up his position again (having first instructed John to kiss no closer than six inches from his hand) – possibly he was in fact a true clown, born with a sense of comic timing and the natural ability to keep a straight face.

The door opened. Father Morrissey.

Instantly the boys stood up straight and serious and silent. She stood up too and turned to face him, ready to explain.

'Sounds as if you're having fun,' he said, making it sound as if *fun* were a full-blown sin. But he closed the door and went away without further comment.

'From your line as Thisbe, then, John,' she said, sitting down again at the cramped desk. '*O wall, full often has thou heard my moans…*'

This time they got through to the end. She applauded, and from outside the open window came the sound of someone else clapping heartily. Father John stepped into view and leaned over the sill. 'Bravo! Bravo, boys! Really that was very good! Especially the Wall.' Thomas blushed coyly. 'Now, as you're all here – who's for a game of football?'

The next minute the room was empty, all of them gone except for Thomas, and one of the boys whose deformed foot meant he couldn't run. They helped her put the room straight, and pushed the heavy teacher's desk back into its rightful place.

'What we do now we finished reading dat?' Thomas asked.

'Nothing. I'm going to Kumasi the day after tomorrow. I shan't be back until just before the beginning of term.'

He looked crestfallen. Suddenly he brightened: 'But we could do a play! A proper play, with costumes. Next term we could do one.'

She looked at his shining eyes. He's right, she was thinking. We could.

18

Kumasi, late August

Dusk was settling like dust among the trees where white blossom glowed alongside the lemons and oranges hanging dense and dark among the leaves. Pale moths fluttered. The air was heady with fragrance, but Josh had begun to grizzle and Jo was agitated. The others had come back long ago, their horses flecked with foam and dark with sweat. She had declined their offers of a lift, preferring to wait for Anne. She hadn't been worried at first, but now it was beginning to get dark and she was sure something must have gone wrong to keep Anne out so late. Especially as she was apparently alone with Daoud, the Syrian trader with the sultry eyes, whom Jo instinctively disliked. Far too charming to be trustworthy, that Daoud. She lit another cigarette and chided Josh irritably as she walked him up and down under the citrus trees.

It was nearly dark when she heard Daoud's voice say, 'Aha, a smoking Jo and a sobbing Josh.'

The horses snorted as they ambled down the slope. Jo could just make out the grey pony Anne was riding, pale as a ghost behind the big dark horse that was Daoud's. Trust him, she thought. Trust Daoud to ride a straining great stallion.

'Jo! Are you still here? Why didn't you go home with the others?'

She heard the edge of irritation in Anne's voice and was stung. 'We were quite happy waiting,' she said in her own defence. Even as she said it she realised it was probably the wrong thing to say, but the truth would have been worse. *Because I needed to know you were all right. Because you're only here for a week and you're wasting it on bloody horses!*

She waited miserably, with a miserable baby on her hip, while they handed the horses over to the stable boy. Very mean, she thought, to have made the boy wait for them so late and then to leave him with work to do. The sight of Daoud pushing some *cedis* into the boy's hand didn't make her feel any more charitable. She suspected Daoud of ostentation. That gold chain round his neck, for a start, and his great big Land Rover! Not to mention the two valuable horses.

'Jump in,' he ordered, opening the back door of the Land Rover, 'we will run you back home.'

She climbed in, resenting the *we* and feeling more than ever like a sulky teenager, sitting side by side with Josh in the back while the two adults in the front conferred in low voices. They were discussing plans for the evening, which they'd obviously made while out riding and were now having to adapt in order to take her home first, but Josh was grizzling again and she couldn't hear what they were saying. She lifted him onto her lap, wondering, had she and Josh not been waiting at the stables for them, would Anne have gone straight out with Daoud without thinking to let her and Kevin know where she was?

When they reached the bungalow Anne got out as well.

'I thought you were going with him.'

'I want a shower first. He's coming back in an hour to pick me up.'

234

Jo heard the unspoken warning – *This is not something you and I are going to giggle about together*. Anne would go out with him to a bar, to a club, perhaps even to his house, and *she* was going to be relegated to mere observer, the dull married woman weighed down with a child, who must stay behind at home.

Later, Kevin asked her what the odds were that Anne wouldn't be back that night at all. As if he found it amusing. Jo locked herself in the bathroom and spent a long time weeping silently in the bath. She felt abandoned, betrayed. Friendship had fallen away from her, leaving a black hole in its wake. She knew it was her period coming on and making her miserable but knowing it meant nothing. Images of Anne, pale hair shining in candlelight, big grey eyes gazing into the sly dark eyes of the Syrian, kept coming into her mind. How exciting it must be to be Anne! The romance of being free! But it was Daoud she was jealous of, having Anne all to himself in a way she never could.

She knew she was going to make a fool of herself, clutching and clamouring until Anne recoiled in distaste. She knew she would, as she always did, destroy the thing she loved.

Kevin was the only human being who did not recoil from her. And because he didn't she thought him a fool.

Josh was different, of course.

The thought of Josh immediately made her hot and swollen heart contract in fear. What if something bad happened to him? A snake under the cot? A scorpion! Or he'd stopped breathing…

She climbed out of the bath, dried herself hurriedly and padded into his room to peer into the cot. He lay on his back, thumb in mouth. His little naked belly rose and fell tranquilly above the muslin nappy. The floor under the cot was empty, the shutters tightly closed against the threatening night.

She went to bed, leaving an unsuspecting Kevin reading in the sitting room, and cried herself to sleep.

In the morning when she staggered bleary-eyed to the bathroom, Anne was sitting at the table in the dining room, cool and poised in her pale blue dressing gown, drinking a prosaic mug of tea.

'Sorry, I didn't mean to startle you,' Anne said, amused. 'You look spaced out. Did Joshua have a disturbed night?'

'What time is it?' she asked, stretching and scratching her up-ended mop of hair. 'Eight-thirty? My God! Josh hasn't woken up yet! Better go and check…'

He was fast asleep. She came back into the dining room. 'He must have been totally worn out after yesterday. I didn't hear you come in.'

There was a mug of tea waiting for her on the table. Jo sat down. She could see Anne wasn't wearing anything underneath that casually elegant blue robe, trying not to let it show she was looking. It made her feel scruffy and scrawny and over-dressed in her old pyjamas. 'What time did you get in, then? Kevin bet me five *cedis* you wouldn't be back at all.'

'Oh he did, did he! In that case, you've just won five *cedis*. I don't like Daoud *that* much. We went to a bar but only for one drink. And then to a Lebanese restaurant for dinner. Kevin was still up when I got in so he can't duck out of it.'

'If you didn't sleep with him why are you smirking like a cat?'

Anne laughed. 'I don't smirk!'

236

'Looks like a smirk to me.'

'Well just a bit of a smirk, perhaps. I've been thinking. You're right – it's unhealthy lusting after priests. Much more refreshing to have a good plain old-fashioned flirt. Specially with a good-looking man.'

'Humph,' grunted Jo, her spirits rising dizzily. Flirt, not fuck – she'd heard the critical distinction. Though she might have said that, for herself, she would much prefer it if Anne went on lusting after harmless priests rather than flirting with sultry Syrian merchants. 'I don't know about good-looking. Stuffed full of testosterone, yes. You can see that a mile off. Just like his horse! That man would flirt with a cabbage.'

'Why thank you, ma'am,' Anne said. Then she added, 'It's true though. He could flirt the shell off a tortoise.'

Jo snorted with delight. 'Do you want some more tea?' she asked. 'What shall we do today?'

Anne came out of the airport building and got on the airport bus to go into town. It was nice to be back. The air was drier and paler than Kumasi. It was strange being the only white face on the bus again after the cosmopolitan world she'd just left. Funny world, Kumasi. Not very real, somehow, but Jo and Kevin seemed to like it.

She wasn't sorry she hadn't stayed longer. Poor old Jo. That troubling, unclean edge of jealousy, the undercurrent of neediness: it did get tiring after a while. She watched idly as an elderly man in a white robe came out of the airport building and walked towards the bus. The Buddy Holly glasses looked incongruous under the splendid white turban. She watched the group of men he was with trying to persuade him not to get on the bus. Eventually he turned unwillingly and went back into the terminal, surrounded by his entourage.

Still the bus waited. Even without glass in the windows the heat was nearly unbearable. Passengers fanned themselves with their hands and complained loudly. From beyond the airport building the background roar of aeroplane engines rose in pitch. A few minutes later she saw the plane rise steeply into the air and swoop away, back towards Kumasi. The bus driver started the engine and they moved off towards town.

They were near the police barrier on the edge of Tamale, just outside the big mosque which was painted bright green, when a crowd of men blocking the road forced the bus to a halt. The men surrounded the vehicle, shouting fiercely. The bus driver shouted back. The passengers were getting to their feet and shouting too. Anne looked at the rough-looking men outside. Every one of them seemed to have a rock in each hand. Their faces were ugly with anger. The woman in the seat in front of her had jumped up and was shaking her fist through the window and yelling.

Then, just as suddenly, it was over. The men in the road stood back, the bus pulled away, and the passengers sat down. They were still shouting but now it was with relief. 'What was that all about?' she asked the woman in the seat in front, but the woman just grinned and said, 'Crazy mans!'

The house was hot after being shut up all day. She propped open the front door and opened the back door too, to get the air moving, and then she took her rucksack to her airless room. It was just as she'd left it, only dusty. 'Hello house!' she said out loud, surprised into affection. It was familiar now, and almost homely.

A vehicle pulled up outside, and suddenly there was her dad, his face strained as he hurried across the room and grabbed her to him in a hug.

'Hello, Daddy,' she said in surprise. 'Did you miss me?'

'Thank God you're safe! What happened? We heard there'd been an incident with the airport bus!'

'Nothing happened. Not really. There was a bit of a stand-off between the bus and some men with rocks, that's all. Outside the spearmint mosque.'

'So nobody got hurt?'

'I don't think so. Why? What was it all about?'

He sat down suddenly on the nearest chair and wiped his face on his handkerchief. 'Somebody came into the office saying the airport bus had been stoned and of course I knew you'd be on it.'

'But why would they attack the bus?'

'A visiting Sufi Imam was due to come and speak at Friday prayers. The Sunnis didn't like it so they got up a rent-a-crowd protest. Apparently he wasn't even on the bus – he went straight back to Kumasi on the plane when they told him there'd be trouble.'

'That must have been the little old man in Buddy Holly glasses! He didn't go back willingly. They had a hell of a job persuading him not to get on the bus.'

'The mosque where you stopped was stuffed full of guns, apparently. The police raided it, must have been just after you'd passed. I am so glad to see you and all in one piece! Did you have a good holiday?'

'I did. I had a great time. Did you manage without me?'

'We got by.'

He sat and chatted a little while but now the panic was over she could tell he was anxious to get back to work.

As he was going out of the room he paused by the bookcase and picked up a sheet of paper, torn out of an exercise book. 'In case I forget, there's a note here from Father Stefan.'

She was surprised. What could be so important that it needed to be put in writing? She unfolded the rough sheet.

Deer Ann Pleese you must scuse my no good English. Specially riting. John and Dom and me we goin Wagadoogoo Weds next in car but I bin tinking it long long way and I too old for fancy trips but you nice thin girl – not too big. I like you go for me for treat. It make an old man hapy to tink he give you holiday. (I don ask you do my business for me ha ha. John do dat). Why not you go in car to Wagadoogoo 2 – 3 days with Dom and John. You like – nice place. Your good frend Stefan

She passed the note to her father. He read it and chuckled. 'Don't know about *fancy trip.* That Renault Four's an old tin can, and you wouldn't want to get stuck in the back seat with John, but then he would be doing the driving, so you wouldn't.'

'It's a sweet thought but I couldn't possibly go. It's much too close to term beginning, and anyway I've just had my holiday.'

'But Anne, you can't pass up an opportunity to see Upper Volta! And Ougadougou is fun – lovely food, fantastic market. Full of weaving! You don't see those Mali blankets here. I'd take you myself but you know how it is – such a crazy time of year…'

She was unconvinced.

'Come on, Anne! Why the lack of enthusiasm? You've

got all weekend and Monday and Tuesday beforehand. And you'll have another weekend after you get back before school actually starts. Surely you can get done what you need to in that time, if you put your mind to it?'

She'd promised Rose a last session or two of English practice before she left for London. She hadn't finished the *Tom Jones* notes, or preparing *Romeo and Juliet* for the new Fourth Formers. But most of all, Michael would be back soon. She didn't want to miss a single day of him! She beat the thought down hastily but her dad was too busy telling her what fun it would be to notice. 'Where would I stay? And what would I do all day?'

'What? That's not like you!' He sounded genuinely shocked. 'There are hotels galore in Ouagadougou – it's not like Tamale-here. Upper Volta used to be French, for God's sake. You may not get another chance like this. Go for it!'

'You aren't trying to get rid of me, are you?' she asked in a small voice. 'I've only just come back.'

He stared at her in surprise. 'But we're talking about three days at the most! I'd only be here in the evenings if at all.'

Michael wasn't due back for another week, and anyway she really shouldn't let his movements influence hers. 'Okay then. I'll go.'

'I'll be passing the Mission now, if you want to write a note to Stefan.'

She wrote it quickly and he took the paper from her and stuffed it into his breast pocket as he went out of the room.

'Oh, by the way,' he said, poking his head back round the door, 'Michael got back yesterday.'

19

Ouagadougou, September 8th to 10th

'What's this?'

Michael patted the battered bonnet of the Land Rover. 'Do you like it? This old beast is the result of Father Benedict's latest fundraising drive among the good people of Hastings. Hop in.'

She clambered up into the cab. It was built like a tank. 'Father Stefan isn't going to drive this, is he?'

'We'll keep the Renault going as long as we can, so he and Vanni have something to potter about in.' He started up the engine. The cab rattled. 'I have to warn you, we will probably be nostalgic for that Renault by the time we get to Ouagadougou: she's a rough old beast.'

She let him make small talk as they drove through town. She was still stunned that it was just the two of them. Had he manoeuvred this? The possibility made her tongue-tied, and rather uncomfortable.

It was six in the morning but it was market day and already the roads were busy and Michael's chatter dried up as he struggled with the gearbox. Perhaps they would have to turn back, she thought, as third gear proved elusive yet again. She asked once about his sister – the one whose husband had been killed – but he didn't reply. Maybe he didn't want to talk about it. It felt as if they were a pair of strangers.

The town thinned at last, and so did the numbers of pedestrians and donkey-carts.

'Aha!' he said, changing gear to overtake a cow. '*Now* I've got the measure of you, girl!'

She looked at him sharply but he was talking to the Land Rover. He sat back in his seat.

'Morrissey was shaping up to veto this trip, it was touch and go. I certainly didn't deserve to go off on a jaunt so soon after coming back from my hols.'

She listened to his voice, light and bantering. His holiday voice. John had asked him to come, he said. To share the driving. And then had gone down last night with a bad dose of the runs. Dominic was already sick with malaria. Everybody else who'd thought they might come had decided to stay in Tamale for one reason or another. They had considered cancelling. 'But I'd set up a whole raft of meetings in our sister mission in Ouagadougou by then. Besides, somebody has to go,' he said. 'We've run out of Communion wine, and Stefan needs his plants.'

Not her at all then. Just chance. Michael the Priest. She cheered up. 'I'm surprised he trusts you with them.'

'Oh but he doesn't! He nearly changed his mind this morning when he heard John wasn't coming and it was only you and me. Thank God he didn't – he's a terrible fidget, and he gets carsick too. Do not whatever you do let me set off for home without the bloody plants!'

She looked out of the window at the tall yellow grass, solid as fences, blocking in either side of the road, and wished time could be made to stand still, right here on the road, with the women striding gracefully in the shadow of their massive head-loads towards the town. The luxury of a day driving to Ouagadougou suspended in front of her, a

243

whole day there tomorrow, and then a day driving back again, suddenly rendered magical by the fact of it being just the two of them.

'Now we've got the worst bit done,' Michael said, relaxing back into his seat, 'you can give me the full low-down on what you've been up to while I've been away. I heard about the play-readings from John – sounds like I missed a whole lot of fun! What else? How are the Dagbani lessons going?'

'Rose is great but my Dagbani is still rubbish. I'm no good at languages.'

'It'll come, it'll come. I'm glad you liked Rose. What else did you get up to?'

'I went to stay with Jo and Kevin in Kumasi for a week, as I told you the other day, and I went riding again. That was fun.' She paused, putting out a hand to steady herself against the dashboard as Michael zig-zagged round some potholes. 'And I spent a lot of time with the weavers here. But I've decided not to do a thesis.'

He shot her a surprised look. 'Why? I'd have thought they would make an excellent subject for research!'

She said slowly, 'They would. But I realised while I was in Kumasi that I don't want to do a PhD. I feel… I don't know, I just feel I want to be doing *real* things. Studying the weavers here is one thing, but I don't want to go back to university to be an academic. I want to do something practical, like learn how to teach properly.'

He grinned into the windscreen. 'That's my girl! I knew you'd got the makings of a real teacher in you!' She glowed, until he added, 'As soon as ever I set eyes on you.'

He asked her more about the play-reading and how it had come about. And then at last he told her about his own summer, though he didn't really say much. Pauline was bearing up. The boys were surviving. His dad was getting old. You can't carry events from one world to the other and have them still sound real, he said. But she didn't think it was a question of different worlds: she thought he didn't talk about himself, whichever world he was in.

'I meant to ask you – what happened about that English woman? The one Ursula wanted to embroil you with. With the child.'

'Mandy?' she said, her heart sinking. She'd been so hoping he would have forgotten about it, so that she could forget to tell. 'Nothing much. I think she went back to London in the end.'

'I take it from something in your voice that you *did* get involved then?'

'I did.'

'And?'

'And…you were right. You were right, I shouldn't have. It was horrible. He was really angry with me! And he probably had every right to be angry.'

'So – was going to see him something you did because your head told you to, or because your heart did?'

'I didn't want to get involved but I felt I ought to.'

'Well there you are, Annie. You should trust your instincts more. Forget about the old head, just follow your heart.'

Oh I would! she thought, looking out of the side window. *If only I could, I would!*

Two unmanned police posts a mile apart marked the non-committal border. From here, swinging up and down along the dusty switchback of the road, Upper Volta looked only

245

subtly different, and yet, for all the rolling grassland and the scrub trees, it emphatically was *not* Ghana. The landscape was becoming steadily drier as they travelled north, the trees farther apart and more stunted: true savannah, marching fast towards the desert lands. Above them, the vaulted sky was studded with scudding clouds. Below, cloud shadows raced across the pale, empty landscape. Groups of people walked from nowhere to nowhere along the taut thread of the road. They wore simple, hand-woven cloths in white or indigo, shabby from the sun, very low-key after the printed factory cottons of Ghana. But the goats skittering across in front of the car were the same, and their young kids on stiletto hooves, skidding to a halt just in front of the Land Rover before diving back into the dry grass along the edge of the tarmac.

They passed a series of small lakes, lying like pale, glittering discs among the yellow undulations of the hills. Pink and white water lilies floated serenely on the glassy water.

'Full of crocs' he said. 'I'll show you, on the way back.'

It felt like climbing back inside a second skin, this long slow sensation of relaxing into his company. But when his hand, reaching for something in the glove box, accidentally brushed against her knee she jumped as if an electric shock had fired through her. It was hard to believe he didn't notice. Hard to believe he hadn't felt it too. But when she sneaked a look at him his face was untroubled. Devilry made her ask, 'Should I be here? Shouldn't you have left me behind, if the others couldn't come?'

He shot her a startled look. 'Don't be daft!' he said.

It was nearly dark as they approached the city. France suddenly and unexpectedly came out to meet them: jaunty

Deux-Chevaux tooted, boys on *velocettes* puttered past with fresh baguettes held across the handlebars. But the boys were black, and the dust rising off the road merged in the early dusk with the dark red of a horizon against which stood the thorny desert silhouettes of naked acacia trees.

He suggested she find herself a room at a small hotel he knew of near the centre of town. Standing with Michael in the shabby reception area with the key to her room in her hand, she hesitated, hoping he might suggest they meet for supper. Or failing that, at least he might suggest meeting up tomorrow. But he said only that he would come back for her at noon the day after tomorrow. And suddenly he was gone.

The hotel was scruffy but the family who ran it were friendly and the pretty courtyard with its irrigated shrubs and climbers was a world away from the endless dried-up grasslands they had been driving through all day. She followed the boy up an iron staircase to the long balcony connecting the first floor rooms. In places the balcony was almost submerged in lush growth and hanging creepers. Moths like flying saucers flitted among over-sized flowers and bats swooped. Outside each room, cane chairs and coffee tables suggested quiet reading by day and evening drinks at dusk. But not alone, she thought, as the boy took the key off her and unlocked a door. The empty chairs would make it seem so much lonelier, sitting there as one when it so easily might have been as two... She followed the boy into the room. It was large, simply furnished. On the double bed there was a handsome hand-woven woollen blanket from Mali, very distinctive. The night was warm now, but it would be cool later, even cold, this close to the desert.

She sat on the bed. Through the thin fabric of her summer skirt the blanket was rough against her skin. The weak light bulb flickered as if here, as in Tamale, the power supply was erratic, and she saw there was a half-burned candle on a saucer on the bedside table and a box of matches.

Suddenly she felt too weary to go out alone in search of an evening meal. She ordered a cheese sandwich to eat in her room. Why not? she thought, adding a glass of red wine to the order. She was in an ex-French colony, after all.

The boy came with the tray: half a baguette, the cheese Camembert and very good. As was the wine. And a little bowl of olives, unasked for and somehow more frivolous seeming even than the wine. More confusing as to quite where she was. Europe in Africa, Africa in Europe? But with food and wine inside her she felt a little less lost.

She read for a while, sitting on the bed. Took a long shower, luxuriating in the twin novelties of hot water and cool night air. Went early to bed. But could not sleep. Michael's presence was too vivid. The outline of his forehead and nose against the light of the window as he drove, burned into her consciousness. The light catching in the fuzz of his close-cropped hair. The shape of his arm, the line of his thigh under the thin cotton of his trousers, strong, square-kneed, so tantalisingly close to her own. That electric moment when his hand had brushed over her knee.

Crazily, the same word echoed over and over in her head, out of nowhere. Ridiculous word. *Coitus.*

Coitus interruptus.

Coitus no interruptus?

Coitus.

Tossing and turning. Passing her hands down across the

interesting thrust of her breasts, which had gone so long untouched. The taut nipples aching so much to be stroked. The hard outcrops of her hips. Down her willing thighs. At any moment he would knock on the door after all. How could he not be drawn here by the powerful thread of her yearning? Was that his footfall just then in the courtyard below? Whatever his promises and vows, surely he must be feeling this too? It couldn't just be her, alone in her head! He must, in the end, turn to her as she longed – longed so achingly – to turn to him.

But he did not come. Only the mosquitoes came, whining in the dark. And the cheerful, inconsequential feet of fellow guests, passing nonchalantly in the courtyard.

Once, suddenly, a woman laughed – a throaty, sexy, half-smothered African laugh – in the room below. But nobody climbed the iron staircase to her upper room.

The next day dawned hot and clear. A desert heat, drier and paler than the humid rainy season heaviness of Tamale, which was halfway to the tropical heat of the forests.

She went early to the dining room and ate a decidedly Continental breakfast. Butterflies had replaced the moths among the flowers in the courtyard. Little birds flitted in and out of the leaves. After breakfast she sat in the pleasant shade of the balcony outside her room, reading her book and watching the wildlife, and the small boy who wrestled with the hose in the courtyard below, watering the plants and rather more of the walls and the paving than was strictly necessary but he didn't think anyone was watching.

She went out to explore.

The market was laid out in regimental lines under magnificent baobab trees. In the cloth section, hand-woven blankets were stacked on the ground outside little shops made of corrugated iron. The sing-song voices calling her to come and look were speaking pidgin French and she began to enjoy herself, struggling with her rusty French and making them laugh. She went from stall to stall, bargaining hard. As she moved slowly down the line an incomprehensible commentary fired backwards and forwards over her head from stallholder to stallholder but it wasn't aggressive. It sounded like fun. Besides, there were piles of blankets and hand-woven cloth everywhere. It was a buyer's heaven.

Hours later, two lovely blankets tucked safely under her arm in a large bundle wrapped in newspaper and tied with string, she made her way to the restaurant Michael had recommended: a place run by French nuns but serving such good food that it was, he said, where most European visitors, from priests to businessmen, liked to go for lunch. It was late but the place was still full. The air was loud with voices and heady with the aroma of meat cooked in butter and olive oil, those most foreign of ingredients in the middle of Africa. A nun (her neat, short-skirted habit revealing good legs) led the way to a table recently vacated by two wealthy-looking African men in dark business suits. Following the diminutive nun through the crowded dining room, eyes down but senses acutely alert to Michael's possible presence, she tried not to look self-conscious, but nobody called out her name.

Under cover of reading the menu she surveyed the room. A table of six priests in dog collars and two men without lingered silently over the remains of their meal: none of them was Michael. In the corner, a large group of Latin-looking men in dark slacks and white shirts was getting up to leave. The rest of the tables were small groups of pallid Europeans.

She had just decided on onion soup to start when one of the men from the Latin group paused by her table.

'Anne! What are you doing here? I had no idea you were in town.'

Daoud! Handsome, solid, full-blooded Daoud, with a look of pleasure in his hooded eyes. His neat beard trimmed close, his hooked nose more regal than ever. It had never occurred to her, either, that she might run into him anywhere but in Kumasi, and Kumasi was several lifetimes south of here.

'I'm here on business,' he said. 'What about you?'

'Just visiting for a couple of days,' she said, 'with a friend.'

He glanced down at the table, set only for one, and regarded her quizzically. She knew what he was wondering. She could let him think she was here with a man, or she could make herself available. He raised one sardonic eyebrow. Oh, what the hell, she thought. 'I hitched a lift with a priest from one of the missions in Tamale. Father Michael. He was coming up for some kind of symposium and I thought I'd tag along and be a tourist for a couple of days.' She could see the thought processes going on in his head.

'You mean you're on your own in town?' Daoud frowned and glanced at his departing companions, who were laughing back at him from the doorway. 'Look, I can't get out of my meeting this afternoon but you shouldn't be on your own.' Not noticing her bridle, drumming his fingers impatiently on the cloth while he considered. 'No, really I *can't* get out of this one. But you will come and join us for dinner tonight.'

Was it a question, or a command? She was tempted to refuse. But there was something boyish in his fierce eyes that implored as well as commanded, and she had no other plans, and only unrealistic hopes. Better to be decisive, face up to reality instead of waiting like a pale ghost for the impossible to come galloping over the horizon. She inclined her head slightly. He smiled, looking once again like a confident sheikh as he bowed politely and kissed her hand. She was immediately irritated with herself for not holding out.

'The beefsteak is the best thing on the menu,' he said, gesturing at the menu card in her hand. 'I'll pick you up at 7.30. Which is your hotel?'

Shortly before seven, as she was coming out of the shower, there was a knock at the door.

'Just a minute!' she called, her heart swelling painfully with sudden hope as she grabbed her dress off the bed. She started to pull the dress on over her head but it stuck awkwardly on her wet skin. She threw it down and wrapped herself hurriedly in the bath-towel instead.

She opened the door a crack, her hair dripping onto her shoulders, and shivered in the sudden draught of cool night air. Daoud was standing to one side of the doorway leaning on the doorpost, smiling his lazy, approving smile.

'I thought you were coming at seven-thirty,' she said.

'It was more convenient to come now. No need to rush. I will wait.'

She expected him to sit outside on the balcony but it seemed rude to close the door on him, so she left it ajar and picked her clothes up off the bed to take them to the bathroom to dress. When she looked back she saw that he had taken this as an invitation to come into the room. He bent to pick a scrap of material up off the floor. 'You've dropped something.'

She looked down at the limp little grey rag he was holding out. She felt her face go hot as she took her knickers from him. Felt the answering coolness of his arrogance and was doubly irritated. All the same, she couldn't help being flattered. The undisguised warmth of his admiration made a refreshing change, elderly knickers notwithstanding. 'Thank you.'

She hoped it was a dignified retreat. In the bathroom she towelled her hair dry and brushed it out quickly before tying it up in her standard knot, but she did take more care over it than usual. She wished that the dress hadn't got so crumpled on the journey. She hadn't really been expecting to wear it when she stuffed it into her rucksack as an afterthought.

Coming back into the bedroom she avoided looking at Daoud, acutely conscious of the expanse of the double bed between them, of the intensity of his eyes watching her.

'Beautiful Anne,' he murmured, his husky voice catching. 'You will dazzle my colleagues and make them seethe with jealousy. Here, I have brought you a gift.' He held out a slender package wrapped in scarlet tissue paper. 'You will find you need it – the nights can be cold here, near the desert.'

She opened it warily. A silk shawl, very fine and soft, a lustrous deep pink.

He took the shawl from her, shook it out capably, and (with an intimacy she wasn't quite ready for but couldn't help enjoying) draped it deftly round her head and shoulders. Hmm, well practised! she thought, as his voice said softly, somewhere near her ear, 'How lucky that you are wearing black.' He stood back and scrutinised her severely. 'That suits you. It suits you very well.'

She looked down at the shawl, avoiding his gaze, and fingered the knotted fringe. 'Is this the sort of thing you trade in?'

'Among other things. I import ladies' clothes, I export carvings and gold to Europe. In the main.'

'And your colleagues?'

'Oh between us, a bit of everything. You will find plenty to talk about, from fridges to perfumes. We cover everything that is of interest to women.'

He'd misunderstood who she was but she wasn't sufficiently interested in him to care. It was easier to accept his guiding hand on the small of her back – with that small in-spite-of-herself frisson – and the sneaking pleasure of being guided to his brand new jeep. He ushered her into the vehicle and went round to climb into the driver's seat. He started the engine, and paused, his hand on the state-of-the-art cassette deck on the dashboard.

'You like Stevie Wonder.' Again, the question sounding like a statement, as if her response was only a formality, but he was looking at her with that slight, boyish uncertainty in his eyes.

'I do...'

'Okay then. We have Stevie Wonder. Let's go.'

With 'Superstition' blasting, they swung away from the kerb.

She watched the busy traffic, feeling – just as she had in Kumasi – profoundly disturbed. Without doubt, Daoud was one of the most handsome men she had ever met (apart from the equally disturbing Dr Yiri Jebuni, on that dreadful day she'd prefer not to remember). He looked down at her with those dark brooding eyes, out of his sheikh's face that made her think of hunting with hawks, of camels, scattered tents, and the endless dark expanses of the stars. His was a wild beauty, but when she was with him she felt caged. For all his romantic courtesy, his ancient code of protectiveness, his conversation was oddly banal. Instead of feeling like a romantic heroine when she was with him, she felt caught in the snare of his attention.

There were other inconsistencies, too. He looked like a desert Arab but he was a Syrian Christian from a family of traders. He had lived all his life in cities. He wasn't ascetic, although he looked it. She suspected that in other company than hers he was more a playboy than a gentleman. His protectiveness felt proprietorial: she had suspected in Kumasi that she might be under scrutiny as possible marriage material, for all the slightness of their relationship. It *was* exciting, being with him: he exuded such rich, deep sensuality. The way he looked at her made her stomach turn over. But was it him, or her own susceptibility, that moved her? And if she were to reciprocate, would she fall out of the net of his interest anyway? Instinct told her that men like Daoud bedded prostitutes and wanted virgins for marriage. It felt safer, and simpler, to retain his respect, so she held herself carefully aloof while he flirted about her like a stallion around a young filly. And the more she did so, of course, the more he flirted. It made her feel very odd, sitting beside him in his expensive jeep. She could feel the warmth of his sexuality and her own instinctive response, as if her body were a dog, off following a scent all on its own and leaving her brain behind, and that made her feel treacherous. Which in turn made her impatient. What was the point of being faithful to a dear but oblivious priest? She was being ridiculous. Just get on with it! she said to herself. Have a good time. Stop worrying about it!

'Where are we going?' she asked. But only for the sake of saying something.

'A motel,' he said. Where he and his colleagues were staying. 'A novel place,' he added, but he wouldn't say why.

They drove out of the small city and across a dark stretch of open land towards an arc of bright lights which, when they got close enough to read it, said *Safari Mote*, the *l* blacked out. She couldn't see much to be surprised by, unless you counted the expensive cars lined up inside the gates. I don't think I'm going to like this, she thought as they parked up on the end of the row.

They walked into the low-lying main building, past uniformed doormen wearing white gloves. The circular reception area was lined on either side with two large curving glass tanks a few feet wide. In each tank a single lion paced up and down, a male on the right, a female on the left. For all the splendour of the surroundings the glass was grimy and the lions looked moth-eaten. All the same, she was startled, and Daoud looked satisfied. How could the glass be strong enough to contain an adult lion? Very pissed-off lions too, by the look of it, however jaded. But the staff on the reception desk in the middle of the room looked relaxed, as if they were so used to them they no longer even noticed the rancid smell.

Daoud ushered her into the dining room. Unsurprisingly, it was built on a safari theme: a large circular room with a central core of trunk-like pillars supporting a thatched roof. Around the pillars in a circle there was another glass wall. Lions would have made uncomfortable dining companions, but this tank contained pythons.

Pythons, not carpet snakes, she told herself sternly, staring through the glass. She could feel the edge of fear creeping in under her skin. She never used to be scared of snakes! She refused to be now, especially with Daoud watching. She made herself gaze into the enclosure coolly, studying the thick ropes of the handsomely patterned bodies. The pythons lay in a sandy hollow under the bright lights, three or four of them tangled loosely together. And they were not going anywhere. Indeed, it was difficult to believe they were real, except when one of them shifted slightly, like a sliding of silk, or a dark tongue flicked.

'Thirty foot of living handbag in there,' Daoud said.

They deserve better than this tank, Anne was thinking, but he misread her expression and smiled down at her reassuringly. Which was irritating, but before she could think of a suitable comment the door opened and his colleagues trooped in.

It was a pleasant enough evening. The food was exotic: gazelle and antelope appeared on the menu. 'Probably camel and horsemeat,' Daoud said, and advised her to try snails instead. 'French snails, of course,' he added quickly. 'Safely imported in tins.' So, in the middle of Africa, she ate French snails, secretly horrified at the thought of those giant planes flying them in to a country poised on the brink of drought and famine. They drank a lot of very good wine. Then even better brandy. In the candlelight the dark Syrian faces were gentle and genial, focussing on her, the only woman, as if she too were some rare animal, imported suddenly into their midst. They flirted with her, but deferentially, as if acknowledging she was Daoud's. All the same, she was touched by their amiable courtesies. The wine warmed her like love, the candlelight was generous, and her critical mind, which found the whole place appalling and longed to be out of it, conveniently lay down and slept.

It was very late when Daoud took her back to her hotel. He hadn't made any move to suggest she stay with him so she hadn't needed to decide on a response.

The reception desk was deserted. He reached over the counter and took her key off its hook. She expected him to say goodnight here in the lobby on safely neutral territory but he led her up to her room, his arm still round her waist as it had been from the car park – a light firm touch which she found very pleasant and wished she didn't, because she still didn't know what he was expecting, or how she was going to deal with it when the time came. They passed under the bougainvillea and up the metal treads of the outside staircase to her room. Her alcohol-softened mind was racing ahead, undecided still. Part of her wanted to ask him in, to lean against him and let him run his hands over her body. She didn't want him, and yet she did: her body was clamouring for him, even if her heart was not.

He put the key into the lock and turned it. She stood watching him as if she were somebody else, the seconds of her freedom ticking by. A bat swooped just over his head. The dark hair on the back of his bronzed neck curled with a surprising innocence. As she leaned against the doorpost where he had leaned earlier in the evening she was remembering him riding his proud horse in Kumasi as if he and his mount were fused into one animal. The pink shawl was soft on her shoulders. The fragrance of jasmine wreathed about them. He took the key out of the door and turned towards her.

If I ask him in, she thought, he will stop really wanting me, which is not a problem because I don't really want him. But if I ask him in, I might end up wanting him after all and by then it would probably be too late.

That wasn't what decided her. It certainly wasn't hopeless thoughts about Michael. What decided her was the sudden desire to hold on to the heightened excitement of the moment unresolved. Surprising herself, she took the key gently out of Daoud's hand, kissed him fleetingly on the cheek, murmured a swift thank you, and slipped into her room, closing the door softly but firmly behind her.

She stood with her back against the door, her heart pounding. She waited until she heard him, some minutes later, move away. For a moment or two she felt clever. She thought of Michael and felt honourable. Then her emotions plummeted: she had been too clever. She had won a victory (and Daoud's respect, she was certain) that she didn't even want. What she wanted just now, what she urgently needed, was neither respect nor romance but just a good plain common-or-garden fuck.

She went to bed, more miserable than if she'd stayed in alone all evening and – after so much wine – very, very thirsty.

Next morning Michael, finding his business concluded over an early breakfast, went straight to Anne's hotel to suggest they get on the road sooner than he'd said.

There was no one on the reception desk but the key to Room 11 was not on its hook and he couldn't see anyone at breakfast in the dining room so he guessed she was probably still in her room. It was just after eight-thirty as he climbed the metal staircase to the upper rooms and knocked on her door.

Anne looked dismayed when she opened the door. He was surprised but didn't think much about it: she was dressed, but so tousled and flushed that he thought she had maybe fallen asleep again after breakfast and he'd just woken her. She pulled the door to behind her and stood with her hand on the doorknob while he told her he'd like to get going as soon as she was ready, could she manage that? 'Yes,' she said, still with her back to the door and her hand on the knob.

'I'll sit here then, till you're ready,' he said, pulling out one of the chairs on the balcony. 'If that's all right?' he added.

She started to speak but a voice from the other side of the door interrupted. A male voice.

Michael felt himself go very still and quiet inside. Anne shot him an odd look. She opened the door and said to the man inside her room, 'I can't. Father Michael's here. We're leaving now.'

Father Michael, Michael noted, the formality absurdly hurtful.

A tall handsome man, very dark – Italian, perhaps – appeared in the doorway. He looked Michael up and down for a moment in a proprietorial fashion before stepping out onto the balcony.

'Father Michael…'

Michael took the proffered hand. He felt the cool firm grip and gripped hard back.

'I have heard a lot about you,' the stranger said, then without bothering to introduce himself, the smooth bastard turned his back and murmured something in Anne's ear. Michael saw him bend to kiss her, too. He looked away but he heard the kiss, and when he looked again he saw how

Anne was blushing. Then the stranger shook hands with him again and bowed politely, but still withholding his identity like a card he had slipped back into his shirt pocket against his chest, watching Michael with his cool, hooded eyes. Mocking eyes, Michael thought as the man padded away on rubber-soled shoes, loose limbed as a cheetah.

Through the door he could see Anne hurriedly stuffing clothes into her rucksack, looking very flustered. Behind her, an expanse of crumpled bed. He watched her for a moment, considering. *Who was that?* he might so easily have asked, and saying it might have made things normal again between them. But he said nothing, and neither did she. He went to sit on one of the balcony chairs with his back to her open door.

Michael drove aggressively, crashing the gears. He cursed cyclists and donkey carts. She sat beside him in the passenger seat, shocked into silence. She had never seen him bad-tempered before and it made her feel so guilty she had to remind herself it was only in her thoughts that she'd transgressed, and how could Michael presume to judge her for that? Trouble was, she had transgressed so thoroughly in those thoughts that if she started explaining she was sure her voice would make it sound as if she was lying. Safer to keep quiet.

She cursed Daoud for coming back this morning. He'd forgotten to ask her for her address last night. Forgotten on purpose, she thought now. Though Daoud couldn't possibly have guessed what it meant to her, that he should have run into Michael quite like that.

Or had he guessed? It annoyed her, the way he'd almost seemed to be gloating over Michael's obvious misreading of the situation. It had been written so clearly all over Michael's priestly face: he thought Daoud had been there all night. He might as well have accused them out loud! If he had, she reflected, she would have been able to put him right. But as things were, what could she say? She couldn't think of one single thing she might say and it not seem suspiciously self-justifying or just plain absurd.

It probably hadn't even occurred to Daoud that Michael might be a rival. Daoud just enjoyed people thinking he was her lover. He had strutted so proudly in front of his colleagues last night, with more than a hint that he and she were already a couple, and yet she had a very strong impression that she would have to remain unobtainable if she wanted to retain Daoud's interest. *Might as well have stayed in all evening,* she could hear herself telling Jo when she got back, *for all the good it did me.*

It hurt to be thought of badly by Michael! Especially when he'd jumped to the wrong conclusions. *Bloody Daoud.*

She kept her face turned away, watching unseeingly through the side window as they drove out of the city. Her eyes smarted with the effort not to cry. She was so tangled up with feeling that she kept forgetting to breathe. Whatever Michael might think of her, his anger was shocking. It felt like a physical blow. How he could think *this* badly of her? But if it was a question of guilt, she was guilty. It didn't matter that it wasn't with Daoud. She *had* made love with other men, it didn't matter who or when. Not just one man, either. Three, if anybody was counting.

Well, if Michael had thought she was somebody else then he'd been wrong, and that was *his* problem. This was who she was. Her complicated history was what made the built-up layers of herself, like the inside of a sea shell.

Michael said something.

'Pardon?'

'I said, "Bloody cyclist!"'

They lapsed back into silence. As they got out further out on the open road heading south the traffic eased, exposing the silence hanging inside the cab as heavy as fog. In the back of the Land Rover a tray of potted cuttings nodded their soft green heads sadly with every jolt. She glanced sideways at Michael. His face looked shut off.

An hour later and her mood changed to irritation. Did she really deserve to be considered quite so wicked? And anyway, why should human warmth not be cherished, whatever form it took? What was a pearl but layers around a piece of grit? What business was it of Michael's to judge her for moving about freely in a world he himself had chosen to opt out of? Because he *had* opted out, she could see it clearly now.

Another hour passed and still they drove in silence, and Michael remained as grim. She lapsed into sadness. Maybe his anger was paternal, as fathers are angry when they find their daughters have become women. Most fathers. Her own didn't seem all that bothered. If her dad been there this morning he'd probably have done nothing more than raise one sardonic eyebrow. But raising that eyebrow would have made it possible for her to explain.

Michael braked and pulled up roughly at the side of the road and got out. She watched him, wondering if he'd stopped for a pee, but he jerked his head at her to come. He was walking away from the road, along a path. She climbed out and started to follow him. Surely they should be locking the Land Rover? All those boxes and packages in the back! But he'd walked off with the keys and she wasn't prepared to sink so low as to shout after him.

When she caught up with him he was standing on the crest of a small rise, staring down at one of the small lakes. She had forgotten the lakes. It felt inappropriate to be stopping to look at them now, crocodiles or no crocodiles, a world away from where they had been when they'd talked about it, two days ago. This is getting silly, she thought. He heard her coming up behind him and walked on down the path towards the patch of shimmering blue. He hadn't looked at her once since that accusing look of dismay outside her room at the hotel. She followed him crossly, slapping at the tsetse flies that settled in gangs to feed on her bare arms. Michael was slapping irritably too.

But the lake, when they got close to it, was magical.

Across its sparkling surface sailed a flock of pelicans with beaks like buckets. Improbable and unflappable, ignoring the floating logs that lay here and there in the water with their wicked crocodile eyes half-closed. And everywhere the enormous water lilies, glowing pink and white.

He stood waiting for her, his expression unfathomable in the shadow of his sunhat. It was, she thought, a very unflattering hat. Her own head was bare. The glare hurt her eyes and the hair on the top of her head was growing hot as fire in the sun. She came up beside him. She'd had enough.

'You seem to be judging me. It's not fair, you know! He turned up only a few minutes before you did. He hadn't stayed the night, if that's what you think.' She lifted her eyes from the ground in time to see his eyes light up momentarily like the sun chasing a cloud shadow across the grassland. Then the darkness snapped down again. He frowned at the horizon.

A chasm opened up at her feet. It wasn't anything to do with her at all. Something must have happened yesterday in Ouagadougou. She was the one who had completely misunderstood and she had just exposed herself completely, her voice betraying how inappropriately she cared what he thought of her. She stared at the water lilies in unseeing dismay. What had she just done? In the crudeness of her despicable self-preoccupation she had just single-handedly ruined their friendship. They walked back to the car in silence.

20

September

There was *before Ouagadougou*, and then there was *after Ouagadougou*. As if the earth, shifting slightly, began spinning on a different axis.

After Ouagadougou, the pressure of harvest time kept her dad out of the house all day, seven days a week, and Moses with him. Jo and Kevin failed to come back from Kumasi, though she was slow in realising it, not having rushed to greet them. And Michael, like a ghost, seemed to be for ever disappearing out of her field of vision, exiting stage-left or stage-right, so that the small stage set of her life was left sadly empty, waiting for the action to return. Classes were a relief. Old boys happy to be back, new boys starry-eyed and nervous. But there was no Michael to share it all with and, much as she was loving the classes, she missed him badly.

She pinned him down once in the staffroom. His eyes were courteous but kindly, as if he wasn't quite focussing on her face. He answered her query and remembered an errand. Sidestepped her as deftly as if she were Ursula, Anne realised, mortified.

In the Low Cost House she cooked solitary meals and worked without distraction. They came in late, her dad and Moses, dusty from driving round the rice farms, too weary when they came in to do more than sleep, going out again before sunrise. She went to Jo's house but the door was still locked and dried bougainvillea flowers had piled up in an undisturbed drift against the sill. This time she minded. The slight taste of irksome obligation that had been there whenever she thought about Jo had faded. It left her feeling alone, especially now that Rose had gone to London. There was no one out of school that she would call a friend. Even Ursula – dubious acquaintance that *she* was – had not returned to Tamale: she had stayed in England to put the kids in school and learn to load the washing machine. And Michael was avoiding her as assiduously as if he were carefully writing himself out of her history. It was the jokes she missed most. That was a surprise.

It will pass. I will just have to lure him out, she thought.

The play idea took hold among the boys without her saying a word, the newly incarnated Fifth Formers seeing it as their own baby, the Fourth and even the Sixth showing interest too. Even Third Formers were asking about it. She went to see Father Morrissey.

He looked at her over his praying-mantis hands and did not smile. '*A Midsummer Night's Dream*? Hmm,' he said at last. 'We did *Murder in the Cathedral* a few years ago, but Shakespeare? And hardly suitable material for Christmas or for Easter, do you not think? After exams next July would be better timing. And more in season.' He barked his staccato laugh, making her jump.

July would be useless for boys due to sit their exams in June. Perhaps Morrissey was hoping the idea would die a quiet death. 'But what about a drama club now, once a week after school?' she suggested. 'Without aiming to mount a performance? Would that be possible? And what if – ' she added tentatively because he seemed unconvinced – 'what if we looked at the possibility of doing a Mystery Play instead?' She was ad libbing but seeing him hesitate she expanded – 'The *York Mysteries*, perhaps?' It wasn't only the boys she was thinking of. Surely Michael wouldn't be able to resist a play.

Father Morrissey gave way suddenly, taking her by surprise. A Drama Club, then, once a week after school. They could use the classroom, as before.

She wanted to go to Michael and present him with her victory like an apple in a basket. But she did not want to watch him being deft.

A letter came. Her dad had carried it round with him all day and it was crumpled and dirty, engine grease smearing the UK stamp and the tight, unfamiliar handwriting on the envelope. Inside, a single sheet of paper, Jo's name scrawled across the bottom of the page. Anne read it quickly. There was more lying between the words than lay within them: Jo and Kevin's sudden exodus from Kumasi to London was because Kevin's dad had been charged with serious fraud. His mother was in hospital recovering from an overdose.

She read the words twice over, struggling to absorb their meaning. Kevin's father? Kevin the Epitome of the Happy Family, example to us all? And then she read the last two lines again: 'Don't know if we'll be coming back. Kevin's contract is due for renewal in November in any case. Might try somewhere else – always fancied Kenya. India even! When circumstances here permit.'

They wouldn't come back to Tamale. Jo would have written differently if it were otherwise.

She put the letter on her bedside table with the latest

letter from her mother, awaiting an answer. No, they wouldn't be back. There was just a whisper of relief in the thought. There will be other friendships, she told herself. But then she remembered Joshua, and her heart hurt.

She worked extra hours coaching pupils who were struggling with the syllabus. She spent many more hours preparing lessons. The Drama Club was oversubscribed but it would probably settle to more manageable numbers, given time. Whatever she had implied by suggesting the *York Mysteries*, they were acting out *A Midsummer Night's Dream* again from the beginning, by popular request. The boys were so keen that they might put it on properly, with costumes. With scenery, even. Without an audience, if Father Morrissey wouldn't relent before next Easter.

The Sixth Formers, having decided on reflection that the Drama Club was beneath them, asked her to help them start a Debating Society. 'Competitiveness is not compatible with Godliness' was their first debate, a jibe at the school's football team, which was on its usual losing streak. Father John came to listen and laughed good-humouredly at all the barbed jokes. He looked like Friar Tuck in shorts as he sat there chortling into his beard. His presence made Michael's absence the more glaring. She wondered that nobody commented on it.

What have I done? She mourned at night, in the quietness of the sleeping house. But she was irritated too. She had not done so much! Even if she had, wasn't she deserving of his pastoral care? Was she suddenly worth so little?

Friday night, and her dad was late coming home from a two-day field trip. He had set off in the Land Rover for

Bolgatanga the previous day, taking Moses as usual. They should have been home by early evening. She didn't think much about it at first. It got late and the bad thoughts began to surface; she swatted them back down. They might be delayed until tomorrow and it would be nothing unusual.

It was after eleven when she heard a knock at the front door.

Kwesi at the door (her dad's boss but younger than him), his kindly face clouded with anxiety. 'There's been an accident,' he said. The white bud of panic in her heart flared like magnesium at that single word, *accident*. 'Nothing to worry about.' His face saying something else.

Kwesi, well-acquainted with the hospital (his wife Millie was due to give birth to twins there shortly), led her on foot through the gates where all but the prostrate cases were stopped from driving in. Between the gates and the building, a crowd of people, late as it was, milling about. The moon shone down, leaching out the colour, glinting blue on teeth and the whites of eyes. Smells of food hung in the air, and the smoke of cooking fires: loved ones inside the hospital had to be fed.

The building floated above them like a seagoing liner, a light at every porthole.

Inside Accident and Emergency information came in fits and starts, in tiny doses. Yes, Richard Foster had been admitted shortly after ten p.m. He had two broken ribs (lower right thorax); a wound in his right thigh; a superficial abrasion to his left temple. Moses Kutame, admitted at the same time, had a fractured kneecap (right); a wound to his forehead requiring stitches; a dislocated shoulder (right). Mr Kutame was now on the Orthopaedic Ward. Mr Foster was in Theatre being operated on for removal of foreign material from the wound in his leg.

She sat, as instructed, in the waiting area near the operating theatres. Kwesi went off in search of Moses but she could not. She was too anxious to see her dad. Too angry with Moses, who would have been driving.

Trolleys passed and re-passed. Some bulky, some not, under rough, greying sheets, randomly holed. Each with attendant nurse in soft-soled shoes, holding drips, carrying files. Around her other people waiting, until they recognised in a motionless figure the person they loved and rose to follow the trolley, anxious and meek. But she, whose body on the trolley should have been far easier to recognise, being so conspicuously white, waited in vain.

Eventually she was the only one left in the waiting area.

Kwesi came back and sat with her, reporting that Moses was in pain but he was sleeping now. Kwesi was worrying about his Millie. Anne told him he should go home. He went, reluctantly.

She waited.

No, said the nurse for the third time. Go back and sit.

So she waited again. The plastic seat was hard and still hot, even though by now it was long after midnight. It creaked uncomfortably under her sweaty thighs. The nurses behind the desk were openly watching her, laughing together as they talked. They held her with their challenging stares. There was no pity there for a white girl whose father had been hurt. Whatever vengeance they were wreaking, they took it gleefully. Did they train in Britain and, having suffered, wanted to retaliate now?

A third nurse came, calling greetings, along the corridor. Three nurses now behind the desk. They were whispering

271

behind the screens of their hands, and giggling. The furtive glances made it clear they were laughing at her. What had she done to deserve this? Nothing in this life, or everything – her race, her kind. She would pay, willingly – but not now. The night a long distance. A tunnel with her head in it. Her father flying ahead, always beyond her reach. Dad, oh Dad! Be okay, be safe! I don't want anything more. Not for myself. Only that.

Then, as she sat, a white coat loomed in front of her. From each cuff, an elegant hand, long tapered fingers very dark and finely shaped. A stethoscope hanging. A voice saying with interest, 'It's Anne Foster, isn't it?'

He was different in his white coat. More approachable, less haughty. Or perhaps it was that he was smiling. Dr Jebuni. Yiri Jebuni. Whom she had wanted never to see again. Who owed her no favours. Who had grown a beard since she saw him before, a small beard, neatly trimmed.

'What are *you* doing here?' he asked. His eyes narrowed. 'Is Richard Foster your father? I operated on him earlier this evening. No, no – nothing serious! Just a bit of cleaning up to do. A bit of a car where it shouldn't have been. Nothing that won't heal.'

All the fatigue of waiting, of it being nearly two in the morning, all that time thinking he was in the operating theatre and how serious that made it. The hurt of being the object of the nurses' spite, the pain of feeling so lost and alone. Terrified of the abandonment it might have been, and exhausted now by the relief that it was not. Salty tears started coursing freely down her face. Wiping them away angrily, probably leaving dirty streaks. Embarrassed to be crying in front of *him*.

'Your father came out of theatre a long time ago. You

should have been told,' he added sternly. (It was satisfying to see the nurses on the desk subdued now because she was talking with the surgeon.) 'He is on the ward and he is asleep, as you should be. Come, I will take you home,' he said, brushing aside her objections. 'Come back in the morning.' She started to protest but he silenced her: 'Nonsense, I am going home now – it is not far out of my way. Come.' A favour then, disguised as a command. Which she could accept. Not an obligation, which she could not.

They had made no mention of their previous meeting. Perhaps they never would.

In the car they were silent. She could feel his weariness, a load as heavy as her own. He was the father who had reclaimed his son. She was the daughter who had mislaid her father. As if she had been careless. A lapse of attention. Wanting him but never quite reaching him. Not knowing she had been looking in the wrong places until now.

Dr Jebuni dropped her outside the shuttered house and drove away. Leaving her there, alone. The dark houses, the empty road.

21

2nd and 3rd October

In the morning her dad was, of course, where he should be, on the Surgical Ward, in a small side-ward of four beds. Pale and drawn, but conscious, and pleased to see her. So clearly and unequivocally pleased.

She kissed him as if he were made of tissue paper. There was a dressing on his forehead. He held on to her hand and she thought of babies gripping. He saw the tears in her eyes and shook his head, smiling. Tears glistened in his eyes too.

The Ward Sister came with a list of instructions that made Anne laugh. The Sister bristled, thinking she was being mocked, but it was the length of the list that was laughable, the things Anne hadn't got. *Two flannels?* 'One for tops, one for bottoms,' Sister briskly replied. Her dad snorted from under his sheet. Ghanaian patients would not be given a list like this, surely! This was being rolled out especially for them.

Anne would have to improvise on pyjamas, let alone flannels. And think of food she could make for him. She had brought only fruit, there was nothing else in the house until she went into town. But he wasn't hungry. She was angry with herself for not bringing him drinking water. She had assumed they would have clean water here, but there was no jug, no glass.

They sat quietly, hand in hand. Tenderness made her heart feel raw and swollen.

Michael came in. He drew up a chair on the far side of the bed without looking at her once. Then suddenly he did – a quick, strong look. Her bruised heart turned over. The meeting of their eyes was like a lock catching, like light waves connecting. He looked away.

Her dad was telling Michael about the list. 'She won't have time to come back to school, you know. She'll be much too busy cooking for me and ironing my flannels.'

Michael, very serious, said, 'You'll need to take the week off.' Looking at her again. His eyes were greener than she had remembered. Grey, but with brown and green flecks in the grey. Deep as water.

She didn't want time off. Though she was glad it was a Saturday. So much to do before she came back here tonight: food to find and to cook, the improvising of flannels…

'For Moses as well,' Michael said, concerned she might forget she must look after Moses also. And he had a point: she did not want to. He saw her resistance and said firmly – in his priestly manner – 'Moses needs looking after too.'

'He does,' her dad agreed.

She looked steadily back at Michael. He was a priest but he was also a man. Fallible, just as she was. 'I'm finding it a bit hard to be kind to Moses,' she said. 'I mean, after this…' She gestured vaguely towards the bed.

Michael looked at her dad's feet, avoiding her gaze.

Her dad was looking at his feet too. He said, 'Moses wasn't driving. I was.' He looked up at her. 'And he's the one more seriously hurt: I'm the one who's guilty.'

Her anathema was exposed. There were no excuses for it to hide behind. She was like a white grub under a turned stone.

275

'It's a terrible thing, jealousy,' Michael said gently, meaningfully. He wasn't chiding, he was telling her something else. She knew, but only because he wouldn't look at her as he said it. The old Michael – Michael the priest – would have looked into her eyes. This Michael, the man Michael, was looking at the foot of the bed.

She glanced at her dad, wondering what he made of this, but he seemed not to have heard. As always when the rivalry between her and Moses came to the surface he vacated the conversation. He looked old, suddenly. Frail. She noticed for the first time that there were liver spots on the backs of his hands. The lines around his eyes puckered and he shifted uncomfortably in the bed. 'What is it?' she asked, at once alert to any symptom of pain.

'My leg's a bit painful. And my ribs hurt when I move. I can't get comfortable.'

The bed was high and narrow. A rough grey sheet covered the plastic mattress and another covered him. The ubiquitous holes, gently frayed. A hospital gown of the same rough cotton. 'We'll get you home soon,' she said. 'You'll be much better off there.'

'In the meantime some pyjamas *would* help,' he said. 'Only I haven't got any.'

Michael offered at once to bring him some. Begged, borrowed or stolen, he said. He would come back in an hour, maybe two, bringing whatever they needed, but first he was going to check on Moses. He said it in simple explanation, without the edge his voice had when he was reminding her of things she ought to do. In some strange way they had become equals. She sat for a long time after he had gone, thinking about this.

A nurse came, carrying a cup with six pills in it, two each

of three different kinds. The nurse took her dad's temperature, then gave him the cup. 'Take dem,' she ordered. As they were, she seemed to mean – dry, without any water.

'What are they?' Anne asked, protective and suspicious, but the nurse eyed her impatiently as if this were none of her business. 'Can't I get some drinking water for him somewhere? He'll never get them down dry!' Two of the pills were so big they could have been elephant medicine.

'De drinking fountains are out of order. You must bring water with you if you don' care to drink from de tap in de hand-basin.' The nurse looked at her dad, who was hesitating. 'Are you afraid to take dem?' she challenged, as if he were a mouse not a man.

He looked at Anne and grimaced, then dutifully took the pills, one by one, as if he were swallowing bullets. She smiled into his eyes encouragingly. She felt closer to him than she'd ever been. The nurse tutted, standing over him to make sure he didn't cheat but took all six. When he had finished she sighed loudly in thanks and briskly neatened up the sheet.

'Doctor's coming!' she whispered, standing to attention beside the bed.

For some reason, Anne hadn't expected to see Doctor Jebuni today. But in he came in his white coat with a respectful following of young men and women, similarly dressed, in his wake. He smiled at her dad and looking directly at her he said, 'It's a teaching hospital. I'm afraid our patients are also useful specimens. But we won't be long.' His voice was low and friendly. She looked into his eyes, which were very dark and, she thought now, kind. He turned to the student doctors and explained her dad's case history in brief, efficient terms. Her dad listened with interest. Then he raised one eyebrow at her and whispered, 'Double Dagbani to me,' though Doctor Jebuni had spoken in perfect English. She frowned, not wanting anyone to think they were being offensive.

The doctor signed to the students to leave. He turned back to her dad and said: 'Nurse tells me you're doing well, Mr Foster. We should have you up and out of here in a few days.'

Her dad nodded, smiling like an anxious pupil called up in front of teacher. Dr Jebuni smiled at Anne and as he left he patted her shoulder briefly. She froze in surprise, wondering what it was about her that made men so avuncular. But then she thought he was probably just acknowledging their first meeting and implying that they should disregard it and start afresh.

Her dad gave her a questioning look.

'I met him before. You remember that time when I went to Zigbili? That was him. But I'm sure he'll be kind to you. I'm sure he's a good doctor.'

Why was she sure? She knew nothing about him except that he had been a bad husband (or maybe not), and a good father (or maybe not), everything having multiple faces depending which light you viewed it in. And being a beautiful man didn't make him a good doctor, only an aesthetically pleasing one.

'Tell me what you'd like me to cook for you,' she said, taking her dad's hand again, unwilling to end the pleasure of having him all to herself. Unwilling to do her duty, which she knew she must, of going to see Moses in the Orthopaedic Ward. She felt a lesser person when she thought of Moses, even now.

She wondered, secretly, how her dad could be so sure it hadn't been Moses driving when he could remember nothing else of what had happened.

The Orthopaedic Ward was above the Surgical Ward and mirrored it: the same long line of four-bed wards, the same tired, holed sheets, the subdued yet crowded atmosphere. If visiting hours existed at all they seemed very relaxed. Nearly every bed had attendants (parents, grown-up children and a few small ones, and uncles, aunts and cousins) who sat or stood, or rested on the floor, around each recumbent patient. The health status of the patient could be read in the despondency or the cheerfulness of the attending family, without looking at the bed.

She didn't see Moses but passed him by, surrounded as he was by fat, cheerful aunties. He was drawn and pale and she didn't recognise him until he called her back, his face all eyes, anxious and pleading. Wanting to know, was it true, what Father Michael had told him? Was Dick really okay?

She couldn't help but be touched. The way his eyes relaxed when she told him. The way his voice rose in pitch, in an odd falsetto of relief. Perhaps I have been hard on him, she thought. She already knew she had been mean. It was an undercurrent of disturbing self-knowledge that threaded through her days. A self she would slough off if she could.

The aunties were smilingly silent, eyeing her curiously, nodding politely whenever she looked in their direction.

She asked him what she could bring for him. His list was short and modest. A few clothes, the magazine he'd been reading. Then he asked her suddenly, could she bring him something of Dick's? To keep by him. Being stuck in bed unable to see him. A shirt, a piece of clothing, anything like that. Of course, she said. Wondering what *juju* he really wanted it for.

They talked of this and that. Mainly the accident. Her father had driven into the back of an unlit charcoal lorry parked on the side of the road. Moses had been sleeping when it happened. He only knew it was a charcoal lorry afterwards, when they sat trapped and mercifully alive in the mangled cab of the Land Rover with spilled charcoal raining whisperingly down on them until villagers came and dragged them free. The villagers had flagged down a passing car, which brought them to the hospital. A journey of such excruciating pain that Moses could remember little of it.

It was late at night when she got home, all her duties accomplished: two men supplied with fruit, and bottles of drinking water, toothbrushes, soap, a towel cut in four pieces for flannels (Moses looked askance and uncomprehending when she handed him his), books for her dad and an evening meal, and the football magazine Moses had asked for plus a new one, specially bought in the afternoon when she had gone into town and only two months out of date. His face had lit up with surprised pleasure when he saw it.

She was exhausted. She lay in bed, waking-dreams suspending her between consciousness and sleep. The detail of the day knotted and re-knotted itself. The phone call she had made to her mother from the central post office, the only place with a public phone. She had tried to explain, against the crackling and the disconcerting echo, her mother not hearing what she said. Feeling self-conscious with so many grinning faces watching her through the window of the phone booth: idle boys hanging around the post office, older youths picking their teeth, people queuing for the phone. She had turned her back on them all and raised her voice. She could hear her mother, so far away in the ether, crying. It made her terribly homesick suddenly. Wishing she could just be there by her mother's side and put her arms round her to comfort her. Be hugged and comforted back. She hadn't had a really good hug since she came to Tamale. Not one.

Now, trying to sleep, the phone call circled relentlessly in her half-dreams, reinventing itself: sometimes she got through, sometimes she was struggling over and over to dial the right number. But all the time she felt achingly awake as if she had never fallen asleep at all.

She got up. The house was sombre and still. All Moses's things (his two knives, recently sharpened, his radio, battered now and sadly mute) arranged carefully on the kitchen shelf, the knives placed in their usual precise juxtaposition. His idiosyncratic stacking of plates, dishes, saucepans. A small leather pouch of tobacco at the back of the cupboard and with it an old silver lighter engraved in flourishing italics: 'To Dick, with all my love.' 'Dick' crossed out, and 'Moses' scratched faintly above it in clumsy letters. She wondered at this but didn't suspect him of stealing something so little hidden. She couldn't remember seeing him use it, but when she tried it the lighter didn't work anyway. In the tobacco pouch there was a small, resinous lump nestling in the tobacco. She smelled it. Grass. A Moses she hadn't suspected.

She made herself a mug of tea and carried it through the house. A faint breeze breathed through the louvres of the shutters. It stirred the sweat-damp hair on her forehead and

281

at the back of her neck so that she shivered, though she wasn't cold. She stopped in the doorway of the living room and on an impulse turned back and went instead into her dad's room. Checking under the bed first, as she always did.

The room was so neat, like a sailor's cabin. A fastidious placing of things: her dad's few precious possessions. There was nothing new. She had seen them all before. Yet they all looked strangely different, as if her own placement in relation to her father had subtly shifted, and with that all his belongings looked slightly different too.

She put her glass of tea down on the desk and picked up the photographs. Which she had never got round to asking him about. Who took the photo of her mother, and when? Who was the young black woman, standing with what seemed to be her husband and children and smiling at the camera so radiantly? Why did he have these two women on his desk, the one she knew and the one who was a stranger, as if there were depths to his life she didn't know of? Perhaps – just perhaps – he didn't regret that marriage after all, or her, the product of it. She thought of her mother weeping on the phone today and put the photos back, disturbed, not comforted. If her parents' relationship was other than the one she'd been led to believe, she wasn't sure how much she wanted to know. Some things were better left as secrets.

She *could* ask him about the photographs, though. Tomorrow. In this tranquil solitude which they had unexpectedly been given, and which they would probably lose when the pieces on the board shifted again.

She noticed how dusty everything was and leaned forwards to blow the dust off the photograph frames, thinking about Moses and how small and lost he had looked in the narrow hospital bed, whereas her dad filled his. The curious stares of the other patients and their visitors in the orthopaedic ward, watching the white visitor to the black man. The young white girl coming to visit the young black man. Many ears listening in. The sense she'd had of all conversation being suspended when she appeared, and closing in behind her in a whispering wake when she left. She turned, and her elbow caught the glass of tea, knocking it over.

The liquid ran everywhere and then she was running too, to get a cloth. Guilty. An intruder, leaving her mark. On her knees among her father's things, frantically mopping, she felt like a naughty child. There wasn't much tea on the floor. It took her a while to realise that the middle drawer of the desk was slightly open and had caught the greater part of the liquid.

The drawer was full of files and papers. She pulled them out hastily. The wettest were the ones on the bottom, which had sat several minutes in a puddle while she had been mopping the floor, thinking she hadn't done much damage, wondering at how little mess there was from a glass nearly full of tea. She spread the papers out on the top of the desk to dry, careful to keep them in order so that she could put them back exactly as they were. She looked inside the folder which had been lying at the bottom of the drawer. Letters, the ink smudging on damp corners. She was so tired her bones felt cold. She wanted suddenly to be in bed, lying down, letting go and drifting. Cursing aloud to be where she was and shouldn't have been, she pulled the letters out and spread them to dry.

They were love letters, she couldn't help but see: all written in the same childish, half-formed hand. Phrases jumped out at her here and there, though she thought she wasn't looking. *'Mr Dick you are beutiful man and I want to ly in your arms.'*

283

'Then I was cumming and I so wonted you…' *'De kiss you gave me wen…'.* She laid them out, page by page, like playing cards, not wanting to see, unable to quite be blind. Perhaps this was the unexplained African woman of the photograph? The thought was strangely repugnant. Even though she knew all children find it difficult to imagine their own parents involved in sexual relationships – even so, she couldn't believe in the reality of her ageing father in that pretty young woman's arms.

She mopped the empty folder where the tea had stained it, then went gratefully to bed, leaving the papers laid out on the desk to dry.

Sunday dawned, like all Tamale days, so hot by six-thirty that it was uncomfortable to still be in bed. Red dreams chased her round and round as she rose unwillingly through the curtains of overheated sleep.

She lay listening to the emptiness of the house. Next door's rooster flapped up onto the fence and crowed. A woman began to move pots and pans about, just the other side of the fence, grunting to herself in sleepy sentences.

The weariness of yesterday was still there but with the dullness of anticlimax now. The great fear that had reared up was not so big after all, and in its wake she felt like a mollusc thrown up by the tide and left to dry unsatisfactorily in the sun. She felt terribly alone in the empty house, as if she were living someone else's life and had got lost in it. She thought of Jo in England and for the first time really missed her. A great wave of homesickness (so rare that until yesterday she had forgotten the sly salt taste of it) washed through her. I could go home too, she thought. Then remembered that now, of all times, she could not.

Her father was very quiet when she got to the hospital. His skin was hot and dry. The pleasure and excitement of survival seemed to have worn off, or maybe it was simply that the effect of the drugs had. He was in more pain, and very tired and drawn. He hadn't been able to sleep much, the ward had been too noisy. The occupants of two of the other three beds had changed since yesterday morning. One man was waiting to go down to the operating theatre for a routine hernia operation. Another, with a head wound after being knocked off his bicycle, lay groaning in the next bed. The young man in the bed opposite, who had lost the fingers of his left hand to a circular saw and yesterday had been in a state of excited euphoria, was pale and subdued today with the belated kick-in of shock. Her dad made no complaint but it was clear that today he too was struggling. He kept closing his eyes while she was talking.

She missed him, the dad of yesterday. The brief closeness they'd had. She wanted him back, afraid to waste any of this precious time without Moses.

Dr Jebuni made his ward rounds, this time without his retinue of students. He wasn't wearing his white coat but dark trousers and a white, short-sleeved shirt. He looked smaller and more ordinary in European clothes. He was tall but he had the sloping shoulders and pigeon-chest of someone who'd been malnourished as a child. He spoke kindly to her dad, as he had to each of the other patients in the room before him. She watched him, thinking that in another life she would have liked to be his friend. He had a sensitive, interesting face.

He caught her eye. 'Come, I want to show you what we're planning for the new extension,' he said.

285

In the corridor he said 'That was an excuse – I wanted to have a private word with you about your father.'

An iron fist gripped her heart and squeezed as soon as Doctor Jebuni spoke. She'd known something was wrong! She nodded mutely.

'There's some infection. I am concerned because his temperature is up – he is very febrile. It is nothing to worry about,' he said reassuringly, 'but I did not want you to be too hopeful that he will be coming home today or tomorrow. He may need further treatment. I would like to keep him in for observation, if you are agreeable.'

'What sort of treatment?' she asked warily.

'Drugs – antibiotics. But if the infection gets worse I may have to re-open the wound.' He smiled down at her. 'You will be glad to know your friend Moses is doing fine. He will be up and about on crutches very soon. It will be hard for him, with his damaged shoulder, but he has youth on his side.'

She felt she was going backwards, retracing the progress of yesterday. Her father was subdued, sunk into himself when he was awake, slipping into frequent fitful sleeps.

Then the diarrhoea began. Soon after, the vomiting. A nurse brought a bed-pan, and a bowl of water for him to wash himself, the flannel coming into its own after all. Afterwards she showed Anne where to empty the stinking contents of the bedpan. Her father was as mortified as she was embarrassed. Then he was too weary to do more than concentrate on his own needs. She felt strange, mothering him like this. In the quieter interludes she sat by his side and held his hand as before, but he felt absent now, his hand an empty shell, as if he needed all his energy to concentrate

286

on that which was within. She had given up reading to him. It seemed to irritate him.

At last the spasms eased. When he fell more soundly asleep she went, dutifully, to visit Moses, but he was busy with aunts arranged around his bed in a jolly phalanx. Her presence silenced them. They became all smiling teeth. And she had little news for him. Moses was going down to the operating theatre shortly to have his kneecap removed. 'Den I'll be up,' he said. 'When dey put me in plaster I'll be up from dis bed and walkin' on crutches. Den I come see Dick.'

She felt mean not wanting it.

When she got back to the ward her father was being sick again. The nurse was relieved to hand over: they were short-staffed and she was needed elsewhere.

All afternoon she passed flannels and took away slop bowls to wash them out.

'First one end, then the other,' her dad said with a weak grin. 'We used to say that about you, when you were new.' He so rarely talked about their family past. She smiled back at him, trying not to let him see how scared she was. Thinking of the photograph. That relationship – her mother and her father – which should have been the foundation of their family, the 'we' he had just referred to. Why had they not stayed together? Where would the three of them be now if they had? The questions were too big, too unfathomable. She plumped up his pillow and didn't ask.

Dr Jebuni came in and studied her dad's face intently as he felt his pulse. 'It is the fever,' he said. 'Plenty of fluids, and add a pinch of salt and a teaspoon of sugar.'

'Easier said than done,' her dad said. 'Can't hold it down.' But he said he was feeling a little better, just very tired.

She went home and cooked some food that she hoped would be appetising enough cold to tempt him to eat, when he felt like eating again. How well she understood now what she had taken to be a squatter camp on the road outside the hospital: the mothers, daughters, aunts, sisters, husbands and sons, cooking, cooking, cooking, trying to tempt their sick loved ones back into life, until they were strong enough to emerge out of the labyrinthine deeps of the awesome building which towered so implacably above the people by the road. At night the cooking fires glowed like wolves' eyes in a huddled pack and the blue smoke hung, wraith-like, in a flat pall.

It was hard for her to think of things to cook when her resources were limited and her time was so snatched, and she had no oven for baking. If she'd had an oven she would have made him nursery food – rice pudding, cheese straws, miniature quiches. But then, she had no cheese either. And no milk except for tins of Ideal Milk, or dried milk powder.

In the evening, when he seemed more settled, more peacefully asleep, she walked home through the quiet dusk, wearier than she had ever been. On the road, people she didn't know called out, asking after her dad, sending their greetings. She lost count how many, marvelling at how news had travelled, and that there should be so many who cared enough to tell her that they knew.

She let herself into the house with distaste. The hollowness of it. Not, she realised, *her* house at all. So full of echoes, the real inhabitants not here. Picking at food by candlelight, the power off. Too tired to read. About to go to bed when she remembered the tea-slopped papers. Better tidy them up, just in case he was well enough to come home tomorrow as they had hoped.

Considering this thought she saw she no longer set any store by it. It had become a formality only. Now she wouldn't want him to come home tomorrow. He was safer where he was.

The day had been windy, though inside the hospital this had meant nothing. Walking home, the hot dry touch of the wind had been pleasurable after days of humidity half threatening a late, last rain. Now she cursed it: coming in at the half-open louvres, the wind had stirred the spread papers on her dad's desk and scattered them over one another onto the floor. Intending not to look at them, she had to look now to sort and order them.

She stood a candle on the desk. Phrases jumped out and punched her between the eyes. *'Our love' 'Dick, I want your dick' 'When I put my tongue in dat place and take you in my mouth' 'Dat ting you do...'* The crude, half-formed handwriting as clear and legible as a child's exercise book. But the sense not a child's at all.

She had neatly numbered the pages, this unknown writer. And dated each letter. The earliest was 1966, ten years ago. I was twelve then, she thought. Where was I while this woman was doing all these embarrassing things to my dad?

With my dad. Having to make herself admit he had been the willing reciprocator.

The last letter was dated 8th March, 1970. Six-and-a-half-years ago. There were only nine letters in all, but a total of thirty-three pages between them. And he had kept them, they meant something to him. He who had few photos of his daughter, and not one of her many childish letters, so far as she could see.

She put them back in the folder, slipped the folder into

the drawer and the other papers on top, hoping he would never notice the different order, or the stains and smudges.

Straightening up. Picking up the framed photograph of the smiling African woman with the young man standing a little to one side, and the little girls.

Christ! Perhaps these were her half-sisters?

She stared in horror. They looked like any little girls in Ghana dressed in their Sunday best, hair tied in plaits sticking out at each side of their heads, bubbly smiles and frilly dresses. They didn't look pale enough to be mixed race.

I couldn't bear it, she thought. It was the sense of loss that hurt, the having to share that which she felt she had so little of to start with. It was the betrayal created by secrecy. The indignity of deception. She felt that, moving in a world she didn't recognise, she must look like a bumbling fool. Then curiosity stirred in spite of herself. If she were to read them there might be some clue, something to connect and explain the photograph, perhaps. She shut the drawer resolutely and turned her back.

It was only half past eight. She longed suddenly for Jo. For Jo's over-emotional, down-to-earth common sense. She longed even more for Michael. To feel the heat of his near presence, so carefully poised at a discreet distance. The forbidden fruit she could not reach out to touch, believing now that this was not one-sided. That it was something they shared.

The old days of their easy friendship felt like a past life, a dream. The things she might have done differently not visible.

The wind knocked on the shutters and stirred the lifeless ceiling fan. The ghosts moving.

22

October 4th and 5th

Monday dawned, another standard day: heat oppressive, bright blue skies, high scudding clouds. The humidity of the last two days vanished. The dry season was truly here. A sense of things drying, fading, paling, of furniture contracting and houses settling.

She went to school at the usual time. In the staffroom Michael came looking for her.

'Have you been to the hospital already?' She shook her head. 'Don't you think you ought to go and see how he is before you come in to school? Set your mind at rest before you start lessons? If he does come home today, won't he be needing you at home?'

She looked at him. Yes, all these things could be true. But she didn't believe they would let her father come home for a while yet, and she was beginning to hate that house and her loneliness in it, and that hospital ward. School had the lure of a refuge.

He seemed to be too busy trying to be helpful to understand. 'I'll sort out your classes. You don't need to worry. Off you go – we'll manage.'

She felt dismissed. Was she needed? By whom? She wanted Michael to need her too much to let her go. And her dad. But she was afraid of being needed again as she'd been needed yesterday.

The nurses greeted her now. In the ward, the other beds had all changed occupants again. There were seven visitors in the small space. In the corner, her dad solitary in his bed. The red febrile spots of colour on his cheek-bones had faded. He looked grey, wan. He smiled when he saw her as if he had been waiting with his eyes fixed on the entrance. Relief washed through her, having expected so much less. *Dad, Dad! Oh Dad...* But she said nothing. She held his hand tight and smiled as calmly as he did. 'How are you feeling?'

'Totally awful.'

But no sickness or diarrhoea so far today. His lips had cracked. Dark shadows made hollows of his eye sockets and his beard no longer looked neat. When he spoke, strings of mucous threaded between his teeth. She helped him sit up and heard the moan of pain that he failed to quite suppress. He felt hot to the touch. His skin papery and dry. And his breath was rank with an aura of drains.

'I'm afraid I've wrecked these,' he said, gesturing at the borrowed pyjamas. 'Look.' He pulled the sheet back to show her.

'Oh Dad!' A ragged brown stain on the side of his upper thigh, with a black dot the size of a large coin at the centre of it. 'Why didn't they change the dressing?'

'They did. They've changed it several times. But it keeps coming through.' He peered down, bending cautiously because his ribs hurt. 'It's funny, it comes out that colour. Not like blood at all.'

She heard the edge of fear in his voice though he tried so

hard to sound unconcerned. Neither of them said it out loud: the wet stain looked as though he was rotting on the inside and leaking outwards. She said, eerily calm, 'You'd better take those pyjamas off. I've got you a clean tee-shirt and some shorts here, which would probably be cooler anyway. I'll take those home and wash them tonight.' Though she didn't see how she would ever get that stain out. She wondered how much Father John would mind sacrificing his pyjamas. She helped her dad pull off the loose jacket and get the tee-shirt on. It was like helping a child. An apologetic, half-amused, oversized child. She caught his eye and he smiled a wry smile. In the white tee-shirt he looked more himself. More filled out. More everyday and less like a Marx Brothers extra. But when it came to getting the pyjama bottoms off, the pain from his ribs and the wound in his thigh made it hard for him to lift himself off the mattress. He struggled feebly for a while before giving up.

She tried to maintain his dignity. Then merely to stop him frightening himself. Finally, in the odd panic of simply trying to achieve an end, she did most of it herself – pushing down and pulling off, feeding in feet and pulling up. Seeing more than she wanted to, of parts so private and glimpsed unwillingly in another woman's letters. Those letters were so far from this – the hot indignity of a hospital bed, caught in the unrelenting glare of the sun through the unshaded windows, sticking sweatily to the plastic mattress through the sheet. Which was itself stained. Not old stains, perhaps – perhaps the same dead stain that was seeping out of her father. She struggled through bravely, turning a blind eye wherever she could, and when they had finished she was rewarded with a weak smile and a look, intense and tender, from eyes whose blueness she noticed as if for the first time.

He put his hand round her wrist. 'Anne, I'm so sorry. I never wanted to hurt you.'

She thought he meant by his helplessness and was touched. 'Nonsense,' she said. But the new certainty that he wouldn't be coming home yet stood like a closed gate in front of them.

Time blurred. The days merged into a slow blur of non-event.

The major non-events were the continually changing occupants of the other beds. Her father's increasingly difficult daily struggles into clean clothes. Moses being returned from the operating theatre to his hospital bed upstairs in a full-length plaster, startlingly white against his glossy black skin.

The minor non-events marked her dad's slow slide downwards while Moses gained in strength.

'I get my crutches tomorrow!' Moses told her jubilantly on the Tuesday. She heard his tone as meaning: 'Then I'll be able to go and see for myself.' But she was too worried to mind losing sole care of her father now.

School had ceased to be even an intention. She simply ducked it, grateful in the knowledge that Michael would make sure her classes were covered. All day she scrubbed stains that wouldn't come out, cooked food that would not be eaten, walked the dusty road between the Low Cost and the hospital, sat long hours in the uncomfortable chair by the bed where her dad lay so quiet, so concentratedly motionless, that she knew the measure of his pain more by the care with which he avoided movement than by the occasional groan which escaped him.

Dr Jebuni was coming each day, giving them more of his

time than any one patient merited. He didn't mention re-investigation of the wound again. She was sure her father's problem was more a failure of medication in the face of excessive challenge than a failure of surgical skill. It was obvious that the whole hospital system was overstretched. The sheets that were worn to holes; the simple things like the window blinds that no longer worked. Although it had not long been built, this was a ship which was gently sinking at its mooring. She thought of it as a ship. Its big engine drumming deep in the hold, its generators liberating it from the erratic town supply. A ship slightly adrift on its moorings, straining at the ropes that held it safe. Yiri Jebuni and those like him a strangely quiet, studious crew. His visits to the ward made a high point in her small days. But the grave concern in his eyes when he examined his patient made her sick with worry. It was obvious her dad wasn't getting better.

Then it began to be obvious he was getting worse, even though the vomiting and diarrhoea had passed. Changing his clothes was almost more than he – or she – could bear. He spoke little, just held her hand. Even listening wearied him. He seemed to be shrinking in front of her eyes, his solid self becoming smaller and flatter in the bed. Her pureed soups (laboriously pushed through a sieve) and mashed fruit went untasted.

They were sitting in silence when Moses appeared at the entrance to the room. He balanced for a moment on his crutches, gazing at her father where he lay in the bed. Hastily she went to help Moses to the chair where she'd been sitting, amazed that he had managed – on one crutch (because of his bad shoulder), and with the plaster still wet and very heavy – to get all the way from one ward to the other. Now that he was here she could slip away and get some jobs done. She hadn't swept the house once in five days and the tide of dust was rising relentlessly.

'You'll both be home soon!' she said, knowing it couldn't now be true. 'They want your beds,' she added. But however pressed they were on the ward, there was never any suggestion that her dad's bed would not be there for as long as he needed it.

Moses was eager to get away from his.

'Are you coming back to the Low Cost, now?' she asked him.

He shook his head distractedly, his eyes on her father, gazing with anxious devotion. 'I go stay with my cousin. It nearer de hospital. Den I can come every day. From de Low Cost I could not walk.'

His cuts were healing already, scabs lifting like dark insects, the new skin underneath startlingly pink and clean. Her father was gazing back at Moses. She felt they were both waiting for her to go. She was the perpetual outsider. She said sadly 'I'll go home for a bit, Dad. Leave you with Moses for a while.'

His hand briefly covered hers on the bed. 'You have a break, love.'

It was not what she'd meant but she was touched by the rare endearment all the same.

She was sitting in the kitchen, on the low stool Moses sat on to cut up vegetables or when he was cooking on the gas ring on the floor. The setting sun cut in at an angle through the window, patterning the room sharply in terracotta light and black shadow. She had come in here intending to cook for tomorrow but she had done nothing, only sat with her head resting against the edge of the table, her thoughts blanked out in a fog of weary nothingness, watching the sun.

She looked round the room at the things Moses had left behind him and might soon come back to. Had innocently believed he was on his way back to, the night of the accident last weekend. Which now seemed a lifetime ago. The innocence of actions interrupted.

Looking at his things she felt unexpectedly nostalgic for his presence. How homely their little household, peopled, felt from this empty vantage point. Everything in here was neat and ordered in his way, not in hers. She had tried to preserve his order. But there was thick dust now on the shelves and on his little treasures which were carefully laid out there: the transistor radio, in need of new batteries; the calabash bowl he liked to eat from sometimes; a little carving of an antelope. The much-sharpened kitchen knives arranged in their usual perplexing juxtaposition – knives which her dad must have brought from England, along with Mrs Elizabeth Bramwell's cookery book – that strange tentacle of the past which snaked out to grab her every time she set eyes on it.

She got up wearily and reached the book down. Its old-fashioned certainties seemed so alien here. It was hard to believe that Moses could have found much inspiration between its covers but she knew better now, and the orange stains of palm-nut oil here and there and the faint aroma of ginger and chilli confirmed it. She turned the pages, seeking inspiration herself.

A loose page torn from an exercise book fell out, a recipe for goulash copied from some other book. She couldn't remember Moses ever cooking goulash but maybe she hadn't recognised it in the adaptation. She looked idly at the recipe, written out in a childishly unformed hand, then went back to turning the pages of the book. But something nagged at her mind. She turned back, looking for the loose page again. She was sure it was her imagination. Then she wasn't sure. She took the piece of paper to her father's study.

Michael came round the side of the church and locked the main doors. In the early dark he didn't see her standing by the bougainvillea, half hidden under its heavy droops of flowers which were grey in the lamplight, leached of their brilliant daytime colour. He didn't see her until she moved forwards to speak to him and then he jumped visibly. For a brief moment his face brightened, snuffing out like a candle flame almost immediately afterwards.

She hung back out of the light, not wanting him to see her ravaged face but when she spoke her voice betrayed her. He peered at her then, leaning down to look into her face. The old Michael. Taking charge. Leading the way firmly into the refectory of the priests' hostel. Father Giovanni was sitting smoking his pipe and reading by the feeble light of the single overhead bulb. Michael having made some signal, Vanni stood up and announced affably that he was just on his way to bed, although it was barely nine o'clock. Michael pulled up two chairs. She sat in one but he didn't sit down. He paced about the room listening as she told him what had been happening at the hospital. When she had brought him up to date and stopped talking, he seemed not to realise there was something more. He probably thought she had come to tell him that her dad was dying. Because, telling him, she admitted for the first time that she thought he was.

He came and sat down opposite her, at a careful distance

but she could feel his eyes on the top of her head as she sat looking down at her hands. She wondered how to go on. The urge to talk to him had been too powerful to resist any longer. Though she had thought, briefly, that she would not need to go to him: as she walked past Jo and Kevin's bungalow on her way to the Mission she'd seen a Land Rover parked below the house and thought they were back. But when she ran up the drive it was only Kevin's colleague from the Water Corporation, come to pack up their things and send them back to England. Her crazy heart had plummeted like a rock. She realised then how much she missed them, as she walked back down the dark drive. She'd wondered what she would do if Michael, too, were not to be found. She hadn't seen him since Monday. But there he was, coming round the side of the church.

'What is it, Annie?' he asked softly now.

She was silent, not looking at him. She didn't know how to say it. No words could fit the tumult in her heart. And she would find disbelief or empty reassurances very hard to bear just now.

He reached out and very lightly, with the back of his right forefinger, stroked the back of hers.

'Tell me, Annie. What is so troubling you?' His voice sounded as if he had swallowed it.

She told him in small sentences. Her innocent guilt at spilling tea on the papers. Her less innocent guilt in reading bits of them. These admissions she must make in order to reach the bigger truth. The glaring, horrible, inconceivable truth that made her feel sick, as if spikes were turning in her gut: the writer of the letters was no woman, but Moses. And there was no way her father was not reciprocal in this relationship. Not just the acts described, but the fact of his keeping the letters, like small treasures in his sparse desk. And all the other things that were falling into place now, all the little signs and clues to which she, in her naïve clumsiness, had been blind.

She came to a stop and sat with bowed head waiting painfully for his astonishment, for him to contradict her, or worse still to laugh at her. But it was more terrible when he didn't. He just said, 'Poor, poor Annie.'

She began to sob helplessly. Michael watched her and let her cry. So he'd known all the time and he hadn't told her! She was furious. Angry with herself, too, for being so stupid and so blind. Everyone had known, perhaps, except for her. She couldn't bear to be in the same room as him but she was crying too hard to stand up and get out and all she could do was turn her back on him and bury her face in her arms on the back of the chair. She heard him quietly get up and go out of the room. The pressure eased slightly as the door closed behind him. But even though she tried to breathe deeply, the gulping sobs kept rising. I must get out of here! she thought wildly. Except that she had nowhere to go.

'Drink this.'

She buried her face deeper to block him out.

'Anne, drink this. It will help.'

She glanced up at the glass. 'What is it?'

'Chamomile. Drink it.'

'I don't want your poxy drinks!'

'Annie!' A smile twitched at the corner of his mouth.

That was the last straw. 'You betrayed me!' She didn't care who overheard. 'You should have told me! You knew how much I minded that I felt the way I did towards Moses. Didn't you! You knew, didn't you? I didn't have to feel so

300

bloody guilty for *that*, at any rate. How could you do that? How could you let me go on not knowing? If you'd told me, I'd have known it wasn't just me being horrible. Be nice to Moses, indeed! How *could* you! How could you, Michael!'

His face had gone white but he said firmly, as if he was talking to a child, 'Come on, drink this. It will help. And then I'll try to explain.' He sat back down. 'Annie, I owe you a huge apology. I never thought you were horrible for feeling jealous. You are not guilty. You're certainly not a failure! Now drink that up and catch your breath.'

She glared at him. He stared her out. The indignity of it! Trapped, she took a token sip of the chamomile. He waited. She took another.

'I honestly thought you realised how complicated it was. I didn't *know* anything until just now, when you told me. And even now we don't really know for certain, we can only conjecture on the basis of half-facts and suggestions, feelings that you have, handwriting that might belong to Moses or it might not. But yes, I admit I did suspect their relationship was more complicated, and I really did believe you suspected too; I thought we were thinking along the same lines.'

'It isn't conjecture,' she objected. 'The letters make it disgustingly clear!'

'Even if Moses did write the letters, you don't know your father's side of it, do you?'

She knew he was waiting for her to look at him. She would not look up.

'I really did think you had guessed more or less as much as I had, Annie. I thought, *That girl! She's amazing. If it had been me I'd have been so mad!* It was me that was stupid, not

301

you. I'm *so* so sorry. I should have realised you weren't suspecting. And why should you? You're younger and more innocent than me, and anyway I'd known your dad and Moses differently to the way you know them. I probably picked up on things differently because I've known them as…as a unit. And from longer ago.'

'All this time I've been feeling so badly towards Moses and I thought it was me being mean. I thought I was pathetic – a jealous only child wanting to be Daddy's girl. And look what Dad was doing to me all that time! His daughter and his lover – his *male* lover! – living in the same house! How *could* he have done that? And why didn't he tell me? If only he'd told me I'd have tried to understand.'

His patient voice, explaining. If their suspicions were true, he said (and they mustn't lose sight of the fact that they might not be), it had to be this way. Could she not see some of the reasons? Homosexuality was illegal in Ghana, even if the law had changed in the UK. Her dad and Moses – *especially* Moses – would have had to be careful, very discreet. It would be very dangerous for them otherwise. 'People here find that sort of thing terribly shocking, Annie.'

Well, so do I! she thought, but she could not say so. She was supposed to be a modern woman. And anyway, maybe she only minded when it was her own dad. She felt Michael watching her.

Quite apart from the danger, he went on, think how hard it must have been for both of them when she came out to stay – letting her in and fitting their relationship into the space that was left. Even *before* she decided to stay on another year.

'Couldn't Dad have let it be, just while I was here?'

He said, not looking at her, 'Wouldn't you find it hard to abstain, if someone else came into your territory? Wouldn't the need of each to reassure the other make it more complicated? And six months is a long time. Let alone another year or more, as it will be now.' In any case, he added, she was assuming the physical relationship (if there really was one) was still current but maybe that had stopped long ago, before she even arrived in Tamale. Would she feel it so badly if Moses was more like a son now, a sibling rival but no longer a lover? Surely she had come to terms with some of that already?

She listened. And some of the time she didn't listen, her mind wandering off. Her thoughts tangled like fishing nets, all the fragments of her shattered illusions clinging to the net like mother-of-pearl. She had the odd sensation that they had all risen to the surface again, the illusions she'd thought she had put aside, but in pieces now.

Suddenly she remembered she'd told her dad she would go back to the hospital this evening. The thought of sitting there with her fragile father when she felt so angry with him, not to mention Moses, was unbearable. 'I can't go! I just can't!'

'I'm going to walk you home,' he said. 'And then I'm going to go to the hospital to tell them you're not feeling too well but you will be in tomorrow. You're going to go home and you're going to have a glass of whisky, if you've still got any in the house, and then you're going to get a good night's sleep.' His teacher's voice, kind but firm, not to be argued with. 'And tomorrow morning I shall come round to fetch you and I'm going to take you to the hospital. Because you've got to go, Annie. You know you have. I'll come with you tomorrow and walk with you, and

I'll sit with you. And if necessary I will talk to Moses.' She shifted in her chair, wanting to protest, but he took no notice. 'It's difficult, but you know you do want to deal with this. If your dad comes through you've got to face him, and if the worst should come to pass – in the unlikely event that he were to die, which surely he's not going to – you've got to forgive your dad before that happens. It's probably the most important thing you've had to do in your whole life. If you love him you must accept him as he is, Annie. And Moses too. You must accept Moses for your dad's sake, whatever it costs you. You know now that Moses is feeling as much as you about what is happening – maybe even more. You thought he felt less, but he doesn't. You have to give him space for that, and respect him too, Annie, however hard it is for you.'

He looked at her steadily out of his clear grey-green eyes. He was the only person in her life who had ever called her Annie.

23

October 6th and 7th

'Have you had breakfast?' he asked.

She shrugged.

'Come on, Annie. This won't do. You must eat or you'll not have the strength to give your dad the help he needs.'

'Did you see him last night?'

'I didn't go in. The Sister said he was sleeping and shouldn't be disturbed as he'd had such a bad day. She promised to tell him you weren't well when he woke. I said it was nothing serious. But you really should eat something, Annie. You're getting terrible thin.'

'I couldn't. I'd only puke it up again.'

'You Cambridge girls do have such a way with language,' he said. 'I'll let you off on one condition – that you come and eat with us in the Mission tonight. It's not very exciting food and the company is crazy but it would be better than you moping and starving yourself here. Is that a deal? Come on then, let's go. I have to be in for classes by eight at the very latest.'

They walked through the pale early morning, the sun just flushing out the colour of the earth from under a milky haze of dawn mist. The day smelled fresh and lovely. There was dew in the long, fading grass, and spiders' webs catching the sun. It might have been a morning in late summer at home except for the power of the sun, barely muted by the earliness of the hour. He entertained her with tales of the refectory. He could hear the slight desperation in his own voice trying to take her mind off the day ahead. He had talked to the doctor last night. Anne had not been exaggerating the gravity of Dick's condition.

All the same, when he saw Dick he was shocked. The man had shrunk. His skin was like paper, his hair had gone dry and thin-looking and was no longer dark but colourless. It was as if the light had begun to shine right through him and out the other side. He lay motionless in the bed, and there was a faint stench of death hanging about him. Michael stood very still, staring down. It was, as the doctor had said, a situation the limited facilities of the hospital had simply not been able to grapple with. Had Dick been in England he would probably be back on his feet by now. But they were so short of drugs here, and the sterilising equipment was always breaking down, and the wound had probably been hopelessly infected from the foreign material that was in it to start with. Poor sod, Michael thought, he probably knew quite well what was happening to him and what his own prognosis was. They had moved him into a small room on his own, to save the other patients from having to cope with the smell. That had caused a panic in itself, the empty bed in the ward, Anne not surprisingly jumping to dire conclusions until all was explained.

In the hot little room she had sat down beside the bed and taken her father's hand in hers. Dick muttered and opened his eyes. The lids fluttered down again. Moses had got up when they came in. He was crying. Michael patted him on the shoulder.

'He bad, Father. He so, so bad.'

Michael took him by the arm and led him gently out of the room.

Michael and Moses were gone a long time. She sat there with her dad's dry listless hands in hers, listening to the harsh sounds of his laboured breathing. Whether he was asleep or awake, or even unconscious, she couldn't tell. She didn't know whether to talk to him or let him rest. To try to pull him back, or to let him float to the end of the long rope of his consciousness.

In the corridor, Michael and Moses talked with Dr Jebuni.

'What about shipping him out?' Michael asked bluntly, when Dr Jebuni had explained again that the problem was a national one – too few drugs, too narrow a spectrum of antibiotics. 'I mean, back to the UK.' He was aware of the stricken look Moses gave him.

'Has he changed his mind then?' Dr Jebuni asked. 'He has been most emphatic whenever I have discussed this with him that on no account does he wish to be moved anywhere else.' He added, a note of defensiveness in his voice, 'He really was quite clear about this.'

Michael looked at Moses and saw the conflict of pain and relief in his face. Moses would want what was best for Dick, even if it meant separation.

'Actually,' said Dr Jebuni, 'I think moving him now would not only be very painful for him, I think it would be actively detrimental.' Moses looked up quickly. His gaze fixed fearfully on the doctor's face. 'I mean,' the doctor explained gently, 'he is fighting his own battle now. He needs all his strength. If we were to move him, even by air, we would only make that battle more taxing. By road, it would be impossible. I think you take my meaning?' They both nodded. 'I haven't told the girl so much but I think she understands the essence of it. Now, if you'll excuse me...'

They let him go and went back silently to the ward.

Michael sat down next to Moses, on the far side of the bed from Anne. He had a little time still before he must go in to school. He was a priest and this was his pastoral duty. It was legitimate, but he hated himself for thinking like that.

He looked at her, this confident young woman, and he could see only a lost and frightened child, walled in behind the pallor and the un-communicative eyes. Being un-communicative, they freed him to be here. Because he *had* stayed away, though he didn't know if she understood this.

He watched her trying studiously to ignore Moses. He frowned at her, but she ignored him.

Before he left for school he said, 'Don't forget to come and eat tonight, Anne. Seven o'clock. I'll tell them you're coming.'

Her dad tossed and turned through the long hot day. Sometimes he was turned towards her, sometimes towards Moses, but his eyes were always shut.

She read her book, making notes. The new books had come. They could begin to work on *Tom Jones* as soon as she was back in class. She wondered how they were managing her lessons without her. If the Drama Club had been cancelled. Probably not, Father John had only been waiting for an opportunity to step in and take over, she thought.

Moses sat with the strange waiting calm that Africans have, waiting for buses, sitting by their stalls in the market: looking into the middle distance with dreamy eyes, hands loosely clasped between his knees, cracking his knuckles rhythmically one by one. She'd thought she couldn't bear to be in his company but there was a strange comfort in it after all. His quiet sharing of the same grief. The two of them suspended in a no-man's land, waiting for they knew not what. His tears had dried. If only he would stop clicking his knuckles...

The hours passed. Her dad slept all day. The nurse said he had hardly slept last night, after about ten o'clock. She wouldn't say anything more when Anne probed, the questions agitated her. But no Doctor Jebuni came that day to explain, and she had missed his rounds the day before.

Moses went to eat in the early afternoon. Her dad was still sleeping.

The day was dragging so heavily, and though she wasn't hungry she was desperate to move around in the open air. She didn't know what she was waiting for but she was afraid that if she went away she would miss it.

Then her father woke at last and lay on his back, very still. He looked at her when she leaned over him to plump up his thin pillow, but listlessly, as if human contact tired him. She sat on a long time, not reading, just holding his hand. Sometimes she thought he was asleep again but when she stood up to stretch her legs she saw he was quietly awake.

At last she said, 'Dad, I'm going to go out for a bit. Just to get a bit of fresh air. Moses will be back soon.' She bent over him and kissed his dry sunken cheek. 'I'll come back later.'

His eyes focused on hers, then slid over her shoulder as if to look at someone behind her. She turned to find Moses had come into the room. Her father was still looking at him as she slipped out.

When she came back fifteen minutes later he was sleeping. He was still sleeping when she left to go to the Mission for supper, as ordered.

Eleven priests, a girl, a mouse in a glass jug. The priests and the girl are white. The mouse is black. This is the way it is in Ghana, Michael thought, regarding his brother priests. Tales of a religious life, chapter one.

The cook is also black. The priests eschew the employment of servants, being servants of God, and do their own cleaning, up to a point. And live with the cleaning they have not done, beyond that point. Because, for all their good intentions, they are all of them too busy to spend much time sweeping. So there is a tidal wave of dust in the corners and under the tables, beyond the reaches of the cursory once-a-day broom that one or other of them will wield after breakfast, to some mysterious, un-ordained rota (one which, each of them separately notices, does not include Father Patrick, who seems to escape all obligations). But they do employ a cook. Long ago it became clear that if they were to perform in the community they needed some basic nourishment, and they were always too few to spare the manpower needed to scour the markets and spend hours preparing food for a dozen hungry men. And now Ishmael the cook has become one of them, he has been there so long.

The girl is here because her father is dying. Michael looked at her, sitting in their midst like a flower in a

Japanese pebble garden. Her sadness gives her an ethereal beauty to which the man hidden within each of them, Michael thought, like toes peeping out from under a soutane (except for Father Morrissey, who has pared the man in himself away to nothing), cannot help but respond. They move about her with the peculiar energy of excitement of a group of men in the presence of a single woman, for all that they are priests. Even Father Christopher, the only one of them who is remotely near her in age (though in Michael's opinion Christopher, with his stoop and his anxious eyes behind the thick spectacles, must have been born old) – even Christopher has a buzz of excitement about him tonight.

The mouse is here because Father Dominic caught it in his room and wants to keep it as a pet, to the consternation of some of his brethren, the encouragement of others. The argument is bouncing round the refectory, a vehicle for the excitement, safely impersonal. Each of them is working hard to entertain the poor child in their midst. Each of them apart from their Superior, Father Morrissey, who preserves his habitual ascetic glumness as if he believes he carries responsibility for all their souls on his own shoulders. The mouse is inspected, considered. Fed on a stale crust, which it ignores but uses as a convenient step in its attempts to escape.

'Oh look at the sweetie!' exclaims Father Giovanni in his thick Italian accent. (Vanni's accent is so much part of his character, Michael thought. In his own language does he have a different persona?) 'Isn't he clever! And just look at his lovely little whiskers!' Vanni says, leaning over the jug, crooning.

The mouse balances on the bread on its long narrow back paws, reaching upwards with its front paws dangling, its slender snout trembling. The bright black eyes stand out like tiny jewels. Its belly is white, and the skin beneath the pale hairs of its paws is fragile and pink. But the rest of it is glossy black. It is a very healthy looking mouse.

Father Dominic persists: if François would make him a cage in the carpentry workshop he could keep the mouse in his room. It would live on scraps and leftovers from the kitchen. It would be no trouble. Vanni says he will help look after it.

'How do you know it's a he, Dom?' (There is a malevolent edge to Father Patrick's voice.) 'It might be a she, and then you'd be keeping a female in your room.'

Father Dominic ignores Father Patrick but blushes nevertheless.

'And if it is a she and it's already pregnant, you could find yourself with babies.' Father Patrick sits back grinning.

'I think you should let it go,' says Father John.

Father Dominic objects: 'The cat might get it!'

'You could take it out in the jug and lay it down under a bush in the garden. Let it come out in its own time when the coast is clear.'

'It mightn't know the cat is there,' says Father Giovanni. 'It might think it was safe to come out and then – splat – the cat might land on it out of nowhere. It's a very clever cat. It's probably watching us now and listening, waiting for its dinner. It's thinking, you have your dinner, I'll have mine. Thank you. Yum, yum and what's for pudding?'

Father Dominic, thinking there is a continental indifference showing up here after all, hovers protectively over the jug. In which the mouse is now busy washing itself as if it is in the privacy of its nest and not exposed like a goldfish in a bowl in the middle of the refectory, under the one bare light bulb.

Father Klaus says 'You can't let it go outside. I don' want it making itself at home in my pig feed. You should just kill it.'

'Yes you must!' agrees Father Stefan, but he giggles nervously as though he isn't quite confident of the conclusion. 'I got enough mouses in my garden, eating all everyting! I don' want no more!'

A great debate broke out then, on morality and ethics and the relationship of man to the world around him. Michael looked at Anne and forgot the story he had been telling himself about priests and their foibles as he watched her sitting so motionless in the centre of the room, silent, smiling, weary. Her eyes didn't smile. She perched on the uncomfortable chair as if carefully holding her exhausted bones together, but he could see she was touched by the way they moved around her as if she was fragile and precious, a foreign body unexpectedly lodged, the pearl in the midst of their celibate oyster. The intellectual discussion seemed to be washing over her but he watched her incline her head gently, to one, then to another, as if she was conscious of their eyes, turning and turning to her, concerned, approving, anxious, wanting to amuse her. They were all a little rivalrous, but he felt very quiet tonight himself. There was an element of proprietorship in the fact that he was accepted by all of them as the one who knew her best, *de facto* the one who was closest to her. Her friend.

The debate was still heatedly jumping backwards and forwards when Ishmael came in with the soup.

'What ting is dat? Heh?'

He banged the soup down on the table, making the mouse jump.

'What you done doin' now!' he said disdainfully to the

313

room at large. 'Dat ting no good. Kill it. Anyway, why you keep de cat for? De cat makes a poor servant when de rat is king.'

And he stomped out of the room. All the struggles of Ghana were summed up in Ishmail's retreating back. The priests looked at each other, shamefaced. Even Christopher was shamed out of groping for his notebook.

'He is right, you know,' Klaus said. He picked up the jug and carried it outside. Distinctly, through the windows, which were open to the noisy West African darkness, they heard Klaus calling the cat, and then the growl of a jumping cat, the faint, sibilant squeal of the mouse. Dominic gave a little wail. They had all momentarily forgotten Anne. Except for Michael, who saw, with a painful constriction of his own heart, the dark tremor that passed across her face. But she didn't cry, as he feared she might. Just held herself the straighter in the mean chair, the smile a little more glazed on her exhausted, lovely face.

Thursday morning. Her father in the hospital bed. He had slipped, at some indefinable point that night, from restless sleep into passive unconsciousness. The change so gradual it couldn't be measured except in subtle shifts: the stillness of his dry hand upon the sheet, the abandon of his slack mouth, the finality of his closed eyelids beyond which he still existed, somewhere. Shut in. Unreachable. His sour, frail breath like a barrier left standing. He'd been like that when she called in on her way back from the Mission last night. When she came in the morning there was no change.

The nurses were also subtly shifting – no longer quite so friendly, a hint of impatience about them. As if she and Moses were of the past while they were busy with the

314

present. As if the old tyranny of empire stretched even to here, the taking up of beds from the urgent living by the slow white dying.

Time blurred, little changing. The threat within that. Doctor Jebuni – Yiri, as she thought of him now that they were on first name terms – came in as he had done nearly every day. He was kind to Moses but to her he was friendly. She was aware that he sought her out. But that he was also embarrassed. As if he was an ambassador of health care in Ghana, and that she, seeing its underbelly, must be an unwilling critic. He explained too much and made her head spin with technicalities. She in turn was embarrassed, feeling stupid for her inability to understand clearly what he was explaining. But it was clear, whatever the nuances, that the outlook was bleak.

She looked at her father, so inert and frightening in the bed, and wondered, when he regained consciousness, would he be brain-damaged? She didn't ask Yiri this question, afraid he might take it as a criticism.

They sat, she and Moses, one on each side of the bed through the long hours. Two grey shadows, one dark, one pale. Moses, with his amazing ability to sit for hours at a time, continued to crack his knuckle joints and after a while it ceased to irritate her. It became like the rhythmic clicking of rosary beads, counting off the hours she dreaded to see passing, as if their massing in number was a measure of the dwindling of hope.

There was a point when she knew for certain what her last memory of her conscious father would prove to be: that moment of his eyes sliding off her face to look at Moses behind her. Whether it was love, or simple curiosity to see who had entered the room, for her the experience was the

315

same – abandoned by his eyes, abandoned by his attention, her last real moment with him corrupted by this, but so small a detail, so meaningless: just distraction, a moment of inattention. So accurate a summary of her life with him that the hurt was not angry, merely resigned. As if anger had been bled out of her by the long slow hours at his bedside. There was no logic for anger, only for acceptance. Moses, beside her, was no less hurt than she was, she knew that now.

But that wasn't the all of it. She wanted the place that Moses held at the centre. She did want it. They sat one on each side of the dying man but they were not equal. She could never not be female. The guilty race.

Thursday evening. They sat at either side of the dying patient, the priest and the girl. Moses had gone out for a smoke.

He cleared his throat. It was so long since either of them had spoken that he couldn't find his voice easily. And what he needed to say was difficult. 'You do know, don't you Annie, that he isn't going to make it…'

'No! Don't say that!' She glared at him. Her blue eyes were dark and hollow with fury and from lack of sleep. 'We mustn't give up hope! We just mustn't. He's going to be all right – I've got an instinct that he is.'

She went on glaring as if he had let her down, then turned away so that he wouldn't see that she was crying. Of course he did see, and was silenced. But he had sat by many dying people in this hospital, and in hot rooms and dark huts all over the town, and he knew the signs.

Moses came back in. He, too, looked terrible. He sat in the other chair on Michael's side of the bed but the heat,

316

which was still heavy though it was nine-thirty in the evening, was making the plaster on his leg excruciatingly uncomfortable and he had difficulty sitting still for long. He fidgeted, and fidgeted. Got up, sat down. Got up and went out to stand for a while in the corridor. Anne by contrast was as still as if she had been turned to stone. Both she and Moses seemed to have been here all day. Perhaps they both understood, in their secret hearts, that they were waiting for the end. Whatever she said, normally she would have gone home by this time at night. He had only come in for a few minutes but when he saw Dick he decided he must sit with them as long as he could. He watched Moses and the girl and felt himself a failure because he could not think of words to ease the pain that ran backwards and forwards between the two of them like a clumsy saw.

Time passed slowly, marked every now and then by Moses getting up to shift unevenly round the corridor on his crutches before coming back to the little room to sit again with his crutches laid on the floor beside him like folded wings. Anne sat so still, sideways on the seat, her chin resting on her hands on the back of the chair – she might have seemed to be sleeping, except that her eyes were fixed on her father's face. Every half hour she did as the nurses had taught her and turned Dick gently over to alleviate the bedsores that were making lurid raw patches on his knees and elbows, his hips and his buttocks. Then she sat and gazed as before, but now at the back of his head instead of at his face.

Michael watched Moses watching Anne turn the inert man in the bed, excluded because he could not stand and lift, and hurting for it.

Some time after eleven, Moses went off to eat.

'Have you eaten today, Annie?' Michael asked.

'Yes.'

He watched her intently for a moment. 'I don't believe you.' She didn't reply. 'Annie. Annie!' he said softly. 'You must look after yourself better than that. You'll get sick, and that will never do.'

'I don't want to eat. Just the thought of eating makes me feel sick.'

The slightest of movements in the bed distracted them. There was no change, and yet there was a transformation: the man in the bed had not so much moved as drawn energy inwards, as if all his being was focussed and concentrated behind the closed eyelids. Michael guessed at once what was happening. He got up and came quickly round the bed to stand behind her.

She did not make a sound as she watched her father tense in the bed, though he lay intently still. A slight frown condensed almost imperceptibly in the mask of his face, his faint breathing suspended as if he was gripped in a last struggle. Then he breathed out a long, last, rattling sigh and the tension went out of him. His face, slack and suddenly subtly empty, looked tranquil.

For a moment she was silent. Then a single wail of despair broke out of her, so desperate that Michael took hold of her rigid shoulders, gently massaging them as if he might pass some of his own strength to her. He felt the collapse as she crumbled. Gently, he rubbed the back of her neck.

By the time Moses came back they were sitting quietly, one on each side of the bed, heads bowed in stillness. As if we are praying, Michael thought. Moses seemed to know at once from the way they were sitting – their strange, cold,

European way – what it was that had changed. He threw himself across the motionless body, shaking and wailing, so that the nurses came running and everyone knew it was over.

24

Friday, October 8th

Late, so late that they had lost all idea of time, Michael walked her through the familiar dark, thinking how often this week she must have walked home late and alone to that empty little house. Nothing had outwardly changed, but for her it was no longer the same world as it had been yesterday, and the day before.

When they got to the house she seemed about to close the door distractedly, almost in his face. He held it ajar and asked if he might come in for a few minutes. He followed her into the living room.

'Annie, I need to tell you something.'

She looked at him, startled for a moment out of the weary depths of her numbness as if she had only just realised he was there in the room with her.

'Sit down,' he said, and sitting in the chair next to her he leaned forwards to look into her face. 'You need to understand, Annie. They bury people with what can seem like unseemly haste here. The reasons are obvious enough. The hospital will want arrangements to be made first thing in the morning. They're taking your dad to the mortuary now but they'll want him claimed as soon as possible, and it would be best to bury him tomorrow afternoon. Have you had any thoughts about what you want to do about all that?'

He'd been so afraid she would react angrily, but she seemed to have no fight left in her. She just looked at him, her big eyes darkly circled with exhaustion and dumb with sorrow.

'Moses came to me yesterday,' he said gently, taking one of her limp hands in his. 'He asked if your dad might be buried in the Mission graveyard.'

Her eyes woke up at that. 'The *Catholic* graveyard? But he's not a Catholic! Neither is Moses. Why did he ask that?'

'But Moses isn't *not* a Catholic, is he? I mean, he is from a Christian family, and he does sometimes come to Mass.' She stared at him blankly. 'It seems to be very important to him—'

'It's important to me, too! And I couldn't imagine putting Dad in a Catholic graveyard! Especially when he didn't go to church and certainly wasn't a Catholic. That's important to us too! You might not understand it, but it always was. We were never a family that needed religion.' She glared at him but he didn't take up the challenge and she looked away. 'I suppose I'll take his body home. I'm sure that's what Mum will want.'

It was Michael who was startled now. Possessiveness by the living towards the dead always made death more complicated, but this was an angle he hadn't foreseen. She was too tired to be reasoned with and it wasn't fair of him to try. 'Look, Annie,' he said gently, 'I'm only pushing you about this because there's so little time and I want you to have a chance to think it over before tomorrow. But think about it carefully. If you were to take the body home to England it would mean a horrible expense, though of course your dad *might* just possibly have an insurance policy to cover that. And it would certainly be a big bureaucratic challenge – so many arrangements to be made in a very short time. And what would it achieve? *Of course* it's hugely important to you, even more than it is to Moses. But you will always be connected to your dad. You don't have to lay claim to him, he was your father. But Moses has no public claim at all. What has he got, except the knowledge that the man he clearly loved, whatever other people might feel about that, is somewhere close by? Besides, if you let your dad be put to rest here he will be among his friends. If you take him back to a place he hasn't lived in for fifteen or twenty years he will lie among strangers. If that matters. Maybe it doesn't. You have to decide. It's about how *you* will feel, in the time to come.'

'But he wouldn't be only among strangers. I will be there.'

'Will you, though? You might be anywhere. You might even be here.'

The silence filled up with the pulsing, persistent beat of cicadas. On the far side of several walls, in the next-door house, a man coughed in his sleep. She was staring obstinately at the floor. He turned her hand over and traced small circles on its unconscious palm. 'Annie, Annie. I do know how you're hurting. But you have to forgive. You only hurt yourself if you don't. Believe me, I do know.' She looked up at him through eyes full of tears. 'Listen, Annie. It's been hard for you. I do know how terrible hard. But don't hate Moses for your father's mistakes in trying to hide from you what it would have been easier for you if you'd known. Your dad didn't understand that. He misjudged the situation, he misjudged you, but don't blame Moses for loving him, or for being loved by him. To love your dad truly don't *you* have to understand him? And that means understanding Moses's part in his life, even if that makes it harder to understand your own part in it. He did love you, your dad. Deep down you know he did. He just wasn't very good at handling it.'

There was another long pause filled with the noisy sounds of the Ghanaian night. Cats yowled and insects shrilled. Somewhere nearby a confused cockerel mistakenly greeted the dawn.

'What do I need to do then?' she said, so low he nearly missed it.

He rubbed her hand between the two of his. 'If you want me to, I'll ask the others if they'd be willing for him to be buried in the Mission. Very little is black and white in Tamale after all, and your dad did come to Mass once or twice, just as you have. It might only have been out of curiosity, but that's not for any of us to judge.'

He looked at his watch. It was half past four and he had to be up at six. 'I've got to go, and you must get some sleep.'

'I couldn't sleep!'

He stood up and gazed down at her for a moment. He was feeling very crumpled and tired himself. 'Have you still got that whisky? No, don't get up – I'll go and have a look in the kitchen. I'm going to make you a stiff drink of whisky with some lemon and honey, if you've got any. It'll help your mind settle enough to let you get to sleep for a bit.'

He came back a few minutes later. She hadn't moved. He handed her the glass and stood over her until she had drunk all of it. She took it like a child taking medicine, with a grimace.

'Go to sleep now. Don't try to make up your mind about any of this until the morning. Don't even think about it before then. I can't get out of the first lesson tomorrow morning but I'll come round straight after and see what you've decided. And then I'll go and sort out all the arrangements, whatever it is you want to do. You won't need to worry about the detail, you can leave all of that to me. Just make up your mind what you want me to arrange. Either way.'

'Thank you, Michael, for being such a friend.' She slurred the words slightly, her eyes closed.

'I want to be.'

'The best!' she said, grinning up at him without opening her eyes. It was the first time he had seen her smile in several days but she looked smaller, as if she had shrunk, and older by years. In a few moments she was falling asleep on the sofa where she sat. He let her be and left her sliding sideways into the cushions, fearing to wake her if he tried to make her go to bed. He crept out of the house to walk through the dark, noisy night back to the Mission and the longed-for haven of his own empty bed.

Friday morning. Anne heard him knock softly on the front door. She heard it from the stifled depths of the grief that hugged her in a straitjacket, its rhinoceros hide shutting all comforts out. The front door wasn't locked. She heard him open it and kick off his sandals on the porch step, and the faint padding of his bare feet on the concrete floor of the passage.

He didn't see her at first, in the chair behind the door.

'You're awake!' He stood over her, sizing her up. 'Did you manage to get any sleep?'

She had slept a dreamless, unrefreshing sleep, until the grim grip of the heat had pulled her awake not long after eight.

'I've brought you some breakfast. I knew you wouldn't have had any because I looked in the kitchen last night and there was none to have. I've brought a bag of treats. Everyone is worrying about you. They all send their love and I'm to take you back with me for lunch and also for supper tonight because they want to see for themselves that you're eating. But in the meantime I've been sent with this – ' he pulled the coffee table over in front of her and knelt on the floor to unload his string bag with great care onto the table top. She watched him, feeling untouched and untouchable. He was trying too hard. 'The bread was made by Ishmael, specially for you this very morning. Look, Annie – look at this.' He carefully unwrapped a small bundle in a red and white cloth. Inside was a miniature cob loaf. He tipped it towards her. 'Look!' A large 'A' had been cut into the golden crusty top before it was baked. He saw her looking, and catching at the limp hem of her attention, he rolled out the other treasures from his bag one by one, like somebody carefully blowing on a weak flame. 'This little pot of jam is from Giovanni, brought back from Italy. His mama made it. Though she must be 90 if she's a day, as he's no spring chicken. Unless he's been hoarding it for years. No, no – it smells good and there's no tell-tale fluff on it, I don't think it's too ancient. And here – ' (he took the top off an old jam jar) 'this is a great honour, this is! Here we have a morsel of Klaus's very rare and special cheese.'

'What! From pigs?'

He peered at her in surprise but she wasn't joking. 'Don't be daft! He keeps goats as well as pigs. He makes very good cheese but precious little of it. Come on, have a taste. It's a curd cheese. Doesn't keep, but it's very good with jam and new bread. Come on, Annie, help me eat it. Even if you only have a taste. So as not to hurt their feelings.'

'Tempting me with titbits – you're making me feel like Dominic's mouse.'

He laughed and looked her up and down. 'I have to tell you frankly, Annie, that you're not half so sleek as that damned mouse. You slept in those clothes, didn't you? You're going to eat something, and then you're going to get in that shower while I go and sort out the hospital. But first, try a bit of this bread.' Little by little, as if he were landing a fish, he wheedled her out of her obstinate sorrow, as if he knew she was trapped there by guilt as well as by grief. 'Tastes like cardboard, doesn't it?' he said gently, watching her chew and chew, and swallow with difficulty. 'Grief does that to you. But it does get better in the end. Only *you* can't afford to wait till then, you must keep your nourishment up or you'll fade away. I'm going to boss you remorselessly until you're eating properly again without me interfering. We don't want you going down with something like Victorian ladies used to in the days of the Empire. But now you have eaten something, a bit of business. The others agree, if it *is* what you want now you've had time to think about it, your dad can indeed be buried in the Mission graveyard. They feel that in the circumstances this would be appropriate. If you do want this it can be done this afternoon. But if you don't, and certainly if you want to take the body back to England, we'll have to go about things rather differently. Have you decided?'

She nodded. 'Bury him here in the Mission graveyard,' she said quickly, before she could change her mind. 'But it does hurt! I'm very unsure about it. And it's far too quick. I never expected to have to decide anything so soon.'

'I know, I know,' he said. 'But really it is for the best. And you will feel better when this bit is over, trust me. Now, there are a lot of boring but important bureaucratic things that have to be sorted out first. Notifying the embassy, all that sort of thing. Because he's a foreign citizen. I'm going to do all of that for you, you don't need to worry. But I do need you, as next of kin, to write a letter authorising me to act on your behalf. That is, if you want me to?' She nodded her agreement, her thanks. 'Good.'

He stood up. 'Right, first things first. Tell me which is your bedroom.'

Surprised, not least because he must know really, she gestured to the door off the living room that led to her room. A moment later she heard him going through her cupboard, talking to himself as the hangers in the wardrobe clicked: 'Would this do? Mmm, a bit on the frisky side. Something a bit more sober, I think.' What *was* he doing? But she knew he was performing for her, a one-man off-stage show, wanting to make her laugh. And she knew she was resisting. 'This might do. No, too sombre. Hmm... perhaps. Aha! This is looking more like it! And – yep, I think *this*.'

He reappeared, her long flowery skirt draped over his arm, and her white cheese-cloth shirt.

'I've done the big bits – you've just got the itsy bits to do. I always wanted a little sister to mother! Plenty of sisters but all of them too big by half.'

Little sister? A small spark of disappointment briefly penetrated the armour of her misery before snuffing out.

'Go and get in that shower now while I get some papers together. I need your dad's passport and stuff. Do you know where I should look for them?'

She led the way into her father's bedroom. She hadn't been in here for several days. It was so hard to think that Dad was never going to come back into it and she looked around dimly, feeling her mask slipping.

'In here?' he asked, beginning to open drawers on the right-hand side of the desk.

'No, not there,' she said hastily. 'That's where the letters are, in there.'

'Oh yes, the damned letters.' He slammed the drawer shut again. 'This side then?'

'Perhaps. I don't know,' she said. She didn't want to look through any of his papers ever again. Was glad Michael was there to do it. But she would have to in the days to come, wouldn't she? She couldn't expect that Michael would do it all. All the bills and administrative things, too. This was just special, to tide her through. She wished suddenly that it might not be special. That she could lean into him and have him here. Let his warmth and his strength melt into her. Today, tomorrow, next week. Carrying her on his big capable back. 'I'll go and have a shower.'

'Good girl. I'll be off just as soon as I've found his passport and his immigration papers. I'll come back in about an hour and take you to the Mission. You're going to stay with Dominic and Giovanni until it's time for the funeral. We'll do that later, when it's cooler.'

'Where will you be?'

'I've got lots of things to sort out. Coffin, truck, hospital. You don't want to worry about any of that. But you could give Dom and Vanni a hand. They're very busy in the dispensary at the moment, stocktaking. They'll keep you occupied until it's time to lay him to rest.'

She wondered listlessly how Dominic and Giovanni

would feel at having her awkward company foisted on them.

'You'll feel better when he's been laid to rest,' Michael said. 'And you'll feel better when you've been in that shower and got into some clean clothes. Off you go now. I'll pick you up in an hour.'

In her long blue skirt with the little white daisies she felt like a broken flower. The two fathers closed around her tenderly, as if she were one, each in his own way trying to do the right thing. There was comfort in it. The day passed in a daze of kindliness, and of other people's actions leading to final acts.

She hardly saw Michael. He scurried, like a large angel dressed in grey shorts and a pink tee-shirt emblazoned with *Stop the World* on the front and *I want to get off* on the back, from Mission to hospital to Regional Office and the Lorry Park, and back in reverse order. Dominic and Giovanni kept her busy. Even Father Morrissey was kindly.

At five-thirty, just as the suspense was becoming unbearable, Michael drove into the Mission compound in the old Land Rover with Moses in the passenger seat. Shortly afterwards a clapped-out pick-up drove in with a coffin roped down in the back.

He's in there! she thought. Horrified at the sudden thought that he must smell bad. This heat so powerful, the rate of decay so rapid in its iron grip. But Father Stefan was tucking her hand into the crook of his elbow and leading her off towards the church.

'You not been able to come to our garden lately,' he whispered. 'But some of it come to you.'

Inside the church, with its white walls and lurid white

and gold scrolls, its painted cherubim and blue Madonna, the soaring nave was surprisingly cool. There were white lilies everywhere, standing in big earthenware pots on the tiled floor. Their heady perfume was nearly overpowering, their perfect shapes glowed in the shadows. She felt her spirits ease a little in the solid tranquillity with its comforting certainties. Somewhere out of sight Father Christopher played meditatively on the old harmonium. The wheezing of the bellows which powered the harmonium, and the slight unevenness of Father Dominic's pumping, punctuated the quiet chords.

Moses hopped up the aisle on his crutches with Michael at his side. He stopped, hesitating over where to sit. Michael gestured to him to sit in the front row next to her.

Moses was very pale. The dark shadows round his eyes made him look as if he'd been punched in both eyes. But he nodded to her with dignity. Suddenly the bitter dregs of her feelings towards him dissolved. She wanted to reach out and touch him. His grief was hers, and hers was his. No other two people could come near to sharing the feelings that they shared. He was the brother she had never had, in this at least.

He stood beside her in the row, balancing on his one good leg and holding on to the rail in front as he bowed his head for a moment or two in prayer, then sat down carefully, his plaster knocking rudely against the prayer rail for all that. She caught his worried look and smiled reassuringly. He was no more at ease in here than she was.

Kwesi came in, looking scrubbed and anxious, and behind him a group of faces she recognised from the Rice Corporation. Michael went to greet them and show them to seats. They nodded and smiled at her, looking around them furtively, sitting upright and agog on the edges of their seats like new students at school. She was touched that they should have come, and amazed that Michael had managed to arrange even this.

More people came in, most of whom she didn't know. Nearly all of them men. Colleagues perhaps. Some were neighbours, she was surprised how many. A few white faces, mostly from TAT, including the American she'd met in the market that time, the one who'd been so rudely astonished that her father had a daughter. She looked at him sharply, wondering. What had he meant, that day? The man saw her looking and inclined his head gravely, giving nothing away.

All of the priests were here, of course. And suddenly, surprisingly, the boys arrived, washed and polished and unusually sombre – Joseph Appiah and John Aburiya, Thomas Nanfuri and nearly all of their class, and a good number of the Sixth Formers too, quietly filing in, and when the chairs were full, standing at the back of the church.

The service was short and simple. The Latin, being unfamiliar, sounded the more beautiful in her ears. She had expected to feel excluded by its foreign-ness but the singing rhythms cradled her instead, modulations of sound behind which the lowering sun slid slowly up the further wall and that time of evening came, the lovely, glorious time, when the world lost its own colour and hung in a sheen of gold against the deepening of the shadows in the trees and bushes. The coffin, draped in a purple cloth, was carried by four of the Fathers to the rectangular hole that had been rudely dug in the graveyard. Stefan appeared again at her side and took her hand. She looked down – in her palm he had placed a single red rose, the thorns carefully clipped. Her eyes flooded with tears so that she couldn't see. He held her elbow tightly. She could feel his wiry warmth at her side, breathing comfort. Father Morrissey was intoning the last words of the burial service, a dark shape against the light. The white sleeves of his surplice caught the sun like gilded wings as he raised his arms to make the sign of the cross. The faces of the small crowd were marked out in red-gold brilliance etched with black shadow as they stood in a circle round the grave.

And then earth and stones were falling rapidly onto the wood of the rough coffin, covering the wilting little rose. The hired men in grimy shorts and singlets worked quickly to fill the grave before darkness fell. Dominic took her gently by her free arm and he and Stefan led her quietly back to the refectory.

They walked down the road as they had so often walked in the friendly, noisy dark, he and she. He was wheeling his bicycle. But tonight they were silent and it was not like other nights.

All evening the other priests had been gently teasing her, drawing her kindly into their intimate world. Calling her their mascot. Saying that they wanted to keep her to themselves and feed her and look after her. 'Better than the mouse,' said Dominic. 'Prettier,' said Giovanni, and blushed as if he'd said something dangerous.

They told her she should stay, that she could sleep in the guest room in the hostel, that she didn't need to go back to an empty house tonight. That they were her family. Then they asked her what she meant to do and destroyed the illusion, because of course she was without family now and they expected her to leave them. Would she go back to England? And she said of course not, she wanted to stay and teach. She would be back at school on Monday! She loved it here, she said.

But she was more worried than she admitted about what she was going to do. Kwesi had already said to her that she could stay in the house as long as she needed, which she knew, even as he said it, meant she could take her time to leave but leave she must. The house would be needed for other workers. And there was no Jo any more. No Ursula, even. Only Michael, her friend, whose eyes had been watching her so intently all evening, who walked beside her now and was uncharacteristically silent and sad. The Fathers had competed over who was to walk her home. Dominic said he wanted to. Patrick argued it was his turn. But in the end, by some mechanism she didn't see, it was Michael, her customary guide and angel, who accompanied her. And she was glad.

She looked at him as they passed under a street lamp. He was still wearing the bright pink tee-shirt, though like the bougainvillea it was colourless in this light. But trousers, not shorts: for the funeral, and now to keep the mosquitoes at bay. The trousers swished slightly as he walked but his sandaled feet were silent on the road. She remembered that she asked him once, wasn't he afraid of getting hookworms? She'd been told always to wear shoes. And he had said self-mockingly, 'I'm doing God's work. If I get hookworm, He can sort me out.'

Her mind was swinging dangerously in the warm darkness. Ferreting among all the different things that had been said during the last twenty-four hours. She could not bear the thought of leaving Tamale, not least because it would mean leaving him, this friend at her side. She thought she would rather stay an old maid and teach alongside him and be his friend than go back to Britain now, to its staid certainties and dull convictions. But she felt out of her depth. Unfledged still, and unsure of her connections. The Fathers meant to be kind but their kindness made her more aware how far removed from them she was. Too young, too foreign, too female, to be quite accepted. A mascot, not a brother. She could never be that, of course. And amongst them she would always be an outsider for that simple reason.

She sighed. Michael looked at her quickly.

'What did you say?' she asked him. The grey mood had lifted just a little but the light, which was glinting in, was bleak and she wanted the safe blanket of the numbness to descend back down.

'Nothing. I didn't speak,' he said, and they were silent then until they got back to the house. It was ten o'clock and the street was quiet. No one was around to call out to them and she was glad of it, not wanting to have to leave the cocoon of her privacy and explain anything to outsiders yet.

The house looks forlorn. She stands dejectedly in the middle of the living room, regretting now that she didn't let the Fathers persuade her to stay in the guest room at the Mission. She doesn't want Michael to leave but she can't say it. All their life must be like this, the felt and the unsaid. She looks at him and sees for the first time how tired he is. There are lines in the sun-tanned skin around his eyes and his mouth and he looks haggard. Her heart goes out to him in a hot flood. But she doesn't move. Just looks.

He moves towards her and unexpectedly puts his arms round her and draws her to him.

'Oh Annie. Little Annie! You look so terribly miserable. I hate to leave you in this empty house looking so forlorn.'

She stands where she has ached for months to be, against the warmth of his big chest, his surprisingly firm belly, holding her hands carefully limp at her sides, hardly daring to breathe. Surprise is what she feels most. Wondering what he is doing, terrified of breaking this brotherly gesture and not trusting herself. He is so close. She can feel him, breathe him. She could so easily move wrongly and break the spell.

His breath stirs her hair. She can hear his heart beating loudly. She isn't sure whether he is comforting her or she is comforting him. She leans ever so slightly against him and the pain falls out of her, as if it is puddling on the floor at her feet. She breathes more easily. They stand there a long, silent time. Then she feels him turn his face into the top of her head and she leans into him and cautiously puts her arms around him at the same moment that he begins to kiss her hair. He kisses her ear. She reaches up and kisses the strange foreign intimacy of his neck. His arms are about her now, hard-muscled and full of tension. She is crying, she realises, and laughing at the same time. He is kissing her face, her neck, under her chin, his arms still tight about her. They sink slowly, inevitably, onto the floor. He touches her breasts, his hands passing over her body as light as moths. She passes her hands over his chest, feeling the sharp bumps of his nipples through his tee-shirt. He is moaning her name, and crying too.

Afterwards, that was all she remembered. How they had rolled tightly on the floor, both of them crying. No clothing removed, not touching one another's bare skin, but the shocking frankness of how they were lying together making

335

them seem naked. He'd held her so tight she thought he would suffocate her, his erection pressing hard against her stomach through their clothes. No thoughts in her head, just Michael. Michael filling her blind senses. The dark shapelessness of it, until he convulsed urgently, stretching his head up and away from her and trembling violently all over as if he would break in pieces. Then he turned his head away and lay very still.

She stroked his hair tenderly. 'Michael. Oh Michael.'

Abruptly, he pulled away. Got up, not looking at her. Rubbing the tears roughly from his cheeks and saying over and over, 'I'm sorry. I'm so sorry.' And there was a wet patch on his crumpled trousers, at the top of his thigh. So that she knew for certain. She couldn't pretend now that she did not know.

He turned away as if ashamed. The tangled love rushed through her chest like a tide-race. Poor Michael! Standing there with his hand over his eyes like a man in shock.

Michael I love you! The words she could not say, not yet. Letting him take his time. Her own heart exulting: I knew, I knew! This is who we are!

Of course it was complicated, especially for him.

The timing was awful, but Dad of all people would surely understand.

They *could* make it work.

She sat on the floor, her back against the bookcase and her clothes all awry, her mind racing and the love beating in her veins. *It's going to be all right. Love versus outdated clerical vows. And love winning. Surely.*

Suddenly, he was gone, his last words hanging in the air behind him. 'I'm so sorry, Anne. Forgive me.'

25

Saturday and Sunday, October 9th and 10th

She stayed around the house all day before she was forced to acknowledge he wasn't going to come. At least, not today. She had been so sure he would. Not having slept all night herself, except in fits and starts, going over and over the events of the evening until they got slippery and hard to hold onto, she knew that he must be even more disturbed. Surely it was obvious now that they were meant to be together. He would come to her and they would discuss what they were going to do, now that everything was so altered. It needn't be complicated. They could stay in Tamale. He would have to make difficult and complicated changes, of course, but there was no reason why they shouldn't both continue to teach, and he could fulfil all his other duties too but as a layman, not as a priest. They would probably have to be formal and get engaged, she realised that. No sex before marriage, either, whatever Michael's private beliefs on religion might really be. She would do that for him, of course she would! She would even be prepared to become a token Catholic, if it mattered to him. Or to anybody else. She realised the Fathers' generosity might be a little stretched, faced with all these changes and herself no longer the innocent, passive mascot, but she couldn't believe they weren't capable of adapting, in the end. Even dry, antagonistic, woman-hating Father Morrissey.

As the long day slipped towards night her understanding shifted. He had not come. Her feelings, on such a high in the morning, had cut a huge arc. There was a plateau in the early afternoon when the possibility that he might not come began to prick at her through the exhaustion of prolonged tension and excitement. Then a long, slow crashing as the day wore uneventfully on. He didn't see their future as she did, after all. The disappointment was so bitter that for a while she was angry with him. How could he feel sorry for her and then let himself embrace her like that? But she was glad he had, because now she knew it was real.

She went to bed in a state of strange, sad calm and slept through for once. But was troubled by confused dreams.

Next day, Sunday, she woke with a start. In all the pressure of waiting for Michael yesterday she hadn't even thought about phoning her mother, but of course she must. She couldn't tell her by letter. Tomorrow, she thought. Tomorrow after school will be time enough. There was nothing to eat, Ishmael's little loaf and Giovanni's jam finished yesterday, but she didn't dare go far from the house, terrified of missing Michael if he came while she was out. Wondering what had stopped him from coming yesterday, unwilling still to admit he might not come at all. Going round in circles in her mind on this.

Other thoughts began a corrosive drip-drip-dripping. That photograph. The suggestion in it of continuing relationship between her parents when they themselves had always suggested there was none. Why? Was it a cover for something else? Did her mother already know about Dad and Moses, then? Such an abyss of unknowing yawned suddenly at her feet. Layers and layers of implication. If her mum knew, shouldn't she too have been told? Was that the real reason her mother had been so anxious about her coming here?

She rattled restlessly about the house, picking things up, putting them down again. Staring for a long time at the photograph. Feeling left out. Absurdly left out.

Around midday she walked out of the house quickly, at the hottest time when the sun pelted down from so directly overhead that shadows were shrunken to almost nothing and people avoided being on the road if they could. She climbed the path at the back of the house to where Abina made bread in her round clay oven. Abina greeted her with warm concern, hugging her hard, telling her how sad she and her husband had been to hear of Dick's death. The Dagbani phrases familiar now for death and loss and regret. Abina took two loaves and pressed them into her hands but would not accept any payment. Anne was embarrassed. She argued, but ineffectually.

The same thing happened with the banana seller up on the road, an elderly woman with a kind, wrinkled face, her greying hair tucked neatly under a kerchief: the sad and courteous phrases, the sorrowful look the old woman gave her, the warm, dry hand gripping her arm. And no money accepted for the fruit.

She hurried back to the house. Michael might have come down the road while she was going up the path.

There was a bicycle leaning against the house wall.

In the porch, Kwesi was sitting on the small stool Moses used to sit on when he was sorting rice. He jumped up shyly when he saw her. 'Dey tellin' me you just gone out so I waited,' he said, shaking her by the hand. He wouldn't come

339

into the house. He had brought her some letters that had arrived in the post for her father, and a file of personal papers from his office. And to see how she was.

She brought him a warm bottle of Fanta from the crate in the kitchen and sat beside him on the porch step while he drank it. He was awkward and self-conscious. But when she asked him about Millie his wife and the imminently expected twins he became animated. She watched his face as he talked, the ungainly mouth, the bright, intelligent eyes, the welts and bumps of the tribal marks that patterned his forehead and cheeks. Wondering, not for the first time, how they made those marks and how painful it must be when they did it.

She thought he might be going to invite her to a meal and was relieved (and then disappointed) when he did not. He didn't stay for long, anxious to get back to his Millie. And really it was very generous of him to spend part of his precious Sunday afternoon coming to see if she was all right, she knew that. He shook her by the hand and promised to come again soon. She remembered then what she wanted to ask him. Said carefully that she knew they needed the house back for their employees but what was the rent for a house like this? The sum he named was so large, compared with her modest salary. She couldn't possibly pay anything like that and have enough left to feed herself. And besides, as Kwesi said, there were no such houses available to rent anyway. What about rooms, she asked? He looked doubtful. Oh yes, there were plenty of rooms to rent but they wouldn't be good places for her. Whether he meant as a foreigner, or as a single girl, she couldn't tell.

He left, and she felt terribly lonely after he'd gone. Tried to immerse herself in preparing lessons for tomorrow. Tried not to listen for footsteps. Went at last to bed and dreamed terrible dreams. Her mother insisting she bring the body back home, so that all night long she was scrabbling with her bare hands in the cold, gritty sand of a dream graveyard, trying to find him.

'Anne! I didn't expect you to come in today.' Father Morrissey sounded momentarily flustered. 'Did you not want to take some time off?' She shook her head to the question, not trusting her voice. 'In that case, could I have a word.' He had recovered himself quickly. It didn't sound like a request. Suddenly wary, she followed him back down the corridor to his office. Father Morrissey was small and neat but he had few graces and it was obvious something was amiss as he sat at his desk and motioned her to sit in the chair on the further side. He put his elbows on the desktop, his hands clasped as if in limp prayer, his back very erect. This was the way they had sat at their first interview, so long ago, it seemed. Six and a half eventful months. A lifetime.

A whole lifetime, she thought, and swallowed the rising sob. Father Morrissey tapped his thumbnails against his teeth. She sat watching him and willing herself to be calm. Don't jump to conclusions, she instructed herself, listen carefully before you speak. He may know nothing. But Michael had not been in the staffroom this Monday morning and she hadn't heard his voice anywhere in the corridors, though all her senses had been waiting for it. No one had mentioned his name in her presence. But then, nobody had had occasion to, and they had all seemed their usual selves and not as if they were concealing, or watching.

At last Father Morrissey spoke. It took a while before his

341

words sank in. '… and therefore our funding situation has changed. So we shall not be able to continue to employ you.'

What funding situation? She hadn't actually heard and could not ask now. She looked at him. He gazed calmly back, his grey eyes a mask. He was firing her! She was so astounded by this that the implications took longer to sink in. And the tone. The curt edge in it. And the fact that he didn't say anything about the misfortune of the timing, at such a point of crisis in her life. She thought he must believe she was no observer of such niceties herself. Guilt flamed suddenly from the corner where it had been hiding, waiting to be summoned. She felt her face go hot and dropped her gaze to the floor. The large black ant labouring past was carrying a remnant of Father Morrissey's elevenses. He was talking now about cuts and economies, the fact that he was sure – *now that your father is so sadly no longer among us –* that she would want to go back to England. He spoiled his succinct bombshell by saying too much after all. Forgetting her shame she lifted her head to watch him, and began to resist. He was lying to her. It wasn't for the sake of economy he wanted to be rid of her. It was something to do with Michael, but it wasn't Michael's initiative she was watching.

She knew, suddenly, how to stop him in his tracks. She said calmly, 'I'm very sorry to hear you've got to make cuts. But that needn't stop me teaching. I'm not planning to go back to England. I can go on teaching on a voluntary basis, just as I did at the beginning, even though it's full-time now. I'd like to do that and I can afford to do it. You needn't worry about paying me. When and if things improve you can take me back onto the payroll.'

His eyes hardened. He frowned, and looked distractedly

at the papers on his desk. Ha – got him! she thought. And waited, curious to see how he would get out of that.

His eyes met hers. All right, they seemed to say, have it your own way. Out loud he said, 'I'm afraid there is more to it than that. As you are well aware, Miss Foster. Let us just say that your services are no longer required and leave it at that. You may take your things and leave after this interview. I had hoped to save us both from embarrassment but it seems you choose otherwise.'

'What are you talking about?'

'I am not prepared to spell out details. Suffice it to say – your presence has had an unfortunate impact on this Mission and while I acknowledge this may not have been intentional on your part, I want the situation remedied as quickly as possible. It is not appropriate for you to remain in our employ. I think you understand why.'

She stared back at him, half in horror, half in defiance. She wanted to know what had happened to Michael. She was sure Michael wouldn't have betrayed her to Morrissey but she thought Morrissey wanted her to think that he had. He stared back, but something in the back of his eye was – just slightly – flinching. He was bluffing, she was sure. But she was also sure that he would tell her nothing. She stood up with all the dignity she could muster. Michael's voice, teasingly mocking in her ear, was all that stood between her and howling mortification – that she the good girl (the girl guide, the hockey captain, the school prefect) should be found so very much in the wrong, whether or not Morrissey was bluffing about the details.

Having nothing left to lose, when she got to the door she asked him the question she'd been holding back. 'Where is Michael? Where is he?'

343

He wouldn't tell her. But he couldn't quite stay silent. Father Morrissey always, in the end, reduced his own power by saying too much. 'It's not the first time he's been in trouble, you know.'

And then he added with barbed satisfaction, 'And I don't suppose it will be the last.'

Father Klaus looked up from feeding the pigs. When he saw her, he emptied the bucket into the trough and came over to the side of the pen.

'Where has Michael gone?'

He hesitated. 'I cannot tell you that. If he wants to, he will tell you. And actually I do not know. He went so suddenly already. I have not heard from him yet.'

She looked carefully into Klaus's face and thought he was telling the truth. So, Michael *had* gone away, he wasn't just hiding. 'But you will hear from him, won't you. He will write to you – you are his friend.'

'I cannot tell you anything unless he asks me to,' Klaus said gently. 'These things happen sometimes and when they do they hurt very bad. But you must let it take its own course. It is between him and his conscience, what he does now.'

'Who did he get into trouble with before?'

He looked puzzled. 'Before? Who told you that?'

'Father Morrissey.'

Klaus's ugly features relaxed slightly but he didn't say anything.

'Did he lie to me then? Did Father Morrissey lie?'

'No, not lie. But he let you think something other than what is true. Perhaps he did not mean to.'

'What did he mean then? If Michael *wasn't* in trouble before?'

'Oh Michael was in trouble, sure. Before he ever came to Ghana. And Father Morrissey knew him in that time and he did not like him for it. That is why he would let you misunderstand. Perhaps also he thought it would be easier for you if you did. It was not trouble for a woman, it was for apostasy.'

'Apostasy?'

'Abandoning his God. Abandoning his faith. That is what they thought Michael did.'

She was silent. If Michael had lost his faith, why hadn't he left the Church?

Klaus said quietly, his eyes on the pigs as if he was talking to himself, 'If a priest loses his way he is a lost and lonely man. This happened for Michael one time, I think. Not complete loss of his faith perhaps, but he lost his sense of God. It is a hard life if you do not live it with a sense of God. You must work out everything for yourself and sometimes your conviction is shaken. For Michael, I do not know. I think perhaps you shook his conviction, too.'

'Am I guilty then?'

'How can I answer that, child? I do not know your story.'

They stood on either side of the barrier and watched the pigs in silence. The sows had finished their feed and were nosing round Klaus's legs. He scratched one of them behind the ears and the animal leaned against him, trembling with pleasure.

Klaus said gently 'Sometimes a man runs to God, away from himself. It is a terrible thing if then he loses God, because what does he have left to keep him from himself? I do not know if this was true for Michael. We never spoke of it. But I do know that he must have time now to work out what he must do. Possibly his future may include you but it would be false to hope so. It is more likely, I think, that it will not. Priestly habit dies hard, you know. He has long ago decided what in life he must give and how he will give it. It would be hard to make space for another in this, even without God.'

'But surely loving another human being is a state of blessedness in itself?'

'Ah, but do you know that he loves you in the way you mean?'

She flinched. She didn't know. How could she, when hope unbalanced all her judgement?

'But surely if he doesn't believe in God he would always regret it if he ran away now.'

'Ran away from whom? From you, or from God? We do not know what is happening for him. Maybe in his own way he has always believed in God. Maybe the pain he is suffering now, having to go away and leave his beloved school behind, the questions about himself he is having to answer – maybe *this* will bring God to him, if he did not already have Him in his heart.'

He smiled at her kindly but she knew that in his eyes she was something negative, bringing trouble to Michael. She had wanted Klaus to say something so different and she couldn't quite believe she hadn't heard it. Her one last hope. She lingered by the pen, staring unseeingly at the ground.

'I am sorry, Anne – I must finish feeding the pigs. Come back tomorrow and we will talk.'

She nodded, but she knew she wouldn't see him again.

As she walked up the slope away from the pig-shed she heard voices in the garden. She couldn't leave without saying goodbye to Stefan and Emmanuel. If she wasn't to go on teaching she wouldn't be able to come to the garden again either. Blow after blow falling on her head.

And then she thought, maybe Stefan wouldn't want to see her now, if he knew? Her heart was heavy and unwilling as she turned in at the little gate but a small part of her brain was also urging, *Go on – they might have news of him!* She walked down the path towards the shelter. She could hear, from under the fading thatch, their two voices rising and falling.

They fell silent, looking up at her in a mixture of surprise and confusion that she couldn't interpret. It was clear they knew something but she couldn't tell from their expressions what, and in any case she was too choked with sudden emotion to say anything at all. She stood looking down at them where they sat on their low stools. Then Stefan got up, so sharply that he knocked over the stool he'd been sitting on, and rushed off. Not towards her, as for a moment she thought he was going to, but past her and out of the shelter. She was shocked by his crumpled face, like a child in tears.

Emmanuel stared at her. 'He very upset 'bout Michael.'

'I came to tell you I won't be coming here any more.'

'We know dat. Stefan very sad 'bout dat too. What about de play?'

The play? It seemed irrelevant. But Emmanuel didn't sound hostile. He bent over the charcoal stove while she stood hesitating. If she waited would Stefan come back, or was he angry with her?

Emmanuel looked sideways at her, openly curious. 'What you do now, now your daddy dead?'

She shrugged. Then words and courage deserted her. She muttered goodbye and fled.

Stumbling, tear-blind, she walked quickly away from the Mission towards the centre of town. She couldn't bear to go back to the house. Couldn't bear to do anything. She felt like a limpet pulled out of its shell, all her tender privacies exposed in the sun. Even Stefan condemned her now. His good opinion and his affection, which she had accepted so easily and taken for granted, probably destroyed.

All her brave opposition had crumbled in shocked self-disgust. She'd thought herself so clever standing up to Morrissey but what had she done except confirm his suspicions? (She was sure it could only be suspicions, she still clung to her faith in Michael.) Morrissey thought her bad. She who had always stood in the ranks of the good! Her pride hurt as if it had been dragged out of her body and chopped into little pieces. She crossed the road blindly and a lorry blared its horn.

Of course Morrissey would think her awful, if he had any inkling at all of what had happened. As Stefan seemed to. Her father freshly in his grave. And she *was* awful. She pushed her way through the crowds on the pavement outside the Post Office, wondering that it had taken her until now to think so. Blind, selfish, and disgusting.

Her head jerked up. *So* selfish. She turned back and pushed her way inside the building.

In the phone booth, she stood with her face to the wall so that she need not see the grinning faces peering in at her and listened to the phone ringing in a far-away house, steeling herself for the tears and recriminations. On the dirty wall all manner of hands had written phone numbers, and Kofi declared his love for Kisi in green marker pen. Her mother's voice spoke in her ear. She opened her mouth to say *Mum?* but nothing came out. Her mother's voice said, 'Darling, is that you?'

No tears, no scene. No accusations. Her mother unusually dignified. Her parting words hitting the harder for that. *Darling – come home.*

Anne came out of the Post Office and turned towards the market. She had very little idea where she was heading now. Food. She ought to buy food. But it was merely clutching at the straws of normality: she would never want to eat again. In the crowded alleys between the stalls, dust rose from underfoot. She stared at the colourful piles of vegetables and fruit with unseeing eyes and stopped at a stall selling pyramids of tomatoes, their red waxy skins giving off a rich aroma in the heat that verged on the putrid. The woman selling them haggled languidly, a bored expression on her face. They agreed a price. Fifty *pesewas,* Anne thought, but when she handed over the money the woman shouted angrily, 'What dis? I say seventy-five! I no want you cheat me!'

It was the last straw. Or, Michael's voice said in her head, the last tomato. She burst into tears and rushed away, tomato-less, leaving behind the package of peanut butter which she'd put down on the table while she counted out the money. People turned to look at her curiously as she made her way out of the market. She brushed the tears away furiously and walked fast. But to where, she did not know.

A car she didn't recognise drew up beside her. Tooted cheekily. Bending to look through the passenger window she saw it was Deepa, Ursula's friend.

'Anne, I was so, so sorry to hear about your father. We've only just got back from leave. I was going to come and look for you tomorrow. Are you all right? You look dreadful!' The cut-glass accent. Deepa the dignified.

349

'I'm okay. Just feeling a bit strange. It was very hot in the market.'

'Get in. I'll give you a lift back home.'

'No. No, it's all right…'

But Deepa got out and came round the car, shading her eyes with one hand to scrutinise Anne's face, making her feel pale and ugly as she stood there exposed in the bright light. Was it obvious she'd been crying?

Deepa, neat and elegant as always in dark slacks and a white silk shirt, kohl accentuating her handsome eyes, her silky black hair pinned up on her head. Deepa with the haughty bearing of a Rajput princess, and a voice to match. Taking Anne by the arm she said gently (but in a tone that was not to be opposed), 'Get in the car. I'm taking you home.'

She did as she was told. Deepa got in behind the wheel. 'With whom are you staying?'

'No one.'

She felt Deepa's keen look of surprise.

'No one? Surely you're not living by yourself at such a time! Do you not have a houseboy?'

'I'm living by myself now.'

'Have you been eating? You don't look as if you've been looking after yourself at all. You must eat, Anne, or you'll get sick.'

'I'm sick of people telling me that!'

Deepa said, 'But it's true.' She drummed her fingers on the steering wheel. 'Look, come home with me now to my place. It will be good to have a talk, and you can stay for lunch. I'll take you home afterwards.'

'I don't want to put you to any trouble.'

'Nonsense. You've got loads to tell me about. And I've

got things to tell you, I've just been staying with Ursula in England. Come, let's go.'

The bungalow was set in a big garden in a wooded area of the town Anne had never been to before. Hidden birds made loud tropical noises. Now and then bright feathered things swooped or flitted half out of sight among the leaves. In this garden, time seemed to have no relevance. She sat beside Deepa at a wicker table with a glass top, under the shade of a tree, drinking tea spiced with cardamom and ginger. Butterflies danced in the sun. It was like another country in this garden, quite unconnected with the Tamale she knew.

Deepa was talking about Ursula, how she was settling back into English life. 'She is drinking less. Which means she is fun to be with again.'

Anne regarded Deepa, who looked cool in spite of the fierceness of the sun which sparked down through the leaves above them. It was impossible to tell how old she was. She might be thirty-five, she might be ten years older. She wasn't beautiful, but in her assurance and her sense of herself she was handsome. I would like to be like that, Anne thought. When I'm older. But I'm the wrong colouring – I could never be so handsome! Aloud, she said musingly, 'Tamale to Luton. It's a bit brutal, isn't it?'

Deepa laughed. 'Yes, I must say I didn't take to Luton.'

They fell silent. A large azure-blue and Omo-white crow landed awkwardly on the grass, eyed them askance, and took off again. Nothing in Ghana was mediocre, not even the crows.

'Tell me about it,' Deepa said softly.

She told the outline. The accident. And then the dreadful

351

slow plunge into an ending, which even now seemed like a bad dream from which she would wake in a while. She told about the priests being so kind, how they had picked her up and looked after her as if she were a rag doll. Then she told what Father Morrissey had said, at their meeting today.

'But Anne, that is quite awful. He can't do that! Surely you have a contract?'

'No. It was a very informal arrangement. He can't keep me on if they haven't got the money.'

'But how thoughtless of him to drop you just now! He must know this is the very time when you need support. And besides, my house-girl Isobel has a son in one of your classes and from what I hear you've been doing very well. They are fools to let you go. Utter fools!'

Anne shifted uncomfortably in her chair. 'I've made it sound more simple than it really is. There is, umm – there is... a complication.'

'What do you mean?'

She looked away, avoiding Deepa's piercing gaze, into the blue-green canopy of the leaves, the bright sky beyond piled high with summery clouds. At home, she thought disconnectedly, it is autumn now. 'It's not that simple. He had reason to think...badly of me.' Deepa looked disbelieving. 'Actually, he must think very badly of me,' Anne added, trying to control her voice, which was threatening to betray her. She stopped and swallowed back tears. If only I didn't cry so easily, she thought furiously, wiping at her eyes.

Deepa passed her the box of tissues that was lying on the table. 'Why don't you just tell me.'

Sympathy alone would not have seduced her but loneliness and isolation did. She didn't tell all of it, but enough. In synoptic, careful phrases. And then sat waiting to be condemned.

The silence was unnerving.

'Do you think I'm wicked?'

'I don't think you're wicked,' Deepa said at last. 'Muddled, perhaps.'

'I don't know what to do. He must be feeling terrible. He might even feel guilty towards me. But he shouldn't! He wouldn't if he knew how I feel about him. But I don't know where he is so I don't know how to tell him. And anyway, perhaps it's me who makes him feel bad – perhaps he feels I make him a bad person. It can't *be* bad, can it? Love can't be a bad thing, even when it's messy?'

'Ah. Love. I can't understand why all you Europeans make such a burden out of love.' Deepa stared at her for a moment, one neat eyebrow raised. 'Sunni and I married for love, against our parents' wishes. It caused a hell of a lot of trouble at the time. But that was a long time ago and we have had our ups and downs. I look at my friends whose marriages were arranged and it seems to me that the average arranged marriage is not any worse than the average love marriage, once the first few years are over. All marriages are an arrangement in the end.'

She didn't want to think like that! That wasn't the world she wanted. She sat in silence, sadly watching the sun-dance shadows on the table and thinking the world she wanted had fallen away out of her grasp. She couldn't even see it any more. 'I can't imagine the future. I'm not sure I even want one, without Michael in it, and without my dad.'

An elderly man dressed in loose white garments came out of the house and crossed the garden towards them, the sun beaming on his shiny bald head.

'Ah, my husband,' Deepa said.

'Were you waiting for me to luncheon?' He turned to Anne and bowed with a grave smile: 'Whom do I have the pleasure of meeting?'

'Sunni, this is Anne, Dick Foster's daughter. Talk to her for a while.' Deepa stood up. 'Please excuse me, I must go and organise lunch. Anne, you will stay and eat with us and then this afternoon you will have a rest here. I don't believe you have slept properly for a long time. In fact, I think I will insist that you stay with us until tomorrow. So please don't bother to argue.' She rested her hand lightly on her husband's shoulder and bent to murmur something in his ear before leaving them.

Sunni said, 'She is telling me I must not chunter on and bore you. I was so very sorry to hear about your father. He was a very intelligent man. I didn't meet him very often but when I did we had good chats. I liked him very much indeed.' He sat in silence for a moment, contemplating his generous abdomen. After a suitable pause he looked up and asked whether she liked Dickens and what she had read. He had a comfortable voice. While he talked he fiddled with a leather tobacco pouch, filling his pipe. That hurt. She turned away to look at the garden, trying not to think about her dad by concentrating hard on what Sunni was saying about Dickensian London. She had the strangest sensation of not knowing where she was. Africa, India, London – it all seemed so distant. All reality receding. The past and the future far away. The two of them floating in a garden like a green boat in a sea of tropical trees.

Deepa called from the verandah. Sunni said 'Better go, the Memsahib is calling. Now, do you want the Penny Room before luncheon?'

A bedroom like a boudoir, rich with textured white cottons: massed cushions, an embroidered bedspread, white on white. The filmy gauze of the mosquito net (they didn't have them in their house) making her think of four-poster beds. Muslin curtains at the windows, through which the garden floated by, firmly shut out by the glass panes. The air-conditioning hummed gently. She shivered in the cool air. Deepa was moving about, putting towels on the chair, showing her the electric switch outside the bathroom for the shower, turning back the crisp white sheets of the bed.

In this room she felt dirty and scruffy. The bed looked so fresh and inviting, she thought perhaps she could sleep after all. The unusual sensation of having eaten well made her drowsy. A new cake of soap lay on top of the fluffy towels. The luxuriousness tempted her out of any last idea that she might go home just yet. What sort of home was it anyway, with only her in it? As she watched Deepa turn down the bedclothes she felt mothered, though Deepa was the last person she would think of as motherly, with her proud face and her hawkish profile, her clipped phrases. And half of her felt she was copping out, letting herself be mothered. But it was like sinking into a warm bath, this sensation of giving herself up to being looked after, and she couldn't resist it.

Then she was appalled at herself. Five days ago she had been giving herself up to being looked after by Michael. Was she so fickle? Or so childishly helpless? She felt ignorant and gauche, and suddenly so very weary that it was too much effort even to shower. As soon as Deepa had left the room she fell onto the bed, rolled under the deliciously cool, crisp sheet and white bedspread, fully dressed as she was, and slid downwards into dark, remorseless sleep.

26

Early November 1976

The bright, empty beach stretches in a taut, straight line to her left and to her right. The wind makes the dark blue water choppy and turns the coconut palms inside out, bending them landwards on slender trunks. She has come out from Accra in a taxi, meaning to swim, but the sea claws at the sharply shelving beach with such an abrupt line of surf, the long rollers rearing up steeply and crashing down almost vertically, that she lost her nerve. That, and the solitariness of it. There is no one here except for a couple of boys walking along the shoreline in tattered shorts and the suave taxi-driver who leans against the bonnet of his car on the road which runs along above the shore, smoking, and watching her. She had expected to pay him off and take another when she was ready to go back into the city, but there are no taxis here so she has asked him to wait. No taxis, and no crowds either. Nobody at all except the driver, and the two boys, and her sitting alone on the sand.

She flew down from Tamale this morning, and tonight she will fly to London on the midnight plane. Crossing back up the country again like a fly over an atlas, back into the familiar arms of November Britain. A late and (her mother informs her) glorious autumn, after the hottest, driest summer on record. There. But here it has rained more than normal, there has been no drought. And her father has died and left her, more definitively, more totally, than he ever did before.

She does not want to go back but she is resigned to it. She was unable to resist the logic of Deepa's argument. 'Go back,' Deepa kept saying. 'Get yourself trained. And then come back to a proper contract. Here, or somewhere else. The world is enormous, the possibilities are infinite. There is nothing for you here now, as you are, that does you justice. Go and come.'

That lovely, evocative Ghanaian phrase. *I will go and come*. So she does. And she will.

Far away her mother is excited at the prospect of her return but, for her, returning is an obligation she must endure on the way to something else. All those things she must tell, or not tell, the questions to be asked or left hanging, and she is still undecided. What difference will it make, knowing more or knowing less, to either of them now? Her father's real life is a secret she shares with one person only. Perhaps she should leave it that way. She hasn't told Deepa, even.

It isn't uppermost in her thoughts. Her heart is lumpen with the pain of leaving. How can she leave not knowing whether, or when, she will come back? Even if she had assured Joseph she would, when he came to the house to ask for her address. How can she leave with such a suspense of experience begun and not completed? My boys too, she thinks, watching the long unfurling of the breakers. Has she let them down, whatever Joseph might assure her otherwise? Will the feeling she has deserted them stay with her for ever?

Sitting on the sand, sifting it gently through her fingers,

her chin on her knees and goosebumps on her arms, she shivers. The chilliness in the sharp, salt wind is almost shocking after so long of feeling only different gradations of heat.

It need not be the end. She thinks of Yiri's parting words, the day he came to see her at the Low Cost House a week ago. He'd heard she was leaving and came to say farewell. He was such a fine-looking, clever man and she was shy and awkward, hyper-conscious of his presence now that they were alone together in the house after so many conversations in public places. But he was relaxed and expansive as he sat drinking a bottle of Fanta in the one remaining chair while she sat on Moses's low stool. Yiri was in his European clothes, his smaller self, but she liked both his identities now. She was aware of his long slender fingers holding the Fanta bottle, his proud profile with its high forehead. She believed him when he said he was sad she was leaving. It was a simple statement of fact, without overtones or obligations. As she too was sad, and unable, talking to him, to be clear why she was going, except that she had no job, no money, and very shortly – nowhere to live.

'These are details,' he said, gesturing expansively with his second bottle of Fanta.

But her ticket was booked, her mother was expecting her.

He said, with calm assurance, 'You will come back. Some time, you will come. Your father is buried here, you have roots now in this soil. When the grass and the bushes grow over his grave it will be here that his spirit speaks in the wind and flies with the birds. So you are one of us, now, and you must come back.' And he stared steadily at her until she looked away.

Was it a challenge or an invitation? She wasn't sure then

358

and she isn't sure now, though she has thought about it a lot inbetween. He stimulates her curiosity. She would like to be his friend. But she isn't sure whether friendship is on offer, or only something more extreme, something risky, uncertain in its outcome. It made her feel afraid, and relieved when he had gone. But the hope that she might, one day, see him again makes a faint, pleasurable buzz in the depths of her mind. As if a large, handsome bumblebee was nosing in a flower somewhere deep within her psyche.

The day his plaster was removed, Moses came to the house in a taxi, hobbling painfully, a livid scar with oversized stitch-marks drawn taut over his strangely under-sized knee, now minus its kneecap. She was in the kitchen when she heard him call uncertainly at the front door. It seemed odd that he should hesitate on the threshold when this was his house as much as hers. He had never moved out of it, his things were still in the little room, neatly folded and stacked, just as he had left them. She called him in hastily. But as soon as he was in the house the old rivalry reared up oddly as if out of nowhere. A slight aggression, an exaggerated politeness veiling animosity. As if they were both grabbing faintly for ownership of the dead in an echo of the old selves they had been when they had fought wordlessly for possession of the living.

She went through the mechanics of the actions she had already planned, which now seemed loaded with unexpected overtones. Offering that he should take anything he wanted from the house, anything and everything he could make use of. It had seemed – last week, even yesterday – only fair, since she would have to give most of it away. But she said it less than graciously now, as if there was a bad goblin inside her. He stared back at her, as if he could see straight through her and give as good as he got. She noticed he was no longer wearing the amulet.

But when they went into her father's room, still at that point almost untouched because she had found it so hard, so painfully final, to start to dismantle this last echo of him, Moses sat down suddenly on the bed, put his face in his hands and wept.

She watched him for a while before she went to sit beside him, awed by the intensity of his grief. Feeling herself at first the smaller because she had hardly wept for her father at all. Until eventually the sheer fact of his tears unloosed hers. Then she put her arm round his shoulders, leaned her head gently against his, and quietly wept beside him. There was a strange release in this, a companionship. No one else had cried with her. Nor, she supposed, with him. They were, after all, like brother and sister.

He wouldn't take anything at first, apart from the Ashanti carving that her dad had kept on his bookshelves. Suddenly she really did want him to take everything. Everything she couldn't fit in a suitcase and take with her. She wanted to be free, and she wanted him to have possessions. And she especially didn't want to give things away to strangers. So she pressed him. *Come with a taxi, borrow a truck – whatever you can – take it all. Sell it if you don't want to keep it.*

Make it easier for me, she said, and in the end it *was* easier, just as she had said. She could think of her father living on in some small way, in the daily use of his modest possessions. In someone else's consciousness, not just in her own. *And his desk,* she said. *Could I leave you to sort out all his papers?* Watching his face, which gave nothing away. Wondering if he knew what those papers were. Well, this

360

way he need never know that she had seen them. They parted as friends, in a fragile sort of way. And if on his return there had been no sign of tears but only a brash matter-of-factness in the brusque way objects were packed, stacked and removed, at least that absolved her of the further pain of missing Moses, too. Though she did promise to write to him and gave him her own address, care of her mother.

'What are you going to do?' she asked as he was leaving after picking up the last boxes.

'Oh, I driving for Mr Kwesi now,' he said carelessly, and she was needled with jealousy on her father's behalf, as if her father had been passed by and left behind.

She went to the graveyard at the Mission, choosing the hottest time of the day when the priests would be eating or resting and she could hope to slip in unobserved. She longed to hear news of Michael but she couldn't bear to be shunned, to be the leper in their saintly midst. Their abandoned Mary Magdalene. She slipped through the gate when the sun was near vertical and the shadows minimal, all colour and subtlety flattened in the midday glare. The grave looked raw still, though the turned earth had dried and powdered until it was the same colour as the bare soil round it. Already, even though it was the end of the growing season, nameless plants were springing tiny leaves in the red loam and a creeper was sending tendrils coursing over the surface of the mound. She stood a long time looking down at this speedy green embrace. Her father seemed a lifetime away, not here beneath her feet, slowly melting into the soil. For a while after his death he had seemed to hover somewhere just out of sight, mournful, homeless, restless. But not, she felt, all seeing. She had never once felt that. He had died with his emotional myopia intact.

361

He hadn't been hovering when she and Michael had rolled on the dusty floor in their one strange – and now, it seemed, final – embrace. But he was outside the house, in the wind, a half-seen shadow against the sun, a bird-cry at dusk, an anxious spirit.

She realised, as she stood looking down at the grave, that his spirit had gone quiet. As if he'd found his destination and was at rest. 'Poor Dad,' she whispered. What a strange half-life he seemed to have lived. She couldn't tell whether he'd been happy.

One by one she ticked the other duties off her list.

She went to the Tamale English Language Library in a taxi and gave them all her dad's books in two heavy boxes, Moses having no use for them. Mr Issafu Nigeria, the young librarian bobbed in earnest sympathy under his abundant Afro and welcomed her in. She and Jo had spent so many hours in here, hushing Josh while they chose their books, reading bits of Mills and Boon to one another in whispers behind the stacks and trying to keep their giggling under wraps, always afraid Mr Nigeria might think they were laughing at him. Now he peered at her sadly through his heavy glasses as she told him she was leaving. He thanked her effusively for the books. Asked if he might put her name on his list of donors, and wondered if she might see her way to raising funds for the library in Britain when she got back? She was glad to say yes because it made her departure seem less final.

When she wrote her name and her mother's address in his file she was taken aback to see Jo's details in the same folder, as if at the last minute they had come to rest side by side after all. Mr Issafu Nigeria obviously worked hard at his donors' list.

He shook her warmly by the hand as she left and repeated (as nearly everyone did) the necessary mantra: 'You will go and come.' And she, as always subtly reassured by the gentle routine of the words, replied 'Yes, I will go and come.' The mantra of parting easing the betrayal of leaving others behind.

Deepa and Sunni said it too, when they took her to the airport to see her onto the Accra plane. Sunni cried when she kissed them good-bye, and so did she. But Deepa, wiping a tear surreptitiously from one eye as if removing a speck of grit, said only, 'We'll see you in London when we come in February.' And she knew they would. In a matter of weeks their warmth and friendship, their kindness and capable generosity, had forged the foundations of a lifetime's relationship.

The plane rose steeply, then, from the little airport with its low-lying buildings and colourful windsock (Sunni and Deepa just visible in the crowd waving on the tarmac), before casting over the silver roofs of the town and swinging away south over the huge tracts of a land she barely knew, apart from a few small details scratched on the retina of her eye and under her skin. From the plane she looked down at the great breadth of Ghana, laid out in tiny detail beneath her, and felt painfully her own smallness and insignificance.

That was this morning.

And now she is sitting, a solitary speck on a broad expanse of perfect beach, and for the moment her insignificant smallness is perfect. Tonight the space which is Ghana-here will swallow up behind her, and tomorrow she will be back in that grey, passionless country she calls home. But in this small island of time which is left to her and which is still Ghana she sits alone on the beach, a little

363

self-conscious of the fact that she has inadvertently put herself into the hands of a taxi-driver she doesn't know, and she ponders the great imponderable of her life. Where is *he*? What is he feeling, what is he thinking? Has he forgiven her? Can he forgive himself? And will she ever see him again? Life is too mysterious to be comfortable. She would give anything – anything at all – to be with him again. Even a life of celibacy, if she might live it side by side with him.

These preoccupations are the greater because yesterday an unlikely thing happened. Ishmael the cook came looking for her at Deepa's house. Refusing a drink, he wouldn't sit but hovered just inside the door as if he was afraid of being caught red-handed. Every question – *How are the Fathers? Has Father Giovanni gone on his vacation? Has Father François come back from his?* – was met with a monosyllabic reply.

At last he said, 'We hear you goin' tomorrow. I bring you small-small ting for say goodbye.' He thrust the package he'd been clutching into her right hand, shook her left hand in both of his, and hurried out.

'Well, *he* didn't stand on ceremony,' Deepa remarked, raising one amused eyebrow. 'What conciliatory gift are they sending you at the eleventh hour?'

'I think it's from Ishmael, not from them,' she said, because inside the neat package of re-cycled paper were two large biscuits. She tipped them gently onto the table and looked at them. Two gingerbread men with *agushi* seeds for eyes.

Deepa came over to look. 'One of them seems to be a girl.'

What did it mean? She sat looking at the two figures with large heads and small bodies like the woodcarvings that were sold in the market. It was true – the smaller one had what might be clumsy breasts, and a skirt.

'If it's supposed to be you it's not a flattering likeness,' Deepa said. Pointedly not questioning who the male figure might then be.

'Maybe it's just chance it looks female.' But she didn't really think so. Something in the way Ishmael had kept looking at her, as if what he was trying to communicate couldn't be put into words, made her feel there was a message here somewhere, if only she could see it. And the way he'd said '*we* hear': had he come representing all of them? A priestly subterfuge behind Morrissey's back? She could imagine how it might have been: murmured conferences over lunch or dinner when Morrissey was safely in his office, a gesture at (as Deepa had observed) the eleventh hour. A small, slight, affectionate, meaningless gesture. Because she was sure it wouldn't have been *their* idea to send the figures. That was Ishmael. Strange Ishmael, with his abrupt and unexpected kindnesses.

But had he meant to convey some special meaning? The biscuits were freshly cooked but the distinctive, faintly stale smell of the Mission kitchen, an aura of weevils and of mice, came up to greet her like an old friend.

Deepa said, 'Are you supposed to eat them or keep them, do you suppose?'

'I don't know. But they are rather fine, don't you think? As examples of African art? I don't think I'll eat them.'

She began to rewrap them carefully in the paper. Then froze. The paper, crumpled from the office bin and smoothed out in the Mission kitchen for re-use, was an address-list of next-of-kin for all those living at the Mission. They were all there. Halfway down the list was Michael Murphy, his next-of-kin listed as a sister living in Belfast, and an address and a phone number.

August 2007

Thirty-one years later she sits again by the same beach, on this her first day back in a country she remembers only in blurred images like a dream. She knows it is the same beach but she doesn't recognise anything about it except the steeply rolling sea clutching at the pale sand. As far as the eye can see there are bodies lying in the sun, most of them white, while black figures move among them selling handicrafts, cold drinks, ice cream. And she is sitting not on the sand but in the expensive bar of one of the exclusive hotels that cluster now among the palm trees, and in places tower above them.

On the table in front of her the moisture looks frosted on the glass of white wine. Wealthy Ghanaians, bright as birds in their leisure clothes, fill the tables around her, but she is alone. Still unused to her single state. Just as she is never-endingly unused to the fact that she is fifty-three years old. A sense of loss sits grieving in her eyes. Her elegance is brittle, a thin veneer masking pain and insecurity. An illusion, the elegance, like a sleight of hand, but unconscious, and unintended.

She has come because invited, but that is only the surface reason. Privately she is making a pilgrimage: to her long-dead, nearly forgotten father, to her own youth, and to the new beginnings that were forged here once, long ago. A pilgrimage to hope and energy, and to pain and loss absorbed once before and grown through, as a tree grows round a broken fence; part of that which holds her up, even now, long years afterwards. And she knows with hindsight that the experience which, last time she was here, formed the whole pulsing largeness of her life was really only the prologue. Her *life* has happened since. She smiles as she thinks this, the painful fragments of her heart settling for a moment into an easier place as she looks up and down the astonishingly transformed beach and feels like a first-time foreigner in Ghana-here.

The next morning she is back at the airport to catch the Tamale plane. Waiting to relive the once familiar journey, looping northwards in two long stitches. To Kumasi in its remnants of forest. To Tamale in its sea of pale grass.

In Kumasi half the passengers disembark and are replaced by others going north. There are Europeans among them, pale and awkward, just as she remembers. Overshadowed by the vibrant Africans. There is no sign now of the dead aeroplane just beyond the runway, which was once emptied by a file of people as a dead snake on the road is emptied by a column of ants. There are fewer trees, and the town is much bigger than she remembers it. She wonders if Daoud still lives here or if he went back to Syria long ago.

They fly steadily north again, the forest slowly giving way to grassy plains. The Volta dam shimmers below them. Tamale is visible some time before they reach it, a hazy blur on the horizon. The town has exploded in size. The airport is a proper little airport now, with a proper terminal building. No longer a glorified airfield.

As she walks through the Arrivals Gate she recognises Mr Issafu Nigeria at once, before she sees the sign held up by the boy beside him which reads 'Tamale English Language

Library 50th Anniversary Celebrations'. The Afro haircut has gone now: Mr Issafu Nigeria is as bald as a baby but the same uncertain, friendly smile and earnest eyes behind thick lenses mark him out. He is greeting a white woman with a young man in the crowd ahead of her, a mother and son, she had guessed, when she saw them board the plane in Kumasi. Now Mr Issafu Nigeria sees her and waves, calling out her name. Her maiden name. In all these years she has never got round to pointing out to him that it had changed.

The woman turns towards her. With a shock Anne realises it is Jo.

Mr Issafu Nigeria has booked them into the brash new International Hotel, an expense she would have preferred to go without. They are a funny little international group: fifteen people with nothing in common except that some part of their lives, large or small, was spent in Tamale. All strangers to each other, apart from her and Jo. And Josh, if that can class as knowing: he is the butterfly, but she was acquainted only with the caterpillar. She smiles inwardly as she steals glances at him, amazed by this transformation, though she shouldn't be: her own two butterflies were not born until Josh was six or seven years old. And he, flattered by her interest and glad of someone new after a week alone with his mother, is attentive. Which, she can tell, is making Jo sour.

When she looks at Jo it is hard to recall the skinny girl with the baby on her hip and the extravagant hair. She is amazed by how many details she recognises, as if all her life since her mind has been waiting to place them again: that way Jo has of turning her head (such a neat head, now), that inflexion in the voice. But it feels like a dream because she doesn't recognise all the other bits inbetween.

Without meaning to she closes herself up, careful to give nothing away. Aware that Jo, too, is doing the same. She doesn't ask about Kevin, guessing from various things said that he is no longer on the scene.

That night, when Jo retires early to bed, Anne sits with Josh in the bar and he tells her all the things she wants to ask but won't. And because she is a stranger to him, he asks her nothing personal at all. She remembers Kevin when she looks at Josh, though he is very like his mother. He isn't good-looking but he does have pretty eyes. 'You were such a beautiful baby,' she says. 'I so wanted a baby of my own after meeting you.' Then she asks him if he knows why they didn't come back to Ghana, all those years ago, but he doesn't. It's too distant, too unimportant. 'Why did you lose touch with each other?' he asks. But she doesn't know the answer to that, either. As far as she can remember there were good intentions and failed attempts, then silence.

The anniversary celebrations take place the following day and are strangely low-key considering how far they have all travelled. There is plenty of time afterwards to revisit old haunts, such haunts as can be found. It is difficult, amongst all the new buildings. The market has been redeveloped, along with the whole of the centre of town, but the Mission of the Holy Redeemer is still there, the school looking very small and shabby. Was it always? The ugly church is overshadowed by bigger buildings and the gardens and the fields have disappeared. With a shock she realises the graveyard, too, has gone. Where once her father lay, melting into the earth, there are foundations now, and concrete and steel.

They are standing in the road staring when the evening Mass comes to an end and the congregation emerges from the church. She looks into the faces of the men for a glimpse of the boys she once knew. Joseph is in London and John lives in New York now, but what of the others? She stares at the Ghanaian priest wondering if it might be Thomas until she realises the priest is too young.

They manage to find the old-fashioned bungalow where Jo and Josh once lived but it has lost its large, empty grounds and is hemmed in by modern houses. Surprisingly, the Low Cost Estate is still recognisably itself, although no longer on the edge of the town. Anne finds their old house with difficulty since it is not now the last road but merely the road at the bottom of the slope in the middle of sprawling suburbs. But when they do find it, the house is just as she remembers, in the gathering dusk. The mango tree is bigger, and the porch has been walled in to make an extra room. She wonders where Moses is now. So much remembering, so many missing people. It makes her very tired. She looks at Jo, knowing from what Josh said last night that she is frail and weary beneath that prickly shell. Jo returns her look steadily. It is a strange moment. As if, more than twenty-four hours after they met, they are silently saying hello.

It is night and the lights glitter on the surface of the hotel swimming pool, empty of people, choppy in the warm wind. A hawk-owl (or is it a bat?) is hunting over the water. Josh has gone for a shower.

Side by side they sit, two women who know how their lives have turned out but they don't know how much of the story they are looking at, how much is yet unknown. A pregnant silence lies heavy between them, each preoccupied with her own tale, each little by little beginning to be curious about the other's story.

'Is this your Dr Jebuni?' Jo passes the newspaper across, pointing to the caption under a grainy photograph of a handsome, light-skinned Ghanaian who looks about Josh's age. The caption reads: 'Mr James Jebuni, son of the esteemed politician Dr Yiri Jebuni, who was Chief Government Advisor on Public Health until his untimely death last year, is seen arriving at the Presidential Palace prior to taking up his post as Assistant Secretary to the Minister for Education. Here is a Rising Star who will go far. Mr Jebuni was married last month to Miss Mary Asiedu, daughter of the Minister for Employment and herself a budding politician. This paper predicts that together James and Mary will form a new Dynasty in the dusty corridors of power. Remember, you read it in the *Daily Star* first.'

Anne puts on her glasses to peer more closely at the picture. 'Is this his son? I guess it must be. He does look as you'd expect after thirty years. Yiri said there was a brighter future for James here than in England. I wonder if this was what he had in mind! Poor old Yiri. Not so old, really. He'd have been…mid-sixties, I suppose.'

'I wonder what happened to Mandy?' Jo says. 'I often wondered about that. I hoped she'd snatched him back but it doesn't look as if she did.'

'No, doesn't look like it. I certainly couldn't imagine Mandy living in Ghana. She looked as if she couldn't wait to get away. Poor woman – there's really no solution to that kind of problem, is there.' Remembering too late that Jo's marriage, too, broke up.

Jo sits staring out over the pool, moodily pulling at a button on her shirt. But at least Jo did keep hold of Josh, Anne supposes. They skirt awkwardly around the unknown-ness of each other's lives. Having so much to ask, they ask almost nothing.

How old Jo looks. And remote. Her clothes are expensive these days and well cut, her hair is neatly tamed but still thick, but such details can't undo the ravages of her illness, the withered look of her skin. Looking at Jo, Anne realises with a shock something deep and hidden within herself: she does want to go on living. She is shaken but still vital. The pain of survival, after all, tells us we are still alive.

She watches the glint of the lights in the blackly hiccupping surface of the pool and wonders how the conversation will begin that she knows, sooner or later, must take place.

Jo says suddenly, as if they had never stopped talking, 'I always wondered what happened to that priest. What was his name? Michael, wasn't it?'

'Ah,' she says. 'Michael. I wondered when we would get to talking about Michael.'

ABOUT HONNO

Honno Welsh Women's Press was set up in 1986 by a group of women who felt strongly that women in Wales needed wider opportunities to see their writing in print and to become involved in the publishing process. Our aim is to develop the writing talents of women in Wales, give them new and exciting opportunities to see their work published and often to give them their first 'break' as a writer. Honno is registered as a community co-operative. Any profit that Honno makes is invested in the publishing programme. Women from Wales and around the world have expressed their support for Honno. Each supporter has a vote at the Annual General Meeting. For more information and to buy our publications, please write to Honno at the address below, or visit our website: www.honno.co.uk

Honno, 14 Creative Units, Aberystwyth Arts Centre Aberystwyth, Ceredigion SY23 3GL

Honno Friends

We are very grateful for the support of the Honno Friends: Annette Ecuyene, Audrey Jones, Gwyneth Tyson Roberts, Jenny Sabine, Beryl Thomas.

For more information on how you can become a Honno Friend, see: http://www.honno.co.uk/friends.php